EVERYTHING I'LL SAY TO YOU TOMORROW

ELÍSABET BENAVENT

sourcebooks
casablanca

Published by Sourcebooks Casablanca, an imprint of Sourcebooks
P.O. Box 4410, Naperville, Illinois 60567-4410
(630) 961-3900
sourcebooks.com

This edition issued based on the paperback edition published in 2022 in Spain by
Suma de Letras, an imprint of Penguin Random House Grupo Editorial.

Cataloging-in-Publication Data is on file with the Library of Congress.

Printed and bound in the United States of America.
PAH 10 9 8 7 6 5 4 3 2 1

1

~~~

I FINALLY UNDERSTAND ALL THOSE SAD SONGS

MIRANDA

The sky is leaden. It's one of those chilly spring afternoons, but you could tell everyone picked out clothes this morning based on the weather they wanted, not on the weather they got. Girls are wearing ballet flats with no socks (as it should always be, if my opinion matters to anyone), and you can see tons of jean jackets and very few trench coats. *Trench coats are made for weather like this,* I think. But I'm also thinking about how pretty people fall in love more. I'm talking about quantity, not quality. They fall in love more. They probably even get their hearts broken less.

Thoughts are piling up in my head; it's chaos.

I don't consider myself ugly or pretty, to tell the truth. I have a lot of things going for me, but stunning and obvious beauty is not one of them. I guess you could say I'm attractive. Once, in a work meeting, they described me as a girl with a unique look, full of character. It's true there's something about my face people remember. They usually remember me, but that could also be because I've always been one of those honest people; I don't even come close to rude, but I do usually tell the truth when I'm asked. Telling the truth politely when asked is revolutionary these days.

He *is* handsome. It hurts to think about and pops up in my head like a red thread tied to the previous thought: pretty people fall in love more. Maybe that's why the man I share my life with is dumping me.

Because he doesn't love me anymore.

Because our time is up.

Because he's really hot and, dammit, hot people have to share their love around with loads of girls, and I'm trying to hog it.

My reptilian brain, the most primitive part, the one that I think will have to take responsibility right now for throwing my survival instinct into turbo drive, wavers. Tristan is attractive. The typical guy who wouldn't turn your head on the street but whom you'd keep looking at on the metro because…what is it about him? At first, you don't know how to put it into words. It's that very Parisian je ne sais quoi, even though he's only ever been a tourist in Paris. Then you realize that he's too much. Tristan is a delicious mille-feuille in many ways; he's got layers. There are lights and shadows that give volume and texture to his attractiveness. His bad sides are what give meaning to his good sides and make them better. Tristan… with his thick, black hair combed to one side, with no prissy part, his nervous smile and his seductive smile, which, paradoxically, are very similar. His long-fingered hands. His full lips… God, they're so full. The leaden sky of the Madrid afternoon in his eyes.

"I'm sorry," he says.

I'm vaguely aware that it isn't the first time I'm hearing that phrase, but I don't think it was really getting through until that moment. Ever since he blurted out, "We need to talk," everything that has come out of his mouth has sounded like Esperanto. And I don't speak it. Esperanto is a dead language, for fuck's sake; no one uses it.

"Miranda…really…I'm sorry."

I'm vaguely aware (or starting to be) that my name doesn't sound the same on his lips anymore. My name that has always taken so many forms in his mouth: Mir, Miri, Miranda, baby. And sometimes "Miss," which he always made sound so cheeky. My name doesn't sound like it belongs to him anymore. Whatever it was that bonded us has broken for him.

"I need you to say something, Miranda." He closes his eyes and presses his knuckle to the hollow formed by the perfect arch between his eyebrow and the corner of his eye.

If I didn't know him so well, I would think he was fighting back tears, but this is Tristan. He doesn't cry in public. He's Tristan, the reserved. He's Tristan, who handles most feelings with his head. I've envied that relationship between his brain and his heart so many times. He is definitely the most balanced partner I've ever had.

"I'm begging you," he insists.

"I don't know what you want me to say. You're dumping me. I feel like this is completely out of the blue."

"That's not fair. We've been fighting for a while."

"Fighting to fix it," I retort.

"Fighting, one way or another," he insists.

Our eyes meet for a second before mine dart back to the cup of tea I didn't realize I was clenching.

"You don't love me anymore?" I ask him.

He huffs. He huffs and looks up at the sky, watching the heavy gray clouds skitter across.

"Of course I love you. That's why we need to end it here."

"You're leaving me because you love me? What's next? You're dying to live?"

Tristan's expression changes. It would be imperceptible to anyone else, but not to me. He's getting tired of this; with each passing minute, he's losing patience and faith.

"Look, Miri…this isn't one of those 'it's not you, it's me' things. It's a 'let's be mature and stop hurting ourselves' thing. We can't sustain something that has one good week, two average, and one really bad. I love you and you love me, but choosing each other over all that means we'll be unhappy, and you have to be able to see that. We don't deserve that."

"Is this about the kid thing?"

He pinches the bridge of his nose. I know perfectly well that's only part of the problem, but in that instant, the only thing I can think to do is wield that weapon. I don't know why. Maybe I feel like it will buy me time.

"We've already talked the kid thing to death." He sighs.

"Maybe next year, Tristan. Maybe next year I…I could consider it. I'm at a point in my career where I want to enjoy my freedom a little more and not have any burdens."

"Children aren't a burden," he objects, putting both elbows on the table. "I think you get more and more confused about that subject the more we talk about it."

"That's not true. It's just that…"

"I'm not going to pressure you about that." He looks away. He's thrown in the towel.

"You're leaving me because I haven't found the time to be a mother?" And I'm trying to cause him maximum pain with that question, even though I know he won't feel as bad as I do.

"I don't know how to do it anymore. I feel like everything I do and everything I am makes you deeply unhappy. I'm sick of your job. The truth is your job at the magazine is worse than having a colicky baby, Miranda. It always needs attention. Because of it, we've postponed decisions, vacations… I can't stand this city anymore. I came for one year…or two. I've been here five! For you! I can't do it anymore. And I can't blame you for not feeling at home, because you don't deserve that. We're both tired, grumpy, angry… We don't even have sex anymore. At most every two or three weeks, and it feels suspiciously like we're just ticking a box because we have to. You're always too tired to tell me anything about your stuff, and I'm not enough of a zombie or alienated enough not to care."

"I'll quit my job," I blurt out without thinking.

And even as I say it, I know I'm lying. I would never quit. The magazine is part of my life. It's my passion. I adore my job as deputy editor. Tristan, who knows that, sucks his teeth. I'm starting to get the feeling that I'm making a fool of myself.

"Miri…you know I would never let you quit your job for me. You love it. And you know what? Even though I've had it up to here with everything it involves, I'm envious of it. I feel jealous. I want to feel like that too when my alarm goes off and I have to go to work. I'd like to love more things, more than you. I… You're the only thing I love anymore." Tristan's voice quavers on the end of the sentence, but he recovers by clearing his throat, which, much to his regret, doesn't camouflage the whimper of pain behind it.

He looks away and taps the table rhythmically with his thumb as he bites his top lip, waiting for the lump in his throat to dissolve. This never happens in movies, and it's difficult to describe in books. When a couple is fighting, there's a lot of silence. Long pauses where no one says anything while they're screaming inside. There are minutes and minutes, all of them violent and uncomfortable, where they both understand that actually, there's nothing they could say that would act as a lifesaver.

"It's not healthy," he tosses out finally.

"You don't think our relationship is healthy? Since when?"

And suddenly I feel like a bag of ultra-processed food while he's a fitness aficionado. I'm a Twinkie.

"For a while now."

"Why?"

"Because we argue too much, we don't talk enough, and we don't understand each other at all. We don't love each other the same way anymore. I don't understand why one of us always has to end up hurt."

I open my mouth to argue, but I hit the brakes because I know it's ridiculous. Yesterday, we got pissed off about something so trivial: one of us had bought chicken strips instead of whole chicken breasts. The truth is neither of us had the nerve to bring up the topic of vacations. He had been asking me for a year to take a month of vacation days so we could go on a long trip. I didn't want to, and I couldn't leave the magazine for that long, and I was frustrated that he didn't get that.

"I feel alone," he confesses, "hemmed in, ignored, and anxious. I know you're not trying to make me feel like that on purpose, but still…I'm tired. And you're always mad at me, like nothing I say is actually enough."

"I'm not mad at you. Why do you say that?"

It crosses my mind for a split second that I have been thinking "this guy's an idiot" a lot lately when I hang up the phone, but I swat the idea away like a fly.

"This is really hard for me," he says apologetically. "But it's like that song."

Tristan gathers up his things from the table. His phone, his watch, which he always takes off when he sits at the table with me, his wallet…

"You're leaving? You're just going to leave me hanging? You're going to be a fucking coward?"

He sucks his teeth again and stares at me.

"No, but as you can see, you've already decided to be pissed at me for something I wasn't even going to do. A perfect example of what I was trying to say."

"That's so stupid."

"Miranda, I want to end this relationship, and you have to respect me, because you don't know how much willpower it's taken for me to make this decision. Please, respect the fact that I feel it's the best for both of us. Yes, I'm putting myself first over a relationship that has kept me up so many more nights than it should have. Let me want to be healthy. And responsible. Because I love you, Miranda, and I don't want us to hate each other. I deserve the things that I dream of. And now, if you'll allow me, I'm going."

He stands up and, without looking at me, distributes his things among the pockets of his suit that makes him feel so disguised. I think about his strong legs wrapping around mine in bed. I think about the short hair on his chest, rough against my cheek... I think, but all my thoughts are so jumbled it's impossible to see any idea clearly beyond not believing anything that just happened.

"If it's okay with you, I'll come get my things from your house tomorrow morning, while you're at the magazine."

"It's not my house," I whisper.

"What?"

"Don't say 'my house.' It's our house."

Tristan stifles a sigh before he responds.

"No, Miri, not anymore. Now it's just your house."

I keep waiting for a kiss goodbye, mostly because I'm an idiot and I haven't absorbed any of the conversation. He dumped me. Tristan just broke up with me. He broke almost five years of a relationship, and the thing that pisses me off the most is that he didn't give me a kiss goodbye when he left. And while I watch him disappear into the crowd, I wonder what the fuck just happened, who I am, who that guy is, what I'm going to do, and how I'm going to get up tomorrow morning knowing that he doesn't want to live with me anymore. Or even kiss me goodbye.

I can't believe it.

There's no way that just happened.

I don't know how much time passed from when he left to when I throw a five-euro bill on the table and get up, not caring whether it's enough money to pay for our two drinks or not.

The wind whirls through the streets, picking up papers dropped on corners, cigarette butts, and dog hair as it goes. I hate the cafés on Calle de Fuencarral because they're all sad chains with fluorescent overhead lights, but we met up in one of them; it was the closest place between both our offices. I appreciate that it didn't happen in one of my favorite cafés, because I would never have been able to go back. Or at home. Imagine not being able to go back to your own house. Though I don't think I can go back anywhere. I think I'm dying.

I walk along hugging myself and go right past the metro stop. I stumble on. My intuition carries me home. To my home. A home that doesn't belong to anyone else anymore. And what will I do with his stuff tonight? With his fastidious side of the wardrobe. With the sheets that still smell like him. With the book he's reading that he left on his bedside table. It's not possible. This has to be a tantrum. Like that other time, right?

I haven't even made it a kilometer when I feel the first raindrop. By the time I get to my door, I'm drenched. My teeth are chattering, but I'd be lying if I said I feel cold. What I feel is a ball of heat in the middle of my chest that radiates an intangible but real pain from my head to my toes. It's a ghost pain that I don't know whether to describe as squeezing, stinging, burning, or stabbing. It's a pain that suffocates, that shrouds my chest, that digs claws into my scalp like it's going to flay me. A monumental migraine that crouches in wait by my temples like a wild animal. I'm a hiker lost on a mountain full of hungry and rabid bears.

I can't even cry. Crying would help me...but I can't.

I peel off my clothes in the bathroom and leave them in a heap on the white-tile floor. I never liked these tiles because they show every piece of hair I shed. But he loves them. Loved them, I should say. The juxtaposition of the tiny white tiles with the black faucets and the iron finish on the showerhead was one of the things he liked most about my apartment. And the light. It's such a bright apartment...exactly the opposite of how

I feel. Right now, I'm darker than Sauron. I'm the Dark Ages. I'm darker than the inside of an asshole.

I crawl into bed just as I am. In my underwear. I pull the duvet over me and slide over to his pillow with my heart in my mouth. I sniff it. His cologne… When I met Tristan, his scent gave me mixed feelings. It seemed too much to me… I don't know. It was overwhelming. I thought it was the typical cologne that dudes who like themselves too much would pick. Stupid, preconceived images from working where I work, I guess. It seemed to me like the cologne a guy who just wanted to brag about his conquests would wear. Someone who wasn't special. Someone with no style but with money in his pocket. How wrong I was about that first impression. He was always the complete opposite.

Over time, among other things, that intense, dense smell with a touch of the exotic, that trace of bergamot and vanilla excited me, calmed me, made me feel at home and ready to leave my life behind to run away with him…all at once. Fucking Tristan.

It's not possible. He'll be back. It can't be. I'm going to die without him. Fine, nobody dies from love, but I'm going to succumb to this pain in my chest. A pounding and horribly hot, throbbing headache settles in above my eyebrows.

What am I going to do without him?

What's going to happen to all the things we were going to be? We're not "us" anymore. Have we died? How can something that was never born die?

The phone and internet bills are in his name. I'm going to have to do paperwork. For fuck's sake.

How am I going to tell my father? He adores him.

And Ivan? Ivan will say something tremendously practical like "There's a reason for everything" or "Just say fuck it and dance, darling." And I'll feel miserable because my best friend won't understand that I'm going to die. Because this has to be what it feels like when you're dying. I'm not fucking around.

Has he told his family? Definitely his sister…and that pig would have celebrated. His sister and I never got along, and she definitely will have poisoned his head, telling him that I'm too independent for him. That I'm too strong. That I'll never want to have kids and he'll be miserable with a life he didn't choose.

God. The pain. I open my eyes, and a light that shouldn't be there blinds me. Great. I probably have a brain tumor. Or aliens have chosen this moment to take me to their planet. I close them again while the sensible voice in my brain reminds me that it's just a migraine. A fucking terrible migraine. The mother of all migraines. Everything is spinning.

Tomorrow morning, I have to go to a cover shoot. And they'll see me with my face like a newborn rat. Isn't tomorrow the quarterly advertising meeting? I have no fucks left to give about the phrase "our sponsors" being used for the 372nd time to justify decisions about our content that I'm sure we would never otherwise agree to. It all seems a little surreal to me. Is this my life? Are these the "important" things? I can't get my head around having to get up tomorrow with this version of reality dragging me down.

Tomorrow, Tristan will come get his stuff.

No. I need to talk to him. There are so many things I haven't told him. There are so many things I didn't know how put into words. Not today or for the past few months.

What if I call in sick?

Yes. I'll wait for him here. And I'll tell him how much I love him. He didn't give me the chance to say it. I'll explain to him that he can't leave me. That you don't abandon the person you love. The person who is the love of your life, like I am for him. I'll remind him of all our plans. Like starting to eat less meat, buying more plants, or saving up to go to Japan.

I'll promise to complain less, to cook more, to not be a slave to the magazine, to think about us. Yes.

Yes.

Tomorrow, I'll tell him everything. And he'll see that I'm right. And he'll stay.

With a little luck, this headache will have disappeared by then.

Damn you, Adele. I finally understand all those sad songs.

2

~~~

WHAT THE...?

I didn't close the blinds or the curtains last night, so the first rays of light flood my bedroom and hit my face like an alarm clock. Ivan, my pragmatic bestie, always says the furniture in my room is all in the wrong place, that it doesn't have good feng shui. But I like everything exactly how it is. It was already like this before I even met Tristan. I've lived in this apartment since my last breakup, because I've been with men other than him, obvs. I had a very long, lovely, and boring relationship, the kind where we're convinced we need them but we don't really love them. Then I met a man who wasn't good for me...the kind who we want but we don't need. I discovered too late that he was married. After him, there were a few fun flings: the polyamorous one, which taught me a lot about jealousy; that skinny doctor who was so funny but I only went out with once; the singer...ay...he was such a fuckboy. But everyone gets tired of it all at some point.

I met Tristan right when I was promising myself I would never fall in love again. I needed to be alone and have some peace. I didn't need a partner, just the occasional hookup to go to the movies with and fuck on the dining room table. Love is a fallacy. The opium of the masses. Blah, blah, blah. I fell in headfirst like an idiot and didn't even put my hands out to break the fall, so…emotionally Tristan broke everything, even my teeth.

I don't know why I'm speaking in the past tense.

The sound of the alarm clock forces me to get up, even though I don't want to, and the first thing that surprises me is that I'm wearing pajamas. Two-piece pajamas with a black button-down top, which I thought I had gotten rid of ages ago. Cock is like acid… It takes you on a full psychotropic journey.

I go to the kitchen and put the coffeepot on the stove and throw my hair into a bun with the hair tie that's always on my wrist and write on my team's WhatsApp group:

MIRANDA:

Ladies, I was up all night vomiting. In charge of the photo shoot today (drumroll please): Rita!! If you have any questions, send me a message. Everyone else, please: behave. I'm staying home today. I'll be by the phone in case there's a disaster, but please, I'm begging you, don't let there be.

I leave my phone on the kitchen counter and cling to it like Rose on the door in *Titanic*. I tell myself: *Don't worry, Miri. You're gonna get him back. This can't end like this. It'll all be okay in the end, and if it's not okay, it's not the end.*

I pour myself a coffee, add in a glug of agave syrup, and dunk three María cookies in it. The saddest breakfast since we all caught a stomach bug at the magazine; we were shitting ourselves like hoopoes, and all we could handle were sips of Gatorade.

A buzz from my phone breaks through the pleasure of feeling the cookies crunch quietly under my molars.

RITA:

Miri, I appreciate you trusting me to run a photo shoot that only exists in your wonderful and sparkling overworked brain, but I'm sorry to tell you the fact that you're not coming *is* the disaster. We have the staff meeting today and the shit show.

I squint as I read it. What shit show?

Eva, the editor in chief, sends another message in case I didn't get it.

EVA:

THE SHIT SHOW.

Wait, isn't today the photo shoot? I press my forehead against the counter and sigh. They're not even gonna leave me alone to cry my eyes out and wallow in this heartbreak. For the love of Harry Styles. Where did the phrase "work dignifies man" come from. More like it tortures.

I turn on the shower, and I'm surprised to see a hanger with an outfit all ready to go on the back of the door. I've been doing that for years under normal circumstances…but I don't think "normal circumstances" is exactly the phrase I would use to describe yesterday's journey. I only get clothes ready the night before because…well, I'm not exactly the regular kind of girl who works at a fashion magazine. I always had to make an effort, and that habit just stuck with me.

When you think of the kind of woman who works at a fashion magazine (and one of the biggest magazines in the world specifically), what comes to mind is the image of a leggy, size zero, young, beautiful girl with long, shiny hair…and I already made it clear that I'm not beautiful. What I am is attractive and full of personality. But I don't have long, slender legs or incredible hair. If a model or an actress had to play me in a movie, it wouldn't be Gisele Bündchen, just to give you a hint. I'm normal. Even though, actually, we're all normal; "normal" is a word that doesn't really mean anything.

This is something we've always defended tooth and nail at the magazine, ever since I started there as an intern. When I got there, I didn't really care about fashion. I ended up there almost by chance, but something about my résumé caught the director's eye, as well as the training I had gotten in my work experience. There were so many impeccably dressed girls vying for the job, and they gave it to the one who showed up in an oversized blazer she got half off from Mango and beaten-up Adidas sneakers.

Taste is refined over time and with practice. You learn what looks good on you, which parts of you should be accentuated, and what garments let you do that. You realize what colors suit you best, which haircuts make you feel powerful, what heels you can handle for eight hours (if you even want to wear them, because you don't have to) and which will have you begging for a toe amputation... You're aware of what fashion can offer you and what you can offer it. Apparently, I have a kind of innate taste that, alongside what I've been trained on since the day I started at the magazine, has equipped me with good judgment. And I'm a good boss... because with a lot of effort and a little luck, I excelled until I got to be the youngest deputy editor of a fashion magazine in the whole country. Right after I turned twenty-eight.

Before I get in the shower, I sit down to send Tristan a WhatsApp and write to him that I'd like to be home so we can talk calmly and maybe even suggest getting something to eat together...but after scrolling, searching, and more searching, I realize that last night I must have been on a bender of infinite sadness and done things I don't even remember, like deleting his phone number, any trace of him in my calls, his WhatsApp chat, his profile on Instagram, and...on top of all that, he doesn't even show up as authorized on our joint account. I mean, come on...

I don't have time to figure out how I was so efficient even though I was half-asleep, so I postpone that. My stomach turns when I realize I've been doing that for at least a year: postponing. I postpone shit shows. I postpone plans. I postpone thinking about things on the back burner. I don't have time. I really don't. Up until yesterday, I had to juggle my life as a deputy editor (on call twenty-four hours a day, seven days a week) with my personal life (a relationship, a father, a few friends), and I always felt like I was doing it all badly.

The clothes I picked out yesterday surprise me. It's spring, but for some reason I can't understand, I chose clothes for the middle of winter. God, Miri. Nothing has made sense since I got out of bed. Still, I open my window and lean out to see what the weather's like: I'm shocked by a blast of frigid air that closes all my pores from now until next year. Maybe I was more lucid last night than I thought…even though I still can't remember a single thing. How is that possible? I'm getting pretty worried, and the hypothesis of the brain tumor is starting to seem more and more likely.

I go through the motions, trying not to think. Black, cropped faux-leather pants, a chunky black sweater, pumps. I pull my brown hair back in a low pony and slap on a little makeup: clean skin, eyeliner on eyelashes with a light dab of mascara, and red lipstick. I look in the mirror right before I grab my leather jacket and my work bag from the hall closet and raise one eyebrow. I feel like I'm stealing someone's look without realizing.

Years ago, when I started at the magazine, our office was on one floor of a terrifying building in an industrial estate, but someone (wisely) decided that we should move to a nice building on Calle de Santa Engracia in the center of Madrid. There are way fewer of us now. I still remember running around an editorial office filled with desks and more desks, organized into segments: fashion, beauty, lifestyle… It's not like that anymore.

We're a pretty small team of women (100 percent women). We survive, we stay standing, we fight to change many stereotypes through glossy paper, to defend sisterhood, the truth behind beauty standards, physical and mental health, and a lifestyle that doesn't feed unattainable goals that only lead to frustration.

Can you tell I believe in what I do?

When I go through the turnstiles at the magazine and wave at the doorman, I have my phone in my hand, as always. This fucking device has become an extension of my own body over the past few years. I check it when I get out of the shower, on the bus, in taxis, under the table at work lunches, while I'm waiting for coffee, the elevator, the bathroom, every-fucking-where. There's always a fire to put out, a question, an email to answer or to ignore or to put a little red flag on so I'll respond to it later.

"Hey, Miri!" the girls already sitting at their desks call out to me.

"Hi, hi… We're going to change the world!"

I rush across to my glass-walled office as fast as I can, but before I can close the door, Eva, the editor in chief, darts in.

"How are you feeling?"

I stare at her in surprise as I slide my bag under my desk, still clutching my phone in my hand. I'm weirded out by her sudden interest in my health but also by how she's dressed: ripped jeans, a rainbow sweater, kitten heels. She could have fallen out of the trends-of-five-years-ago section.

I decide to ignore it. Sometimes people get a little nostalgic about fashion.

"Why?"

"Because of all the barfing."

I raise my eyebrows. Being a good liar means having a good memory, and that's not really my specialty.

"Ah, right. Something I ate for dinner must not have agreed with me."

"You and those poke bowls."

"You know ever since I got food poisoning from that bluefin tuna at a magazine lunch, I never eat poke anymore."

From the look she gives me, apparently she doesn't remember, and that weirds me out too, because it's not that easy to forget someone projectile vomiting in the hallway at the Ritz.

"Well," she declares, "they're coming at 11:30. Right after the staff meeting."

"Who's coming?"

Rita, the fashion director, comes in, and before she's even all the way into my office, she's already nattering away. Rita always likes her own voice to precede her.

"I prepared a few pitches, even though I think we've got it in the bag. Seriously, sometimes working here is like being high AF."

"I'm not going to ask how you know what it's like to be high AF, because I'm scared of what'll come next," teases Marta, the digital director, who just barged in without knocking.

"Why is my office like a whorehouse on payday?"

"Miri, put your phone down already, girl. It looks like it's glued to your hand." Marta laughs.

"She's one to talk…" Rita retorts sarcastically.

The glass door opens again, and Cris, the beauty director, pokes her head in.

"Are you all meeting up without me?"

"We're just kiki-ing before the shit show meeting," Eva answers.

"Can someone explain this shit show thing?" I beg.

"Why do you have your phone in your hand like that, like you're in the FBI and you have to show your badge? Are you waiting for an important call or something?"

The four of them—Eva, Rita, Cris, and Marta—waggle their eyebrows suggestively. Before I can respond to them, with my phone waving very visibly in my hand almost like a flag, a notification dings, and the Tinder icon pops up on the screen.

"What?" I yelp.

There's a plural cackle that ricochets off the office's glass walls. I don't need to look in the mirror to see that I'm the color of a baboon's ass.

"I mean…the thing is, yesterday… Well, actually, never mind. It's just that…"

"Listen, chocho!" Rita cracks up. "It's not a sin to have a little whore tour around Tinder, girl."

I would say from experience that Rita is one of those women who believes in monogamy even more than the indisputable efficacy of the little black dress to get you out of a style predicament. I don't understand this support unless I told them…

Wait.

"By any chance, did I send some of you a message with disturbing content last night?" I ask them anxiously.

"Ah, man, the girl goes out partying and doesn't even invite us," Rita teases.

"No…no…"

"You didn't send anything," Cris rushes to pacify me. My forehead must be covered in sweat. "And the scrolling Tinder thing is nothing new. *Take a breath…*"

I woke up today, and the whole world is upside down. I sigh to try to blot it out and look at my phone. Last night, on top of erasing every trace of Tristan from my phone, I must have downloaded the app and started trying to find a match like my life depended on it. I glance at the notification on my screen.

MANUEL:

Sounds good. I can meet up tonight or tomorrow night.
Then I'm heading out of Madrid for the weekend.

"Holy shit…" I murmur.

"What?" they all say in unison.

"I must be losing it. I don't even remember downloading Tinder."

"They say the accumulation of heavy metals in our blood from sushi can make…"

We all glare at Rita, and she raises her hands in surrender.

"Okaaaay."

"Have you been fishing for salmon in Norway recently?" Cris pipes up.

"It must be a mistake. I'm going to deactivate my account." I put my phone down on the table and look at them again, faking a smile. "So? What are you all doing in my office? Is this about the shit show thing?"

"You can get used to a good thing so quickly, huh?" Marta mocks me.

I don't get it, but I can't be bothered to ask.

"Staff meeting," I say as shorthand, even though I could've sworn we had other things scheduled for today. But my calendar lines up with what these girls are saying…so it must be. "At ten."

"And the shit show at eleven thirty. But don't worry. This week's shit show isn't going to happen," Eva assures me.

"Wow, you're having a pretty crazy first month…" Cris sighs.

Okay. I don't understand any of them. I side-eye them, but they don't take the hint.

"Is Marisol in her office?" I ask.

"Did you come in with no coat?" Rita responds, shocked.

"At this time of year, wearing a coat is a little much, right? Or is Milan street style dictating that we all wear coats in spring-summer?"

I catch the look they all give each other; they're incredulous.

"Miri, are you okay?"

No. Last night, my boyfriend dumped me, and today, the world is even weirder than usual.

"Yes, yes. Of course. I'm going to get a coffee and a bun." I turn on my iMac and pull my wallet out of my bag.

"If you spent the whole night throwing up, are you gonna be able to handle that?"

"I need sugar."

It's the only explanation I can think of before I hustle out of my own office. Out of the corner of my eye, I can feel them still staring at me, stupefied, as I hurry away. Something weird is going on here. Or maybe it's me. Maybe I'm the weird one.

Dori, the waitress in the café across the street, serves me my Americano and my brioche without a word. I just smile. She asks me, like every day for the past few years, how my day's going, but all I can do today is make a face and add:

"Weird."

That's enough for her. Sometimes we gossip about what we're doing at the magazine, and we give her free makeup because she's a doll, and on Fridays, she saves us churros if she sees they're running low. On Fridays, even though we work in a fashion magazine and people probably expect something more glamorous and fancy, the heads of departments and the deputy editor, meaning me, eat churros for breakfast while we go through the agenda for the following week. Dori is our messiah and the churros our salvation.

When I get back, there's already a commotion in the conference room. That's where the planning meeting is held once a month, where we go over the topics for the next issue. We work on the content for the next issue a month and a half in advance, because we have to close everything and get it to the printer, which can be dangerous sometimes: nowadays, a topic can become obsolete in a week. But we've learned to be able to maneuver things thanks to the digital edition, which updates the publication every day in all the different sections.

My role is pretty important in the planning meetings. In the absence of the editor in chief, I'm the highest authority who decides whether a topic is in or out, and our director is usually absent. And it's not because she's blowing it off. Marisol, who has been with the company for many years, has learned to delegate, to give her deputy editor authority while shouldering a part of the job I personally find very thankless: corporate and public relations. You have to be up to it, and she is. She's kind, intelligent, and sweet. She gets more advertisers than the whole advertising department and is the front-facing leader of a newsroom full of women whose voices are always heard. Can you tell I love what I do?

I go into the room with my coffee, my bun, my iPad, and my planner. I'm one of those…analog girlies. I'd rather write things by hand because somehow, I feel like I remember it better that way. It's my way of organizing and categorizing. And my planner is my bible.

I sit at the head of the table, in the position I inherited from the previous deputy editor almost five years ago, and I smile at the girls who are already sitting around the table. Next, I freak out. What the hell are all these people doing here?

"Um…"

Across the table is one of our most beloved contributors who left the magazine the year before to work at a media agency that specialized in fashion. On her right, the perfect girl who we had to fire after the lockdowns. Opposite her, two whose contracts we couldn't renew for exactly the same reason.

What? What's going on? A reunion for old colleagues? The room is full, and they're waiting for me to lead the meeting.

"Good morning, ladies. Um…I'm happy to see some old friends who must be here to share some interesting content with us." I look at the girls in question, who stare blankly back at me, not giving anything away. What I do notice is everyone looking kind of bewildered. "Let's get started then…"

I grab my agenda and open it where the bookmark is. I'm surprised to see the date. November 11. I furrow my brow. I must look like an idiot. The whole room is waiting for me to open with the articles we're going to "syndicate," meaning all the articles we're going to replicate from the main masthead, in this case from the United States. But I could've sworn the planning meeting was in ten days…and that it was April, so I'm pretty lost.

If this is the best part of my life…we're not doing very well.

Is this why Tristan left me?

"Everything okay, Miranda?" Eva, the editor in chief, asks.

"Yes," I say very certainly. "Just lemme…"

I flip through the pages in my planner until I feel a little tap on my leg; to my right, Rita is gesturing at the iPad with her eyes and her perfect eyebrows. I grab the iPad, open the folder called "Current Planning" on the shared server, and glance at it.

"Sorry, girls…I had a terrible night. I had a really bad migraine."

"I thought it was vomiting?" Cris asked.

I look up for a second very seriously and nod.

"Migraines make me vomit. It's fine. We're inheriting from our dear North American mother the Blake Lively interview, which is four pages, where she talks about what this pregnancy has meant for her career." I look up. "I didn't know she was having another baby."

"We talked about it the other day, don't you remember? She wore that blue dress with the Bardot neckline to some event. She looked divine," one of the fashion editors comments.

What she was saying seems to ring a bell…but in the distance, deep down in my memory.

"Um…okay. We're also taking the advertorial, which is coming to us written and produced by the mother ship. It's from MAC about lipstick in grunge colors. The photo is of Lorde. It's two pages. And we're also syndicating…um…a Chanel campaign."

I glance up from the iPad again and pull a face that makes everyone laugh.

"Maybe I'm getting old, but all this seems like the same as always. Give me something good, my girls, because we have to make nice things for the world. Fashion, what have we got?"

"We're going over all the trends that are gonna stick around next summer and which are going to disappear. We're highlighting the following: crisscross necklines, how to use it and where to find the best dupes from models' street style. Athleisure, or how to use sporty pieces in your everyday fits without looking like you're on your way to or from the gym. Oh! And a special on the best rock T-shirts. Then we have an accessories section, our own production, garments from the Dior cruise collection, and in the wardrobe section, we talk about sailor tees." Rita seems pleased after she spews all this in one breathless stream.

"Seems okay to me," Eva confirms.

I furrow my brow.

"Are you within your page limit?"

"Yes. The same pages as always."

They're all looking at me, waiting for an okay. I know fashion is cyclical, but...

"It seems a little warmed over to me, girls. Are you sure?"

Rita is looking at me, confused.

"Miri...it's the most cutting of the cutting edge. We've been going through all the Instagram accounts of the major influencers all over the world and the trends on the runway, plus the fast fashion collections and the prêt-à-porter from the big businesses..."

"No, you know I trust your judgment one hundred, Rita. It's just that... I don't know." I'm not feeling any understanding looks around me, so I decide to make a joke. "Seems like fashion died when Karl did."

There's a stir through every member of the meeting.

"What?"

"Huh?"

"What did you say?"

"Karl?"

"No way."

"Quick, google it."

I'm getting more and more sure that whatever was on top of that bun wasn't sugar.

"Wait, what's going on?" I ask, super confused.

They've all whipped out their phones and are pulling up Google. Is that an iPhone 7 in Rita's hand?

"Miri, girl…" Marta says with a smile. "You're bumping poor Karl Lagerfeld off before his time."

I feel a knot in my stomach. I'm 100 percent sure Karl Lagerfeld is dead. He died two years ago. We did a special on his most iconic designs and his most famous quotes.

I look at my iPad for a second. I take my phone out from under my planner's leather cover. I look at my fingers. A second-generation iPad. iPhone 8 plus. Brand-new. There's no sign of a ring with a blue stone on my ring finger. I don't know what to blame—the migraine, my sadness, or the pain of the breakup, which has been floating in my chest since yesterday—but something isn't working how it should. I'm seeing weird stuff, things that aren't possible…and normalizing them. How did I not realize all this when I've been checking my phone since I opened my eyes this morning?

"What day is it?" I mutter without looking up.

"Miri, are you okay?"

"What day is it?"

"The eleventh of November," one of the younger voices says.

"Of what year?"

Cris gets up and hurries over to crouch down next to me.

"Miri, you're super disoriented. Are you okay?" She touches my neck and my forehead.

I'm covered in a cold sweat.

"Should I call an ambulance?" Marta asks, worried.

"What are you trying to do, make her even more anxious?" Rita responds.

A bunch of birds start fluttering around the room. They're all nervous, and they all want to do something for me.

"What year?" I repeat, my voice shaking.

When she tells me the year five years ago, I feel like I'm going to faint.

"Very funny."

They all look at one another, confused.

"It's not a joke," I confirm. "It's not…" I press a finger into my temple. "Ah…"

They're truly alarmed, and they're still all talking to one another.

"Call an ambulance."

"Could it be a stroke?"

"Too much stress."

"I told you…we should have helped her more with the transition."

"But she wouldn't let us… She has that obsession with doing everything herself…"

I stand up and stumble.

"Give me a second."

"Miri, where are you going? We should go to the doctor."

"Someone should go with her."

I turn toward them and fake the most terrifying grin I've ever smiled.

"I'm fine. I'm just…a little dizzy. Let me go to the bathroom." They all start following. "Alone," I clarify.

I take advantage of them taking a couple of steps back to run off toward the toilets in panic. I'm reassured by the fact that my legs are working. I'm breathing normally, and I can talk, hear, see. I feel a resounding strength in each step I take, each time I notice my strides or the hand pushing on the bathroom door. But...

I go into a cubicle and lock it behind me before I sit down on the closed lid, hugging my knees to my chest.

That was a big year.

I'd like to say it was the most important year of my life.

In that year, I was promoted to deputy editor.

In that year, I went on vacation alone for the first time.

In that year, I met Tristan.

To be exact, on November 11.

Wait...what the...?

3

~~~

IT'S IMPOSSIBLE FOR ME TO BE LEVELHEADED WHEN YOU COME IN AND ASK ME ABOUT US

I met Tristan twice.

I know the concept of "meeting" implies that it's impossible to do it more than once, but you have to believe me: I met him twice. I'm going to try to explain it, but it's not easy.

In that year, I was tired. My professional life was on a roll, I was healthy, I liked what I did, I lived in an apartment I loved, my father was strong and healthy, my best friend always had a fun plan, I went to parties, enjoyed people, traveled… In that year, I bought my first designer bag in a fit of superficiality to reward all the work I had done to get where I was.

But I was tired in my personal life, or actually my emotional one. Wrapped up with a beautiful bow of "I don't need love" was a lot of tiredness. Also some disappointment and a lot of cynicism.

Wait, let's rewind. Sitting here on the office toilet, I keep thinking the same thing: Love doesn't make me who I am. It's not the only way to be happy. But life is a race to share what we have, what we are, and what we feel.

I didn't mean that whole "I don't need love" thing way back then. I didn't want to fall in love because I had loved too much and I was stumbling down a path of lies. Because I had a lot of fun flings, but I had a scar down the middle of my chest that split me in two, reminding me that one day, I fell in love with a guy who, after telling me he would pull the moon down so I could step on it, decided it would be better to…stay married. Two punches at once: "Hey, Miranda, I'm married. See you later, Miranda. I'm not leaving her."

So I had a good time. When the wound had healed, of course. When I felt up to it, when it suddenly sounded fun to me, when I knew I wasn't doing it for the wrong reasons, I got on Tinder. And I had a blast. I had dozens of fun dates with guys who wanted to impress me to get in my pants, and I pretended to be impressed and got in theirs.

Until Tristan.

The first time I met Tristan, he was calling himself Manuel. I matched with him on Tinder. His pictures and most of the information on his profile were true.

MANUEL

32 years old.

I'm one of those uncomplicated guys.

I like what everyone likes, no surprises here.

I don't rock climb and I'm not going to claim I make the best tortilla de patata in the world.

But what I can promise you is I'm good company. And I know a little bit about wine.

I don't blame him for the little white lies. I was called Laura on Tinder. It was easier. Miranda always made guys ask a bunch of boring, weird questions that I didn't feel like answering with the classic "ha ha" that you send when your face is more serious than a nun. I liked his profile for its honesty. In the meat market, where everyone tries to stand out as funny, built, sexy, or sophisticated, this guy was defending normality. He was showing himself as he was. So he caught my eye…but his name wasn't Manuel, and it did get complicated.

We talked for a few nights. In the beginning, it was the same old "Where are you from?" "What do you do?" "Have you lived in Madrid for long?" "What kind of music do you listen to?" "Where do you go out?" We cut through the bullshit pretty fast. I told him I wasn't looking for anything serious. He said he wasn't either; he was just passing through. After two or three days, we sent each other a few photos, no dick pics or anything obscene. We were both chatting from our respective beds, and we sent each other a selfie. We made stupid faces. We suggested a few things we could do when we saw each other and tried to pick a day for our first date in person…a first date that never happened because, of course… I met him for the second time.

At the magazine.

As Tristan.

Thirty-two years old.

Lawyer.

The ones who come to fix shit shows at the magazine.

And remember where they've seen your face…

And that you told them in passing that you like when guys pull your hair during blow jobs.

So…if what I'm afraid is happening actually is, in an hour, Tristan is going to show up at the magazine in a black turtleneck and black pants and a gray wool coat, one of those beautiful, elegant, stylish coats that have already lived a lot but have been well taken care of.

Yes. If it is actually November 11 five years ago, instead of the team of lawyers we're used to meeting, we'll see a partner from the firm in Madrid, one of Marisol's childhood friends, and Tristan, the new hire.

Tristan, the fake Manuel. The man who I spent five years of my life with. The man who dumped me last night.

The door to the bathroom opens, and a few timid footsteps approach the cubicle I'm locked in.

"Miri…" a noble, mature voice that engenders trust whispers worriedly.

"Marisol?"

"I heard you're not feeling well. Can I come in for a second?"

I look at the door in panic. I'm becoming aware that if this is a break in the space-time continuum, I'm violating all the laws for this type of travel, and I'm going to create a really fucking bad butterfly effect, because this didn't happen on November 11 five years ago. What if I wake up tomorrow and I'm a lizard? What do I know?

I open the latch and sit back down, hugging my legs against my chest again. She enters hesitantly and smiles calmly at me. Her perfect, short black hair is combed as stylishly as ever, and her glasses hang on her chest from a chain with oversize black links she bought in Paris on a trip in the sixties with her grandmother…and that broke at the Milan airport two years ago.

"Miri, what's going on?"

"It's not a panic attack," I try to answer calmly.

"Well…" There's a whisker of condescension in her smile, but only a whisker. The type of nonjudgmental condescension you can impart when you've run the gauntlet yourself. "We'll have to see about that."

I suck in air and lean against the wall in front of me.

"They say you were asking what year it is…"

"I just got disoriented." I make excuses, even though I'm still very confused.

"What year is it?" she asks the question back to me.

I echo the year back to her, but I must still have a funny look on my face. She furrows her brow.

"Miri…if this is too much for you, if you need help or maybe a longer transition period, don't worry, okay? We chose you for the position because we trust in your abilities. It's no good for us if you try to take on everything right away and your head ends up exploding. I don't want the cleaning crew to have to clean your brains off your office," she jokes.

"I'm a good deputy editor."

"You will be, of course, but if you need help to handle all this…that's completely fine. You just have to say so."

She says it a lot when we're all running around her hysterical, saying we need everything ASAP.

I have the urge to hug her, to inhale her Bulgari perfume, for her to stroke my hair like we were mother and daughter, but I don't move because everything is incredibly intense right now. And weird. I'm worried I've lost my grip on reality.

"Marisol…" I mumble.

"I'll be with you in the meeting with the lawyers, okay? I know it's really stressful that in your first month as deputy editor, you have to face how the publication handles a lawsuit, and I won't pretend it's normal or that you'll get used to it, but these things happen. We do a story on someone, that someone isn't satisfied with her statements and photos, and instead of telling us, she approves the content and then sues us. Wonderful. It won't go any further… We have all the digital correspondence and consent contracts."

In that year, one of the cover girls threatened to sue us. Or sued us, I don't remember exactly. All I remember is that the lawyers got her to back down. I'm not worried about the lawsuit or the paperwork or that the magazine's image will take a hit…because I already know none of that is going to happen. I'm worried that I've already lived through it.

"Are you listening to me?"

"Yes." I nod.

"Miri, you're really pale. Why don't you pop over to the hospital? One of the girls from the editorial department can go with you, and they can just check you over."

"No, no. I'm fine."

"I'm not going to ask if you're on drugs, because I'm pretty sure the answer is no, and I don't want to risk finding out I'm wrong."

I laugh. It's like the time an actress stole the clothes from a shoot. Some situations are so unbelievable all you can do is laugh.

"That's better. You seem like yourself when you laugh." She sighs. "Let's try something... You go take a walk. I'll finish up the planning meeting. Come back at 11:30, and we'll deal with the damn lawsuit, which is not happening today, you'll see. Does that sound good?"

I feel like I've totally lost my head, so I say yes, trusting that whatever happens, in the current planning folder on the server, the me of yesterday or today or the parallel reality has been uploading all the previewed topics for the next issue.

The door on my father's shop has a little bell on it. I have always loved it because it feels like you're going into a magical store. Like it's straight out of Diagon Alley in Harry Potter. Plus, if I find an invisibility cloak in there one day, I won't be that surprised. My father sells antiques and knickknacks. You can buy all kinds of stuff in his cave warehouse he's turned into a store. It's crazy that, in these times, he can still do that for a living. It's a jackpot for directors of artsy movies and TV shows. If they can dream it up, they can find it in my father's store.

As always, he's not at the counter but sitting in the wing chair that has been on sale since 1995, even though everyone knows he doesn't actually want to sell it. He's drinking coffee from one of the mugs that's also probably for sale and reading a heavy book with yellowed pages and maroon binding.

"Miranda!" He's surprised. "Are you feeling sick? Shouldn't you be in school?"

A giggle escapes from my nose.

"It's been quite a few years since I've been in school."

"Isn't work basically the same? Like going to high school, except you get paid."

"The truth is there are days when I feel like they're paying me to play, that's for sure."

It's a sixteen-minute walk from the magazine offices to my father's store. It took me twelve. I can't see how many calories I burned on this walk on my smartwatch because…I bought it in the future, and apparently that hasn't happened yet.

I can't stay long, but when I breathe in deep and the smell of antiques, dust, and my father's aftershave fills my lungs, I know I did the right thing by coming. I need a little sanity.

"Dad…"

He stands up, worried by my tone, sits me down in the chair he was in a second ago, and touches my forehead and my neck. It's a gesture that many would mistakenly call maternal, but it's paternal too. It's important to remember that the birth of a baby doesn't only awaken protection and care in women (or it shouldn't).

"I don't have a fever."

"You're sweating," he says. "And what are you doing not wearing a coat? You must have caught some strange virus."

"Yeah, the inaugural case of COVID," I joke.

"Of what?"

For the love of the divine cosmos.

"Can I ask you some weird questions?" I propose.

"Of course."

"What year is it?"

"Miranda, sweetie, I'm not senile. Give me a break," he grumbles.

"I'm not saying you're senile. Can you tell me today's date?"

"Well...tenth or eleventh of November. You know I'm terrible at remembering what day it is."

Well, what if I tell you...

"Of what year?"

"Miranda, you're scaring me." He puts his hands on his hips.

I pull my feet up into the chair and curl back into the position Marisol found me in in the bathroom stall half an hour ago. I know he's not going to scold me for putting my feet on the furniture; he's not that kind of dad.

"Dad...something really strange is going on with me. Is there any history of mental illness in the family?"

"Your great aunt Conchi was pretty weird, but that's not a mental illness. She was original. Like me. She went through a phase where she wore purple from head to toe. She looked like a Nazarene with a hood."

I sigh.

"I'm serious."

"No, Miri, there's no mental illness. You're really scaring me."

"Dad, yesterday, when I went to bed, it was five years from now."

My father raises his eyebrows, which peek curiously over the lenses of his glasses.

"My god..."

He perches on the arm of the chair and puts his palm on my forehead again.

"Dad...I'm not joking."

"Sweetheart, you're not well. You've had a lot of very stressful months. And I'm sure you're not taking care of yourself. When was the last time you cooked yourself a decent meal? I have the feeling you only eat things that are delivered to your house by motorcycle."

"What if it's a brain tumor?" I'm freaking myself out now.

Another father might have dragged me by the arm to the emergency room, but he's calmer than that. Maybe less sensible, I don't know. Even I have the urge to drag myself to the emergency room so they can do sixteen scans on me. But he rubs my back.

"Sweetie…you're going to do really well in this job, but maybe you're investing too much energy in it. You're exhausted. Look at you."

I hope I don't look ugly. This is the day I'm going to meet Tristan. Because that's it, right?

"Do you believe in time travel?" I ask point-blank.

"Of course."

His answer surprises me a lot…until he keeps talking and I see where he's going.

"We're always revisiting our past. We travel backward almost every day. Sometimes we need a photo to catapult us into that past, other times just a smell or a song. It happens to me every day. When I get up, I never know what day of my history with your mother I'm going to live again."

I suck my teeth.

"It's not like that, Dad."

"Yes, yes, it is. That's how we learn. In the painful times."

I look at the clock he has in one corner. When it strikes twelve, a bunch of little birds pop out and hellish music plays, which, of course, is the thing that has scared people off buying it throughout the years. It's been rented twice for film sets on horror movies, need I say more.

The hands mark eleven, and I should get moving. I don't understand what's happening, but even in a situation like this, being late seems completely irrational to me. You don't arrive late to places where you respect other people because you're making them waste their time. Something weird is happening to me, but that's not anyone in this dimension's fault.

"Dad, I gotta go. I have a meeting."

"Are you coming over for dinner? You've piqued my curiosity with this time-travel stuff, so you'll have to tell me all about it."

I look at him in complete shock.

"Dad, shouldn't you be worried? I am."

"If I were, then who would you confide in?"

Well, he was definitely right about that.

"Call Ivan and tell him. I'm sure he'll find all this hilarious."

Ivan and I have worked together for a while now. I met him in a showroom where we'd often borrow clothes for photo shoots that we were producing ourselves. He seemed like a fucking blast. We ran into each other at a few soirees for the magazine or brands…stuff like that. And I have no idea how it happened, but we ended up attached at the hip. Now he's a stylist, and he charges through the nose for every job. And I'm glad.

Even though I'm sure that right now he's probably sitting in his apartment smoking and drinking coffee, I don't call him. It's not that I don't want to bother him (I always want to bother him). It's just that I don't know what to say. The whole "last night, I went to sleep five years in the future" doesn't seem like it'll do the trick.

And yet I get a message from my friend right as I'm crossing the street to the office. My father must have called him.

IVAN:

Wait, I must be tripping. You go on an astral journey and you don't even call me? You're a shitty bestie, just so you know.

I would laugh if I wasn't going to find out five minutes from now whether I've returned (I don't know how or why or even when) to *that* day. I'm trying to remember every detail of how things went down, and I suddenly understand why I felt like I was copying someone with my look this morning: I was copying myself. This is exactly what I was wearing when I met Tristan. Except that day, I included a coat in my accessories. I'm not sure if I'm using the right verb tense. This is all so weird.

I think I was sitting in the conference room, going over the agenda and the information I had on the iPad, when I looked up and saw him. And I wanted to die because I had just answered on Tinder that we could meet up whenever he wanted (and I wasn't expecting it to be so soon or under these circumstances) and...of course, also because I had given details to one of the magazine's lawyers about how I liked giving blow jobs and all that. Not to mention that when he showed up, he was even cuter in person. I thought this run-in was going to put an end to my sensual expectations.

I'll be honest, now that I'm sitting in the office: I don't get it at all. What the fuck should I do? Go to the hospital? That's what I should do. I know, I know. But...is it crazy to want to erase any doubt first? It's simple... Maybe it's all a joke. Maybe it's all a dream, like in the movies at the end of *Los Serrano* (oops, spoiler). But I'm sticking around to see if he's going to show up like I remember. I need to see him. I want to smell him. Then I'll go find out if I'm crazy or if I need to find someone to water my plants while I'm gone. And figure out a digital will because I don't want my Instagram account just flapping in the wind for the rest of eternity.

I head out of my office, check that I don't have red lipstick on my face with my front-facing camera, and when I get there and sit down, I realize I left my iPad and my planner on my desk.

I retrace my steps, running in heels; I'm vaguely aware of many eyes following me. The girls must be a little worried about me, and I get it. I think if I had been a spectator this morning instead of the victim, I would have dragged the protagonist of the hallucinations to the ER. It's just that...I've never been a fan of the limelight for some reason.

My phone vibrates, and I'm scared to look at it. Maybe it's a message for time travelers with the phone number for the space-time embassy where I can call in case there's any trouble, but no, it's just a message from the magazine group chat:

MARISOL:

Miri, are you ready? They're on the way in.

"I'm coming!" I yell at the top of my lungs.

"And remember what year it is, babe!" jokes Rita, who's walking behind me.

"I was going to call you a douchebag, but you don't even deserve that, you giant jerk."

I say it right as we're going through the doorway of the room where the meeting is taking place and where, unfortunately, everyone is already seated. And to top it all off, they are staring in slight shock at the mouth where this string of urban poetry just streamed from, which, by the way, is mine. I assume Marisol is cursing me through Morse code with her eyelashes, but I don't notice because all I can see is him. Tristan. In his black turtleneck sweater, standing by the table, looking at me with subtly raised eyebrows. I think he recognizes me, but I don't know if that's because he just realized I'm the girl he's been chatting with on Tinder or because this is all just an act and the five-year relationship is still there, where I can remember it.

"Hi," I say timidly.

"Hi," he responds.

For a few seconds, there's nobody else in the room or maybe in the world. If it's possible that we jumped back five years in time, maybe it's possible that the entire planet's population could've disappeared, except the two of us.

I can smell him from here…and that smell, like so many other times, makes a knot in my stomach, another in my throat, and a final one between my thighs. The body has a memory. Skin remembers. How am I ever going to get him out from inside me? I can't.

It's him. It's Tristan. With him, I knew exactly what every one of the four letters meant in a word I thought I didn't believe in. I laughed. I traveled. I hugged. I argued. I discovered. I fell in love with myself again. All by his side. He can't possibly have forgotten all of it. There must be some trace in his blood, a vestigial feeling that lights up at least a spark of memory. *It's me, Tristan. It's me.*

"Laura?" He raises an eyebrow.

When I was living through this moment for the first time, I responded: "Manuel?" but right now, I have no voice. It was stolen, like in *The Little Mermaid*.

"Miranda," Marisol corrects him.

"Interesting name," he answers, offering me his right hand. "Tristan, nice to meet you. Another not very common name."

I give him a strained smile and sit down. The floor is wobbling, but I seem to be the only one who's noticing the earthquake.

We're sitting around a table in the conference room: the editor in chief and the deputy editor, as in Marisol and me, plus the team that were on the photo shoot and the interview that we are (were? Oof, look, I don't know) being threatened with a lawsuit over: an intern, an assistant, the session stylist, the makeup artist who I haven't even said hi to, and Rita, as the fashion editor of our publication. Then: the lawyers. I remember in the real first year that we met, I recovered pretty quickly from the initial shock; I even called him "fake Manuel" before he left. I was good at flirting. I was in control immediately. Of him. Of his tone. His way of running his eyes over my lips. I bit my lower lip as I looked at how his sweater clung to his chest, and I know he liked that.

Right now, I'm not capable at all. I've lost my rizz.

Maybe a truck hit me yesterday and I'm in a coma, reliving my happiest days?

"Okay, introductions done." The partner from the law firm smiles. "Please excuse Ricardo's absence, but he's at an important trial right now, so we thought this would be the perfect opportunity to get Tristan out of the office."

Tristan had just arrived in the city when I met him. He was still living in an Airbnb, trying to find an apartment. He transferred from the office in Vigo, but he was already making an impression in Madrid. And...he's not going to admit it, but right now, he's overheating and scared shitless that he must be sweating like an animal and making a bad impression.

"He just moved over from our Vigo office."

"Welcome to Madrid, Tristan." Marisol smiles.

It seems like he's about to say something when I interrupt:

"Can someone open a window?" I direct it to the person on the other side of the table. "This room is like a weird microclimate."

"Thank you. Heating and turtlenecks aren't a great combo," Tristan pipes up immediately. He's thinking about how to approach our meeting on Tinder after the meeting, and maybe that's why he holds my eye contact a little longer than is polite. Plus I know he's not that comfortable when it comes to fashion matters. "By the way, is this called a turtleneck?"

"Yes, or a roll neck," Rita helps him, charmed.

I know what she's thinking. I know she's thinking she'd love to get a glass of wine with a boy like him, hoping her ex would see her. Back then, she still wasn't over him, and she hadn't met the guy who would be her husband yet.

And the thing is Tristan is...well...something about his face is intense. The first thing I noticed about Tristan was his mouth. He has a really juicy mouth. The kind of lips that were born to kiss and be kissed. Once, I told him, in bed; we were in the super-rococo room in a hotel in the mountains, and we had just done it. I say "done it" because I'm not sure what happened, whether we fucked or whether we were getting into something even more intimate than that. He cracked up, and even though I was expecting some super-romantic answer like "Well, I only want to kiss your lips," he responded:

"Wow, you say some wild shit."

I land in the conference room again with a bump. I hear people talking, I see the papers they're handing out and the screen in the room connecting to Marisol's computer to project some images, but I can't follow the thread. He's concentrating on the meeting.

This is a nightmare. The Tim Burton version of my life.

This situation seems slightly different from how I remembered it. Maybe time taints everything, the way a child's breath fogs a window. Maybe I idealized him, or maybe I don't even remember clearly how romantic everything was from the beginning with him.

He looks up and catches me staring at him. He smiles discreetly, and I can almost foresee how he's going to approach me at the end of the meeting and invite me out for a coffee or maybe wine. I can almost sense a kind of impatience in the way he's moving in his chair, an inner tension between being very professional and letting himself be carried away by the butterflies.

You give me butterflies. He said that to me before the *I love you* or the *I like you a lot.* Even before the *Why the hell are we paying for two apartments, Miri?*

You give me butterflies. And while some people melt when a man tells them he sees stars in their eyes, this seemed like the most beautiful thing anyone had ever said to me.

"Well then, let me make sure I'm understanding correctly," Tristan says as he stops looking at me and turns back to Marisol. "The claimant never communicated at any time her discontent with the statements that appeared in her interview once it was edited."

"No. On July 6, we sent her the finalized mock-up so that she and her rep could review it…"

I lose the thread again. Reviewing. Is that what I'm doing? What's happening to me? I don't get any of it. I don't get it. Is this a cosmic opportunity for us to try again? So we can rectify our mistakes? Are we going to relive this story from the beginning, already knowing what we've been through, figuring out where we stumbled and where we should have spent more time?

I feel a landslide in my chest getting bigger and bigger and threatening to drag me down with it. Yesterday, Tristan dumped me. He broke up with me, with the life we had, all the plans. He didn't ask me for time. He didn't say he needed to think or get some space and distance, just that he didn't want to be with me anymore and that I had to respect that. And today, the day after he left me, leaving no time for the things I like about him to fade away, here he is again. For the first time.

Him, the guy who always knows what to order for me at the bar counter, who never opens a single door for me but sticks his foot in so it won't slam in my face. I love the way he buttons his pants, like a little kid concentrating really hard on his homework or, sometimes, like a playboy who wants you to know he's going to take them off again. I can't resist the way his thick eyebrows arch. His innocent fingers around a rocks glass from the bar below our house. How he's not silent or noisy or somewhere in the middle: he's like that song by Los Piratas that I like listening to at any volume.

His everyday shoes. His winter pajamas. The slightly tacky ring he wears on his ring finger now but that I got him to take off three years ago and he would always twist when he was nervous. The hair on his chest, which seems a little unkempt, consistent but not very dense, like a thicket that is quickly dissolved by the shower of kisses I rain over it when I have it in range.

His legs. His feet. The way he moves his hips, like he never learned to do it like this with anyone else...with other women...like I had always been there: up, down, to the side, game.

The way he says certain words: "ay," "go ahead," "goodbye," "speed," "heat," "umbrella," "useless contraptions"... The fact that he still uses the word "contraption."

When I met him, when I actually met him, I liked that he was weird, just like me. When we met that morning in the middle of this cluttered world, I felt like my weirdness didn't actually matter. And neither did his. And life is a grab bag of random stuff, and it's impossible for me to be levelheaded when you come in and ask me about us.

4

~~

THE WEIRDEST WOMAN ON TINDER

TRISTAN

I'd be lying if I said I wasn't surprised. I wasn't expecting to be flirting on Tinder and then run into the woman in question at a work meeting. But the thing is maybe I should have started off with the detail that I never imagined I'd be resorting to Tinder in the first place. It's not like I've never needed to. I've had my moments just like everyone else, but I'm really not into it. I don't know. All I know is that after talking shit about these apps, I found myself creating a profile without telling anyone. That's the thing about moving: you start doubting your ability to meet new people outside work, or you feel kind of lazy about the ritual of going into a bar, exchanging glances, going over, striking up a conversation...

Laura isn't the first woman I've talked to or the first I made plans to meet up with. Last week, I had a glass of wine with a charming girl who I had a pleasant fuck with and agreed to contact when one of us wanted to do it again. I'm not looking for a relationship, and I'm up-front about it; I'm not trying to play anyone. But it's not like I walk around saying, listen, sex only, because that's not what I want. I want something warm, a nice time, stimulating conversation, and if it ends in sex, even better. I don't want to Netflix and chill. I can do that on my own. Laura seemed fun, and I was thinking about meeting up with her today or tomorrow. But

Laura's real name is Miranda, and she's sitting here in front of me, looking at me like I just said I was a Scientologist. Or at least how I would look at someone if they said that to me.

Manuel is what my parents were going to name me, but their romantic streak won out, so I'm Tristan. Tristan incites too many questions and dominates the conversation. I get bored of having to explain that yes, it's because of the Arthurian legend of Tristan and Isolde. That no, it's not a family name even though it's so weird. But in my defense, I will say that the rest of the information I gave Laura was real, even though I've also been pretty careful not to spill my whole life story. I don't like saying I'm a lawyer, because I don't think it fits my real personality. I don't like admitting I'm so new in town, because it makes me feel like I'm at a disadvantage. I don't like admitting that I've had kind of a lot of practice in relationships with the opposite sex because I tend to lose interest pretty quickly. That's just being an asshole, and I'd hate to dig too deep and find out I actually am one. My sister says I'm not, I just haven't found the right girl, but she's the kind of sister who no one will ever be good enough for.

Miranda doesn't seem to be following the meeting very closely. She's kind of spacey or distracted. In three dimensions, her face is a little rounder than in her photos on the app, and maybe I imagined her with bigger boobs, but the truth is she's prettier. She would've caught my eye in a bar. Miranda is weird; she can't hide it, but she's not trying to either. And I'm way more into that than stuff like an oval face or hair or body type. I don't have a predefined type. I like whatever I see and happen to like. And I'm attracted to her. Besides, there's something strange in the air, like the way she looks is just the first layer of a cake I'm going to end up eating with my hands.

The meeting is showing signs of wrapping up. We have all the information we need, and it's already being forwarded to us for archiving and analysis. It's going to be child's play. Soon, I'll have the text drafted that will dissuade the "cover girl" from following through with this.

"Some people will do anything to get attention…" I sigh.

Miranda shrinks a little in her seat when I look at her. Maybe she's one of those people who will do anything to get attention? Or the opposite? I think it's probably the opposite. Restrained in public, explosive in bed, I would bet my whole hand.

There's something about her that seems so familiar…

The whole team, made up of almost all women, is saying goodbye with polite smiles and chatting about what they have to do next.

"I have to go do returns," one says.

"I have to compare prices," another reports.

"I have to go over all the material we're going to syndicate."

"I have to call the agency."

And I feel super lost, because I have no idea what any of it actually means.

The partner tells me he's going to grab a coffee with Marisol, the editor in chief, who he seems to be old chums with, and I tell him that I'm going straight back to the office so I can get everything ready as soon as possible, but he tells me to relax.

"Tristan, go get a coffee. It's a nice day. Enjoy Madrid a little. It won't bite."

I've been a little tense since I got here. I guess I feel like I have a lot to prove. The kid from the suburbs never forgets where he comes from, and…it's exhausting. But he's right. A coffee wouldn't hurt.

I catch up with Miranda when she's almost at the door. She hustled out of there, and I feel bad because…I don't know why. Maybe because none of this seemed that awkward to me, although I had been hyperaware since the moment I saw her that she likes having her hair pulled when she gives blow jobs. And the idea of her hair wrapped around my fist got me bad. And bad is a euphemism for horny.

"Hey…" I stop her. "Miranda…or should I call you Laura?"

"Laura's my twin. You'll see. We're like two peas in a pod. You must be getting us mixed up. Don't worry about it. It happens all the time."

She says it without even turning to look at me. When she does, she has a horrified expression on her face, but she tries to cover it up with a polite smile.

"Do I look way uglier than my photos?" I ask her jokingly.

I know for a fact that they're not good photos and I'm the opposite of a catfish, but she doesn't answer.

"What? Don't look at me like that. We all have our games."

Miranda sucks her teeth, and a sigh sneaks out. She's much more nervous than I was expecting.

"It's not that. It's not that at all," she answers.

"So?"

"I'm having a bad day. A terrible one."

"Okay…"

"I'm going to the doctor right now."

"To the doctor?" I raise an eyebrow. "You're not feeling well?"

"I feel awful," she admits.

"Listen…this isn't because of me, right?"

She looks at me so closely for a few seconds that I feel weird. Uncomfortable…but not exactly. It's a look of recognition. It's the look you give your ex when you run into them after a lot of years, and because of how much time has passed, you can suddenly recognize the boy you fell in love with at least for a little while. I smile. I don't know why, but I smile. She does too.

"You're looking at me funny."

"I'm looking at you like always," she says.

Like always, she says.

"You're pretty weird," I tease.

"And you ain't seen nothing yet."

"Tell me more? Let me buy you a coffee. A quick coffee."

She seems to waver.

"I'm really going to the doctor."

"But is it serious?"

"It could be." She nods with a severe expression. "Maybe I'm dying."

That makes me let out a guffaw, even though it shouldn't. She smiles a little too.

"One coffee," I insist.

/

"A headache," she says, clenching a cup of green tea.

Is she nuts? Why am I so intrigued?

"Well, that doesn't seem fatal."

"This morning, I got up, and I didn't know what year it was. Super disoriented."

I blink. Jesus.

"Does that happen to you often?" I ask carefully.

"What? Of course not! That's why I'm freaked out. What if a tumor is pressing against some part of my brain that…"

"Stop, stop." I laugh. "Fake Laura…it's not a tumor."

"How do you know? When you become a lawyer, do you get some superpower that lets you perform MRIs with your eyes too?"

"Yes," I answer securely. "And also the ability to guess what you want in a bar. It never fails."

She looks at me almost tenderly before she sucks her teeth.

"Don't push it," she whispers.

"Push what?"

"I don't know." She clutches her head, and with her fingers in her perfect updo, I can see how real her anxiety is.

"Hey…" I reach out and touch her forearm. "I know I don't know you at all, and who am I to say… Well, I mean, you can tell me to eff off, but it's not that serious."

She looks up, curious, and waits for me to go on.

"I really don't know what's bothering you, but if, for some reason, it's something like you feel ridiculous because of how we met…the first time"—I smile—"or because of the information we've shared with each other, forget it, okay?"

She nods.

"Life is too short to want to be like everyone else, right?" I add.

She studies me with those thick, long eyelashes with just enough mascara. With her slightly smudged red lipstick. Her clean, snowy cheeks with a tint of color. Yes, she's looking at me and actually studying me with something I can't identify. Maybe the situation, her anxiety, the possibilities that are unfolding in front of us?

"Listen, Tristan…I'm going to ask you a really weird question, okay?"

"It's not like anything so far has been very normal, but okay."

"Imagine if one day, you found yourself in a situation, and you know how it's gonna end."

"I know or I imagine?"

"You know. With devastating certainty."

"Okay. And I'm guessing it ends badly."

"Yes," she agrees very confidently. "But you can avoid it."

"How?"

"You can avoid it by turning your back on it. Choosing another path."

"I think I understand."

"Or you can try to avoid the ending by throwing yourself in headfirst and changing your methods."

"Okay. But I don't have any guarantee that it will end well."

"You're getting into the case, huh?" she teases.

"I like these kinds of games." I wrinkle my nose a little as I lean my arms on the table, which I do to get closer to her. And smell her.

She's wearing a kind of powdery perfume. Sweet. Expensive.

"What would you do?" she insists.

"I'm not really sure how my answer matters at all, but here goes: I would weigh the pros and cons of this terrible ending you mentioned. If it means a temporary pain, I would risk it again. But if it means a lifelong scar, the kind where you learn things that don't make you better, I would pass."

She sits up slowly, looking at me intensely.

"You're handsome," she blurts out.

"Thanks. You're not bad yourself. And you smell good."

"You do too. How long have you been wearing that cologne?"

"I don't know. Five or six years."

"It's intense." She raises her eyebrows. "It's the kind that takes us girls some getting used to."

"Yours too, now that you mention it."

I smile at her a little insecurely. I don't feel in control of the situation. I'm nervous. I don't like it. I do like her, but I don't know if it's enough to keep the upper hand. Men lose all their bravado when a woman we don't know challenges us and we know she's in control.

She smiles sadly and puts a hand on mine.

"It's been a pleasure, Tristan."

"Is that a goodbye?"

"I know how this ends."

I take a second to react. She's so sure when she says it. She's not talking about a wound; she's not talking about some trauma. She really believes what she's saying. The warmth of her hand on mine comforts me in a way I can't explain. A kind of tingle. Something, I don't know where. Miranda makes me tingle in some part of my brain where I can't even scratch.

"Seriously?" I ask her.

She pulls her hand away. The magic shatters. The moment.

I hesitate. I'm disconcerted. I see her get up and hang her bag on her shoulder.

"No," I moan, trying to sound sweet, even though I'm not exactly known as a ray of sunshine. "Don't leave me hanging. What would happen if you didn't leave here today?"

"A glass of wine. Since you just got to Madrid, you'd ask someone at the office where you should take me, and they'd recommend a fancy but terrible place, full of tech bros strung out on coke who gross me out. We would laugh a lot, that's true. We'd have sex at my house, sex that's surprisingly good between two people who are as different as us. We would say goodbye assuming we were never going to see each other again, but you'd text me the next day. And the next."

"That doesn't sound much like my normal behavior."

"Tristan…you're going to be a good lawyer, but maybe you should reconsider the possibility that you're getting into a profession you're not in love with."

"I'm not the type who falls in love."

"Yet."

A few strands of hair curl around her ears, escaping her hairstyle and making her look more natural. I don't know why I have such a strong urge to stroke them and wrap them around my fingers. Miranda, who are you?

"Tea's on you, okay? You don't know this yet, but you owe me one."

I watch her head to the door unwaveringly, not turning to look at me, completely convinced that what she says is going to happen, will happen. And I'm sitting there watching her leave, not saying a word.

Miranda, who are you?

I have no doubt about it. She's officially the weirdest woman on Tinder.

5

~~~

IS THAT NOT HOW
ALL THIS WORKS?

MIRANDA

It was torture leaving the café this morning without looking back, but the thing is I know how we end, and I've been thinking, you know? Thinking about why this is happening.

Well…I thought about it after going to the ER, saying I'm having hallucinations, asking them to do a brain scan, and having the neurologist on duty tell me that everything inside my skull is normal for a girl my age. I had the urge to ask him if he had found shit. Because with the flood of shit society and media spews at us, I'm surprised our coconuts aren't full of manure.

Now that the possibility of a brain tumor the size of a Calanda peach is gone, I've started thinking about magical things, but it's not really helping; I'm trying to find the logic in all this. What do I know? If it's not a physical matter, maybe I have some kind of mental illness. I asked the neurologist. Listen, it's not that big of a deal. It's not something you put on your Christmas list, but if it happens to you, you get medication and that's it. Enough demonizing mental health matters. Look, it took me all day to get to this point of self-awareness. But he explained to me that it's very unlikely that I'd start showing sudden symptoms of a super evident mental illness that causes hallucinations. I didn't tell him that ever since

I woke up this morning, I've been surfing a wave through time into my past...just that when I got up, I thought it was a different year...

"Sweetheart, you're under a lot of stress."

I was about to go on a rant about how paternalistic that sounded, but I decided to let it go. Today is not the day to explain to a doctor who could be my father that I already have one and I don't need the world to find others for me. I'm an adult and very in control of my own life. Of course...not today, because control, control, what they call control, I don't exactly have.

When I get home, it's already nighttime. It's November; it gets dark really early. I have a few missed calls from Ivan, but I send him a WhatsApp saying I'll tell him everything tomorrow. Procrastinating has never been as easy as it is today; I'm normally afraid of facing the consequences in the near future made less sweet by leaving for tomorrow what you can do today, but the truth is I have no idea what's going to happen tomorrow.

I've jotted down in my planner a few possibilities that have occurred to me:

1. I wake up the day after my breakup and return to my real space-time.
2. I wake up on the twelfth of November, the day I originally got a message from Tristan. But of course, because I did something different today than I did, that will be an alternative November 12 where I turn into a world-famous flamenco dancer.
3. I wake up on some other random day.

The third option makes me really anxious. How can I live normally with no clue what damn day I'll wake up in? I'm probably in a coma, and all this is a dream caused by medication. Or I'm dead. Or I'm cryogenically frozen like Walt Disney. Maybe I tripped on the rug in my bedroom again, and I fulfilled my own prediction of ending up gaga. The corner of the wardrobe always looked dangerous to me.

It's gotta be something like that.

When I climb into bed, I feel like I'm Dorothy in Oz without the magic shoes, swept up in the folds of the space-time continuum…a girl who has invented a huge lie to flee from pain. But I fall asleep. Like someone bonked my head with a mallet. Immediately. Deeply. I sleep.

The grayish light around my bed wakes me up. It's like smoke. At first, I'm scared something in the apartment is in flames. And since I have crappy vision…that didn't help, like in eighties movies or the *Insidious* series. But no. It's just that it's very foggy, you can't see the sun, and the sky is covered in a whitish blanket.

My head feels heavy, muddled, but for a few moments, there's no pain or worry. Just my bed and sleepiness. It's seven in the morning. At ten past seven, my circumstances are back to feeling as heavy as they did before I went to sleep…and I look at the date on my iPhone screen.

It can't be.

Saturday, December 10, five years ago. Wait…what the fuck?

I don't need to stop to think for a second what's special about today. I already know.

Tristan and I met on Tinder, and we acted accordingly. We grabbed that glass of wine I told him about "yesterday" in the café across from the office. He took me to a pretty cringe place in the middle of Paseo de la Castellana, the kind that was "trendy" at the end of the noughties, that attracts the most flashy suited and booted cokeheads in all Madrid. Total bummer. But we giggled a lot at the tasseled loafers and the fancy hairstyles. And we had an amazing first kiss and even better sex at my house.

We said goodbye in my doorway, convinced we'd probably never see each other again. But like I said before, he texted me the next day. We met up to fuck two more times…until our first date, which was something neither of us planned on.

I sit on the toilet with no trace of glamor in my body, but to make up for the 232 pounds of anxiety pressing against my chest, I contort my body to rest my head on the laundry basket in front of me. I remember what Ivan said when I told him about our sporadic encounters:

"Ooh, girl…you're both going to regret starting off like that."

"What are you talking about?"

"Well, say whatever you want, but this isn't a fling, and in two years, you're going to have to answer 'fucking' when people ask how you met. It's the worst story…ever."

I liked Tristan, but the way you like a boy you drink wine, talk about interesting things, and have great sex with. The kind who the most intense thing they've shared with you is an orgasm and the worry about not finding a decent apartment to live in.

No. Tristan and I didn't have a fairy-tale start, but…what couple really does? Every day, love stories are sparked that start with a "Let's get a beer" or "You have to meet my friend. He's perfect for you." And so what? I never understood the universe's insistence on grandiloquence. I've always been a fan of things that just work.

"I don't understand why we have to be bigger fans of champagne than the wheel," I said once at the magazine. "Is it prosaic? Sure. But it makes the world turn."

"Yes, but champagne makes it fun."

I don't remember who came up with that retort, but they were right.

In the beginning, Tristan and I were a wheel. The wheel of a car, a taxi, a shopping cart… We were something simply practical up until a month after we met, when we learned the magic of champagne.

And that day is today.

For that day to happen exactly as it did, I should get in the shower now and get all dolled up because I feel like it. Get a coffee in the Café de la Luz and read *Madame Bovary*. Go buy flowers in that little store where, depending on when you go, you'll be helped by two kooky old sisters or a very cute boy. Although if I do all that and I do it right, I won't make it to my last plan, which is buying sushi and a bottle of white wine to share with Ivan at my house, because on the way, serendipity will cross my path in the form of a tremendously handsome, tremendously bundled up, and tremendously overwhelmed man.

I grab my phone without thinking and call Ivan. It's 7:30 in the morning on a Saturday, but I don't have time to think about how people like to take advantage of these moments to sleep. I've always been an early bird. Ivan's not like that. He likes to sleep. He enjoys it. He says it's one of the great pleasures of life. We've never been able to agree on that point. I don't understand how something you don't feel can be a pleasure; you just do it, and that's it.

He picks up grumpily when I'm about to give up.

"Bitch, are you crazy? Please tell me you're dying or something, because that's the only way I'm going to forgive you. It's seven fucking thirty in the morning."

"Ivan…"

He knows me like the back of his hand, and I don't need to say another word. Just his name and the tone are enough for him to understand it's something serious.

"What's going on? Are you okay? Should I come over?"

"No, no, listen."

"Are you pregnant? Ay, no, even worse…did you do an STD screening? Do you have syphilis?"

I look at the tiles on the bathroom wall, bewildered. What the fuck is going on in my best friend's head?

"No. Listen to me. I'm going to ask you something that's going to seem really weird, but I need you to play a game where you answer without thinking too much, okay?"

"It's really early. I don't think I could think even if I wanted to."

"If you could change your past…would you?"

There's a silence on the other end of the line; all I can hear is his sheets rustling. Then I identify the sound of his feet going down the metal stairs that separate the bedroom from the kitchen in Ivan's tiny duplex. He's going to make coffee.

"Is this an existential crisis?" he asks.

He's buying time while he thinks about whether the best answer to my question would be hailing a cab in his pajamas and showing up at my house. I know him well.

"It could be."

"Are you having an anxiety attack, Miri? A panic attack?"

"No. That's what I mean about not thinking too much. Just answer the question." And I squeeze my eyes shut so hard that I see sparks. "If you could change your past, something that hurt you, would you?"

"Say more."

"There's no more. Would you erase a love that hurt you?"

The semiautomatic coffee machine he bought himself for Christmas makes a sound that won't let us talk for a few seconds, but this gives Ivan time to think about his answer.

"It's fucked up that I have to answer when I don't know what you're talking about, but I don't think you woke up worried about Ander."

Ander was my first boyfriend, my stable relationship, the one you get into because you think it's what you want, but it's actually what you think you should do.

"No. I don't have to be thinking about someone specific, right? I can just be asking myself things about life. I'm a woman in my thirties."

"It's barely seven thirty in the morning on a Saturday. If it's not about someone, you need medication."

"It's a simple question." I say impatiently.

"Fine." He sighs. "Let's get rid of some extenuating circumstances here: obvs, if you're talking about an insane relationship, abusive, unequal, toxic…I'd say yes, I'd erase it. But if your question is not actually about 'a love that hurt you' but how much the heartbreak of falling out of love hurt, I'd say that anything beautiful has the capacity to hurt us when it disappears from our lives because it leaves a void. But that doesn't eliminate all the positive feelings that helped us grow and believe."

This throws me off. Ivan has always thought that love is something kind of cringe. I mean, the romantic idea of love. I guess we all think when other people fall in love, they're kind of corny…and I'm the first to admit it. It's a topic that has caused me some issues, obviously.

"Okay," I say.

"Is this for an article? Did it send you on a hormonal spiral?"

"I'm going to forgive the hormonal spiral comment because it's you, but that's gross."

"Some months, your period hits you really hard, girl. That's just the truth."

I roll my eyes.

"I'm at an age where I'm considering things about my life," I say, not wanting to get into too many details.

"Did you see a rom-com yesterday that made you go crazy?"

I am a little crazy, but how can I explain it to him?

I come out of the bathroom and perch on the high stool at my kitchen bar, where I find my planner. I flip through the pages absentmindedly.

"A book," I lie. "Sometimes novels can make you think a lot."

"That's why I don't read."

I let out a cackle.

"You shouldn't brag about that."

"You have to respect that some people don't like to read, buttercup. I respect that my best friend calls me at dawn on a Saturday. When I should be telling you to go find other friends. The fact that I'm all you have makes me sad."

"I don't only have you. I have a lot of girlfriends."

"So why don't you call one of them?"

"Because they're not you."

My smile is tinged with sadness. I love my girlfriends a lot, and I believe strongly in the importance of investing time and care in every social relationship that matters to you, but Ivan will always be Ivan, and my relationship with him will always be special.

"Fine, what are you doing today?" he asks me.

I managed to soften him up, but he doesn't want to admit it.

"Well, I was thinking about going to get breakfast…"

I stop dead when my eyes run across something in the planner I'm holding. Something that brings me crashing back to reality. The very unrealistic reality I've been living since yesterday. The reality that I can't be sitting here calmly talking to my bestie on the phone like nothing is happening because I'm traveling through fucking time like I'm on a Ferris wheel.

There they are. On a random page are the notes I made last night that guessed where and when I might wake up tomorrow. This might not seem that important, but it really is. Why? Well, I made the notes yesterday, right? Yesterday, reliving a specific day five years ago. The day I really met Tristan. And if the ink of the pen I made them with is still there and it hasn't been erased in the same magical way that I'm moving through the past, that means I can change it. That I can make things happen that I didn't do, and the consequences should withstand time. And that maybe my decision to leave the café, to say goodbye to Tristan and say no to the possibility of seeing each other again, could have changed the wheel of events.

Is this my new past?

"Miranda?" Ivan complains.

"Yeah…I'm here."

"I thought you hung up on me."

"No. It's just…I remembered something. Listen, I'll let you go, okay?"

"Are we meeting up at your house to eat sushi and drink wine?" he asks.

I think about it…

"I don't think I'll have time. I'll let you know."

December 10, five years ago, I had a super-chill morning that has nothing to do with this version 2.0. Chill doesn't really get along with the whole time-travel thing. The first thing I do is go downstairs to buy a newspaper, just to double-check that this isn't some stupid joke orchestrated by all my friends. The logical me isn't ready to throw in the towel. But no. It's not.

"Sanchez leaves without clarifying his candidacy for the PSOE," a headline screams. Messi is still playing in Barça. And fashion doesn't lie either: in the street, skinny jeans and thigh-high boots are everywhere. There's no doubt about it; we're in the past.

I have a copy of *Madame Bovary* in my bag that I found on my bedside table, but as much as I want to recreate that day, I have to be honest with myself and admit that memory is not my strong suit. I don't remember how late I was getting to the café or how long I spent there. I don't know if I went straight to the florist or if I stopped to pet a dog, because the truth is I'm one of those people who smiles at dogs I come across on the street. So I'm nervous because I have no way of being able to find out empirically whether everything changed with my decision from yesterday or if this really is a parallel reality where, at any moment, ferrets and cats are going to revolt against humans until they control us.

To break it down: the fact that "yesterday" I left the café without agreeing to see him again could have led to the result...

a) That in this present, we never fucked, so the opportunity of being an "us" has passed us by and we're not going to randomly bump into each other today.

b) That my decision had the equivalent effect on the universe as when I say "I'm not going to drink even a single glass of wine this month": as in, it hasn't changed a single thing.

I try to repeat the steps I can remember exactly. I order the same thing: an Americano and a piece of pan con tomate. I try to read, but I can't. I go to the bathroom. I give a friendly answer to a girl who asks where my sweater's from and stroll unhurriedly to the florist. I don't remember what flowers I bought or how many for the bouquet, but I know it had some pale-pink flowers and white ones, branches of eucalyptus and everlasting flowers in lilac, plus some other stuff. I do my best to describe it to the shopkeepers, not knowing if these are important details.

"I want...like...lilac, pink, and white. I know that's kinda boring."

One of the women helping me smiles, and I feel just like the bouquet: totally cheesy. Especially compared to her, because this woman owns a floral shop, but she looks like someone whose favorite flower is broccoli.

I'm nervous. I need to somehow figure out how time behaves when something changes. Today, I woke up on a different day again, so nothing makes me think that the same thing won't happen tomorrow. And I need to understand it.

I stroll along with the bouquet in hand, just like I did, but I'm not in the same mood. I was happy that day. I felt like I had managed to make my life my own and not be constantly worrying about relationships or crushes. I thought I had learned how to live without needing anyone. And I liked it that way, mostly. It was my life. My independence. Saturdays. My house. My routines. My chaos. Family. Friends. Fun. My sheets. Which is to say everything I decided and how I decided it. Now I know that meeting Tristan today diverted me from that path. Or maybe it simply transformed it into a love story.

It happened when I turned onto Calle de Fernando VI. And no, it didn't happen like it did back then. I didn't see him from afar, at the same moment he recognized me. We didn't approach each other with a slightly bashful smile because the last time we saw each other, we were naked…or because we'd seen each other more naked than dressed, to be honest. This time, it happened out of the blue, leaving me no time to prepare myself and decide what to say.

I turn the corner, take three steps. Bam!

"Miranda?"

The voice comes from behind me, out of nowhere, like magic makes everything possible materialize wherever it feels like it, wherever I least expect it. I turn around, and there he is. His beard is a little messy; his hair brushed to one side haphazardly, definitely with his fingers; his eyes full of that fog that never lets you see what color they actually are, whether they're green, honey-colored, gray, or dark. He's well dressed, in a checked shirt and jeans, and wrapped up against the dry Madrid cold in the same good wool coat with worn cuffs as always.

"How's it going?" He smiles.

"Good. You?"

I don't want to say much. I need to establish our relationship to each other. Did I change something yesterday by behaving differently? Have we slept together yet? Yes, no, a kiss, a hand job?

"Good. I mean…a little overwhelmed." He wrinkles his nose. "Finding an apartment is impossible. I guess I told you… I just moved to Madrid."

"Yeah, that rings a bell."

"I would've told you more, but..." He flashes me another flirty smile, a little charming and nervous at the same time. Now I know he believes it doesn't do any good to be nice with strangers. "You told me you know how that glass of wine I wanted to invite you to was going to end and..."

"Yes."

"Sorry, I just rushed right over to you, and you were probably on your way to something. Did I catch you at a bad time?"

I'm aware that I was answering him almost monosyllabically, but I'm trying so hard to figure out where we stand, he should consider himself lucky I can even manage that.

"No. I'm actually on the way home," I say, brandishing the bouquet. "I just came out to run a few errands. You know how it is, grab some breakfast and read a little, go buy some flowers for the house and something to eat... What about you?"

"Well..." He looks around. "I came down to buy some food to make lunch. My fridge is completely empty, and I don't feel like spending the whole weekend eating takeout. Plus... I wanted to cook something delicious, you know?"

Yes. Yes, I know. A steak tartare, with the sirloin cut by hand, patiently. A bottle of good wine, a Pago de Carraovejas, a little foie, to which you add some thin slices of caramelized apple and serve alongside warm bread.

That Saturday was the first time we ate something together. We usually just had a glass of wine and went straight to bed. It was the first time I saw him cook, but not the last. When we first started dating, Tristan liked to cook for me because he said he thought it was sexy when I told him interesting things while he made food for me. We discovered a lot more in each other that day than we had ever expected to see, and...we were left wanting more. It was...sexy but also magical, interesting, maybe a little cheesy. A beginning.

The bouquet I was carrying, or actually its twin from another reality, stayed at his house. He dried the flowers. Five years later, they were in my living room, slightly faded but hanging in there in a beautiful white vase with rabbit heads from Abe the Ape that he gave me the day he moved in with me.

"Hey, do you wanna come with me? It could be fun, right? We could go to the supermarket." He tilts his head toward it. "We could buy a few things, and you could be my sous-chef while I pour you a glass of wine."

I stare at him. His lips. That mouth born to kiss. That perfect nose. Those foggy eyes. He's just as handsome as I remember. Actually, it seems like years haven't really passed for him. And it's not just that I don't know what to say to him. It's also that I get a little dopey thinking about nineteenth-century romance novel bullshit, and I lose my train of thought. And since my silence makes him nervous, he launches into speaking again, this time a little more awkwardly.

"I guess you're still thinking you know how this ends, huh?"

"Yes." I smile sadly.

"I bet you've met a lot of morons like me and you're a little sick of it all, but…I'm just asking you to come eat and talk. Maybe it's not that big a deal."

I know how lonely he felt back then. The original back then. He missed his group of friends, the most diverse gang I've ever met, who were nothing like him. That he was questioning his decision to accept the position in Madrid and that sometimes, when he got into bed, so tired and so alone, he thought the capital, hulking and hungry, would end up swallowing him. But still, I have the power in the palm of my hand to avoid our whole story, and maybe tomorrow, when I wake up, I won't even remember him. So maybe it's possible I won't be hurt, and I'll keep being fine being alone or, who knows, maybe I'll end up falling asleep in someone else's arms… someone who doesn't want to leave me, who doesn't break my heart after years of dinner, wine, plans, trips, and I won't end up scarred.

I can't think about it clearly.

"The plan sounds really nice, thank you so much," I say, being very, very friendly. "But I have plans to eat sushi with a friend at my house."

He raises his eyebrows. He thinks I'm dating someone. I guess he's wondering what the hell I'm doing on Tinder, but he doesn't say it.

"Ah." He makes a face. "Sorry. Umm…I didn't mean to make you uncomfortable."

"You didn't make me uncomfortable. It's a great plan, but maybe I'm not the right girl."

He nods, and I take a step back, in the direction of fleeing. Just like yesterday in the café, I'm not sure I have enough willpower. Because every urge in the world is pushing me to live that day all over again, to forget that in the end, as I know all too well, he's going to leave me. Living through it with him, opening up to him, seeing him again with the eyes of someone discovering themselves through someone else.

But it hurts.

A lot.

I loved him. And he stopped loving me.

"Nice to see you again," I say. "Hope Madrid treats you well."

I don't wait to see his reaction. I turned around and start walking. I feel a kind of relief mixed with pain, but tomorrow, all this will have passed. The man who I loved and trusted, who I wanted a future with, won't betray me, telling me he doesn't want me by his side, that I'm not his happy place anymore. Because I love him, and maybe I'm tempted by the idea of taking refuge in memories, but if I can save myself the anxiety of knowing he'll leave my side, I'd rather go to sleep and forget about him. I wish that tomorrow, all this will be no more than a fuzzy feeling that's hard to shake after a really vivid dream.

Or is that not how all this works?

6

~~

I THINK IT'S A PRIVILEGE
TO KNOW BEFOREHAND

Ivan is watching me scarf sushi with a slightly horrified look on his face.
The truth is I am doing it kind of anxiously. It's not pretty to watch. I'm
eating my feelings, and even the people who sold me two hundred sushi
rolls know it.

"Are you okay?"

"*Yeth,*" I say through a mouthful.

"Well, you're eating like a nutjob. Did you even hear a word I said?"

"Yes. They have to raise the skylight on your terrace because they think
that's where the water's leaking into your downstairs neighbor's house
when it rains."

"Oh, I mean, yeah," he says, surprised. "But I said some other stuff too."

"Well, I guess the last thing didn't register."

I wipe my mouth with a paper towel, staring off into the distance.

"Seriously, Miri, what's going on?"

I pout. I can't avoid the internal battle, the hundreds of conflicting
feelings that are fighting to the death in my stomach, in my chest and my
head. I'm oscillating between relief and sadness, anger, confusion. Am I
really going to forget him tomorrow? Is that the solution? Am I in a coma?
In a digital simulation of my life? Am I in the Matrix?

"If I say the name Tristan...does that mean anything to you?"

"An opera?" He takes advantage of me talking to stuff a roll in his mouth. The truth is I haven't given him much of a chance to eat. "Who or what is Tristan?"

"No one." I shrug. "Nothing."

That's what I wanted, right? For him to stop being anyone, to stop meaning anything, for the letters that spell his name to stop being glued to years of my life. So why do I have this feeling then? Why do I feel like I've thrown away an opportunity?

Ivan is eating absentmindedly, and I keep staring at his eyelashes. Holy shit. I'd never noticed. They're so long. But...like *Drag Race* long.

"Ivan, do you have eyelash extensions on?"

"Do you have cunt-hair extensions on? Of course not!"

I burst out laughing.

"Dude...but they're so long."

He touches them, weirded out.

"Well, they're like always, dumbass. You're such a dumbass."

"No. I swear. You look like a Mariquita Pérez doll."

"Nice. Really subtle way to insult your queer friend."

I roll my eyes.

"Come on, man! I'm serious. Your eyelashes are fucking giant. They look like fans. You have to be careful with them. They're a weapon of mass destruction! Seriously...lemme see? Wait, they're hitting your eyebrows! How did I never notice this before?"

"Oy! You know what we should do? Get all dolled up and go out and get a drink," he proposes, all hyped up.

"Where?"

"I mean, I dunno. El Corazon. Is that what that place you love so much is called?"

Jesus...El Corazon. I haven't been there in centuries. Well, in the present, I haven't been there in centuries. Five years ago, I knew the names of the bartenders. I loved the little blondie who looked like a surfer.

"I don't know what the hell is going on with you, because you're even weirder than usual," he insists, "but there's nothing a few gins for the price of eighteen-carat gold can't solve."

I waver. Maybe that is what I need.

"I dunno. And the whole getting dolled up thing…do we have to go to your house so you can change?"

"Me? No way, lady. I'd be hot in a hospital gown."

It's barely even 8:30, but El Corazon is packed with regulars. On Saturdays, hell must be empty, because all the devils are here. And the devil knows more because he's been around forever than because he's the devil. Which makes me think of myself, because inside, I'm five years older than what I see in the mirror. And it's not like it's a generational leap that makes some huge difference, but it makes me look at things differently. Is it possible I've matured? At twenty-eight, everything seemed so much easier than now. My father always says the years strip away our blindfolds and show us life is much simpler than we first thought. But I think it's a roller coaster. Sometimes, everything is too hard, and sometimes, life is child's play.

Next to the window on the left, right as you come in, at his usual table is the pastry chef we've all been half in love with at some point. He comes in a lot. He used to come in with a blond; now he's here with a brunette. The way things are going, you'd guess that next he'll be in there with a redhead or a strawberry blond, but no. One day, he stopped coming, and later I ran into him on the street with the same girl, pushing a stroller. I watch them laugh and clink their glasses together, with those sparkly eyes people have in new relationships, and in a way, I feel powerful. They don't know that they're going to be parents soon. But I do.

"Ivan, do you think what gets us jazzed about love stories is not knowing whether they'll work out?"

"Well." He takes a sip of his gin and shrugs. "If you think about it, that makes sense. Anything too secure ends up being a little boring. It's like, if we don't fight for it, whatever we win is worth less."

"Yes, that's true. Human beings are shit."

"Human beings are shit, darling." He smiles at me. "But the good ones are the strange exceptions. Come on…drink up. We have to spend our whole paychecks here, and we're falling behind."

The music they play in El Corazon is what a slightly nostalgic and unjudgmental millennial would play. That means that even though one of Nirvana's most famous songs is playing, Backstreet Boys could be next. And it's all good. In a few years, noughties-themed bars will start popping up everywhere, but these people don't know that yet. They're going to get sick of dancing to Sonia and Selena or the Spice Girls.

I don't know if it's the gin or the freedom of knowing (or more like guessing) that there will be no consequences tomorrow, that I won't remember, that my history with Tristan won't exist… Ever since I got here, I've been feeling better. It hurts less. And I wonder if this might be some kind of cosmic salvation to live these years differently. What if tomorrow is still five years ago, but Tristan isn't there? What if tomorrow's the present, but my heart is still beating?

Ivan and I have been cheering each other up. We set up camp at the end of the bar, next to the bathroom, where there's more space to move around freely. Behind us, there's a group of preppy boys who look boring but are still making kind of a racket. We, on the other hand, are dancing and singing. It's not even ten, and it'd probably be a good idea to put something solid in our bodies to soak up the drinks, but it's the last thing on our minds. Ivan is belting out, in his baritone, the biggest hit from the *Dirty Dancing* soundtrack, which is playing right now, but in an English that sounds more like he's invoking Satan.

"Stop!" I scream. "You don't know the words!"

"Aaaa jeend de taaiiimm of mai laif, is a nana nana llu bifor, ant ent…"

"Some god of the night is going to hear your prayers, and then what're we gonna do?"

"Well, enjoy it, because I'm asking the lord of the night to get you laid, to wipe that dried-fruit look off your face."

"Dried fruit?"

"You're like that slimy green piece they put on top of a fruit cake. Disgusting!"

Why is giving our friends shit so much fun?

I was caught with my guard down. That's it. The hypnotic movement of Ivan's recently discovered incredible eyelashes. Or the music. Or the dark, windowless environment. Or the gin. Or I just wasn't expecting it. I don't know, but the fact is before I can answer Ivan with some absurd insult, like "cockgoblin," someone touches my arm.

"Miranda?"

I get a glimpse of him out of the corner of my eye and recognize him before my brain registers it. Maybe I'm actually getting the hang of this as I live it. I know it's him before I even turn around.

And of course. It is. It's him.

But…what the hell? I thought I dodged this today. I already did what I had to do so our thing wouldn't follow its course. Why is it so fucking difficult to avoid it? Why…why is he so totally goddamn gorgeous, the big whore?

"Hello!"

"Hey…" I say, because I don't know what else to say, and just straight running away would be really weird.

I look over at my best friend to see if he recognizes him. What do I know? Maybe this is like the enchantments in fairy tales, and suddenly, Ivan's look will break the farce and everything will be revealed. How can that be possible? But seriously, what do I know? I never thought I would wake up five years ago either.

But of course, there's no recognition in his expression. Not even a trace. Ivan is smiling at me, giving me a subtle thumbs-up and taking a few steps back toward the bar, thinking I'm flirting with some cute guy I'm charmed by. I beg him not to with my eyes, not to leave us alone, but the besties communication line doesn't seem to be working. Normally all I have to do is blink, but he turns around before he can intuit the panic in my eyes.

Panic because duh. Because Tristan, the dude next to me right now gripping a bottle of beer, is cute, he doesn't look like someone who buries bodies in his garden, and he said hello like we already knew each other.

"Traitor," I mutter.

"How's it going?" His slightly raspy voice with that touch of suburban boy I've always found so charming caresses me. "Small world, huh?"

"I mean…yes. What are you doing here?"

He tilts his head behind him to gesture to the group of boring prepsters who are still bro-ing out.

"I just got here. It's my colleague's birthday, and since I didn't have any better plans…"

"I wouldn't mention the 'no better plans' thing to the birthday boy."

"I won't. I'll make like the ocean and…just wave."

I stare at him. The dad joke doesn't seem like his style…and Tristan can be really weird. I remember how, at the beginning of our relationship, when we were chatting on WhatsApp a lot, I thought he was a kiss-ass bore. Later in real life, I was surprised when he made jokes and played pranks. But I wasn't expecting this. It's a joke my father might have dusted off in his ancient antiques shop.

"Just wave, eh?" I hit him where it hurts.

"Bad. Really bad. I admit it. I'm just surprised to see you."

"I'm surprised to see you too." I raise my eyebrows.

"It's not normal."

"What are you talking about?"

"I mean, normally, I'm lucky enough that if a girl rejects me as much as you have, I don't end up seeing her everywhere."

"It's Murphy's Law. That's how Madrid works." I hesitate.

"Ah, so you don't deny that you straight up rejected me twice."

"I have my reasons." I smile.

"Are you always so serious?"

"Not at all."

"So then is it me? Do I make you serious?"

"You make me sad." But I say it with a smile.

He nods, twisting his mouth into a kind of contained smile.

"Before we keep talking…is that your guy?"

Ivan is chatting to the bartender like he's known him his whole life. If it turns out I've been making eyes at the surfer bartender and he actually wanted to flirt with Ivan this whole time…

"He's my best friend."

"You left your boyfriend after dinner and…"

I don't let him finish.

"You just assumed I have a boyfriend. I never said that. I guess it's an ego reflex so that my rejection hurts less. You'd rather believe I rejected you because I have a boyfriend, not because I want nothing to do with you. It's the most plausible explanation, right?"

He raises an eyebrow. My answer surprised him. Oh, oh, I shouldn't be doing this. I should be acting dopey as hell, doing something I know will bug him or irritate him or horrify him. I should be making him leave. But I'm not.

"Ah...you're accusing me of being egotistical." He smiles.

"Nah, I'm not even paying that much attention to you."

I know it's the kind of comment that will spark his curiosity even more, that will make me seem more interesting, and yet I'm still doing it. I can't help it. It's his scent. It's the checked shirt from El Ganso. It's how thick his black hair is.

"Tell me then," he says resolutely.

"What do you want me to tell you?"

"The real reason you rejected me."

"You're going to hurt me," I admit easily.

The good thing about time travel is that you stop being scared about what you should say. Completely. What's the worst that can happen?

"No, I'm not." He looks at my mouth as he answers. "I'm going to take you to dinner. I eat a lot."

"Now you're clairvoyant too?"

"I don't know. If you can play around at guessing the future, why can't I do the same?"

"Okay, surprise me. What does the future hold for us?"

"Well, let's see. I'm gonna go back here"—he gestures at the group of preppy guys in sweaty button-ups—"and finish my beer. Then I'm going to make an excuse about needing air, and I'll leave and never come back. You'll be waiting for me on the corner, and we'll go to my house. I bought some stuff when we ran into each other this morning, but when I got home, I couldn't be bothered. It felt depressing to cook for myself, and I just heated up some leftovers. So I have everything to make a steak tartare, a little foie, and a good wine. We'll eat, chat, I'll put on some music, and when you get tired, I'll walk you home."

"You're going to walk me home?"

"Yeah. I like the cold. It wakes up my brain."

I nod slowly, unable to stop looking at his mouth. Tristan. My Tristan.

Not even brazenly rejecting him seems to destroy the possibility of what we have ahead. Maybe this is the moment to start believing in destiny and throwing myself into a little leap of faith or, maybe, considering the possibility of taking a stab at it.

"It's not because you want to find out where I live?"

"That too." He laughs. His smile allows a flash of his white teeth. He has big teeth, but they're not jarring in his smile. They make it more beautiful.

"What about sex?" I ask.

"Listen, young lady...you can't reject me so brazenly and then demand that I perform in bed. No, ma'am. I'm not that direct."

"You don't have one-night stands?"

I know perfectly well that the answer is yes, but he resists giving it to me. I think he's worried about what I'll think of him, and this version of the first Tristan, the Tristan from the prehistory of our story, confuses me. I don't remember him being like this. And it makes me...uneasy. I don't know what he's capable of.

"I do. Of course I do. But"—he shakes his head, a little more serious, like he's weighing his options—"maybe it's the time to admit that I'm not as direct as you."

"Maybe what's happening here is you like being the direct one..."

"Could be. Maybe it makes me nervous that you're taking the initiative so blatantly."

"I didn't offer you sex," I clarify. "I asked you to find out if you're avoiding it because you don't want to scare me off or because that's really not what you're looking for."

He looks at me with an amused expression. He laughs. Laughing Tristan is my favorite Tristan. It's when he's cutest. I've always known that. Of the dozens of men hidden inside him, that one is the apple of my eye.

"Let's try something." He holds out his pinky, waiting for me to link mine around it, like when we made promises when we were little, but I don't. "I promise not to try anything if you come have dinner with me."

"And leave my friend all alone?"

"You spent the whole day with him. Lie to him. Tell him you're tired."

"That wouldn't make me a very good friend."

"Then tell him the truth." He shrugs. "I'm going back to my colleagues. I'll wait for you"—he takes his phone out of his jeans pocket and checks the time—"in half an hour. At ten thirty."

"Where?"

"On the corner. When you go out, turn left…the one next to the plaza."

"I don't know. I don't know if you're convincing me."

"I'll wait for you until ten forty. You decide."

He says goodbye with an eyebrow lift. I'm so into his eyebrows.

As I head back to where Ivan is propping up the bar, now staring at his phone, I weigh the possibilities. A fan is opening and closing as I make decisions. Maybe it's always like that. Maybe every tiny decision I've ever made in my life closes one path, but I've never had the opportunity to discover it so empirically.

Now though…

If I reject Tristan again, will he be put in my path again? Who's going to put him in my path? I don't want to mention destiny. I'd rather think about a kind of gravitational force that is swaying my timeline. Whoever invented this DeLorean I'm traveling in now.

"Hey…" I say to Ivan.

"He was cute, right? I mean…not obviously cute, but your type. Like, with the nose of a strapping lad from the north, with good hair and a mouth you want to eat."

"Shut up," I beg, cracking up.

"Who is he? You know him?"

"From another life." I turn to look at Tristan fleetingly.

He's fully immersed in the birthday group, but he doesn't seem like part of the gang. He's not saying much. He doesn't interact much beyond the occasional smile and nod. So distantly attractive. So attractively distant. I've always liked that about Tristan. How he handles silences. I think that was one of the things that made me fall for him.

"From another life? Whatever. You're nuts."

"What were you doing?" I tap the now-blank screen of his iPhone.

"Nothing." He smiles.

"Tinder?"

"A little scroll," he confesses.

"And?"

"Nothing new. Or I'm not into any of the new stuff…I dunno."

"Are you still talking to that boy?" I pretend like I'm trying to remember.

"I'm still talking to that boy, yes, but…I dunno."

"What don't you know?"

I do know. I shouldn't intervene…right?

"Well, I don't know if it makes sense to keep talking and talking and talking. He told me a while ago that he's going to grab a drink with some friends. They want to go home soon, but he wants to get a bite to eat somewhere and…"

"And he asked if you want to go get dinner?"

"Yes." He nods. "But I don't know if I feel like it."

I think about it for a second. Only a second. And a second is all I need for my curiosity to take the wheel.

"If you go get dinner with him…I'll go get dinner with this guy." I point behind me.

"There's no fucking way you're gonna do that."

"Wanna bet?"

"You're fucking with me."

"No. I'm not fucking with you. What did you think we were talking about? The weather?"

"If you go to dinner with him, I'll be so freaked out." He raises an eyebrow. "You don't know him at all. What if he roofies your drink and you wake up tomorrow without a kidney in Canillejas?"

"Why Canillejas?"

"Why not?"

In any other situation, I would never do what I'm about to do, but I think in these circumstances, it's allowed. I'm about to lie to my best friend.

"I'm going to take him to grab a bite around here. In Malasaña. So the only thing you'll have to worry about is the highway robbery of what they'll charge me for a burger and that it'll probably be vegan."

He smiles and glances at his phone out of the corner of his eye.

"Come on, tell him you'll see him in half an hour. We'll get one last drink and then leave."

I'm not going to tell Ivan because I'm not even sure what I want to tell him, but I know that he went on tons of dates and had dinner with people he wasn't into...but it helped him realize how over his previous breakup he was. And made him feel strong. And free.

The guy from that night isn't going to be a great love, but they'll be great friends. And I think that's beautiful, incredible, and a privilege to know beforehand.

7

"WAY MORE WEIRD STUFF TO SHOW EACH OTHER."

I had forgotten that back then, Tristan still smoked like a chimney. He was an inconsistent but intense smoker: if he didn't have tobacco, he could go three or four days without going to the tobacco store. If he had a pack in his pocket and he was outside, he practically lit one off the other. I had also forgotten that I smoked too. Look, at twenty-eight, I hadn't quite figured out how ridiculous it was to breathe in smoke from a stinky stick that you lit on fire.

That's why I was so surprised to see him with a stogie between his lips and his left hand in the pocket of a jacket that wasn't the one I saw him in this morning. This jacket… I'll be blunt: this jacket has some flossy overtones. Does it have sheepskin lining? It has sheepskin lining. Would you defend it as an iconic piece and a fashion statement? I wouldn't. Does it turn me on? Like the thirstiest girl in the world. It fits him like it's been licked on by the god of sexiness himself.

I bitterly mourned the "death" of that jacket when, during lockdown, it suffered an accident on the clothesline. What a time we haven't lived through yet.

He throws the cigarette to the ground with a half smile when he sees me on the corner, and I half smile back. He offers me a cigarette as he puts away his lighter.

"No thanks."

"So weird." He makes a face while he concentrates on putting the lighter into the soft pack of Marlboros and slips it into his pocket. "I had the feeling you were a smoker."

"I used to smoke," I confess succinctly.

"I want to quit."

"You will. When nobody's trying to make you. You're one of those."

He raises his eyebrows as he points me in the right direction.

"Oh yeah? What's going on? Can you read minds on top of being able to predict the future?"

I let out a giggle. The proud Tristan. I don't like this one as much, but it always made me a little horny.

"I could profile you better than the FBI right now. No margin for error."

"Is that why you're avoiding me? Because you looked inside me and you don't like what you saw?"

My only answer is a mysterious smile and a fleeting glance. He's a little tense. I'm not…but only because I've slept next to him so many nights that I could count the freckles on his back with my eyes closed.

"Do you like Madrid?" I ask, even though I already know the answer.

"Well…I'm getting there. Sometimes I find it intimidating. It's… huge."

"I know it can feel that way. But we all end up going to the same places over and over."

"Who? The beautiful people?" he teases.

"I don't know what 'beautiful people' means to you, but I can almost guarantee that, if it exists, I wouldn't be among their ranks."

"Ooh…false humility. It doesn't suit you."

"I'm not a cool girl."

"Ah, no…okay. You're the deputy editor of the most famous fashion magazine in the world, right?"

"*Vogue* is the most famous," I defend myself. "And I don't fit the *Vogue* girl profile."

"Why not?"

"Well, because…" I furrow my brow. "I mean…I don't know. Because I'm not a cunt?"

He cracks up, and it spreads to me. It's cold as balls, and we're both clutching our coats around us.

"You finally decided to do it," he notes without looking at me.

"Do what? Have dinner with you? Well, yes. It was mostly convenience. My friend was leaving, and I have an empty fridge."

He smiles.

"You seem sweet," I clarify as I return the smile.

"I don't know if 'sweet' is the word."

"So what is the word?"

"You know what word you girls use a shitload and I hate to the depths of my soul?"

"Yes." I nod.

"There's no way you know." He focuses on studying me with serious but amused eyes, so intensely that he's about to bash his shin on a metal bollard. He dodges it nimbly and laughs at himself. "Ow. That was close."

"Cute," I say.

He stops in the street and grabs my arm softly to make me stop too. Then he stares at me even more intensely. One eyebrow lifts.

"What?"

"You hate the word 'cute.' You think 'You're so cute' is an awful compliment."

"I'd rather be told I have a shitty face."

I let out a cackle. He does too.

"Huh, I guess I'm finally going to have to admit there is some evidence that you know what's going to happen."

"Backward and forward."

He nods slowly. He licks his lips, and my clit tingles. I want him to kiss me. I want him to kiss me more than anything in the world. And I don't understand when I stopped paying attention to our kisses. To the good days. To the goodbyes. To seeing each other again. To the sex. To the…

Tristan takes a step back, still looking at me, before he turns around and pulls me along with him.

Tristan is staying in an Airbnb in downtown Madrid. It's one of those nice, very traditional buildings, with a newly renovated facade and fresh white paint. But inside, the apartments are small and kind of ramshackle, like houses that are furnished just so they can be rented for a few days. There's no attention to detail. Everything is pure practicality, but he doesn't seem to mind it at all. He's a man whose aesthetic awareness can be selective.

As we go in, he tosses his keys onto a plain white entrance table and hangs his jacket in a closet as nondescript as the table. He asks for my coat and bag so he can hang them too. Before I hand my bag over, I WhatsApp Ivan to tell him everything's fine, don't worry, we're having a drink in another bar, and I'm not going to take him home. I don't wait for a reply, because Tristan is standing there patiently, waiting to hang the bag on the rack.

He'd hate it if I said it, but he's so cute.

Why do men have such a problem with the word "cute"? Just because you say someone's cute doesn't mean you don't want to have wild sex with him or that you don't respect him as a person. Beats me. After so many years of dealing with men, I still don't get them.

The house is pretty much a perfect square made up of a kitchen, a living room, a separate bedroom, and a bathroom. The kitchen is small and has a bar connecting it to the living room, which is furnished with a sofa, a table with two chairs, an almost-empty bookshelf, and a rickety, bland piece of furniture with a TV balanced on top. Through a door left slightly ajar, I can see the bedroom; I can describe it perfectly, even though I haven't been in it yet. It's small, with a double bed, two bedside tables, and a built-in wardrobe next to the door of a cute but cramped bathroom. It makes me smile remembering how we almost killed ourselves trying to fuck in his shower. I've probably changed the beginning of this story so much that however this works, that scene will never happen.

"Do you think it's funny?" he asks, coming over to me on his way into the kitchen.

"No."

"You're smiling."

"Would it be better if I was crying?"

That makes him let out a little chuckle that disappears as soon as I hear it. I never thought of Tristan as one of those men who can be seduced through laughter. The stomach and the mouth...you already know.

He asks me to sit on one of the stools at the bar, in the part that opens into the living room. Then he puts two glasses and a bottle of wine on the wood surface, which I take in my hands, along with the corkscrew.

"You do the honors. I won't take long."

But he will, because Tristan is slow. Slow in almost everything. He isn't at work. And he's not when it comes to the hyperfocus needed to take on difficult tasks. But when it comes to how he moves, in anything except walking, Tristan is so slow. So dicing the steak into tiny cubes by hand, chopping the red onion and capers, and stirring it all together will take him an hour. I don't mind. I'm not in any rush. I'm spending time with the person I love, who's going to leave me in a few years...and right now, he doesn't know any of that. Not that I love him or that he's going to leave me or that he'll love me so much it'll drive him crazy.

"Wanna put on some music?" he asks.

"Sure."

"Just connect to that." He waves at a Marshall speaker, and I crack up.

"I'm more analog than an abacus, babe. I'm not going to be able to figure it out."

He sucks his teeth, takes his phone out of his jeans (ay, his jeans), and hands it to me unlocked. I always liked that about him: he's open. He's not one of those guys who guard their phone like its pharaoh's gold.

"Open Spotify, and put on whatever you want."

It takes me a little while. Everything I think of doesn't exist yet; plus I don't want to fall into the mistake of putting on some corny playlist of ambient jazz that will make us feel like we're shopping for tablecloths in a Zara Home. It takes me a while, but I end up with something pretty appropriate for the situation: *Home*, the album by Rudimental.

"So good," he mutters, focused on his task, when the eponymous song starts playing.

"Rudimental. Do you know them?"

"No. But I like their sound."

I already knew that. I don't deserve any credit. All I had to do was search my memory a little.

I uncork the bottle after a short struggle and pour wine into both glasses. He wastes no time grabbing his and holding it up to mine for a toast.

"Do you want to say a few words?" I tease.

"Apparently I don't need to."

There it is: his ability to wield silence, his panty-dropping weapon. Well...one of his panty-dropping weapons. Tristan is hot when he's silent and when he laughs. But when he shuts up, an aura of mystery grows up around him that makes him simply irresistible.

I take a lap around the living room, but nothing in here would tell me anything about him. Until he finds a more permanent apartment to rent, he's not going to bother adding a little warmth to his pad.

"You grew up in Madrid, right?" I hear him ask me.

"Yes." I nod. "Not a cat, but yes."

"What do you mean, a cat?"

"You're only considered a 'cat' if you're a third-generation Madrileño."

"Oh wow. There are castes."

"Duh. My mother was from Salamanca."

"Was?"

"She died when I was really little."

"I'm sorry."

I look over into the kitchen to watch him. He's chopping the ingredients with so much concentration his brow is furrowed in an expression that almost makes him look angry.

"Don't worry. I have an incredible father who never forgets a single detail about my mother, so I grew up with hundreds of stories about my mother. She feels...close."

"That's good."

"What about you?"

"Me?" He seems confused by the question, like he wasn't expecting to have to talk about himself.

"Do you have family here?"

"No. They're all in Vigo. Not many and in Vigo." He smiles.

"I'll bet you anything you miss your friends more than your family."

"You're very witchy." He smiles to himself and then looks at me. He looks at me, and he wants to devour me.

Tristan has a whole range of looks. Icy ones. Hot ones, which make you melt inside. Funny ones. Some of them are a little bit shy. Nervous. And contrary to what some of his smiles can do, they're all very similar even though some of them say no, some say yes, and a few of them leave no trace of doubt. When he wants you, there's no room for error in reading it. And when he looks at you with disdain, there's no mistaking it either.

My heart skips a beat when I remember how he was looking at me two days ago, sitting outside the café on Calle de Fuencarral. How he looked at me when he told me he didn't want to live with me anymore. That he didn't want his life and mine to keep hanging by the same thread. I guess I suddenly look worried, because his expression changes.

"It was a joke," he clarifies. "I don't see you cursing anyone."

"I know. Sorry. I lost my train of thought."

He doesn't add anything else, and I sit on the stool looking at how meticulously he's chopping and preparing the mixture. It's almost hypnotic, and I can't help myself: I get wrapped up in the image of our breakup. It would've been so easy to become engrossed in his hands or to float away on the scent of his cologne. But I don't.

For the first time in two days, I wonder if there could be someone else. People always say men don't break up with their partners unless they've got someone else lined up. That devastates me. So much that I grip my wineglass hard.

A question nestles deep down in my brain. A complex one that I have no way of answering because…I'm waking up in the past, but does our timeline still run its course? Is Tristan with someone else right now on the couch in another house, kissing her neck, thanking her for helping him break free of me? And if so, then what am I doing? Where am I? Is there an "I" still sleeping, lying there, dead?

I don't ask permission. I just jump up and fling open the doors to his tiny balcony overlooking the street and lean against the railing for a long time. The image of Tristan kissing someone else turned my stomach.

The footsteps of his boots on the parquet floor precede his scent, which quickly engulfs me. I don't know if I'm angry, sad, worried, or everything all at once… I don't know. But suddenly, I'm back on the idea that avoiding all this pain is the only possible answer to the question of why I'm reliving all this.

"Everything okay?" He hands over my wineglass, and I take it, nodding. "You ran out onto the balcony so quickly I thought you were going to throw yourself off."

"I don't have suicidal urges. You don't have to worry."

"I figured. Dinner's ready."

I nod with my eyes on the street, and he leans against the balcony's side wall with his glass in his hand.

"Can I be the one who plays at guessing things now?" he asks.

"Of course."

"You sure?" He raises his eyebrows.

"Yes. If you offend me, I can always throw my wine in your face and make a triumphant exit."

He's smiling gently when I look at him.

"Some guy hurt you."

"Oof," I reply. "You have no idea."

"What happened?"

I roll my eyes. "The same thing that always happens. It ended."

"I'm guessing he broke up with you."

"Good guess."

It seems unbelievable to be having this conversation with him when he'll never know that I'm talking about his future self.

"Was there someone else?" he asks.

"I don't know. One day, we were fine, and...the next day, he dumped me."

"That can't be true," he says. "There must've been signs."

"And I was blind or stupid? Neither of those options really appeals to me."

"Or maybe you were looking the other way. I'm not saying you did it on purpose. Maybe there were too many things fighting for your attention."

For a moment, as I look at him, it seems like there's something shining in his eyes, the truth about our relationship, and he knows it perfectly well, but it's just a mirage.

"We argued and stuff. I don't know. I've always been really in love with my work."

"More than him?"

"No." I laugh bitterly. "Wait, why are we talking about this?"

"Because I get this weird feeling that I remind you of him. Or I bring up similar feelings for you. Maybe the breakup is too recent. I don't know. You tell me."

And that can only mean one thing: that he's really into me. He doesn't want to waste time or get into a weird mess or drama. That's my Tristan.

I want to laugh, but I turn around and lean against the railing. Tristan comes over to me decisively and tugs on me. I think he's going to kiss me, but he just pulls me away from the edge.

"You're making me nervous perching there," he confesses, and his voice scratches.

"Nothing's going to happen."

"Well, just in case."

He puts a few more centimeters of distance between us when he goes back to leaning against the wall and takes out his pack of cigarettes. He'll quit in a year or so because one morning, when he gets up, he'll feel like he's coughing too much and that he's too young to be getting out of bed with a death rattle, plus he'll admit to me he's tired of always airing out his jacket so it doesn't stink of smoke. He'll quit cold turkey, and he won't need any help. Just like when he quit me two days ago.

"Can I have one?" I ask him.

"You sure? Didn't you quit?"

"Apparently it's time to revisit some vices."

He gives me one and holds out his lighter. I take my first drag without breaking eye contact. He lights his own cigarette. The air fills with smoke and the smell of the strong, blond tobacco that he smokes.

"Let's have dinner, and then I'm leaving," I say, diverting my gaze to the ciggy.

"I know. That was the deal."

I nod without looking at him. Suddenly, I'm really mad...really hurt. I like his voice so much, the patchy beard on his chin, how thick his hair is, the undefined color of his eyes, his mannerisms, his caresses, his fucking cologne...that it makes me angry. It makes me angry that I lost him, that I still love him, having him so close, our thing not being strong enough to follow him to this past that isn't what it was, that we're changing. He should remember, shouldn't he? If he loved me so much, if I was, as he said, the woman who made him understand what it meant to really love someone, he should remember me. A spark. A glimmer of recognition. Something.

I feel like slapping him.

"What?" he says, breaking the silence.

I take another drag and stub it out in a pot full of dry dirt and cigarette butts hanging from the railing.

"Let's have dinner, and I'm leaving."

"You've already said that quite a few times. And I said that was cool, and I agreed," he teases.

"Yes, but this wasn't part of the deal, and it doesn't mean that anything's going to change."

"This what?"

He wasn't expecting it, but his lips seem excited to meet mine once they recover from the surprise. Yes. I kiss him. I don't know why or if there is a why. Because I always kissed him. Because he's Tristan and there's still a kind of right floating in the air, like he belongs to me and his mouth should be attached to mine. And his tongue to mine.

We both have the taste of cigarettes lingering in our mouths, and we're still holding our wineglasses, but none of that stops us from delving deeper into the kiss and pressing closer against each other.

Tristan kisses like always. Like he kissed me the first time. Well. Very well. There's a hint of hesitation superimposed over passion; I think these are the two sides of pleasure. He abandons himself to pleasure. I run with it. I need the intensity to make me feel more real and tangible. He has his own rhythm, which he always imposes. In his kisses. In his fingers. In his mouth. In his hips. And that turns me on and pisses me off.

His tongue tangles with mine, tracing wet circles that I chase. He's trailing his mouth violently across mine, then gently grazing, and I melt into him. He bites my lower lip a little. When I do the same, a low, sensual growl emerges from his chest.

I would never stop kissing him. I would die of starvation, thirst, cold right here. But he wouldn't. And after a kiss probably longer than appropriate for a first kiss, he pulls his head back a little and looks at me. He seems stuck somewhere between embarrassed, excited, and a little offended because I'm still calling the shots, and he doesn't like that, even if he won't admit it because he wants to be way more modern than that.

"Wow..." he whispers. "You're so weird."

I can't help but laugh, even with all my sadness and my rage. He laughs too.

"The weirder, the better. That way, you won't ask for my number when I leave, and you won't call me tomorrow."

"I'm walking you home." His hand holding his glass is resting on my hip, like he's trying to soften the way he pulled back from the kiss.

"You don't have to."

"But I want to. And I want to ask for your number too."

"Why? If I'm so weird."

"Very weird," he insists, his brow furrowing. "But you make me feel really comfortable. And at home. And that's weird too."

"Yes. It is." A flame of heat rises to my cheeks.

"I'm probably a pretty weird guy too. I'm probably so weird you'd look normal next to me."

I laugh, and as I do, like I have so many times over the last few years, I go over, lean my head on his shoulder, and we half hug.

"Or not," he adds. "Come on. Dinner's ready."

We don't kiss again.

Not even when, true to his word, he goes down to the street with me, intending to walk me home. I guess, knowing him, that he'll want to kiss me when he gets to my door. Kissing in the middle of the street would seem barbaric to him... These northern boys and their modesty. But I have no intention of us getting all the way there. I've had enough for today. In fact, I've already had too much. And I'm bloated, swelling up with all the things that were, the things that maybe won't be, and the things that are. I need to go home, curl up in the fetal position under my sheets, and find out where I'm going to wake up tomorrow. Or more like...when.

"I'm going to get a cab," I decide.

"Oh...um..."

"I already told you, you're not walking me home."

"I mean...fine. It's cold."

"Thanks for dinner."

"Thanks for the conversation. And the kiss." His eyebrows arch into an expression somewhere between teasing and seductive.

"Take care then."

I throw my hand up at the first green light on a taxi that comes down the street. I don't want to see him anymore today. Plus, I'm starting to get the feeling that I'll have to do this all again tomorrow.

"Hey..." He stops me as I'm stepping off the sidewalk.

"What?"

"Will you give me your number? Just in case you want to return the dinner invite."

The taxi stops, and I take a few steps toward the car. He doesn't move. As I open the door, I say yes. He takes out his phone and taps in the numbers as I call them out to him, three by three. He smiles as he slides it back into his pocket.

"Good night," he says.

"Good night."

The door closing swallows up the sound of my goodbye; it gets lost, split in half, between the street and the inside of the taxi. Tristan doesn't move; he stands there with his hands dug into his jacket pockets even when the car has pulled away. I try to follow his figure through the rearview mirror, but I lose him when the taxi turns around the corner.

I have a bubble of helium floating in my chest, and I don't know if the feeling is pleasant or unpleasant. I don't know if I'm doing the right thing.

We're crossing Alonso Martínez Plaza (this has got to be the shortest ride this taxi driver will make all week) when my phone buzzes. I look at it out of habit. Just for something to do. In case it's Ivan.

But it's not.

TRISTAN:

I wish we had hugged.
Next time. We have way more weird stuff to show each other.

8

~~~

"I HAVE TO PREVENT WHAT'S GOING TO HAPPEN THIS AFTERNOON."

I lift my head up from the pillow and hold my breath like I'm waking up from a nightmare. I still have the cold from last night on my cheeks, even though it's starting to warm up under the bedspread. The heat of a spring morning.

I look over to the window to see if I can guess what time of year it is from the color of the light coming through the curtains, but my eyes stumble over a naked back. A man's back. Svelte. Firm. I could study anatomy running my fingertips over what's on display under his skin.

I don't understand. I don't understand this jump. Shouldn't I have woken up the day after our second "date," strictly speaking? That time when he fingered me in a taxi on the way back to my house after we drank a bottle and a half of wine in a Japanese restaurant. Is this part of the domino effect? Is he the person sleeping next to me?

I get closer to his skin and caress his shoulder. It's soft. It smells like his dense cologne. I know the pattern of freckles that start on his left shoulder and form an almost-exact replica of the Little Dipper. It's him.

I bury my nose in his back and press myself into Tristan, who shifts and clears his throat. I don't know if he's asleep. Tristan has a couple things that aren't exactly fitting for the hunky protagonist of a rom-com, like how he snores. His snores sound like two brawling kangaroos. The first time I slept with him, I barely slept a wink. He snores like a brown bear, and he does it even when he's face down. It depends a lot on the conditions: when he's drunk, it's like the rumble of a train; when he smoked, he sounded like a jumbo jet…but in the last few years, it improved a little. So I don't know how to use it to figure out the timeline. Is he not snoring because he quit smoking already? Is it at the beginning or at the end of our relationship? Is he awake already?

"Mmm," I hear him moan hoarsely when I press myself against him.

I clamber up him until I can smell his neck and the place where his short, dark hair starts. My left hand is working its way into his short locks of hair while the right is pulling him closer to me.

"Are you already causing trouble?" he murmurs, his voice much rougher than normal.

I don't answer. I just want to smell him. Touch him. I think the kiss from yesterday made me weaken. God. Couldn't I just stay and live in one of these pleasant memories? Hunker down, hide from time.

"Are you awake, or are you trying to violate me in your dreams?"

A giggle escapes, and he looks at me over his shoulder before he turns all the way around. Fuck. He's so hot. I'd screw him even in a coma.

He kisses me, but it's a restrained kiss, just two closed mouths pressing against each other. It's the typical good morning kiss when you haven't brushed your teeth yet. When he opens his eyes again and looks at me, I'm watching him raptly, and that seems to make him uncomfortable for a few seconds, but I put my right hand on his face and stroke his skin with my thumb, down to his lips, juicy, full, swollen from sleep. I'd like to kiss him again, stroke his nose with mine, leave my mouth hovering near his…but he pulls away.

"What time is it?" he asks.

"I don't know. I don't even know what day of the week it is."

"Saturday." He smiles.

Blessed time jumps, from Saturday to Saturday. Does that mean I could spend a month waking up on Mondays? Don't fuck with me.

I don't want to worry now about how long these jumps will last, but I can't help it. It's obvious nobody can live this way forever without losing their mind.

I curl up on Tristan's chest, nuzzling into his chest hair with the tip of my nose and my upper lip. I get the feeling that he's stiffening up a little.

"Listen... I have to go home," he murmurs.

One doubt dispelled. This "memory" isn't from the last two years. It's earlier. Maybe I shouldn't be so affectionate? Or maybe I should? Why not?

He turns onto his back, and I snuggle into his side.

"I can't." He laughs. "We fucked three times last night. At my age, these feats get a little more complicated. You should've met me when I was nineteen."

"Shut up."

It's true the pulsing between my legs seems to hint of good sex. Good and pretty intense. An exhausting exercise. I try to remember as I sling my leg over his thigh until it's wedged between his legs. My fingers meander across his skin, and my nose finds his neck. A little purr escapes him.

What day is it today? We're in my room, so it can't be that jaunt we took to the mountains. I think that was our record for most times in one night. We practically only did one thing the whole weekend: fuck. We stopped to eat, shower, and sleep. Those good memories only wake me up more.

My hand runs down his flat, tight belly. If the comforter wasn't covering him, I'd see his belly button, the shadow of the muscle that sports have developed over the years, and the obliques that draw down and disappear under the elastic of his underwear. Tristan plays sports like someone who smokes, drinks coffee, watches television, or reads. It's partly for entertainment, partly a vice. He finds a certain pleasure and peace of mind in feeling completely exhausted. He doesn't do it for aesthetic reasons, although he likes what he sees in the mirror when he comes out of the shower. Me too, for the record, because years ago, I learned to be grateful for every inch of my skin and to stop wasting time wishing I were someone else.

"Miranda…seriously, I have to go home."

"Why?"

I need to get on top of him. Get naked. Feel how he pushes into me and how my body welcomes him, wet and hot.

"Because I have that call I told you about yesterday. And because I want to shower and change my clothes. And because"—he reaches up to my ear and whispers—"I can't. It's going to fall off."

He pulls away smoothly and climbs out of bed. Under his boxers, there's something shyly protruding, but I won't insist. Watching him walk around the bed to where he left his clothes is enough pleasure for me. That and the memory of tiredness in my body. I follow him to the bathroom with my eyes. Then I squeeze my thighs and feel a slight pain inside. Yesterday's session must have been…muscular and passionate. The bedside table proudly displays the silvery remains of, at a glance, three condom wrappers.

He doesn't take long to come back into the bedroom. As he does, he's pulling a white button-up over a white T-shirt, with his pants open and the belt clinking against him with a pretty sensual noise. It doesn't improve my situation. Now I want him on top too.

"Come here." I pat the bed.

"No fucking way." A polite smile quickly disappears. He washed his face, and he still has a few drops clinging to his temples. "I'm serious. I can't. Plus my fucking contact lenses are stuck to my corneas."

Wait.

Wait…he slept here and he didn't bring his "stuff"? His contact lens case. His toothbrush…

"What day of the month is this?" I ask.

"When you do that..." He shakes his head and sighs.

"When I do what?"

"When you ask what day it is and all that...you sound super weird."

"I'm scatterbrained."

"It's the twentieth of February," he clears up.

He seems kind of serious. Or tense. Or...what?

"Okay, I'm going," he says after he buttons up his pants briskly. "I'll message you later."

"Okay. Do we have a plan?"

Tristan, who is kneeling on the bed to give me a kiss, furrows his brow.

"We haven't decided on anything, no."

"Oh, okay."

"Why?"

Oy, everything is so tense, right? I don't answer, and he kisses me on the lips, with his mouth closed again.

"I'll text you later."

"Wait, I'll walk you to the door."

"Don't worry about it."

I catch up with him almost in the entrance hall, where he's pulling on his coat. He pauses in front of the door for a second when he sees me, and I open it for him myself as I try to adjust the tie on my silk robe. We stay there, halfway out of the house, very close to each other, not sure whether to talk or kiss. If he gives me a hug, I'll burst into tears. I know Tristan well enough to know that he wants to leave because he's uncomfortable. And before anyone asks, I'll tell you motu proprio that I am too.

"See you later," he says, looking at my lips.

"Yes."

I almost add an "I guess," but before I can, he leaves me hanging with a quick peck on the lips, his feet heading down the stairs. As soon as I close the door, I run to the table I use as my "office" in the living room, where I always leave my planner right when I get home. I don't find it.

After I turn everything upside down, I find it in the bag I use to go to the magazine: a black sack du jour from Saint Laurent, which fits absolutely everything I need to survive a workday. I think I could even fit myself in there if I curled up tightly enough.

I put a Post-it in the margin of the current week's page, so I find it quickly. Right. Saturday, February 20, four years in the past. And the worst part is that date doesn't mean much to me. I spent New Year's Eve with my friends in Ivan's parents' house in a village in Toledo. It's a special day for the gang, since we can't always see one another as much as we wish we could because of work. It was a fun party where I didn't worry about anything besides laughing a lot with Ivan and everyone else.

Tristan went to Vigo with his friends. He texted me at one in the morning to send me a picture of a dog that was hoping to be petted under the table. The only caption he added was "Happy New Year, Miranda."

Everything was good in January. Normal. We had that weekend in a little rural hotel where the sex started to become kind of intimate, and I don't remember anything else that would be important. Wait... I sit down on the sofa and make an effort to remember. January, fine. January, normal. January, a little mini break. And in February...was February when I went to Milan with the magazine? No. That was in March. But in March, he and I...so in February...

"Shit!"

Ivan opens the door dressed in one of those free marketing T-shirts and navy blue track pants that he must have worn to gym class in high school and are now a little short on him.

"You're the worst-dressed stylist I've ever met," I blurt out.

But of course, I blurt it out before I realize what's crowning his head: a bun. A bun the size of a pineapple.

"Wait, what the fuck is that?" I point.

"Jesus, babe, what's going on with you? Stop yelling."

"What's that on your head?" I ask, horrified.

"A bun, for fuck's sake. It's not like it's the first time you've seen me like this. I was going over a few things on my laptop, and having my hair loose was bugging me."

As soon as I step into his apartment, he yanks out the hair tie holding the bun up, and his hair falls loose. Long black hair, straight and shiny, falls like a waterfall down to his chest. I have no words. Ivan's hair is famous. This long hair thing is new. Is it a wig? He wouldn't get extensions, would he?

"What are you looking at?"

I swear, my voice won't even come out. I point at his hair.

"I did a keratin treatment the other day. That's why it's so shiny."

"Ivan, you look like you're wearing the wig they put on the wolf in the second Twilight movie. Or the third."

"What are you talking about, you nutjob?"

He's so quick smacking me on the back of the neck that I don't even see it coming. And I don't complain. I deserve it.

I flop down on the couch and stare at him in shock. I can't explain it. I saw him yesterday, and he had short hair. His usual hairstyle, a little longer in the front, with a swoop that makes even me jealous. I can't imagine how jealous it must make men who are losing their hair. There's no way his hair could've grown this much in the two months between yesterday's "memory" and today's. I can't even string together coherent thoughts.

"Can you stop looking at me like that?"

"Can I ask how long you've been growing out your hair?"

"Are you stupid or what?" He's glaring at me. "Look, girl, you've been really weird lately. And by the way, it'd be nice if you could call before you just show up here. One day, you're going to find me with someone, and you're going to want to die."

I roll my eyes. I wish I could tell him I know exactly when I'm going to find him with someone. I know now.

Listen, what if…?

"Ivan, how tolerant are you to paranormal stories?"

"If there's a ghost in your house, I don't wanna know about it. Hey, your face looks good. You've been fucking."

"Yeah, shut up. Can you answer me?"

"With Tristan?"

"You know Tristan?" I exclaim.

"Well, you haven't talked about anything else since the day you met him at El Corazon."

I'm changing the story. Just the details or can I change the fundamental parts?

"If I tell you something really weird, do you promise not to admit me to a mental institution against my will?"

"I mean, it depends."

"I'm time traveling."

Ivan leans against the corner of the living room, next to the kitchen, and blinks exaggeratedly while he twirls his hair around a finger.

"Are you on drugs?"

"No. You know I vomit if I even take one hit of a joint."

"Pills? Shrooms?"

"Ivan, nothing. I hate drugs."

"Then explain it to me, because now you're freaking me out."

"I'm time traveling, Ivan."

"Like, how? You get in the freezer, you clap twice, and you show up in the Pleistocene era?"

"You think this is funny?" I ask him very seriously.

"No, exactly the opposite."

"Ivan, listen to me. Three days ago, when I went to bed, it was the spring five years in the future. When I woke up, it was November 11, five years in the past. I don't know how I did it. Or how it's happening. Or how it works. Because the next day, when I woke up, it was December 10. And the next day, today…February 20."

"Are you trying to tell me that you've spent three days reliving days in the past?"

"Yes."

"Okay. Give me the winning number for the lottery."

"It doesn't work like that."

"Oh no? What'll happen, you'll violate some interstellar travel law?"

"Do you think I'm fucking with you?"

"I mean, of course. I think your phone is in a group call right now, and your whole gang of hyenas are laughing your heads off at me."

I take my phone out of my bag and give it to him. I take off my coat and yank my sweater up, defending myself like I'm deranged.

"See? No wires!"

He asks me to stop.

"Do you always wear such slutty underwear? For the love of the universe. You look like a bag of oranges."

"It's called lace."

"It's called 'buy a fucking cotton set because that must be bad even for your tits.'"

"Ivan…" I flash him a look that's begging him to focus. "I can't tell you the winning number for the lottery because I don't know. I wasn't paying attention to that. I don't play, you know that. If I woke up tomorrow in five years and then came back to this year, duh, I'd bring you a clue so that you would be filthy rich and not just filthy."

We're driving each other nuts. He's looking at me, not even trying to hide that he doesn't believe me, and I'm looking at him, incredulous that he doesn't believe me. Fuck, this is like a tongue twister.

"I can't give you that fact, but I can give you something else." Something just came to me.

"Okay, so spill the tea."

"But you're going to have to take a leap of faith, Ivan, because you'll know it's true when it happens but not today."

"Well, you tell me the whopper, and then we'll see."

He flicks his hair off his shoulder, and I balk. But when did he decide to grow this Renaissance virgin hair? Enough.

"Wait, I'm trying to remember what happened that year."

"Of course, you must have so many memories to choose from…" he says sarcastically.

"You're an asshole, but you know what the problem is? There's so much mess in your life, and there's no way to remember it all."

I stand up and stare at him like I can see through him, remembering all the stupid things this human being has done over the last few years. And suddenly, I remember. I remember one of the famous things we still reminisce about at group dinners.

"I think it's next month. Or the one after. I don't remember exactly, but…you're going to be on a work trip, and suddenly, when you're on the way back from the bathroom, you're going to find Thalia barefoot in the hall, and she's going to ask you to help her hook a sequin bra."

He looks at me with his brow super furrowed.

"Girl, you're nuts."

"Please…I'm your best friend. You have to trust me."

"Are you hearing yourself? You sound like you stuck your finger in a socket and it made you gaga. You're really freaking me out now."

I collapse back onto the sofa, defeated. He's my partner in crime in all the crazy shit I've done in my life. How can he not support me in this?

I mean…the truth is if he showed up at my house with a similar story, I would think he had been hit on the head and needed to go to the hospital.

"I went to have a brain scan in November," I inform him. "The first time it happened. Everything looked fine, whatever that's good for."

Ivan is squinting at me with his arms crossed.

"Now I'm going to be unhinged until I run into that whore Thalia."

"But you're going to have so much fun that night."

He sucks his teeth, grabs a chair, and sits across from me.

"I don't believe you. You know that, right?"

I nod.

"And right now, I think you drank spiked gin and you're going to spend the rest of your life delirious."

"Okay."

He sighs.

"But we're going to pretend like I believe you."

I clap giddily a few times and pounce on him, covering him in kisses.

"Get off," he says and shoves me away. "Based on the premise that I believe you, then what?"

"I have to prevent what's going to happen this afternoon."

9

~~

GO TO HELL

In February four years ago, and to be more specific, on the twentieth, Tristan and I had an argument. A misunderstanding. As a result, we went a few months without seeing each other or calling or texting. That's not why I want to stop what happened. It's because I came away from that episode covered in scars. The truth is I don't really understand why. Maybe, just maybe, preventing it will solve a few things at once. Or maybe I just need to shut him up before he says "We need to talk" again, because right now, I don't think I can handle it.

Was what happened that day that deep? No. It was so boring it's almost embarrassing that it turned into a hiccup in our history. I guess we all think we're special. And actually, we're all the main character in our own stories, which means they can't be relevant to everyone.

Tristan got overwhelmed. It's as simple and banal as that. Tristan must have thought that I was in a rush to, I don't know, marry him, and he made a graceful exit when he gleaned that I was expecting things from him that he didn't want to give me. He started to think about how he was just in Madrid temporarily, how he wasn't looking for a relationship, how he was burned out at work, and how, besides all that, he wasn't even that into me. So he slammed the door, metaphorically.

Ay, I'm doing a shitty job of explaining this.

That day, we woke up in my bed, just like this morning. And like this morning, I was very affectionate. We had been sleeping with each other for almost three months, and back then, we slept over at each other's houses at least one night a week. We weren't official, and I hadn't even talked about him to practically anybody: just to Ivan and Rita at the magazine. I was trying not to take this thing with Tristan seriously because it made me scared and anxious. I didn't want what everyone assumes you should want: to fall in love, be happy by his side, build something together.

Even the idea of all that made me cringe. All I wanted back then was to fall in love with myself, to be happy alone, and to achieve a life that was my own. I couldn't conceive of sharing something that still didn't feel like my own. So even though I thought about him way more often than I would've liked to admit, I had him categorized as a "fuck buddy."

But that day, when I woke up, I was affectionate because I've never understood why attachment and affection have to go hand in hand with commitment. Because I think that we can be very affectionate with someone temporary. Affection, respect, and caresses aren't linked, and they don't mean you think someone is the love of your life just because you're clinking glasses with them. That's how I see it. Apparently it wasn't Tristan's. He was coming off a tense week already. And he started thinking our ties were becoming tight enough that it wouldn't be out of place for one of us to start wondering "What are we?" We had been seeing each other since November (in the real past), we were falling into a kind of routine, and we were building trust. And he wasn't into that because he didn't feel ready, because he had just arrived in the city, because we didn't know each other that well, because he felt like he was in a different place in his life, and because...he always believed that his lifestyle wouldn't fit with mine. Or more like my rhythm of life had nothing to do with him. Apparently, he was brimming with reasons.

So he left my house a little tense, but when he got back to his, after a shower, putting on clean, comfortable clothes, and a boring work call, he thought maybe he was being an idiot and gave our Saturday "another chance."

If I'm not mistaken, I'll get a message in a few minutes: a photo of him lying on his couch, with a short text: "Let's do something this afternoon?" Four years ago, I said sure, why don't we take a walk? He had found an apartment a month before, and he was still looking for a few things to spruce it up a little, so he suggested going to a "tiny little antique store" that he thought looked interesting. It was my dad's store, of course, but I didn't tell him that. I threw it out there when we were already there. And giving me no time to explain that my dad didn't give two fucks about formal introductions even if I had been dating my "boyfriend" for two weeks, he immediately assumed I was pressuring him. But nothing could have been further from reality.

Remember the wheel and the champagne? I was still very much a wheel back then. Tristan kept saying he wanted a shelf to store his records, and I remembered my dad had one at a pretty good price. That was it.

We were both idiots.

When I said, "This is my dad's store," he grabbed my elbow, trying to stop me from going in the door, and with the same face you would make when you were giving your condolences to someone at a funeral, he threw out that we needed to talk.

And I'm just realizing now that I'm not ready to face that conversation again. I'm too sensitive to hear him say again: "We need to talk." It's too recent. Way too recent. I don't know if I can handle it without tearing his hair out. Or ripping my own out.

I have to stop it. Maybe something changed and tomorrow will go back to being the year it's supposed to be. Maybe over the next few months, I won't fall into the trap of seeing our relationship as a delicate dance between discretion and fear. Being discreet can be a form of capitulation and have nothing to do with loving. With falling in love. With living. With sex. With kisses. With love stories, even if they are just for one night, born of desire, respect, and affection. I only understand discretion when it comes to things I'm not putting my heart into.

It might seem very easy, but it's not.

"So don't take him to your dad's store, darling," Ivan says to me.

"I got that far, moron. Are you listening to what I'm saying? I tried to prevent it twice already, and life keeps throwing him in my path. I don't know what's happening, but I'm getting the feeling that I can't change things too much. Or I can change the way things happen but not the result. Does that make any sense?"

He nods, intrigued.

My phone buzzes. Ivan still has it in his lap, and the lit-up screen shows the preview of a message from Tristan: a photo of him lying on his couch with the brief text: "Let's do something this afternoon?"

Ivan looks at me, bewildered.

"If all this turns out to be true, I'm really gonna flip out."

"You better not wake up tomorrow and forget all this."

"Of course, because what if you go back to being aware of the time jumps…I mean…maybe the Miranda I see tomorrow isn't jumping through time and has no idea any of this is happening, right?"

"Jeez…that's trippy," I say, overwhelmed.

"Are there two Mirandas out there?"

"I guess so, but they're never in the same space-time."

"Girl, this is a crazy trip. Like seeing Thalia and her asking me to fasten who knows what, I'll shit myself."

I give him a serious look that means "I told you it sucked," and then I wave at my phone.

"Tell him you'll take him to the IKEA in Alcorcón," Ivan demands.

I can't help cracking a smile.

"Ivan…please."

"Come on. If it gets messy because he thinks you want to 'introduce him to society,' I would consider heading in the opposite direction."

"And what's that?"

"Well, something super intimate."

"Given that he got overwhelmed with my shows of affection this morning."

"Men are trash."

"As far as I know, you identify as a man."

"And sometimes I'm trash. So…"

"It's better if I just tell him I can't," I decide. "I can't meet up, and… I stay far away from his neighborhood, mine, and any streets with a lot of stores on them. I tell him I have plans with my friends and that maybe we'll see each other another day."

"One of the girls did message the group chat asking if we're hanging out."

"Yeah, I saw."

"So tell him that. It makes sense. If you don't see each other, there's no danger. And then we can go get a beer with them and tell them this crazy shit…"

"No, no," I stop him. "Please."

"What?"

"You can't tell anyone, Ivan. You're my best friend, and even you didn't believe me. Just imagine how everyone else would react."

"I'm still worried about your mental health, to be honest."

"And I'm still worried about your Pantene hair."

I grab my phone and concentrate on answering:

MIRANDA:

Hey Tristan. I have plans with my friends.

We can hang out another time if you want.

Tomorrow? Kisses.

I send it and lock my phone.

"Come on. Take a shower. I'm going to call the girls and see if they want to meet up."

Ivan stands up and heads toward the bathroom.

"After all that, the solution was pretty basic for all the drama you kicked up, huh?" he mutters. "See, you didn't even need me to come up with this Machiavellian plan."

"I'm time traveling," I remind him. "Don't mess with me, hunty."

Carabanchel is an up-and-coming neighborhood that is going to become super cool in the next few years. Soon it'll be jam-packed with bars that will draw people from all over Madrid, like Patanel, where they serve their own craft beer and tapas, or La Cortá Ultramarinos, where you can have coffee and pastries or a few beers with a good tapa and buy some cheese to take home.

The thing is none of these places are open yet, and we haven't reached the age where we want everything to be a little luxurious. At twenty-eight, even in this time-traveling farce, drinking a beer on any patio in the plaza next to the Oporto metro stop seemed luxurious enough.

It didn't chill me out much, to be honest, but it's better than sitting at home, going around and around this carousel of dates and Tristans. I wish I could say something else, like that I'm deeply relaxed, enjoying the conversation, or even that the beer is hitting me hard enough to think that none of this is that deep, but no. There's a lot of noise in my head, and anyway, I'm scared I'll say something that didn't happen the first time, and tomorrow, instead of having hair like one of the Azúcar Moreno girls in the early nineties, Ivan will be a whole different person. Or he'll turn into a lizard. I don't know what I have against lizards today, but I'm still scared.

Our friends are kiki-ing about how one of them met someone at the door of a club or how another is sick of having two jobs, barely any money, and no time. They're the kinds of old friends who are so close it doesn't matter where or how we met, who introduced whom to whom, or the details or our day-to-day lives or our pace of life. And that's amazing. And I'd like to participate, tell them that maybe in a few years, it'll all be better, but I don't want to fuck everything up with the butterfly effect, so I'm staying pretty quiet. At least until they ask me...like they're asking right now:

"What about you? You've been pretty quiet."

Ivan laughs to himself while he studies his split ends. I just can't get used to it, but none of them have even mentioned the long hair, so I assume that in this new micro reality, Ivan has always had long hair.

"Why is this one laughing?" one of our friends asks.

"Because he's an idiot," I reply. "I just don't have much to tell."

"No hookups and no gossip from the magazine?"

I bite my lip.

"Nope." I shake my head with a guilty little smirk.

I feel bad lying to them, but the thing is, telling them all this doesn't make any sense. My phone buzzes on the table, next to my beer, and I glimpse his name on the screen. Saved by the bell.

"Sorry, sluts, no news and no gossip important enough to repeat. Pass."

I grab my phone and wink.

TRISTAN:

Hey.
What are you up to?

MIRANDA:

Having a drink with my friends on a patio.

TRISTAN:

Isn't it too cold to be outside?

> **MIRANDA:**
> In Madrid we sit outside until it snows.

> **TRISTAN:**
> Right.
> Listen...can you talk?

> **MIRANDA:**
> Of course. Is something up?

> **TRISTAN:**
> No.
> Well. A little.
> It's just that... I don't know how to say it.

I look away from my phone. NO FUCKING WAY. *Don't say it. Don't say it. Don't say it.*

> **TRISTAN:**
> I've been thinking and...
> I think we need to talk.

I side-eye Ivan, and when he sees my expression, he instinctively cranes his neck to see the conversation on my phone.

> **MIRANDA:**
> Go ahead.

"Tell him he should at least call you to do this," he hisses.

"I'm not going to say that."

"Why?"

"Because if he didn't think of that himself, why would I ask him to?"

TRISTAN:
I'm not really sure I want to get into where we're going
with this.

MIRANDA:
Be more specific.

TRISTAN:
I think we should stop seeing each other.

I look at Ivan, who's making a shocked Pikachu face.

MIRANDA:
If that's what you want, what are we gonna do?

TRISTAN:
I just think we've taken it a little too far. I mean…it's fun. All
the time I've spent with you has been, honestly. But I'm not
looking for anything like this right now. And I don't want to
hurt you.

MIRANDA:
Well, you could have thought about that before you slept
at my house last night. Now I feel like a dumbass.

"Delete that," Ivan prods me.
I listen to my friend. I erase it and draft a new message.

MIRANDA:
I've had fun with you too.
If it's over, it's over.
It's all been working for me.

TRISTAN:
I understand.

I stay silent, staring at the screen, not knowing what to add. Ivan seems like he's holding his breath when the app shows that Tristan is typing again.

TRISTAN:

I feel really bad, but the truth is I don't want to lead you on and end up with you thinking I'm playing you.
I'm not playing you.
It's too intense and too soon for me. I just moved here and I have a lot going on. Being in a relationship was never part of my plans or my priorities.

"Can't I tell him that nobody asked him for a relationship?" I ask Ivan in a small voice.

"No."

"Why?"

"Because, according to you," he whispers, "you're going to have one."

"But the thing is I don't think I want one anymore."

Ivan is surprised to see my eyes well up with tears.

"Hey, babe!" all the other girls chorus when they realize.

"What's going on?"

"What happened?"

"Miri! Are you okay?"

I open my bag as I nod and give various excuses. I take out some money and thrust it at Ivan, who refuses to take it. I leave it on the table, stand up, and struggle to say goodbye.

"I think I just wanna go home, girls."

"Wait, don't go like this! How are you gonna leave this upset?"

They're all babbling over one another. Ivan is silent.

"No, no, I'm just not in the right mood." I flash a fake smile. "I'll be fine, I swear. It's just that…something unexpected came up."

"Let her go. She'll feel better on her own." At least Ivan is helping me out.

I don't even look back. Who cares? Tomorrow we'll probably all be giant talking potatoes. Who knows what the collateral effect of all these changes I'm making will be? Ivan has hair down to his armpits. Anything could happen.

I hail a cab, and when I'm inside, rage pours out through my eyes. Fuck. I'm an idiot. How can I be going through two breakups from the same guy in three days? But with four years between one and the other.

I should never have gotten back together with him. Maybe this was the sign of how things were going to be in the future. I don't know why I didn't learn. I don't know why I tried so hard.

I read through the conversation again, digging my nails into my thigh. I feel like an idiot, just like the first time.

I want to write him something like erase my number, I'm dead to you, never even think about contacting me again, I'm done, I don't want anything you'll ever give me, but what I do instead is open the window.

"Are you hot?" asks the taxi driver, who has been glancing at me in the rearview mirror every once in a while, a little alarmed by my tears.

"No, no worries."

As soon as we get out of the tunnel, I grab my phone and hurl it angrily onto the shoulder, where it explodes and shatters. The cab driver clears his throat.

"Any objections?" I ask him.

"Señorita…turning it off would've done the job."

And he's right. I don't understand what the point of reliving all this again could possibly be. What's the purpose? Because I can't change the outcome no matter what I do…but I'm going to figure it out. And if this still hasn't gotten him off my back, if it's still going to happen again, if I wake up next to him tomorrow, even if we're on that beautiful trip to Lille we took one fall, even if I wake up the Christmas when he gave me that ring, even if whatever it may be…that dude can go to hell.

10

~~

"BEING FREE TO DECIDE WITHOUT HINDRANCES."

If I could control the time compass that's dragging me from one point to another in my history with Tristan, right now I would ask to go to the end, to the café on Calle de Fuencarral, so I could flip the table as soon as I got there and toss that fucking cortado in his face. I wouldn't add much else. Maybe flip him off and toss out a "This is what I should have known from the beginning, you piece of shit."

Just like in fashion, less is more when it comes to this stuff.

Why am I so mad? Come on. Getting dumped twice in the same week (the last seven days I've lived through should always be called a week, even if they're in different years), especially by the same person, sucks. But falling asleep running through all the sharp edges of our relationship doesn't make it any easier, I promise.

Always demanding attention.

Always saying his sister's right.

Always pressuring me to make important decisions.

Always hiding behind his "I hate Madrid."

Always blaming me for all our problems.

"It's not a good time." "You love your job too much." "You spent too much last month." "I need a little peace." "You're too restless." "I can't handle all these plans." "You seem annoyed that I want to spend time with you."

Before I fell asleep, I did something I don't recommend. These stunts are performed by skilled professionals; don't try this at home. I made a mental list of all the things in my life that weren't going well, all the ones that I could possibly blame on Tristan. And there were way more than I thought there would be…but the first one would've been plenty. I didn't need all the others that came after. It's his fault I'm going to bed today and I'm going to wake up who knows when, in what fucking month, in what fucking year. And how do I know it's his fault? I mean, it never happened to me before. The first time was after he dumped me. This is his fault. I don't have proof, but I have no doubt either.

I hate his turtleneck.

I hate the ring he wore on his right hand when I met him.

I hate the way he always looked at other women.

I hate how insecure he made me feel for the last year.

I hate that he made me consider choosing between the time I spent on work and the time I spent on him.

I hate a lot of things right now but most of all that he dumped me.

I should add one aggravating circumstance: today, when I woke up, I discovered something about my new time-traveling condition. Turns out I'm not just capable of changing the "when." Also the "where." What does this mean? Well, that I can wake up four years before and in a different bed. And if not knowing the date is worrying, opening your eyes and not recognizing the room you're sleeping in is a nightmare.

All I see is darkness, and it's not a familiar darkness. There are thick curtains over the windows, like in a hotel. I rub the sheets with my feet, feeling how soft they are. The temperature is pretty high, probably because two bodies create a lot of heat under one blanket. Two. Because there's someone next to me, and I curse when I glance over and get a glimpse of his black hair and hear a slightly muffled snore.

I want to smother him with a pillow and see if tomorrow he shows up with no warning on my own fucking mattress. I want to pounce on him like a shit-throwing gorilla and slap him until my arms get tired. I want to wax both his eyebrows off before he wakes up and make his life a hell where he can't make facial expressions for a few months.

I shoot my hand out of the sheets and grope around the bedside table until I find my phone. A new one, of course. One that's not in a ditch, with the screen smashed, in the middle of the M-30. One whose screen lights up when you touch it.

07:02 Monday, September 25

Great. What year?

I never thought asking that question would start to feel so normal.

I try to remember, but it's impossible because I'm enraged and half-asleep, so I grab my phone and open the calendar app, where a hellish schedule is laid out before me. There are more than fifteen events (meetings or things to deal with) on every day from here to the day after tomorrow. Why am I in a hotel with so much to do?

Wait. I know where I am.

September 25, four years ago. Paris. One day before fashion week starts.

When it's time to hire new people for internships or work-study at the magazine, I'm usually part of the team that conducts the interviews. I hate it because I never know if I'll be too strict or if I'll crack up in front of the wrong people, but the truth is there are some pretty funny moments. One of them is when we give the new girl (and I say "girl" because most of the applicants are women) the opportunity to ask questions about the position she's being interviewed for. I'm usually with the head of the department the newcomer is interviewing for, so both of us, whoever we are (Marta and I, Rita and I, Cris and I), hold our breath waiting for the question. The question.

"Can I go to Paris fashion week?"

"Yes, sweetie, and the one in New York. Would both be okay?"

I'm not an idiot. It's just…how gullible can they be? In a magazine like ours, where we all get along really well, much better than you would expect from most work environments, there are still tension and (metaphorical) fisticuffs every time the opportunity to go to a fashion week comes, wherever it might be. Because we all want to go, duh. And as deputy editor, I wish the whole team could experience it at least once in their lives, but we do the best we can. The fashion world, and all of us who fall under that umbrella, is no longer the land of milk and honey. So there's not always the opportunity to cover the act in person. Sometimes we syndicate the content, which means someone from our North American "mother" flies to Paris, covers the runways, and then doles out the material, which is then translated or adjusted for each country. There have even been times when our French colleagues take care of everything.

But there are good years. Of course there are. I've sat front row at a show in Tokyo's fashion week. And in Paris in the second row several times. I even went to New York once. For years now, the best opportunities have been offered up by brands; that year was one example.

A really famous cosmetics brand teamed up with a few sponsors to invite some of the editors from fashion publications to the most anticipated event of the year, which was a total luxury. Marisol was one of them, but…

"I don't feel like it."

When she said that to me, I felt like someone had to pinch me so hard they'd draw blood.

"Excuse me?"

"I said I don't feel like it." She shrugged and took off her black plastic glasses, letting them dangle on her chest. A little smile floated on her lips. "You go."

"But, Marisol..."

"You don't want to? Should I ask the intern?"

"Wait, hold up..." I was standing in front of her desk, looking at her, unable to believe what she was saying. "A suite in one of the most beautiful hotels in Paris, the Shangri-La. Passes for the second or third row to Christian Dior, Saint Laurent, Lanvin, Chloe, and Isabel Marant. An invitation-only cocktail party at the Louvre. A gala. Invitation only. At the Louvre. I don't know, Marisol...I feel obligated to insist."

"You're going to have a great time." She smiled.

And then some. That fashion week was kind of my baptism as deputy editor of the magazine, and she knew it. It was something special. Magical. Hard because it pushed me to my limits, but magical.

We had to call in a lot of favors to make sure my look was always on point. And I wanted to go unnoticed, but there are certain idiosyncrasies that come with attending a runway show. If you're ever in doubt, you should wear black. That's what I did and what I always do in my normal life, so it wouldn't be a problem out there. But I'm the deputy editor of a publication, not an it girl, influencer, or hot actress of the moment, so my wardrobe didn't have many special pieces. A few, because when I started working at the magazine, I felt like I had to invest in a few pieces that would last years and wouldn't go out of fashion, but not enough to build the carousel of styles I needed for this trip.

So we called in favors. And I tried on a lot of things that weren't my size. Some of them zipped up (watch for the skirts, they're tricky), others we forced to fasten with some tricks, and for the rest…we had to use our imaginations. Anyway, it wasn't like I was going to be posing in front of the photographers. I just couldn't get caught in a fashion faux pas, like wearing white Decathlon socks under my suit, being identified, and making the magazine look terrible.

Two thrilled interns were dispatched to my house to help me pack. Rita too, because she'd been packed for weeks already and had even included a portable steamer to keep the outfits in mint condition. And I was gripped by a kind of terror the whole time. And I say "kind of" because I guessed it would be an extraordinary experience and because I'm leaving out one of the most important parts about that trip when it came to my personal life: I was going to Paris with Tristan.

Okay, okay. Rewind. How?

Well. Okay. In February of that year, he told me, standing outside my father's store, that he didn't want what we had, but remember that back then, I thought it was simply a misunderstanding. So…well. I guess after two months without seeing each other or talking, when it started to become obvious that I couldn't get him out of my head, I started operation "run into each other randomly." And it must've been mutual, because it didn't take long for us to run into each other in a café one day.

And we said hi awkwardly.

And we chatted.

And he asked me if I would mind if he joined me for a coffee.

And we walked home together.

And he texted me that same night.

And the next day.

And the next day, I was wildly fucking him on his couch like the world was ending.

What? Don't look at me like that. That's what a rekindled love story calls for, right?

Now I think, what a shitty love story. It was like reverse ghosting. First you kick me to the curb, and then, when you think about it in the light of day, you come looking for me. I should wax one of his eyebrows off right now.

We easily fell back into the relationship that seemed like too much before, and before we realized what was happening, he was coming to Paris with me. Marisol told me that as long as having company wouldn't stop me from doing what I was there to do, I could take whomever I wanted, as long as they paid for their ticket. And the big whore paid.

Lying here, I know that if I let everything go the way it actually went, it's going to be a fucking awesome trip. Despite all my predictions, Tristan won't get bored. Not at all. It's going to give him time to miss me and make how he feels about me a little clearer. It will only make him admire me more, as a person and as a professional, which, if anyone asks me, is the base of the pyramid true love is built on. We'll live through incredibly spectacular experiences, like a cocktail behind closed doors at the Louvre. And we'll come back very clear that this is what we want.

Beautiful, right? Well, I'm not in the fucking mood.

I jump out of bed and wrench the curtains open tactlessly. The light is too thin at this time of day to have the dramatic effect I was hoping for (burning his retinas, for example), but it wakes him up at least and not how I think he'd like to be. In the original memory, I woke him up with a fucking blow job. I'm an idiot.

"Good morning," he says in a small, raspy voice, peering at me from the white sheets of the huge bed in the Chaillot suite in the Shangri-La hotel, which is truly spectacular. He checks the time on his phone and then turns back to me. "What are you doing up so early? Come on, come back here." He pats the bed next to him.

Tempting.

"Up. I have a million things to do," I reply dryly.

"Can I help you? Like last night." He smiles like a saint.

During this so-called "last night," according to my memory, he helped me unpack my suitcases and steamed everything that seemed wrinkly. He also, under my guidance, organized the accessories according to looks, so that when I got dressed, I had everything ready and I would have a little extra time. And then he went down on me.

So cute.

No, he's not cute. He's a death trap. He's like an anaconda dressed as a baby. He's still an anaconda. Just like the one he has now standing to attention under his boxers, fuck.

I look away when he gets up and head into the bathroom. He follows me.

"Tristan, for god's sake, I want to take a piss," I blurt out rudely.

"Um."

I pull away and slam the door in his face. What's my plan? I don't know. To make the trip go badly. Badly enough that he gets fed up, wants to leave, and changes his flight. Or so that the two days left in the trip (which I'm not even going to experience because with my luck, I'll wake up tomorrow on our trip to the beach, probably, unfortunately) don't make up for what an asshole I've been today. He'll find himself with a woman he's not going to like. A cold woman only interested in her own comfort and desires. A woman who he's not a priority for, not even close, because he's really not used to that.

So why don't I just tell him to leave and be done with it? Because it's becoming clear that if I'm the one to reject him, the next day, I'm still stuck in this same old song. Let's see what happens if he gets sick of me.

I take a long shower. I get ready calmly. And with the door closed and locked. His bladder must be bursting at the seams, which doesn't exactly push me to hurry.

But when I go out, he doesn't show any signs of being in a bad mood. He just goes to the bathroom and, before he closes the door with a smile, tells me I look very pretty. My hair is still a little damp, and I'm wearing a bathrobe. I look like a yeti on vacation, but he thinks I look nice.

We'll see each other at the end of the day, my love, if you're not fuming by then.

A few minutes after he goes in and closes the door, I hear the shower, and it's not that I weaken, but something makes me feel miserable. It's easy to remember when we were happy, but now it all seems like a lie to me, a fucking farce that will end up with me licking the floor. Could I be in the bathroom right now? Yes. And I'd definitely be in the shower with my face pressed against the tiles, moaning like a cat, but I'd rather be out here. Here, sitting on the bed in a room that's six thousand euros a night, very bitter, wishing he was too.

There it is. Time travel turns you into a bad person.

When he comes out of the bathroom, he's wearing a robe too, and he's barefoot. He dried his hair with the blow-dryer (such a fucking shitty peacock) and combed it to one side with his fingers, like always. He's disgustingly handsome. With his five- or six-day-old beard. His slightly cloudy gaze because he hasn't put his contact lenses in yet.

"Did you see where I left my glasses last night?" he asks.

On the coffee table in the living room, right when you enter the suite. "No clue."

He spends a long time looking for them, irritated. He keeps saying "How can this be possible?" while he crisscrosses the room, but just when I think he's never going to find them and that I could sit on them, some knuckles rap on the door, and when he comes back, he sees them.

"There they are! Phew."

I hate his glasses. I've always hated them, even though he looks cute in them. They're trendy. I never told him because I didn't want to offend him (I don't like commenting on people's bodies or preferences as a matter of empathy. He could tell me he didn't like my double chin, and it wouldn't feel good), but I don't like them. He'd look so good in plastic ones...

With his glasses firmly on, he opens the door and then moves to one side, making way for two waiters decked out in uniform to roll a cart into the room and straight out to the balcony. It's one of the details the brand who sponsored the trip has gifted us. Every guest is awoken with a room-service breakfast. Ours is served al fresco.

The spread they lay out for us before they disappear is a true marvel. There is coffee, juice, toast, eggs, croissants and pain au chocolat, butter, jams, fruit, and flowers. In the background, there's a spectacular view of the Eiffel Tower with the morning sun bouncing off it. This city's light is so special it turns out it's impossible to find it in any other city in the planet.

Fuck. It's pretty hard to be bitter in Paris on an all-expenses-paid trip.

He's dressed when he takes his seat next to me. He's wearing jeans and a blue cotton shirt that looks especially good on him even though there's nothing special about it. It's a blue cotton shirt, but he's wearing it.

I switched the hotel bathrobe for my silk robe that makes me feel powerful. I packed it so that I can do my hair and makeup without staining any of my outfits. But today is a relatively relaxed schedule, because the brand is wining and dining us for a day in Paris before the city turns into a madhouse tomorrow. That...and the cocktail party at the Louvre that I managed to snag a plus-one for.

Ever since he sat down, I've been trying to give him the cold shoulder, but he seems content and calm. This guy is too fucking good at silence. I hate him even more today because, in spite of everything, I can't stop seeing the good in him. He eats breakfast quietly, looking out at the view, snapping photos on his phone, putting his hand on the nape of my neck sometimes, affectionately, as if the silence doesn't bother him. Of course. It actually doesn't bother him.

I look at my phone, trawling the emails and details of the day over and over again even though I already know it all by heart. I start drafting an email to Marisol that I'm not going to send because it's pointless, and when he tries to talk to me, I raise my phone, thrust it between us, and declare:

"I'm sending an important email. Please, be quiet."

He seems weirded out by my behavior, but instead of the effect I thought it would have, he leans toward me, kisses my neck, half-seductive, half-complicit, and whispers:

"Don't worry, you're going to kill it. It's all gonna go great. You have no reason to be nervous."

I want to push his head into the table, but I don't do it. I. Don't. Do It. It's called anger management.

"Do you want to go for a walk?"

"I'm still in a robe," I retort.

"When you get dressed."

"I'm not getting dressed yet."

"Well then, let's go back to bed for a bit." He smiles, and his row of pearly whites is like a middle finger.

It's not possible. This dude can't have this much patience.

"Why don't you go see the city for a bit by yourself? I have stuff to do."

He seems disappointed for a minute, but he fixes his face fast.

"Oh, of course. Fuck…I'm sorry. I didn't want to… I didn't mean to bother you." I almost feel bad. Almost. Until I remember the café on Calle de Fuencarral. "How about this? I'll go walk around, and we can meet up at lunchtime. Okay? I'll send you my location right before and...I'll have a glass of wine while I wait for you. Sound good?"

What a piece of shit.

I spend the morning in the hotel, pretending to be really busy. Actually, after a while, I get so bored that I end up working on something for the next issue that I can get ahead of myself.

Rita's eyes bulge when she sees me.

"What are you doing here working? I didn't call you because I assumed you were making the most of the free day with Tristan."

"Tristan is sightseeing," I respond, my eyes glued to the laptop screen.

"He seems so cute," she says, because I introduced them at the airport and they chatted a little. "Pretty shy, that's true..."

"He's not shy. He's cold."

"Not at all!"

"I would know."

Rita yanks the laptop away and fills my whole range of vision with her face.

"What the fuck are you working on? You're in Paris."

"But there's a lot of work."

"Well, fuck that. Call Tristan right now, and go meet him. Tomorrow, the whirlwind starts, and you won't have a chance to enjoy the city. The most you'll be able to enjoy him is if he gives you a foot rub when you get back from the shows."

I curl my lip, but I don't add anything. I try to snatch my computer back, but she flicks me on the forehead.

"You're acting like a jerk. And you're not a jerk, so explain it to me.

Either you had terrible sex last night, or he has such a small thing that the rest doesn't make up for it. Or you've had another of your psychotic breaks where you don't know what year it is."

My eyebrows shoot up. So that wasn't erased! If she remembers the first day this happened to me, Ivan must remember yesterday too. I need to call him...

"What's going on?"

"Nothing's going on," I defend myself.

"Is this about the magazine? You proved that you deserve this position a long time ago, Miri. You have to relax and enjoy, or you're gonna die really young. And that dude is worth it."

"That dude is going to hurt me," I say, unable to hold it in. "A lot."

Her look is dripping with pity, and that kills me even more. I don't want anyone to pity me. Did Tristan pity me when he dumped me?

"But, Miranda," she says, sounding worried. "Are you really going to lose him over that? I thought you were brave."

I don't answer because I don't know what to answer, but she takes advantage of the silence to keep talking.

"I have a very wise friend, my friend Tone, who says life is what happens to us. Maybe we die a little when things don't happen. Haven't you ever thought about that? While you're hurting or laughing or running or crying or clapping...you're living. Everything else...everything with no danger, is basically the same as being asleep. And you've always been really alive, girl. Don't make yourself dead now."

It's a striking argument. I can't fight against it. But I can ignore it a little, just a tiny bit, just enough so that I can't justify the pain Tristan has put me through as "being alive."

I tell her I'm just going to finish something up and then I'll go. The thing I have to do is navel-gaze a little more. But right when I'm about to leave, Tristan texts me again:

TRISTAN:

Sorry to be annoying, but I'm sending you another
location, okay? They kicked me out of the other place.
They had people waiting.

Fine.

Between my heels and the traffic in Paris, it's obvious I'm going to get
there pretty late, so late I'm scared he's going to send me another location,
but the guy is smart, and he must have found a table somewhere with a
"waiting list," so by the time I spot the place, he's just being seated.

The restaurant is called CoCo and it's next to the Opéra Garnier. And
it's beautiful. Amazing. Disgustingly special. Light floods every corner,
bouncing off the art deco touches in the decor. It's pretty new but is clearly
trying to be a time portal that takes us back to the beginning of the twentieth century. I hope I wake up tomorrow in those years, very far from
Tristan.

They've given him a spot in the corner where the little tables for two are
lined up without much separation. He's sitting on the bench that curves
against the wall, and opposite him, a comfortable velvet armchair awaits
me. He smiles. He's handsome. So handsome. He must have changed
at some point when I was ignoring him and…he really gave it his all.
Because when you go with the deputy editor of a fashion magazine on
a work trip to Paris, you better work. At least if you like her. And I don't
remember him liking me that much, which makes me really, really, really,
really sad.

Fuck. Seriously. Make it a little easier on me, for fuck's sake. I was sure
my changes would leave us eating shitty food in a tourist trap where the
French onion soup would give us diarrhea. Not this.

He's wearing a fine gray cashmere sweater so good it screams in your face. Paired with tailored pants but with a modern twist, cropped at the ankle, and Chelsea boots. Next to him, on the sofa, a black suede biker jacket lined with sheepskin. Fuck. I didn't remember this.

I put my trench coat and bag on top of his jacket and sit down. We stare at each other for a few seconds before I pluck up the courage to speak.

"Your outfit…"

"Yes?"

"Is the total look," I say in English, "from AllSaints?"

"What does 'total look' mean?"

"That you bought the whole thing from AllSaints."

"Yes." He nods. "I changed before I left. I thought you saw me."

"No. I was busy. Listen…in Madrid, they only sell AllSaints clothes at El Corte Inglés, and they don't carry much men's stuff."

"I bought it online." He smiles. "Is it okay?"

I nod. Of course it's okay, for fuck's sake. It's one of my favorite brands. It has that touch of grunge but still stylish…

"And how did you come across that brand?"

He calls the waiter over. I can tell he feels awkward. I know he does; that's the point. I'm sick of feeling like he can handle every situation.

"Are you avoiding the question?" I insist.

"I mean, it's not every day you get invited to spend a few days in Paris during fashion week. I was a little worried about fitting in with the crowd and standing out…in a bad way. You know what I mean."

"Yes. I know. Well…looks good."

"You always think I look good."

He smiles at the waiter heading over to us, and he's about to order when I snipe…

"No. Not always."

He shoots me a side-eye, surprised. I don't think he always looks good, but maybe in the past, I might have gone overboard telling him when I did think so. I'm not going to make the same mistake again. He takes a deep breath and, in pretty fluent French, orders a bottle of Perrier-Jouët. Is the universe hitting me harder with every change I make? This is not how this went. After we strolled around Paris, we sat down in a little restaurant in Le Marais, and we ate unflashy food and drank a couple of glasses of house wine. What's with this display?

"Did you have a chance to look at the menu?" he asks.

"No. Are you paying?"

An embarrassed chuckle escapes him.

"Well, yes. To thank you for the trip."

"Right. Well…" I open it and decide at a glance. "The lobster linguine."

If he doesn't like that, he doesn't say a word. Or give anything away. He just orders a rare entrecôte and adds a bottle of still water.

When the waiter leaves, he smiles at me.

"I hope I got the clothes right for tonight too. I've never been invited to something so…formal."

I bite my upper lip carefully. I don't want to smudge red lipstick all over my teeth, but the suit he wore tonight popped up in my head (how strange, conjugating in the past tense with the word "tonight"—I can't get used to it). It was super expensive, and he bought it just for that trip, hoping to "get some use of it" in the coming years. A suit done right. A fucking suit that cost him that year's bonus. This year's. I can confirm he was able to use it again, and it always looked as good as that first day.

"I don't know if you're going to be able to come tonight," I toss out there.

He raises his eyebrows.

"Oh yeah?"

"Well. It's a pretty exclusive soiree. I'm here for work, not for pleasure."

"I know." He nods. "Well…um…it's fine either way. Don't worry."

It stings a little, I'll admit it. He dropped four figures on the perfect suit for the occasion, and he had a great time at that party. I know he was especially excited about it. But I realized how much I liked him that night, and I don't think that's really what I need right now.

"I'll let you know."

I look away toward the window and try to concentrate on the people walking by, but my head keeps turning over how worried he was about pleasing me on this trip. When did he stop caring about what I thought or felt about him?

"Miranda…" he whispers.

When I look up, his brow is slightly furrowed.

"Go ahead."

"Did I do something that pissed you off?"

"No," I answer, looking away.

"Why won't you look at me?"

I look at him. Jesus. That mouth. So gross.

"No." I give him a fake smile. "Nothing's going on."

"So why do I get the feeling there is?"

"I mean, I don't know. Did you do something that should have pissed me off? You probably did, and I didn't even notice."

"Okay." He sighs, like he's working up to a speech, but the waiter interrupts him with our champagne. Yes, champagne. We are in Paris, you know.

The minutes drag on eternally as the waiter completes the champagne protocol. When he has finally opened the bottle and served the glasses and leaves again, Tristan sighs and leans forward over the table.

"Miranda, I know we never talked about it."

"About what?"

"About how we stopped seeing each other for a few months because I wanted some space."

"You wanted us to stop seeing each other."

"A nuance."

"An important nuance." I nod. "And what does that have to do with right now?"

"Well, maybe you're...hurt."

"No." I shake my head.

"But you don't trust me."

"I shouldn't, no." I'm getting more pissed off by the minute.

"Why?"

"Well, because I can see it coming."

"You see it coming or you're playing fortune teller again?"

"I'm not playing. I think if anyone's playing here, it's you."

"Why?"

"Because. Because you're inconsistent. Because you don't like anyone long enough for them to become important. Because you don't know how to commit. Because..."

"Slow down. Hit the brakes," he says seriously. "When have we ever talked about committing?"

"Ah, here come the brakes." I laugh disdainfully.

"No, no, Miranda. I'm just saying that you can't blame me for not doing something we've never talked about."

"Are you fucking other people?" I toss out.

"No." He shakes his head. "But if you're looking for an excuse to tell me to go to hell, I'll say yes."

I'm about to respond, but he puts his hand on mine to stop me.

"Miranda...I really like being with you. More than I was expecting. You're a surprising woman. Like a minefield. And I can't stop thinking about you, even when I don't want to."

I grab my champagne glass, evading his hand, and take a long sip.

"I don't know how to talk about tomorrow, even though I'm not gonna tell you I don't think about it. I'm rigid and not very brave. That's why I need everything in order and to be really sure about what I'm doing. But I'm in Paris. With you. And the truth is right now there's no place I'd rather be."

I'm about to swig the last mouthful in my glass, but he leans across the table and stops me.

"Can we toast?"

"To what?"

"To anything. To all the possibilities. To nothing. To being free to decide without hindrances."

11

~~~

AND WE RUN TOWARD IT

TRISTAN

I know everything would be infinitely easier if I hadn't taken a step back, if I hadn't left the house that Saturday with the intention of running into Miranda. My life would be calm, affable, comfortable. Because Miranda is uncomfortable, let's be honest. Uncomfortable like the cheapest sofa from IKEA, like a transoceanic flight on a budget airline, like when your mother catches you with eight condoms in your jacket pocket and asks if you think you're Billy the Kid. And like a ride on an extreme roller coaster. And that's the problem, I guess.

Miranda loves her work over everything else. She loves it more than her personal life. If she had to choose, I know what she'd say: to hell with everyone.

Sometimes she sounds like she's nuts, even though she's not. She snores. A lot. And I know I can't throw the first stone on that, but she snores. When she gets nervous, she talks too much. She's awfully direct. She's obsessed with fucking me every time she has five free minutes. She doesn't sleep much, which means that when I'm with her, I don't either. She's one of those crazy people who don't care if they are and seem like it. She made me promise that if she ever had something in her teeth in a restaurant, I would tell her. It was one of our first dates, and before the first course, she had practically drunk me under the table. I'm not sure how I didn't end up literally under the table or on the hood of a car or on a bench at the bus stop since she was so eager to have her way with me. I've never met anyone with such a voracious appetite. Ever. And I've had some pretty demanding lovers. Miranda is a fire that never goes out, that always wants more. Her body is a temple that she doesn't care for much but that she respects with devotion. She loves praying on her knees in front of me, you know.

She's crazy. Crazy like a fox. Crazy curious. Crazy with the memory of an elephant. And elegant. With those curvy hips, slightly drooping breasts, toned arms, and dimpled ass. With everything.

The classic crazy person who wears black and always walks around the city with a book, who drinks coffee without milk and kisses with tongue and a lot of it. Once, after a few glasses of wine, when we started seeing each other again after the monthslong break, she told me that she didn't want anyone to clip her wings, but she can't stop the anxiety from gleaming in her eyes when she thinks that maybe nobody will ever ask her to build a nest together.

She likes really loud music, my cologne (she breathes me in and sniffs me like it's the most normal thing in the world, but, buddy…it's not), sex in the dark, and saying goodbye with a filthy kiss on the mouth and another blown in the air. I suspect the latter is in case the first kiss hints at some hope and the second sweeps up the pieces of what she wants to be given but doesn't dare ask for.

What the fuck am I doing in Paris?

Well, falling. Falling head over heels. For a crazy girl. For a girl I don't understand. A girl who sometimes scares me a little because I don't know if she's getting the best out of me, boring me, motivating me, or making me feel small. Maybe that's why I'm falling for her, to be fair. Because she challenges me. Constantly. Maybe, at some other time in my life, I wouldn't have gotten back in the saddle, but she makes me curious. She's intense…so much that I stopped caring that I moved to Madrid planning to head back home as soon as possible.

So the fact that she's been such a weirdo since we woke up doesn't freak me out that much. She is weird. After ignoring me all morning and a lunch that wasn't exactly idyllic, I had to cut her off because it was starting to get really awkward.

The rest of the lunch went well. She got something stuck in her teeth, and when I told her, even though she tried to be dignified, she couldn't help laughing. Smiling. She's beautiful when she smiles, even though sometimes her cackles sound like loose change rattling around in a pocket. She's noisy when she wants to be, this lady.

After lunch, we strolled to the Madeleine, the gardens around the Place de la Concorde, and the Tuileries, and opposite there, we found a café with a patio where we could have a coffee.

While she people watched, I watched her. The wind had ruffled her hair a little. She got a haircut before we came, and it's barely two fingers below her ears, which have two heavy gold earrings hanging from them that give her a special shine. Her long eyelashes (so long that I've almost succumbed multiple times and asked whether they were really hers), covered by that black line that makes her look kind of feline. And her lips. Those lips…

"Can I kiss you?"

She looks so weirded out it's like I just asked if I could lick her forehead, and I like that. It always throws me off a little when she's the one pouncing on my mouth, because it makes me feel like I don't have the reins. And I need them.

She's wearing a black suit with a double-breasted blazer and pants, and she's wearing a turtleneck that's practically see-through. I wonder what underwear she has on today. She always wears the wildest stuff, like assless panties.

The trench coat, which is perched on her shoulders, never actually with her arms in it, is folded on the seat opposite her right now. The lining doesn't lie; it cost an arm and a leg, like her bag. But I don't want to ask her if she bought it for the occasion, if she already had it, or if she borrowed it, because I'm going to feel silly if I'm the only one who spent more than I should have to fill my suitcase for the trip.

I'd rather kiss her, even with that bright-red lipstick that promises to make my mouth look ridiculous.

"Hey, can I kiss you?" I ask again.

"Here?" She asks me, suddenly a Victorian.

"Of course. Here."

"Ay, no."

"No?" I'm surprised.

"No. And you should be the first to not want to. You're from the north. People from the north don't like PDA."

"You're the worst at stereotypes." I laugh, even though in my case specifically, she happens to be right. "But I remember the second time we met up, I had to stop you because before you even said hello. You were like: 'Let's go fuck in the bathroom.'"

"See? Let's calm down."

I get the giggles. I really like her idiosyncrasies. Shit.

I want that kiss.

"We're in Paris, in a café opposite the Tuileries gardens, watching the drizzle through a beautiful portico…you're not going to kiss me?"

I take a pack of cigarettes out of my bag and put one in my mouth.

"You're going to smoke."

"Why are you being so stubborn? Last night, you kissed me everywhere," I say, laughing.

She furrows her brow. She doesn't remember. I do, and that's frustrating because it was really cool.

"Ask for the check." She looks at her watch. "The party starts at seven, and I have to slap on the war paint. I'm definitely gonna need help with my hair."

"Great. I'm really good at doing women's hair."

She glares at me.

"So gullible," I provoke her, laughing.

A tiny, contained smile appears, which seems to make her even madder.

"You sure you're not mad?"

"Didn't we already talk about this? This is how I am. I'm...well..."

"Weird. But not grumpy. When you get like this, it's always because you've gone too far."

"Too far to you because you're made of ice. But you should've thought about that before you looked for fire as a dance partner, sweetie."

I open my mouth to answer, but she hurries to give me an explanation that I don't need:

"The 'sweetie' was ironic, eh. I don't want you going around thinking I go too far with my cutesy nicknames for you."

"And all that." I raise my eyebrows and call over the waiter, making the universal mime to ask for the check.

Nearly eighteen euros for two coffees doesn't seem like that much after what I paid for lunch. This woman's pace of life is going to drive me crazy and leave me broke as a joke. But this time, she puts down a twenty-euro bill, and as she stands up, she takes the receipt and folds it carefully into her wallet.

"I'm gonna expense it," she explains.

"And you can't do that for lunch too?"

"Don't be a mooch."

The drizzle patters our faces as we emerge from the shelter of the awning. I keep looking at her, but I don't know why exactly. The way she looks at everything around her kind of fascinates me. Because her eyes roam the surfaces so quickly, devouring everything in their path. That hunger is what makes her so indefinable. Because she takes on the whole world without thinking twice, and her interior expands like a galaxy. She's crazy…she goes from talking about shoes to explaining her view that everything we take as absolute truths is actually just a social construct. Sometimes she seems so lost…so completely lost that I think we're similar. Just on the basics.

She's not my type.

She's not.

It's not going to last.

It can't last.

Two worlds. Two natures.

I'm not even that into her.

The fine drops of rain are clinging to her ruffled hair and her eyelashes. She has eyes the color of a cat. What color is that? I don't know. She invented it for the world when she opened her eyes.

What is this? What's going on? Why does it feel like the honking horns, the sound of conversations, and the noise of the city are suddenly singing in harmony? Like this chaotic city is wrapping everything up with a bow.

"Hey…" I call her.

Tristan, what are you doing?

When she turns back to me, her hair, now wavy from the humidity, sways. And I want to put my hands in it and smell it. I want things I've never wanted.

I stop her there, on a corner between two magnificent buildings, wrap her in my arms, and before she even realizes, in a twist she wasn't expecting, I kiss her. Even though I think she's going to reject me for a moment, both of us open our mouths. Her tongue wastes no time finding mine, like she has no choice. Are our tongues completely in love with each other? She kisses so well. So well.

People swerve around us grumpily, zipping in every direction across the sidewalk we stopped in the middle of, but instead of undoing this knot, I squeeze her tighter. Paris suddenly sounds like "Often" by The Weeknd, which I've thought for a few years now was the dirtiest and most romantic song in the world. I wish it were playing right now. Screw "La Vie en Rose." Right now, in her mouth, Paris sounds like The Weeknd.

She lets a moan escape from her throat, but I swallow it quickly because I don't want it to stop. Her, the feeling, the void, the spiral we're wrapped up in that isolates us from the rest of the world. I've kissed Miranda many times, so many, but there's something in that kiss that keeps me hooked to her mouth. The suburban boy who lives inside me whispers that she's too much woman for me, but the adult shuts him up and clings to her even harder. Harder and harder. Left hand on her neck, right hand running down her back, under the trench coat thrown over her shoulders.

She's not your type, I repeat to myself.

She's too extreme.

She's weird.

She's a complication.

She wants more than you want to give her.

I don't care.

Her tongue and mine dance the same way an old couple would. One of those who don't know whether they love each other desperately or whether they need each other out of habit. It's a wise kiss that makes me recognize some things I don't even understand. I just want to press her tighter and tighter into me.

And the magic is breaking. I can feel it. The edges of the world are starting to define themselves again. Something elastic is constricting and expanding between us, trying to smash us into pieces. Her hand pushes against my chest, trying to put some space between us. I refuse. I shake my head no while I keep clinging to the kiss, but finally we pull a few millimeters apart.

"Let's go to the hotel," I beg her.

"To get dressed."

"To fuck. On all fours. Standing up. You on top. I don't care. Fuck me."

"No." She pulls away from my face a little. "This is not how this goes. I'm in charge here."

I don't doubt it. I suspect I lost the rudder a long time ago.

Shit.

She's not my type.

I don't like her that much.

Why do I have so much blood in the wrong part of my body?

That's it. My erection is impeding the necessary blood pumping to my brain.

She pushes on my chest, and I pull back.

I could swear I can see a spark of rage in her eyes, and I don't understand it, but it makes me like her even more. A spark of rage that gets lost like fireworks that explode and then fade into the night. And that rage disappears completely when Miranda bursts out laughing.

"What?" I ask her, a little offended.

She points at my face. Judging from the state of her lipstick, I must be hard to take seriously.

"You're covered."

"You should talk…" I smile at her. "Do you have a Kleenex or something?"

Before I can wipe my face with the back of my hand, Miranda leans in and rubs her thumb over my mouth, from side to side, leaving the tip of her thumb red. I'm about to ask her if that made it better when, she stands on her tiptoes and runs her tongue over my mouth. A second. One fucking second. But her lips dart over my mouth so quickly, from top to bottom. This nutjob licked my mouth in the middle of the street. This crazy lady is going to make me lose my head. And I'm suddenly filled with a tingle that I can't locate or scratch. Because Miranda makes me tingle, and that's something I've never faced, ever.

"Crazy," I whisper, unable to take my eyes off her mouth.

She moves away, tugging me along with her.

"Let's go."

I want to take her hand, but I don't. I don't do these things. All I do is clean off my mouth while she takes out her phone and uses the selfie camera to do the same. She's ready before I am.

She won't let me touch her in the hotel. I try it in the elevator, the hallway, up against the door. She says no very sharply, so I let her be. She must be nervous. I stay silent while she spins around the room like a top, seemingly aimlessly, until she locks herself in the bathroom with her phone clenched in her hand. It's not long before I hear her talking to someone very softly, but I can't eavesdrop because I fall asleep.

At 5:30, she's getting dressed. She's a tsunami swirling around the room, which wakes me up and not how I'd like. I could've sworn Miranda is the type who wakes you up carefully, sweetly, hotly…but if that part is true, she left it in Madrid.

I wasn't expecting her to ask me, but I'm a little disappointed to see that she called over her colleague from the magazine to dress her. I could have done up the zipper on her dress or whatever she needed. Fine, I couldn't have helped with the makeup or hair, but I wanted to be alone with her for a bit.

When Rita comes into the room, I get a little anxious, but because I can't name the root of the feeling, I try to keep it busy with work emails.

And Rita barges in like she owns the place, like I'm not even there. It's not like it bothers me, but...I appreciate my privacy when I'm in a hotel room. She came in with "her own" key card. I guess it's a logistical thing because of the next few days, but *chill out, Rita.*

"Hi, Tristan!" she greets me.

I keep myself busy with my emails, but I look up to greet her and...I wish I hadn't.

"Hi, Rita, how's it's going?" I answer with a smile.

It's not out of kindness. I'm stifling my laughter. I have no words to explain this girl's outfit. Sometimes fashion gets too avant-garde and I stop understanding it at all. All I can see are layers and layers of black-and-gold ruffles... I hope the designer of what she's wearing forgives me, but she looks like a baroque cabbage.

"You're not even dressed yet?" she asks me.

"I'm waiting for Miranda to tell me whether I can go."

Rita rounds on Miranda and glares at her. All her layers, which are pretty light, tremble around her.

"You can. We arranged all that in Madrid," she answers me, although she's still looking at her.

"I wasn't clear," Miranda points out, calling her out with a gesture.

"Well, I'm clearing it up now."

"Ladies." I smile. "I can get ready in five minutes, so however it turns out, don't worry."

I can't understand the details, but they're arguing in the bathroom. And in spite of it all, I find it funny. I wish I was close enough with my colleagues to call them cocksuckers to their face and not just behind their backs when I'm ranting to my sister on the phone.

Miranda takes what seems like an eternity, and I mean, I'm slow, but I have to admit that every minute she used was worth the effort. When she comes out, she's spectacular. She pulled her hair back in a low, slicked-back ponytail, which reminds me of how she looked when I first met her. A few loose strands are curling around her ears, making it all look less formal. She made up her eyes with the most feline cat-eye eyeliner in history and the reddest and juiciest lips in the world. She's a caramel apple. She's wearing a black tea-length dress that fits like a glove with transparent cutouts at the hips and waist. No bra, because her breasts are visible under the stretchy fabric, and judging by the positioning of the transparent fabric, I can't be sure she's wearing panties. She put a rigid, golden necklace around her neck, which makes her look like a Greek effigy, a bust to revere. An Athena with powerful and generous hips, who's wobbling but trying not to wobble on the very high heels of a pair of open-toed shoes with thousands of straps. I don't understand fashion, but I think it's a good choice.

"What?" she asks after I study her in silence.

"Nothing? What do you mean what?"

"Are you making fun of me?"

I point to my chest, surprised.

"Me?"

"I don't know. You made a weird face when you saw me. It is too tight on me?"

"You look beautiful," I abridge myself. I'm not the kind to regale someone with compliments.

"Of course she looks beautiful. She's wearing Balmain," Rita retorts, as if it were obvious.

"I don't know what that means." I shrug and smile. "But she's very beautiful."

"What about you?" her colleague asks me.

"Me? Well…" Since they haven't said anything up until now, I assume I'm not going. "I'll go out for a walk, get something to eat, and come back to the hotel. I brought a book."

They side-eye each other. Miranda seems like she's in a bad mood.

"Get dressed," she says, brushing past me.

I feel like telling her to fuck off, but I get up from the armchair and head toward the closet.

"Okay, kids. I'll see you downstairs."

The dark cabbage disappears through the door with a less dramatic exit than her wardrobe demands, and I take the opportunity to turn around and look for Miranda.

"Hey..." I call out to her.

She's sitting down, concentrating on stuffing lipstick, a few cards, her phone, and a compact into a minuscule purse.

Is she wearing underwear? Tristan, forget it, you can't ask her that. If you're lucky, she'll have one of her outbursts and suggest fucking in the bathroom.

"Go ahead."

She doesn't look up at me when she answers.

"If you don't want me there, I won't go."

She looks up, but she doesn't move her head. Her eyelashes are brushing against her eyebrows, and the effect is very strange.

"Why do you say that?"

"Well, because it doesn't seem like you want me to go. And...I kinda get it. It's a work drinks thing...at a job in the fashion world. I'm a lawyer, and I grew up in a neighborhood where tracksuits were considered highbrow. I don't fit in there at all."

She savors her words before she lets them escape her lips.

"It's just that I don't know if I can go with you."

"I understand." And I do understand, but I feel disappointed.

"I'll spend the whole night worrying that you're uncomfortable and it'll become a vicious cycle..."

"I get it, really."

I nod, put my hands in my pockets, and we both look at each other without talking. This is uncomfortable, not strolling around a room in the Louvre drinking champagne, but I don't say that to her. I should but I don't, because I want her to feel free to decide how the night ends. I'm glad I had the idea not to get dressed yet, because this conversation would have been pathetic in a three-thousand-euro suit.

"It's work," she says in a thread of a voice.

"I know. That's why I offered you a…get-out clause. You wouldn't have had to worry about me anyway, but this way, we can eliminate that from the equation."

"Well, I appreciate it." She nods.

"Fine. Well…see you when you get back."

"Yes."

I would go over and kiss her. In spite of everything, I'd give her a kiss before she left, but I don't fucking feel like it. Self-love stops me.

"Don't get bored," she throws out.

I will say, in her defense, that she seems sad.

She heads to the door seeming undecided. Before she goes out, I take my right hand out of my pocket and raise it in a goodbye. She looks like she's going to double over and vomit on the carpet. She opens the door, and…the sound of the door closing echoes through the hall. I don't know what it is about hotel doors. It's impossible to slam them, but you can't close them without slamming them. And here I am, in front of the door, with my left hand in my jeans pocket and my other hand dangling limply, like an asshole. There's something rumbling in my stomach that has nothing to do with hunger; it's a kind of strange dignity. It's a kind of nervousness that she's decided not to leave.

Miranda looks up at the ceiling, sucks her teeth, and, after a sigh, says:

"Please, don't take too long getting dressed. We have to leave right now."

And I'm lost. Lost. I suspect it, but I still don't know.

Five hours later, we're crossing the Louvre esplanade together, heading toward Rue de Rivoli, where Miranda says there's a car waiting to take us to the hotel. We left Rita with her cabbage dress saying "yes" to the proposal of having one more drink, and we escaped. Miranda would never admit it, but I think she's tired, and those shoes don't look very comfortable.

The Louvre's esplanade is beautiful at night, with the glass pyramids glowing through that very Parisian mist. I try to imagine what we must look like together, like we're in a French movie from the seventies. I love it.

The whole night was…incredible. Seeing her in that environment, seeing her work, seeing her need to create an empty space between us. Seeing her. Fuck. Is there anything sexier or more terrifying than a woman who doesn't need you?

Now, Miranda is walking securely on her heels next to me. She's wearing a coat over her dress, a long, flowing one in something like black suede. Like the trench coat she wore at lunch, this one is balanced on her shoulders too. It's not much protection from the wet wind whipping the city, but she's not complaining.

Now, by her side, I worry my long strides will leave her behind as I look for my tobacco inside my suit. What a suit. Because I don't want to blow smoke up my own ass, but I'd definitely devour myself with this on. I just have to look at Miranda's eyes to see that I'm right.

Even tonight was erotic, and it made me think. For months, I've been asking myself why I'm such an idiot; maybe I inherited it, or that's just an excuse I give myself so I don't feel like such a dumbass. But the truth is the more distant I find Miranda, the more I like her, and the more I like her, the more that distance bothers me. It's irrational, because what seduces me about her are her strength, her independence, her bravery, and her shamelessness. She's driving me crazy. This is a dangerous game.

We walk together but separately, and I keep on imagining us from the outside.

"We're cool." I say the word in English with a wink, only half joking.

"I feel like the star of a Clara Luciani song," she says suddenly.

"Who?"

"'La grenade.' You've never heard of her?"

"Nope. Doesn't even ring a bell."

"Ah. Maybe she's not well known yet. But I promise you when you hear it"—she winks—"we'll be the shit."

She's fucking crazy.

As we cross the street, the wind lifts her coat up a little, and I can see her goose bumps. I want to warm her up, but instead I take a long drag on my newly lit cigarette before I look at the color of the burning embers.

"I'm going to quit," I tell her.

I look at her out of the corner of my eye, and she's smiling with restraint. She isn't looking at me. It feels like she can't look at me for the same reason I can't stop looking at her. We like each other. We're not each other's type. It's not going to last. We shouldn't like each other this much...

The boy from the suburbs tells me to take off my jacket and put it on her; the man that I should be knows she wouldn't like that, so I pull her into me and wrap an arm around her.

"You're freezing. That coat is pretty, but maybe it wasn't the best choice."

"It's called fashion. Look it up."

We both crack up at the same time. Our shadows stretch beautifully across the sidewalk. More beautiful than we actually are, I'm sure. So elongated they look like they could reach anything, slip into anywhere, so intertwined it's impossible to guess where she begins and where I end. That joint shadow seems like a more dangerous promise than the game we've been playing for almost a year now. Almost a year, Tristan...

"I ignored you all night," she says with a note of regret in her voice.

"Yes."

"You didn't have to come."

"Did I complain?"

"No. I guess you're not the type who complains."

"No, I'm not."

I squeeze her a little tighter.

"Fuck..." she murmurs, looking at the ground.

"What?"

"You smell good."

"You say that like it's a problem."

"It is. You smell too good."

"Can you have too much of a good thing?"

"Yes." She looks at me out of the corner of her eye. "Too much is where things we can't control grow."

"Well then, we'd have to burn the wheel."

I don't know if I can even find the brake pedal anymore. But I let her take me.

And we run toward it.

12

~~~

WHO KNOWS WHAT'S COMING NEXT?

MIRANDA

Last night, I should have fucked Tristan. I should have thrown myself onto the hotel bed brazenly and savagely used him as a way to get pleasure. Why? I could tell you some whoppers, but the truth is I'm in Tristan withdrawal, big-time. I'm always staring at him and asking myself stuff... transcendental stuff, like why am I going through this, why me, is this a second chance, maybe I should've concentrated on trying to fix things instead of pushing him away, whether I should be learning from this time-space journey...but suddenly he looks at me out of the corner of his eye, shoots me a smile, and says something in that voice of his, so coarse, so ragged...and then whatever I'm thinking magically transforms into an image of me sitting on his face.

I'm the worst.

But I didn't. We didn't sleep together.

I took off my heels and my dress, took a deep breath (because I hadn't been able to in that dress), and put on "seductive" lingerie. And right when I was about to throw myself dramatically on him in bed, he went into the bathroom.

The bed was so comfortable... It had been such an intense day... I've been so tired since all this started…that I felt like I was pinned to the pillow. Why are hotel sheets so, so soft?

"Come here. I'm going to blow your mind," I slurred forcefully when he came out of the bathroom in navy pajama pants, his chest bare and his stupid, trendy glasses on.

I was half-asleep, but I uncovered myself and showed him my red lingerie.

"Incredible," he said in a sweet kind of way.

"It's for whores."

"Ah…" He lay down beside me, covered both of us, and, to my surprise, snuggled right up to me. "It's great."

I tried to touch his turnip, but he pulled my hand away gently, brought it to his mouth, kissed my palm, and then turned it over to kiss the back.

"This bed is comfortable, huh?"

With the little strength I had left, because this bed was sucking all my vital energy out of me, I tried to slink closer until my mouth was on his neck. But in a masterful twist, like a wriggle, he shifted me onto his shoulder and then his chest, wrapping his arm around me.

"You're exhausted," I hear him say.

Far. It sounded a little far away. He was stroking my back like it was a harp. I realized I was falling asleep when I was scared songs would start playing from his fingers. I was mixing dreams with reality.

"No," I answered stubbornly.

"You know what I liked the most about today? Being able to see the *Winged Victory of Samothrace* in an almost-empty Louvre with that beautiful lighting. It was an extraordinary experience. And the Lady of Auxerre. I didn't know it was called that. Well, actually I didn't even recognize it, but I snuck off when you went off to talk to those people from the cream brand to google it. It's from the seventh century BC. You know what? It shows possible signs of polychrome decoration."

That little bastard…he knew I was about to drift off.

I fell asleep not knowing what colors he thought were painted.

This is going to start affecting my health.

I wake up in bed. In my house, all of a sudden. In a jump. From the innards of Paris to the center of Madrid in a wink. And alone. No idea what day it is or what year, ripped from sleep by the usual alarm clock but disoriented. It's seven in the morning on October 26 four years ago, and I have no idea why I jumped to today. And why I feel like I can still smell his cologne.

While the coffee maker warms up, I check my planner. Today is a normal work Thursday. At least that's how it seems from what I have planned. The October issue has already gone out, of course. We're finalizing the details for the November one, and we're already working on December and the end of the year. There are no photo shoots today, no events, and there's nothing urgent this week. Flipping through the next few days, the priority is closing the last issue of the year soon and doing it well.

But I have to get moving, because the thing that stresses me out most is this paranoia that I'm going to hinder the future and then I'll be stuck in a loop where I can't move forward. So while I drink my coffee, I turn on the water in the shower and text Ivan to ask him if he has plans for lunch. I glance over at the closet to figure out what to wear, but my past self continues to be very efficient, and it's all hanging in the bathroom, neatly laid out: mom jeans turned up at the ankle, a Motorhead T-shirt, maroon suede shoes with a low heel, and a black leather jacket.

Ivan answers right when I'm going through the turnstiles of the magazine with a simple "I'll pick you up at two" that doesn't clarify whether he remembers our phone call "yesterday," because if he does, I actually called him from Paris. Yesterday for me. A month ago for him. Thalia did ask him to fasten her bra in the hallway of an event, but the weirdest part is that he only remembered I predicted it when it happened to him.

"Every other day, it seems like this stuff isn't happening to you and it's surgically removed from my brain."

I didn't fully understand him, but I told him we would talk it all through whenever we could. Jesus Christ…there's another Miranda out there doing stuff. Okay. She's from the past, so it's still me, but it freaks me out. In my imagination, she's like an Annabelle doll, and she's going around out there with those eyebrows drawn on with a 0.5 Pilot pen. Chills.

"Good morning!" the few girls who are in their offices call out to me.

"Good morning, girls. Let's make the world a better place."

Over time, I've accumulated a few phrases and pep talks to motivate the team (and myself) to get our spirits up even on the most somber days. Sometimes we wonder if we're dedicating our lives to something too frivolous. It's good to be reminded out loud that we can make the world turn, even just a little.

If I could at least focus a little more…but who could concentrate on their work when they're going through something that seems so crazy?

I put my bag down in my office, turn on the computer, and go out to "the wall." The wall is where we hang up the laid-out pages so we can see the order clearly. With everything going down the digital path, it might seem a little anachronistic, but the truth is the result is very visual. In one glance, you can clear up a bunch of doubts at the same time, and that map shows you what part of the process we're in when it comes to closing. And so I stand there, my hands in my pockets, studying how we're doing.

"Miri…"

Marta, the digital director, just bustled in, loaded down with a giant bag and a coffee almost as big.

"Good morning."

"Do you have a gap today where we could look over a few things?"

"Of course." I struggle to tear my eyes away from an article about "the worst Tinder dates" and turn back to my office. "I don't think I have anything scheduled, but let me check."

"It'll just take a second. If you want, we can look at it now over coffee."

"SEO positioning?" I guess.

"Just taking a glance at the positioning of our digital content. And I have doubts about our communication strategy on social media."

I look at my planner. I have a meeting scheduled at noon.

"Okay, come in and sit down. Should I call Diana?" Diana is our community manager.

"No. I'd rather talk about it just between the two of us first," she says. "I think we need to handle it with kid gloves."

Marta sits down and spreads a ton of stuff over my desk. I'm kind of a stickler for organization, but I don't mind because I know that as soon as she leaves, everything will go back to its natural order. I go to close the door, but Rita yells at me from the hallway:

"Miri! We have to decide for once and fucking all what we're giving as a gift in January."

"Ask Marisol." I try to wash my hands of it.

"She says she doesn't care! I'll come over, and we'll talk about it."

"Right now, I'm dealing with the SEO positioning, and at twelve, I have a meeting to see the pieces for the watch article. Ask Eva."

"Eva told me all three of us should talk about it. Save half an hour for me, and we'll talk it over."

If time travel weren't bad enough…a typical day at the magazine.

And my terrible memory was working overtime to not give me any hints about how to take a shortcut through all this. And I already lived through it, for fuck's sake. Couldn't it be condensed to a couple of hours?

Well, no.

The truth is I didn't have time to think too much about the fact that every time I've seen Ivan since this started, there's been some radical change in his look. The first time, eyelashes that belonged on *Drag Race*. The second time, he had hair so long a rock star would laugh at it. So I'm not even thinking about it when I go to meet him for lunch, but I run into him out of nowhere, and the sight is stunning.

"What?" he asks.

Is the ground shaking, or is that me?

Ivan doesn't have the long black hair from last time. Or his super long eyelashes or his usual quiff. I wish he did. I wonder if this is like reincarnations. Whatever it is, I prefer the previous ones.

Ivan has cenicero hair. You don't know what that is? That means you either grew up somewhere very far from the hood or you're very young. I'm from the hood, and as Tristan once told me, being from the hood doesn't matter as much as what you have inside. Under my couture clothes, inside my designer bag, keeping warm under the tongue that speaks English in meetings, the neighborhood is lurking there, but not hidden. Because for me, Carabanchel, my neighborhood, makes me feel proud, not embarrassed.

But cenicero hair is too much. It's aesthetic terrorism. And what is it? Put it in Google Images, please. I'll wait.

Ready?

So…what do you think about that circle of hair shellacked straight up, crowning an otherwise shaved head? Is it like a castle's moat? Is hair like that defending anything other than bad taste? Oh, wait...he's got a mullet in the back. I'm dead.

To make it even better, he's wearing some kind of bell-bottom jeans, which are completely passé for any year after 2000. A studded belt. A white polo shirt with blue trim and a popped collar. With the collar popped, did I say that already? Sorry. I'm in shock. On top of this, he's wearing a tight tracksuit jacket. He has two fat hoops in one ear. And around his neck, a gold chain as thick as my thumb.

"What the fuck?" I exclaim when my voice will finally come out of my throat.

"What?"

"What are you wearing?"

He looks confused by my surprise.

"Are you saying this because of the polo? It's new. Do you like it?"

I'm going to faint.

"Okay, Ivan...rapid-fire question round."

"You're such a weirdo..."

"What do you do for a living?"

"I'm a stylist."

"And they let you dress like that?"

"What are you talking about? This is my signature, my brand!"

I hope reliving today is worth it, because this is really heavy.

"One more question. Do you remember the super weird conversation we had at your house one afternoon in February? About Thalia."

He looks at me and furrows his brow. I'm scared I'm going to have to explain everything again, especially when he's dressed like this, but no. Finally, a spark of recognition shines in his eyes, and he nods.

"Yes. And the one from last month."

"Okay." I calm down.

"Can we go get something to eat and sit down while we talk? I had a few tests this morning, and I'm exhausted and starving to death."

I say yes and head to the bar across the street, but then I think better of it and turn around.

"Where are we going? We're not going into Dori?"

"No. I can't go into that place with you looking like that."

"The truth is the vintage rock tee thing is over, babe."

I want to shove my bag in his mouth, but it's a beautiful Coach, and I love it.

We settle on a bar that has a ten-euro set menu and a discreet patio where, more importantly, I had never been before, so we took one of their tables and ordered two beers. I can't stop looking at him. He's the guy who always dresses in black. That's why our group was always nicknamed "the cockroaches"... Why does the universe have such a sick sense of humor?

"Stop looking at me like that," he requests. "And start talking."

"Ivan, I don't want to scare you, okay? But it's just that...with every time jump...you have a completely different look."

He puts his beer down on the table.

"Define 'different look.'"

"Your life is the same. I mean...the basics. You live in your apartment, you work as a stylist, our friends are the same as always...but you... Every day, you're different. The same features and all that...but there are days when your eyelashes go halfway up your forehead and others you have hair like Brad Pitt in *Legends of the Fall.*"

He arches one eyebrow. I just realized that he even shaved little lines into the end of it. Jesus, take the wheel, this is unhinged.

"And I'm not aware of..."

"No."

"What about you?"

"If I'm changing, I'm not aware of it. But I could swear that the rest of the world, including me, is staying the same."

"And I always look good?" he asks coquettishly.

"Have you looked in the fucking mirror, Ivan?"

"Look, girl, this is trendy, okay?"

I snort.

"Then…how does it work that you forget that I'm jumping through time?"

"Yeah." He shrugs. "All I remember is the days that you're…reliving. I don't know if that makes sense."

"You mean…"

"I mean that when the Thalia thing happened to me, I suddenly remembered what you said that day at my house, but then I didn't think about it anymore, like it had been erased from my head, until you called me from Paris last month."

"That was yesterday for me."

"I know, girl. This year is flying by."

I have the sudden urge to slap him upside the head with his fanny pack, but I'd rather no one ever see me touch one of those.

"I mean I relived it yesterday, you dry turd."

"In all your realities and timelines, are you always this rude?"

"Yes."

He shakes his head, as if giving me up for lost, and stares at the waiter who's on his way over.

"I want spaghetti and fried chicken."

"Pretty carb-y," I answer.

"And give her the same thing. Let's see if those carbs soak up the terrible fucking bile you have inside you."

I don't have time to tell the waiter I don't want to eat that because he turns to go back inside immediately. Fine, everyone knows that carbs can salvage a bad day. Even if you are eating your feelings. My therapist told me you should avoid emotional hunger. Maybe filling my ass with carbs in a bar on Calle de Luchana wouldn't be so bad.

"And what are you reliving today?"

"This doesn't seem weird to you?" I ask him, confused.

"Look, there are two things in life that I believe, even though I have no logical reason to support that belief: the first is that there will never be a better club than Pont Aeri, and the other is that you're time traveling. You guessed I was going to help Thalia with her bra. It's not like… I don't know. It's not a normal thing you could just throw out there and get lucky."

"If I told you all the things that are going to happen, you wouldn't believe them in a million years."

"Like what?"

"In February 2020, buy toilet paper and nonperishable food. Trust me."

He gives me a really weird look, but I keep going because I don't want to freak him out with a postapocalyptic vision of the whole world confined to their houses. I don't even want to remember it. I lived through it, and it's behind me now.

"I don't know why I'm reliving today."

"What do you mean?"

"Well, all the other days… I don't know. They've always been pretty symbolic, important. The first was the day I met him. The second, our first date. The third, the first time he dumped me. The fourth, the trip to Paris…our first trip."

"And nothing important happened today?"

"No. I don't even have a memory to use as a reference point. End of October… I dunno."

"Let's see…what happened later? Maybe we can figure it out that way. Mostly so you don't just go around improvising."

I thank God this guy is playing along. Even though I don't believe in God. And I don't know if I trust someone with such a terrifying hairstyle.

"We came back from Paris…at the end of September, four years ago. We had been going around in circles with this thing for almost a year. We had gone a few months without seeing each other or talking and then, when we got back together, we didn't ask too many questions. It was a whole year since we first met before we even tried to put a label on it or assume a little more commitment. October doesn't ring any bells."

"This is so weird." He scratches the nape of his neck, ruffling the locks of long hair that hang like a curtain down the back. "Do you think you're going to stay here forever?"

"I hope not. And you either because…as handsome as you are, Ivan, Jesus…you look so ugly in this getup."

After a plate of spaghetti as deep as a bowl and fried chicken with fries that were so good they made you want to scream, we still haven't figured out why I'm reliving this day. Unless the universe has deemed that I've had too many weekends or holidays in a row and wants to make me work one day just because. It's just… I haven't even heard anything from Tristan.

"You should write to him," he says with a poker face.

But I don't dare. After everything I've relived, who knows what's coming next?

13

~~~

EVEN ON SOME RANDOM DAY

I spent the afternoon fighting (but the good kind, there are very few bad fights here) with the fashion and lifestyle teams to make them change the focus of two articles we're going to publish. One of them was very criticized, with good reason. If you're a publication that supports women in all their versions, you can't take up half the fashion section with a "how to dress best for your age" article.

"It's gonna be pretty short, Rita: dress however the fuck you want in your twenties, your thirties, or your eighties."

"Come on, you're so rude," she complained. "You all thought it sounded fine in the planning meeting."

"Well, in the planning meeting, I must have been overdosing on coffee or something. Rework it with your girls. This is offensive and horrible. Eva agrees. If the deputy editor and the editor in chief suggest a change... I don't know, Rita. Think about it..."

She cursed at me bitterly. She also told me that when I'm seventy, I won't be able to wear what I'm wearing today. I bite down the urge to tell her that in four years, she'll still be rocking the same schoolgirl haircut, and nobody's going to throw it in her face. But I take a deep breath and bite my tongue. I bite my tongue, and I wonder why I still haven't heard from Tristan and why I'm not messaging him myself.

I think I'm not because I'm scared all the things I've done in the past, in the days I've been reliving, have rewritten our history, and right now, he's with some other girl or…he's decided to fully embrace the bachelor life.

Maybe that's why I wasn't expecting to find him as soon as I left, right on the sidewalk outside the magazine, leaning on a sign saying parking prohibited. He looks handsome, but he seems tired and a little bored. I wonder if he's been waiting long.

"Hi," I murmur when I'm closer to him.

He hasn't looked at me yet, he's fiddling with his phone, but he doesn't startle, he just answers in a muted voice.

"Hi."

He puts his phone in his pocket and gives me a kind of hug. This is how we greeted each other in the beginning…with a hug. It's always like that, right? The hug is the most useful greeting because it's not a formal handshake, a polite kiss on both cheeks, or an intimate kiss on the mouth. A hug implies affection but enough distance so that no passersby would think we're a couple. A hug in public is a friendly greeting; it's a safe zone.

"Am I late?" I ask cautiously.

"A little." He wrinkles his nose and shrugs, like he's saying it doesn't matter. "We'll still get there on time."

"On time?"

"The play," he points out.

"What play?"

"*Oleanna*," he reminds me. "You were dying to see it. I snagged two tickets and…"

"Ah, yes. Sorry. I'm still kind of…" I move my hand in circles in front of my face. "In magazine world. I haven't acclimatized yet."

He nods, like he wasn't really listening.

"Hey…are you okay?" I ask him.

"Yeah, why?"

"I don't know. You look like you're pissed off with something, and it's possible that something is me, so I'm asking."

Seriously…the freedom not caring gives you.

"No, shit." He rubs his forehead with his thumb and forefinger. "It's work. Come on. Do you want to get a cab or the subway?"

A beam of light, a sudden flash has illuminated my memory of this afternoon. It's true I was really looking forward to seeing that play. I was even pretty annoying about it; I was hoping he would show me who knows what by getting two tickets…and he did. I remember feeling a little empowered. I enjoyed the play. I don't remember anything else. Not that he was tired or that it was a special night.

"What if we don't go?"

His forehead wrinkles.

"What?"

"What if we don't go? I don't know. I don't feel like it."

"Seriously?" He looks stunned.

"You don't seem like you want to."

I don't know if I'm screwing this up on purpose so he will leave without looking back and takes away this pain from inside me or because I really don't want to see the play again.

"Miranda…" he says very seriously, "you said over and over that it had to be today because your calendar will be crazy from now on because the December issue will be closing. And I got the tickets."

"I know. And I appreciate it. But…"

"But what?"

I think I can glimpse a slight smile behind the question, but I'm not sure. It's probably more like that face you make when you want to rip someone's head off.

"You look like you'd rather get fucked in the ass than go to the theater right now."

"Pretty much, but I feel the same way about not going and wasting the fucking tickets. They cost me fifty bucks."

That raspy, husky voice, which seems like anything but a lawyer's voice… and he curses like a sailor. Fuck. I'm resisting it, by the way. But…what if I take him home and use him like a blow-up doll? He looks so hot in that blue suit.

"Miranda, you seem so spaced out. What's going on with you today?"

"Nothing. I'm weird, you know that."

"Yeah, I know, girl. I know." He rubs his eyes again with a sigh he seems to use to muster up some patience.

"It's just that you can't say both options suck. Then what do we do? Do we kill ourselves in a collective suicide pact like a cult from the seventies?"

"Calm down, Peoples Temple."

I smile. I've always liked that he gets my weird, freaky references. Is that why I fell in love with him? *No. Don't think about that. Do stuff to make things worse between you. Focus. You want to get away from him,* my conscience's voice says.

"I don't want to go to the theater. I'm really sorry the tickets cost you so much."

"So you're flaky now?" he asks seriously.

"I mean, yeah. Listen. I'm a shitty flake, but I'm tired, and I don't want to go see any plays. I'm sorry."

"And what do you want to do now, if I may ask?"

"Well, I want…to go to my house, and we can order some greasy Chinese food or a kebab." I'm throwing out the least glamorous thing I can think of. I don't fart because I don't need to. But I'm not exactly trying to make a good impression. "We could watch a war movie or a kung fu movie or one of those romance movies that are sickeningly cheesy. And then we can go to bed and fuck like rats in heat."

"Does it have to be rats? Can't we be some other animal?"

And he says it so seriously, you wouldn't believe.

"I said rats. Ah…and you're going to go down on me. For at least half an hour."

Tristan opens his mouth, takes a deep breath, and lets it out slowly. Here it comes. He's going to tell me to fuck off.

"What?" I prod him. "Is there something about the plan you're not into?"

"Let's see." He crams his hands into his pockets, probably so he doesn't strangle me. "I'm sick of everything today. And everything is putting it lightly. A client gave me a lot of shit because she wanted her dog to inherit everything, and there was no convincing her that *that's not legal*. One of the partners is a fucking psychopath about the rules, and he told me I'm *not putting in very many hours*. The fourteen I spent there yesterday aren't enough apparently. One of my colleagues spent the whole lunch break talking my ear off about the difference between loafers with tassels and without. And now you're telling me you don't want to go to the theater? And you want Chinese food and a movie and…"

I prepare myself for an explosion. He rubs his face.

"Fuck. And you couldn't have told me earlier?"

"Well, I'm telling you now. I've been really busy all day."

"Come the fuck on."

Tristan's chest swells. That slender but sinewy chest created by swimming every free second he gets. That chest that looks so good in cotton shirts. That chest that has a thin smattering of hair, like it's scatterbrained. That chest…

"Jesus, Miranda, you're gonna drive me insane." He rubs his eyes.

Here it comes, here it comes.

I can already hear it: *The last thing I need right now is a girl who drags me around on a wild-goose chase, Miranda. The rest of us have a life too, beyond your whims. I'm sick of you. You stay here.*

"Let's go to my house first. I need to take off this suit. And get a change of clothes. And my contact lenses. This nomadic life is the fucking worst, you know that."

When he starts walking, I can't believe it. Either he can handle more than I thought, or I don't know this dude at all, or the universe is a real bastard son of a bitch.

"Are you coming or what?" he asks from ten meters away.

I have to speed up and almost run to match his pace.

Two spring rolls; an order of combo fried rice, another of shrimp noodles because he doesn't like rice, the texture makes him cringe; a lemon chicken; and a prawn toast. Plus, two sodas; mine is diet, as if not adding sugar to the drink could stop the torrent of bad fats, salt, and carbs. What a day I've had. I hope the time jumps burn a lot of calories or something; otherwise with this surplus...

Wait, since when do I lose sleep over calorie surpluses? It's not like I'm walking on a runway next month. We have to fight so hard against the ideas that society has ingrained in our heads.

"Do you ever worry about your weight?" I burst out.

He's stuffing himself with noodles, so I guess the answer is no. But I still wait for him to answer while the war movie we chose plays on the TV.

"Mmm, I dunno."

"You don't know?"

"I've been thin my whole life. I never worried about it too much. Well...I'm lying. I worry a little about looking like a sack of bones. Stress makes me a mess. And so does eating badly. And not exercising."

"Do you get thinner if you don't exercise?"

He nods while he crams in another huge mouthful of noodles.

"Do you worry about it?" he sputters.

"Your weight? Not at all."

"Yours, you idiot."

I waggle my head.

"Yes and no. For me personally, it's never driven me crazy. If someone doesn't like me because of my size, good riddance, but then... there's a kind of social pressure, you know? Society as a mass. There's a lot of hidden fatphobia. Like the stupid person in movies is always fat. Or associating the word 'fat' with concepts like 'insane' or 'ugly.' There's a hostile climate toward being overweight in general. If you go to a Zara to buy pants that are on trend, they won't have your size... so you go home all annoyed and thinking you're the problem because everyone else can wear them, but you can't. I guess the same thing happens to really thin girls. The problem is that they want to impose a mold on us, whatever it may be. The imposition. You know what I mean?"

Tristan is looking at me curiously.

"I get it. But...you look in the mirror and you like what you see, right?"

"I look in the mirror, and I see me, which is what matters. There are days I like it and days I don't even want to look at myself, but there are also days when I don't even want to see you, and you have the torso of a Greek ephebus."

"I play sports to unwind, Miranda, not to have the torso of a Greek ephebus."

"Well, you could unwind by slamming me against the headboard too."

"If it were up to you, I'd be slamming you against the headboard twenty-four seven."

"Does that mean we're gonna fuck?"

"No."

He dishes a little more food onto his plate and focuses on the film like he didn't just reject me. I lost track of the plot a long time ago, more or less since the first tank came out. I get up from the living room floor, where we were sitting to eat, and take my plate to the kitchen.

When I come back, I realize Tristan is staring at me.

"What?"

"Are you mad?"

"Why?"

"I don't know. I study law, but I'm not good with words. I probably stuck my foot in it."

I pout and shake my head.

"Something's going on," he insists. "Is this about the weight thing?"

"Oh no. I couldn't care less about the weight thing."

"So?"

"I don't know."

He puts his fork down, wipes his mouth with the piece of paper towel I hand him, and turns off the TV.

"I'm listening."

"I said nothing's going on."

"And I said I hear you. You tell me whatever you want. It doesn't have to be because something's going on."

I furrow my brow. This is new. I stay silent. He does too. Ah, I do know this tactic. He gets quiet to make me nervous; he knows that I can't handle these kinds of silences and that I'll end up saying something, even if it's just to break the ice. But I'm not falling for it.

"I'm not falling for it."

"Falling for what?"

"The old trick of seeing who'll talk first."

"Okay." He raises his eyebrows and smiles.

That smile. Fuck. I've been with some hot guys in my life. It's not something that's particularly important to me because I usually end up sprung on the way they smile, their quickness or intelligence, if they awaken something special in me, a spark of something inexplicable... Still, they've almost always been good-looking. Not just to me. My friends say: "So-and-so is hot. Whatshisname is really fine. You always go out with such hotties." I'm not especially pretty, I'm not fine, I'm not trying to be, and I'm not hoping for the guy by my side to have those prerequisites.

Tristan is, however, the best-looking among the good-looking. Or maybe he's not and I just think so because I'm in love with him, I don't know. But he always seemed like one of those boys who I (I repeat, I) couldn't stop looking at for years. And that feeling, the one that I would keep looking at him forever, fills me with sadness now that I know that this thing we have, or had, is going to end.

"Maybe it doesn't make sense to keep going with this." The words escape from my mouth.

"I knew it." He sighs. "Keep going with this... What are you talking about?"

"Us. Keep seeing each other."

"What we have is good," he says very confidently.

"Maybe. But it's going to end. What sense does it make to keep going if it's going to end?"

"What sense does it make to live if we're going to die?"

I suck my teeth and concentrate on going around closing the Chinese food cartons. They're all dripping with grease.

"Do you want to stop seeing me?" he asks.

"No."

"So?"

How can I explain that he's going to be the one who dumps me in four years?

"I don't know. I already told you I don't know. You're the one who's forcing me to talk."

"Miri...look at me for a second."

I stop messing with the containers. I stacked them into a tower without even noticing.

"You think too much." He smiles. "There are days when you flow like you invented the current, but others…" He makes a face. "It's like you know too much and you don't like what you found out."

"Maybe."

"Or maybe you're doing *that thing* again."

"What *thing*?"

"Messing around with predictions. And I don't like you imagining what decisions I'm going to make because it feels like you think I'm predictable or simple or…incapable."

"Don't be stupid. That's not what I'm saying."

"What is clear"—he widens his eyes—"is that I'm not going to listen to a fucking word of this brainwashing. That and, for whatever reason, you don't want me to keep eating."

He waves at the half-empty containers.

"I can't believe you're still hungry after all that," I say.

"I'm gonna finish it all. And then we're going to bed."

"To fuck?"

He lets out a laugh at the same time as he grabs the take-out containers and starts opening them again.

"Let's see…pre- and postcoital chats are so underrated. I'd like to have a few words with the people who started the rumor that men have more sexual appetite than women. That or bring them to meet you. And study you."

"And why would you do that? Am I a rare specimen?"

"Pure fire." He winks. "Pure fire."

After dinner, we stopped trying to follow the plot of the movie. It seemed good, but we're just not very lucid today. We brush our teeth together and, well, that's good, that's normal. Buuuuuutt…then he started pissing with me in the bathroom, even though that doesn't surprise me anymore. We've been together so many years, but I don't know if in this timeline, I should have pretended to be falsely uncomfortable or, at least, surprised by this gesture of intimacy. So the only thing I said to him as he held it so calmly while he talked to me was:

"Intimacy is gross."

I don't care that he pisses in front of me. Or showers. Or that he puts his contact lenses in while I'm in the shower. It always felt to me like those chats we have in the bathroom are part of the DNA of who we are as a couple. Or who we were. Or who we will be. And he seems to agree.

We get into bed and turn out the lights, but the streetlights still fill the room with a soft glow, even with the blinds down, so we can see each other's faces. And here we are, opposite each other, talking about super random stuff. It's been like this all day. Nothing seems to have a meaning or a concrete purpose.

"Wait, you like rap? You're kidding," he teases.

"I swear. I love rap."

"That's not true."

"Of course it is!"

"You don't look like a rap fan."

"And what do rap fans look like? Do I have to wear a baseball cap sideways or something?"

Tristan bursts out laughing.

"Okay…tell me your favorite rapper."

"Natos y Waor."

"Who are they?" He's giving me shit.

"In a few years, you're going to like them."

"Oh yeah?"

"I promise."

"Let's see…sing me one of their songs."

I think about it for a bit. It would have to be earlier than the year we were in…

"You don't sing rap," I say to buy some time. "You rap it."

"Well, then rap to me."

I start rapping one of their hits. This makes Tristan crack up. Me too. I dig my fingers into his ribs.

"Stop laughing at me!"

"It's not at you." He's still laughing. "It's with you, chica."

We play wrestle, jostling each other only to end up much more snuggled together than we had been before. One leg between his and the other over his hip. My hands split between his neck and his hair. I see the thin chain around his neck glinting dully.

"That chain is straight out of communion," I tease him.

"What? You never got so used to wearing something that if you forget to put it on, you feel naked?"

I nod. Yes. Him. Especially him on top, in my imagination, inside, with his cock trying to reach the point of no return, down below, when he looks at me and I know he feels proud, by my side, always…

"Your face changed. What are you thinking about?"

"How I don't want this."

"You don't want what?"

"To get used to having you around my neck and then feeling naked if you leave."

"And why am I going to leave?"

"Because you do leave."

"What about if you leave?"

I sigh gently.

"Listen, Miranda…"

I'm scared I got too intense…although…why is it too much when it's what you feel? Why this fear that we won't be able to handle the things we need to say?

"What? You want me to shut up, right?" I cut him off.

"No. Listen…what if tomorrow, we play hooky from work and we both say we're sick."

"Why?"

"So we can stay in bed."

Umm…

"Or even better," he goes on, "we could book a weekend somewhere and sneak off tomorrow. Tell everyone we're sick and get out of Madrid for a few days."

"But…why? When we can just stay home and…"

"To do things." He smiles. "To have a life outside work."

A stab of guilt travels through my intestines.

"I don't know."

"Let's go to…El Escorial!"

"El Escorial?"

"I don't know that area. It must be beautiful. And it's nearby. We'll rent a car and go walk around, eat, and fuck."

I smile. I can't help it.

"Ah!" He laughs. "You're starting to like this plan more, eh?"

"Let's stay home. We'll call work early, say we're both sick, and then we'll go back to sleep. And then…we'll spend the weekend watching shitty movies, fucking, and eating food that arrives on a motorcycle."

"Or cooking," he suggests. "And going to the movies. Or walking around downtown and drinking martinis on Sunday. I want to get out of bed at some point. I know you too well."

"What if someone from work sees us?"

"We'll tell them we feel better. You don't have to be dying to miss work."

I do.

Tristan grabs my face with both hands and pulls me to his mouth. He kisses me. He kisses me beautifully. It's one of those kisses you would give anywhere but tastes better somewhere intimate, in bed, in the arms of another. It's a kiss that doesn't mean anything; it's not a sorry or a hello or an I missed you or a goodbye. It's a kiss that is given because it's wanted, because we're craving it. It's a soft, smooth, stunning kiss…and it doesn't last as long as I'd like. Then he looks at me and smiles.

"We're not gonna blow off work tomorrow, are we?" he says sadly.

"I think we're too responsible to do that."

"Fine. It's Friday anyway."

I want to tell him we'll see each other when we get out of work, that we'll make plans and we'll follow them through, but it's futile, because tomorrow, I'll wake up on another day, and I won't carry them out. It won't even work to get him away from me. How long did I stay angry? One day? Even though I'm thinking it, I don't have the ovaries to just bluntly say: "Tristan, you're going to put me through horrible pain, and to prevent that, I want you to get out of my life. *Now*." And since I'm not capable of saying it, since I'm weak, here I am, doing this.

"Will you fuck me?" I ask.

The laugh that escapes him first like a fart between his lips spreads to me. I've always been like this. I've never known how to get out of tense situations with flying colors.

"What?" I whimper.

"You're the shit."

He kisses me on the forehead and then on the nose. Then he hugs me.

"Why don't you want to?" I ask worriedly. "Yesterday" in Paris, he didn't want to either.

"I do want to. But you wore me out yesterday."

"Is that a joke?"

"No. Let's leave it for tomorrow. We can fuck like two crazy people when we get back from work. That'll give me motivation to be able to deal with the douchebags who are my colleagues without murdering anyone with a stapler. Why don't I reserve a table at Ostras Pedrín?"

"Great..." I sigh sadly.

"Fine. It's going to be a good weekend."

He snuggles in like a boa constrictor around me and gets ready to sleep. Knowing him, in two or three seconds, he'll be letting out his classic rounds of snores, but a minute passes. Two... And even though I still haven't dared to move a muscle, he doesn't seem to be sleeping either. I twist around as much as I can with his left arm still wrapped around my waist. His right searches for my hand under the pillow.

"Good night," I say to him.

"Miranda..."

"What?"

"I'm not going to leave," he insists.

"Okay."

"Never."

He kisses my shoulder and then my neck. A few seconds later, he's asleep. And I don't know why the fuck I lived through this day that has been so horrifically painful. Because this time with him has been incredible. Because we've always been the best on the humdrum days. Because I don't know if I want him out of my life anymore. I don't know if I can make him leave anymore. And because...what the fuck, I still love him... even on some random day.

14

~~~

FUCK IT

I wake up, but I don't care when. What time, what day, what year. I don't care. I wake up in the kind of "mood" where you have no fucks to give. I open my eyes without an alarm startling me, and the only thing I find is a pale-white glow in my room. I'm alone.

If it's Saturday, I'll spend it in bed and do nothing but sleep. If it's Wednesday, I'll do the same. What about the magazine? Who gives a fuck? Tomorrow will be another jump. Tomorrow, I'll be in another year. It seems like the changes I perpetrate in the past don't have any consequences, so…

I turn over and pull my blanket up to my ears.

It's winter. That much is easy to figure out, because the house is cold and the thin light coming in is like a typical winter morning. And if it's not winter, it's about to be. And it must be early even though it's already daytime, because the building's central heating hasn't come on yet. It must be nine at the latest.

But I don't care. I'm not interested in anything outside this bed, outside the feather duvet my dad gave me when I moved out on my own. I never confessed to him that I don't like it because sometimes feathers escape from the filling and prick you.

Not content with my padded lair, I pull the duvet over my head for total isolation. And I would have fallen asleep again if it weren't for the keys I hear scratching in the lock and warning me. Someone comes in quietly. My ears prick, and I hear that someone put their keys down on the entrance table and slowly close the door. I can hear a paper bag rustling as shoes are pulled off. A short zipper is opened, and if I had any doubts, this would have cleared them up: they're Tristan's boots. I have good hearing, the house is small, and the bedroom door is open…and these sounds are part of what was, until recently, my routine. I roll back toward the window again and burrow deeper.

Maybe I should grab my phone from the bedside table and try to figure out what day I'm living again, but…does it even really matter? I'm stuck in a loop. I'm in a kind of personal hell. It's my limbo. A state of suspended consciousness where everything is spinning so quickly only to end up landing in the same gutter.

Barefoot footsteps padding toward the bedroom rouse me from the drowsy state I'm submerged in, but I don't turn my head toward the door. Not even when the mattress sinks from the weight of his knee.

"Miri…" he whispers into my neck before kissing it intensely, affectionately, stopping to breathe me in. "It's ten. Wake up."

"I am awake," I say, my voice thick.

"Are you feeling okay?"

He puts something on the floor, next to the bed, and with his hands free, he leans back into me.

"Are you sick?"

"No. I'm tired." But my tone of voice seems to express something else.

"Do you need a hug?"

I stay silent. I have a lump in my throat that makes it hard to swallow. I'm enveloped in his scent. He smells good in the morning, before he showers. Tristan's skin holds a delicious memory of his cologne in a low, serious note, like the keys on the left side of a piano. It's a note that reverberates in your chest. And that's how he smells. Of my sheets and yesterday's cologne.

"I went out and picked up breakfast," he says into my ear, getting as close to me as he can in my fetal position. "And I made coffee. You're right…that coffee maker isn't that hard."

"You did it in the Italian espresso one from the back of the cupboard, right?"

"Yes."

That makes me smile a little. In all the years I've been with Tristan and that coffee maker, I've never been able to get him to work it. It's an impossible threesome.

"You just have to push the buttons, Tristan."

"Well, it comes out better from the Italian one. Come on…"

I turn around and sit up a little; he puts a tray into my lap. A coffee, an orange juice, and a Swiss bun. I love Swiss buns. I touch it with the tip of my finger…it's still warm. Fuck. He smiles at me with his white teeth.

"Come on…"

"What about you?"

"My tray's in the kitchen. I have to get ready first."

I wrinkle my brow when I see him efficiently unbuckling his belt. Then the button and zipper of his jeans. He struggles to pull off his pants; they're the kind of jeans that have no stretch, and they fit him so well. Then, before he takes off his sweater and shirt, he tugs his navy boxers into the right position. He takes off his socks and tosses them on the floor, leaves the bedroom, and comes back a few seconds later with his own tray and a few goose bumps.

"Fuck my life, Miranda, it's so cold in your apartment in the mornings."

He does a juggling act to get into bed without spilling his coffee and orange juice all over himself.

"Brr…" He looks at me and smiles. "Aren't you cold?"

"No."

"Well, that's weird, because your pajamas are 'unpajamas.'"

"What does that mean?"

"That you're more naked than dressed in those. They're naked pajamas."

He kisses my shoulder and starts on his coffee.

"It's mizzling."

I stare at him. Him and his myriad terms for identifying how hard it's raining.

"Drizzling?" I ask.

He smiles and nods. A fine rain, not very intense, the kind where you can't be bothered to open your umbrella, but the damp gets into your bones. He loves it. It reminds him of Galicia.

"I was going to say we should go drink vermouth in La Latina, but with this weather…" He takes a bite of his bun and looks at me. "I was starving! We didn't eat very well last night, did we?"

"I don't know."

And the thing is I really don't know.

"You're really quiet. You normally wake up more… I don't know, it depends on the day, of course, but you're usually a little peppier."

"Yeah, right. I don't know."

He downs his orange juice in one gulp and studies me with his thick eyebrows subtly raised.

"Did I do something wrong?"

"No."

That doesn't seem to placate him much, but he concentrates on his bun, which he finishes in two more bites and washes down with his cortado. Then he puts the tray under the bed and turns back to me, where I'm pulling my bun apart into tiny pieces that I put on my tongue so they dissolve in my spit.

"Is this about Thursday?"

"What about Thursday?"

"What you said to me on Thursday. The whole thing about…if this is going to end some day, we might as well end it now."

Ah…mystery solved. The jump was only a few days.

"No. I just woke up on the wrong side of the bed. That's all."

"I get it."

I take a big sip of my Americano, which isn't very good, and then, firmly gripping the tray, get up. I'm wearing one of my nightgowns that uncovers more than it covers.

"Give me your tray. I'll take it to the kitchen."

"Why the big rush? We can take them in later. Come here."

"Come on. Give it to me."

He groans and finds it under the bed; then he rebalances his glass and mug onto the one I'm holding and slides his under mine to make it easier for me to carry. My bare feet stick lightly to the parquet on the round trip. When I get back to the bedroom, I find him at the bathroom door, and he pulls me into him as soon as I cross the threshold.

"Let's take a hot shower."

"Together?"

"We'll actually fit in yours." He smiles.

It doesn't seem like a sexual invitation. Knowing Tristan, it probably isn't; that's not his style. He sneaks in, rubs you, kisses you, and…before you know it, he's on top, inside you. And he's arching with pleasure and you're digging your nails into his back and pulling his hair and biting his bottom lip…

Stop, Miranda. Stop.

I turn on the hot water, but before I strip off completely, he sticks his hand in and turns it up a little hotter. Tristan likes his shower water scalding…if it's not stripping off a layer of skin, it's not hot enough for him. He tugs on the waistband of his boxers, but before he takes them off, I head to the door again.

"You go ahead. I'm gonna grab another towel. Plus it's way too hot for me."

If he finds that weird, he doesn't say anything. When I come back to put the towel down, he's standing with his back to me, facing the stream, a waterfall cascading onto his head, plastering his straight hair across his forehead. I don't want to look too hard because he's naked, and naked Tristan has always been too attractive to me. With that cute little butt. The thin but strong legs. That V his abs make on the way down to his cock… I'm not a very shallow girl, but I like the shell housing Tristan's soul a little too much.

"I'm leaving your towel here."

"Stop looking at my ass," he teases with his eyes closed.

"I'm not looking at your ass."

"You're looking at something…"

He steps back a bit from the stream and looks at me, pushing his hair back. My eyes keep trying to travel farther down, but I resist…

"Go ahead and look."

"I don't want to look at you, you narcissist."

"Do you remember what you said to me the first time I got naked in front of you?" His voice, always a little raspy, has a fun lilt to it now because he's making sure I can hear him over the murmur of the water.

"Yes."

We side-eye each other and smirk.

"Such a dirty girl."

"I just said what I was thinking. Don't hate on me for my honesty."

"You said I had a beautiful cock. Who says that?"

"Me, because you do. It's not my fault." I shrug.

He backs into the water again, shaking his head incredulously. Maybe he's never believed that I think he has the most beautiful cock on the face of the earth. The foam from the soap he's been rubbing all over him falls to the shower floor and slips down the drain. He's smiling kind of enigmatically, somewhere between nostalgia, sadness, fun, and desire.

"I like you when you're like this," he admits. "Even when I'm trying to find the remote control to slow you down a little." He turns the shower off.

He sluices off some of the water clinging to his skin with his hands. He turns around with a kind of pride. I don't look down, but it's there.

"I'm not looking at it," I repeat.

"You're smiling."

"Of course I'm smiling." I try to stifle a laugh. "You're being a cocky jerk."

"Big dick energy." He raises his chin, like a tough guy. "Look at it."

"No!" A giggle slips out. "Get out already."

He opens the door to the shower, and I chuck a towel on him immediately. He cracks up. That laugh I like so much. That laugh that sounds like a fifteen-year-old boy with his bomber jacket and his hoop in his ear, flirting with the girl he likes. I take off my underwear and then my nightgown. I throw it all in the laundry basket, but he wastes no time grabbing the nightgown.

"Not this one."

"You woke up all fired up, huh?"

"We'll see, we'll see."

He dries his hair with the blow-dryer (he couldn't be more vain, my God) while I take my shower. As soon as I finish, he's waiting there with the towel open, making a big show of looking away, like he doesn't want to see me.

"It's nothing you haven't seen before."

He doesn't answer. He just wraps me up, rubbing me gently with the soft, fluffy towel over my skin, tenderly. He has his wrapped around his waist, and…oof. I think decades could pass, trillions of years, before I got sick of his skin, his touch. Why did we touch each other and look at each other so little at the end of our relationship?

"Dry off, you wet rat. And then we're going back to bed," he says to me.

"It's Sunday, it's raining, and there's nothing better to do."

"And what are we going to do in bed?"

"Umm…" He pretends to think about it. "Well, we're going to…vibe."

"Oh yeah. Talking is underrated."

"You underrate it because you're a pervert."

It's raining. A light rain, an almost velvety curtain of water caressing the windowpanes. If it were colder, it's the kind of day Madrid would be covered in a layer of crunchy snow that would quickly turn into dirty water but that would drive many people out of their homes. We Madrileños, who are not yet familiar with the ravages of Storm Filomena, get really hyped about the snow.

But today, it's just raining, and Tristan and I have climbed back into bed to hide from Sunday under the cover of a duvet and my patterned sheets. Behind his back, I'm making a mental list of all the reasons I should stop loving him, but he's shooting them down, one by one, with his fingertips trailing down my back. His breath becomes a light breeze lifting the short hairs on the nape of my neck. I can't focus on anything except him.

"Do you know the freckles on your back look exactly like the Little Dipper?" My usual habit of breaking the silence.

"Yeah?"

"Yeah."

"And that's good?"

"Some things aren't good or bad. They just are," I declare.

"You think so?"

"Of course. Some things simply are. They exist."

"Like what?"

"Like... I don't know, for fuck's sake. I mean...trees."

"Trees are good. They're great. We breathe because they produce oxygen, remember?"

I want to kill him and then devour him with kisses.

"Ay..." When he gets like this, it makes me laugh. "Fine, then birds, I don't know."

"I'm sure birds make up an important part of nature's food chain."

"Do you think there are natural predators in the middle of Madrid?"

"Sure," he says, very focused on tracing shapes on my back. He's only wearing boxers, and I'm in my nightgown.

"There are things that aren't good or bad, Tristan, that's it."

"Like us?"

I crane my neck to peer at him over my shoulder. He's smiling a little.

"What? I can't say nice things to you?" he calls me out.

"I find it kinda surprising that you consider that nice."

"Ah, no? I said 'us.'"

"Oh." I turn all the way around and widen my eyes. "Should I give you a round of applause?"

"You're so feisty, you little minx," he says, leaning over to kiss me. "But you make me wild."

Okay. At least we can both agree on that. I don't remember Tristan saying stuff like that. I had forgotten he could be so sweet.

"I make you wild?" I want to hear more.

"You drive me crazy."

"Because I'm so complicated, right?"

"Weird as fuck. Luckily I'm weird too."

"Sometimes I'm boring."

"Yup."

"And sometimes you are too. Especially your texts, when you're not in the mood."

"I know."

"So?"

"What do you want, for me to tell you I like you?" he teases.

"It wouldn't be so bad. To know that. To understand it."

"What is it that you don't understand?"

"What you see in me?"

He blinks in surprise.

"What's that about?"

"I don't know. I've never gotten it. You're one of the hot ones. Hot people should stick with people from their own species."

"And you're not hot, right?"

"Don't get it twisted. I'm other things."

"Ah," he cackles. "And I'm just hot."

That makes me smile.

"Yes," I lie. "Hot and vapid."

"That sucks. I'd rather be interesting."

"Well, sorry. You didn't get that in the genetic lottery."

At first, from his silence, I think he's searching for a retort, something fast and quippy, but I suddenly realize that's not it. No. Tristan has stumbled down a path to another thought, another feeling.

"Miranda…" he says a little more seriously, "you make me tingle."

Ay, no. Please no.

"Shut up." I cover his mouth with my hand. His soft, full mouth.

He pulls my hand away and repeats:

"You make me tingle. You tingle me. And that's new. And I don't know what it is."

So what do I do now? What do I do now, when he cups my face in his hands and kisses my upper lip? What do I do when he looks me in the eyes?

"You don't know what it is?"

"No. It's like trying to tell someone I don't know what color your eyes are. Because one day, they're brown, then another, they look like the color of honey, and sometimes they're crazy green."

"Do you do that a lot? Tell people you don't know what color my eyes are?"

"I talk about you sometimes," he says in a quiet voice.

"Oh yeah?"

"Yeah. Stupid stuff you'd never believe. Stuff like my friend Miranda…"

"…makes me tingle?"

"No. Not that." He smiles tenderly. "I keep that just for me. At least I keep it to myself until I know what it means exactly."

"What could it mean, Tristan?"

"What's going on? Do you know?"

"Yes."

His expression shifts to a much more serious one. He takes a deep breath and stops stroking my face.

"You've always been scared to put a label on things," I say. "I think you think that labeling something will make it fade faster. It makes it tangible, and tangible things…"

"…are at the mercy of time."

My God, I want him so much.

"A table doesn't hold less weight just because you call it a 'table.'"

Tristan sucks his teeth and rolls onto his back; he rubs his hair with one hand, and with the other, he touches the thin chain he wears around his neck, normally hidden under his clothes.

"Clearly you've always been the one who takes the initiative," he jokes.

"And that worries you."

"It worries me that everything's so clear to you, Miranda." He turns back to look at me. "How hard you are, how you're smarter than me, how you have this job you love, how you can never have enough sex, how sometimes I find sex instead of affection on your skin, how fast you accelerate, how you want to know when you're going to see me, how..."

"If you were overwhelmed, all you had to do was say it, you know?"

"But I'm not."

"You're in love."

He presses his lips together and doesn't answer. He stares at the ceiling. I'm not scared of making a fool of myself, in case you were wondering; remember I have the advantage of knowing what I'm saying is true, even if he hasn't figured it out yet.

"I don't know what being in love means," he says finally. "So I guess I can't say you're wrong, but I can't say you're right either. Is that okay?"

I smile.

"Ay, Tristan..."

He turns back to me.

"You're the first thing I think about when I wake up and the last before I go to sleep. You're on my mind from the courthouse to the firm and from the firm home. I open the fridge with you. I shower with you. I watch TV with you. All of it...and, hell, it's not even the first time it's happened to me, but it's the first time it's lasted more than two months."

"You're the king of jerks." I smile.

"Boohoo, I already told you that."

We both laugh.

"What if I am in love?"

"I don't know, doctor, it seems serious."

"Hey..." He gently whacks me on the arm. "I'm serious."

"Well, if you are, it's no big deal, because even though this is gonna make you have trouble swallowing, I am too, with you."

Tristan swallows.

"We're going to jinx it," he says warily.

"No. Not at all."

"How are you so sure?"

"Because even though I should be telling you the opposite to prevent what's going to happen, I know what's waiting for us."

"Ah, the fortune teller." He smiles, snuggling in closer and wrapping himself around me.

"We have some beautiful years ahead of us."

"Years?"

"Yes. Beautiful. And hard."

He seems to take what I'm saying very seriously.

"Hard?"

"Yes. You and I are very different, Tristan. It's not gonna be easy."

"But will it be worth the effort?"

A waterfall of incredibly vivid images rains down over me. The first time he held my hand on the street…probably the first time in the last twenty years of his life. The wild night of partying at that festival, in the summer, where we discovered that on top of wanting each other and loving each other, we're the best companions in the world. The surprise trip I give him for his next birthday. The sex, all magnificent, wild, affectionate, and filthy. All the plans we'll carry out and the ones we won't, but they'll serve as an engine for our thing. Him moving into my house. The honeymoon first few months of us living together. That trip to meet his family and the dawn on New Year's Eve. The Vetusta Morla concert. Dancing at Rita's wedding, in the pitch-black of the farm's grounds, where noises echoed and bounced back to us so weakly.

I smile at him.

"I guess so. Yes. It'll be worth the pain."

I don't know when I decide. I don't know if it's when I say it to him or when I feel his warm tongue in my mouth. Or if it's when I feel how much talking about love turns him on. Maybe it's when he shifts on top of me while he kisses me. Or when he pulls off my panties. Or I don't know when, but I decide, here and now, that even if I am stuck in a loop, I've been fooling myself thinking this isn't a gift. Maybe it took me a while to understand it or process it or chew it over, but finally I get it. Every morning, every new old day, I'm going to try. Because if this has any meaning, that must be it, it has to have a purpose. And that purpose must be fixing what broke for us one day.

Tristan pushes into me without a condom. It's not my first time with him, but it's his first time with me in this crazy timeline I'm living. He seems repentant and excited by what he's doing…and surprised I'm not stopping him.

He pulls out of me, supporting his weight on the palms of his hands, pressing into the mattress on either side of my head, and looks at me, holding his breath and licking his lips. I don't say anything, I just squirm, and he rams into me harder; a moan escapes his throat. Fuck, I never realized how hot his moans make me.

"I'm not wearing a condom," he reminds me.

"Pull out before you come."

Don't judge me. I wouldn't do it in any other situation; let me get carried away now that I have the advantage of knowing we're both healthy. In January, we'll do an exhaustive medical exam so we know everything's fine and can decide what kind of contraception to use from there. I would have waited if I didn't know everything was fine.

Tristan stares at me so intensely it makes his eyes look deeper. Darker. He says again that it's impossible to tell anyone what color eyes I have, and that makes me laugh because that's exactly how I feel about his. They aren't brown or gray or green. Just murky. And on top of all that, sex makes them hungry and languid.

"God…" he growls, thrusting as deep as he can, burying his nose in my neck.

He grips my right thigh and pulls it up on his hip. Suddenly he's much deeper and harder, and the feeling hijacks him. He loses himself in pleasure for a few minutes, pushing in and pulling out almost all the way, alternating between hard and slow thrusts. I let a scream escape from my throat when he starts pounding me rhythmically again. I let him, loving feeling him like this, so naked, accelerating until the sound of our skin smacking together fills the room.

"Don't come, don't come yet," I say. "Slow down."

"Why?" he groans.

"Because I haven't come yet," I remind him.

That makes us laugh. Sometimes that happens. It's not that he's egotistical; it's just that pleasure clouds his brain. It's just that he forgets the whole world. It's just that he drifts far away, to a place where he believes that his pleasure and mine are so intertwined that it's impossible I don't feel the same as he does.

He flips me over roughly so I'm on top, and I move very slowly. He needs to relax.

"Don't fuck with me," he moans as he digs his fingers into the flesh of my hips. "Go faster…ah…faster…"

I obey a little, but only a little. He laughs. Sometimes pleasure makes Tristan laugh, but I don't think he's aware of it, which makes it even more special. I circle my hips faster and faster, and he takes advantage of each little jolt to grab my ass even harder.

"Like that, like that, like that…" he moans.

"Like this?" I tease him.

"Just like that."

He closes his eyes, licks his lips, and looks up at me again. We don't need words. What we suspected…now seems more like a certainty. Our flesh slapping together sounds sensual and wet. We're sweating, but neither one of us wants to stop. I'm afraid we're not always in control of our bodies.

We roll each other over a few times before he settles between my legs, him on top, and his hips speed up the thrusts inside me without asking permission. It's the signal for me to touch myself. His thrusts are getting faster and more violent, and his breathing is getting shallower. I'm about to ask him to slow down when he pulls out of me in a rush and sprays all over my...nightgown. From my nightgown all the way down my chest to my thigh. From my nightgown to the sheet. From my nightgown to my thigh, from my thigh to the sheet.

"Shit..." he mutters as he comes, watching every drop shower over me. "Shit, fuck."

My fingers are still playing with my clit, and suddenly they hit the right spot, and just like that, covered in come, him panting over me with his cock in his hand, I come until there's nothing left of me but a sustained note on a pentagram. An off-key note, so high no one hears. A note that shatters a distant crystal vase with how hard it vibrates.

Maybe it's true what my friend Marina says, that we're all stupid and our clits fall in love every time we sleep with someone. Or maybe it's a question of being on the same vibration with someone, fitting together, feeling like a membrane is splitting when your skin pulls away from their skin. I don't know what it is, but I know that if there was any resistance left inside me to fight against this, it's drowning in saliva, sweat, and semen now.

I'm going to get him back. Fuck it!

15

~~~

IT WILL BE BEAUTIFUL

Love is much more complicated than we were told. I'm the kind of person who spent my whole life embarrassed to fall in love; I don't know at what point in my upbringing or education I came to understand that love was a weakness. So when my friends would splutter with their mouths full that they were in love or tell me, their eyes shining with excitement, what they were going through in their new relationships (because we only do these things in the beginning), I would sink into my chair and look away, praying it would end soon.

I'm a terrible friend, I know, I know. But come on, in my defense, I do always try to be a good ear for them. If I learned anything from Tristan, it was to empathize with all the poor people in this world afflicted with that ailment called love. But I can't deny that I had a hard time when I fell in love with Tristan.

While I believe that love is the compendium of many things, including a few chemical processes I don't claim to understand because, for fuck's sake, that's the only thing that can explain why we turn into such assholes. I think we all remember the moment when we realized we were crazy in love. That one that you can mark with a before and after. The one we thought would be forever, that would save us from cynicism, that would hold us until the world ends.

I was aware that I had fallen in love with Tristan, like I had been hit with a dart smack in the middle of my forehead, with an overwhelming certainty that left me with half a word dangling from my mouth, unable to finish the sentence.

It was the day I first met his friends. That morning, he asked me, as if it wasn't about him, as if it wasn't that deep, if I wanted to join him for a drink with some of his friends from Vigo who had come to spend the weekend in Madrid. No warning: it was news to me they were even coming to see him. He always does important stuff like this: he strips it down to the skeleton of pure practicality, into facts with no emotional conditions. It's a symptom of how much he respects emotions, how much he fears them, and what sincere and visceral emotions they provoke in him. Tristan, the man of silences, needs to chew things over before he feels them. Tristan, the man who digests his feelings into emotional baby food.

At the time, I already suspected that I had long since left the safe lane; the "don't get involved" rule that allowed me to be a bit indifferent some- how felt that it was important, even if I didn't want to show it, because showing it would be like pointing straight at the bull's-eye of my weak- ness for him. And right there, in the middle of trying to be nice, being so charming that his friends would have no choice but to tell him how much they liked me for him, I realized that I loved him.

I loved him. Does a cornier expression exist? No. But there's no realer one either.

Today, when I wake up and realize that's the day I'm in, I wonder if the fact that I talked about love with him last night (or in the timeline of our story, four months ago now) will have changed anything. But…as embarrassed as I am about love, I can't hide the fact that I'm glad I woke up "today."

"Today" is one of those days.

Those ones. You know the ones.

Despite everything, I never liked waking up at his house, so when I open my eyes, on top of the confusion of not knowing where I am, I'm greeted by the dreary white walls, the IKEA curtains he never hemmed so they drag on the floor, and the sheets he never uses fabric softener on. Tristan is a neat guy, but his place is still 100 percent bachelor pad, clean, tidy, but no extras. We women are much more caring when it comes to nesting. We're detail-oriented, and we treat ourselves. One of my friends says that we know we have grown up when we invest in good towels and pans. I would add candles and flowers. Not that I expected the latter in that little flat in Chueca, but…

Tristan's towels were scratchy. The sheets were clean, but he hardly ever made the bed. The survival prospects in his fridge were awful. And it's not like I'm one of those people who can whip up something delicious with just a few ingredients, but the thing is Tristan only ever had milk, beer, coffee, and ham. Very enticing menu.

"I only have food when I know I'm going to make something. Otherwise everything goes bad, and I have to throw it out. I hate throwing food out."

Well, that's fine. I was never that well stocked either. Plus, I was always happy to pop downstairs and buy whatever I needed or order what I felt like. But at his house…I didn't have my stuff. And I like having my stuff.

Tristan comes into the bedroom in his navy blue pajama pants, shirt-less, with his phone pressed to his ear. Once he checks that I'm awake and have my phone in hand (looking to see what day it is, my sweet, summer child, don't look at me like that), he keeps talking:

"Yeah, yeah…yes. He's like the dinosaurs that survived the meteor." He laughs at his own joke. "But give me a second. I could have sworn I left my card in my leather jacket pocket."

He pulls the phone away from his mouth as he moves toward the wardrobe.

"I'm making coffee. Do you want anything else for breakfast?"

"Ooh, yeah. Serve me a slab of ham."

"Jerk." He smiles.

He rummages in the pockets of a jacket, cradling the phone between his shoulder and his ear until he finds something.

"Here it is. I'll take a picture and send it to you." A pause where he rolls his eyes. Fuck…he's so good-looking. This week must have been stressful, and that's why he dedicated all his free time to fucking me and playing sports because… "No, don't worry. Yeah, it's Saturday, but I was up already."

He shakes his head vigorously at me, and I burst out laughing.

"Fine. Yes. No problem. See you Monday."

He hangs up and hurls the phone dramatically onto the bedside table.

"Remind me why I thought this 'promotion' to the capital was such a good idea."

"Because you had to meet me."

"Ooh, so romantic," he jokes. "Listen…what are your plans for today?"

"I told my dad I'd go have lunch with him," I fib on the spot.

"Ah, do you have time for breakfast?"

"Yeah, yeah. I'll have a coffee with ham and then go home to take a shower."

"You can take one here."

"I'm still not into full-body exfoliation."

"You're an idiot." He raises his eyebrows. "I've told you a million times: in my opinion, towels have to be a little scratchy to actually dry you."

"You're sick in the head. Why were you asking about my plans?"

"Oh, no reason. It's just that..." He turns around and pretends to be very busy folding things on top of his chest of drawers. "A few of my friends are in town...well, part of the crew from Vigo. And they asked me if I wanted to grab a drink this afternoon."

I get out of bed and air out the sheets. I'm wearing one of his shirts. No panties. Whoa, whoa... I didn't remember last night's seismic activities.

"Where's my underwear? Any idea where they ended up?"

He crouches down and tosses them to me. I pull them on without much grace.

"I was just saying, in case you felt like coming," he goes on, but now he's looking at his phone.

Anyone who didn't know him would think he didn't care, that he was just saying it to be polite. But no.

"What time? Because I was thinking of telling Ivan to come have coffee at my dad's house, and knowing how 'punctual' he usually is..."

He makes a barely perceptible face. I'm fucking up his plan.

"We're meeting up at six thirty...but I still don't know where to take them."

"Take them to the Mercado de..."

"Not the Mercado de San Miguel, it's full of tourists, and it's so expensive!" he complains.

"The San Fernando one, you dope, you never let me finish my sentences."

"Is that the one on Calle de Embajadores?"

"Yes." I smile.

"Ah...well..."

I make the bed in two nimble flicks of the wrist and head toward the bathroom. His voice reaches me at the door:

"So are you coming?"

"Of course, I'll stop by for a drink."

Everything's so comfortable when you know how it's going to end.

My father wasn't expecting me, but he's as happy to see me as always. He's surprised when I throw myself into his arms and squeeze him tightly. We're affectionate, but maybe not that effusively. It feels like we're reuniting after a war, but he recovers from the surprise quickly and fulfills his duty as a parent: pulling out enough food for a whole army.

"Ay, my sweetheart!" He's thrilled. "It's so great you came. Do you know what I made for lunch?"

"Stew!"

It's Saturday. And on this day of the week, Dad never fails to make stew. Years ago, he stopped opening the store on Saturdays because he was tired and because what he could earn wasn't worth it. He's been thinking about retiring for a while now, but we both know he won't do it as long as he's still standing.

"Do you want a beer?"

"Yes, but just one. I'm going out for drinks this evening, and I don't want to show up already hungover."

"You didn't brag about being able to drink a Viking under the table, did you?"

"I'm getting too old for that shit, dear father."

"What an embarrassment of a daughter..." he teases. "Are you going out with the gang from the neighborhood and Ivan this afternoon? Or with the girls from the magazine?"

"No. With Tristan and his friends."

I study his face as he hands me a beer and a plate with freshly sliced ham (nothing like the packaged stuff sleeping in Tristan's fridge). There's a glimmer of recognition in his expression.

"You're going to have to introduce me to this Tristan… You've been mentioning his name for quite a while now. Is he your boyfriend?"

"Yes," I admit.

I don't know how I did this the first time, but if I'm going to live with him, it's better to say things as they are. He nods silently and hands me a basket of sliced baguette and then a plate of cheese.

"What?" I prod him.

"Nothing."

"Stop taking food out."

"A few mussels and then that's it. Would you prefer a martini?"

"No, Dad. I'm fine with the beer."

He nods again. I can't tell if he seems sad or worried. But there's no need; he's going to love Tristan. I have to make this end well, or there will be so much pain all around us… I can't let this breakup happen.

"Does he treat you well?" he asks slyly.

"He reads the pamphlets from medicine he sees me taking."

That makes him smile.

"And does he make you laugh?"

"He reads me the side effects in a worried voice. Of course he makes me laugh."

He seems satisfied when he puts a piece of bread with ham in his mouth.

"Dad, was there a specific moment when you knew you loved Mama?"

"Yes," he says nostalgically. "She was wearing a green dress. I trotted out that old Spanish saying: 'She who dares wear green must be beautiful,' and she answered that I should stop drooling all over her. Then I thought: 'She's right, stop drooling, and ask her to marry you.'"

"That's beautiful, Dad."

"That's how it was back in my day. Now you're all sending each other texts with smiley faces."

"And eggplants," I add.

"What?"

"Nothing."

"Do you want noodles in the soup?"

"What kind of question is that?"

"But you don't want chickpeas, right? You wouldn't want to cough and then end up farting in front of your boyfriend's friends."

The piece of cheese I'm chewing threatens to spray out of my nose.

Tristan is laughing very animatedly (I would calculate at least three beers, knowing him) when I find them in the "central plaza" that was labeled on the map of the stalls of the Mercado de San Fernando. They're sitting around a table covered in many empty bottles of beer. In Madrid, we call them "stubbies," but in other provinces, they're known as "fifths," so they haven't actually drunk that much...yet.

"Hi." I wave and tuck my hair behind my ears with a gesture of false shyness.

In the original moment, I seemed moderately shy when I met them, so even though over time, we've all come to know and trust each other, I repeat what worked for me the first time.

"Hey!" Tristan greets me, coming over.

He kisses me on the cheek, like he did the last time, but this time, it doesn't bother me; I know he's learning to manage how he feels. He grabs my waist in an affectionate but not overly committed gesture and gets the group's attention. And what a group: the girls look friendly, but the dudes look like characters from science fiction. He lists their names, all eight of them, including the baby being held in one of the girl's arms, and then turns back to me.

"And this is Miranda."

"The famous Miranda," one of the girls says slightly snidely.

"Just Miranda," I joke, smiling at her. "Any similarities to actual persons are pure coincidence."

They all laugh, and he squeezes my waist affectionately. How nice to relive this day. I feel lucky. Even though it's kind of annoying to have to perform a me that everyone will like, what a gift to go back, with no nerves, and relive these moments and watch Tristan's initial unease transform into calm.

And the thing is I always liked how badly his life fit with mine. His seasickness in my storm. His routine with my chaos. His calm with my tornado. Little by little, I surrendered to that image of what a bad couple we made. He was such a handsome little boy that everyone spent half their lives trying to set him up, but he never found the right one. Me, this over-the-top woman unwilling to let love make her feel small. Him, those full lips wrapped up in a well-managed silence. Me, so Jessica Rabbit, just without the red hair, always surrounded by thunder.

I start thinking, as I make small talk with two of his friends, how I probably got caught up in what a bad idea we were. I got hung up on every irresponsible thing we did.

I fell in love without noticing that I was gambling more than I thought. I, who always had a bet on the line and didn't mind losing it all, going all in, hoping for what seemed like a good hand.

We can't lie to ourselves and paint the fantasy that we were always a perfect couple, because we're a bad idea that ended up materializing into a kind of pure magic. We're a pipe dream gone right. We're a crumpled, wet postcard that somehow arrives at its destination still legible. We're a staticky voicemail message. We are this relationship that ended a week ago but that I'm reluctant to let go of because it's too good to give up. Perfect in its fucking imperfection. I'll make him see it.

They ask questions about my job, and even though I love it and think it's the best, I downplay the glamour with subtle false modesty lurking under comments like "It's still a job," "There's a lot of hype," "Sometimes I feel frivolous," things I don't actually feel at all. Because for life to be bearable, you have to appreciate the beautiful, the frivolous. Because hype doesn't matter when you're passionate about what you do. Because it's a job, but it makes me happy.

And there I am, surrounded by his friends, being nice, liking them, taking an interest in their lives, when it happens again. It comes back...but just like the first time. It comes back, as if something wants to make it clear to me how small I am in the face of all this: everything I felt, everything that is still churning in my stomach. The arrow comes back, and it's more accurate than I remember it, jabbing into my forehead, right between my eyes, and making a throbbing pain radiate all the way down to my chest.

And it passes as if it were just a blip, because in reality, the world keeps turning, and we don't mean anything to it or its future. It looks, to everyone else, like exactly what it is: a completely insignificant act. A man picking up a child who was grizzling in his stroller. It's a man talking to the child's parents as he does it. It's a man searching for me with his eyes as if he could wordlessly tell me everything he doesn't yet know but that will pull us apart in the end:

I want to be a father, and I want to experience this with you. I want our life to be exactly like this. But you won't.

Tristan scoops the quietly whimpering baby up deftly. And the scene seems to be unfolding almost in slow motion. He straightens up with the baby in his arms, one hand holding his little body and the other his little head, which makes the bomb of certainty explode in my chest once again. Because people say a lot of stuff about love, and they're probably all true, but for me, love means dispelling all doubts, believing blindly.

Over the past few years, he has pushed me to the limit with his stupidity, his weirdnesses, how passive-aggressive he is in arguments, his lack of initiative or interest. I would have slapped him a million times…because over time, that silence I first fell in love with started to exasperate me. I would have pulled my hair out strand by strand out of frustration and despair when I saw him holding his breath instead of saying what he felt. Because he may be unbearable, impassive, cold, Martian, but I can't live without him. Fuck, I mean, I can, but I don't want to.

And there, in his green plaid shirt, his jeans, his battered brown boots, his finger-combed hair, his ten-day-old beard, his crazy mouth, and his hazy eyes… There…holding a baby, cradling him…even I, as someone who's pretty sure I don't want to be a mother, feel my uterus blossom at the sight, just as strongly as I felt it the first time. And a love explodes inside me that's so deep, so pure, so innocent…that with a word half dangling from my lips, I apologize to the people I'm talking to and go over to him. When I reach his side, he smiles at me.

"Are you having a good time?" he murmurs so quietly only I can hear him.

I grab his face in my hands and draw him to my mouth. And it's a soft, discreet kiss without fanfare or passion. A true love's kiss, like they talk about in fairy tales, except instead of breaking the spell, it casts it. I can see it on his face when I pull away. He's the restrained one who said he would never hold hands with anyone in the street again, who made fun of couples who kiss in public. But he's just realized that he loves me too. That he's deeply in love. That he doesn't believe in the future if it's not conjugated in the plural we of Tristan and Miranda's story. And here, looking at each other, with a baby who is not our baby cradled between us, we silently sign our love. And everyone around us disappears. And there's no market. And there's no hustle and bustle. And there's no beer. There is just us and the certainty that this us exists.

He smiles. I do too.

"Shit," he murmurs.

"What?"

"You were right. I am falling in love."

He murmurs the words like he's scared they'll stray too far from his lips, but I gather them up with my lips and swallow them. It doesn't matter to me anymore. Never more.

We're going to rebuild it, and…it will be beautiful.

16

~~~

"I DON'T KNOW. BUT IT MAKES ME THROB."

You come down from drugs, but not from this endorphin rush.

I don't understand how I could have been so bitter about these trips in the first place. I mean, fine, this is the closest thing I've had in my life to a bad trip, and I needed some time to adjust before I figured out what I'm living through. I don't know why I've been given this opportunity or who thought it was a good idea to send me, but I'm ready to enjoy it. And make the most of it. It's a gift.

I'm woken up by the soft crooning of Tristan's alarm clock, which gets louder if it's not turned off. It never gets very loud, because he slaps it and stops it almost immediately. I look around. We're in my bedroom, with the forest-green curtains and the bed with soft sheets. I smile. Yesterday, I realized again for the first time that I was in love with him. Uniting the concepts of "again" and "for the first time" is starting to give me chills.

What will today have in store for me?

"What time is it?" I ask when he snuggles into me.

"Six fifteen," he grumbles.

I push my ass into his crotch, which is awake now too. I feel his serious laughter on my neck.

"You can't be asking me for a good time..." His voice warms a little as I move.

"He who riseth early..."

"Shut up, you blasphemer. They're gonna excommunicate you."

Tristan pulls off his boxers without another word. I tug my underwear off, and we hide under the duvet.

"No messing around."

"I don't have time, even if I wanted to."

"Exactly."

He pushes in all at once. I'm not that wet yet, but my body takes him in happily. He groans. Tristan is one of those people who has no awareness of what he's saying when he's in bed. Saying or groaning. Yes, Tristan groans a lot, and I love it.

He lies on top of me, grabs my flesh wherever he can, and groans into my body, as if this animalistic act is the way he marks his territory. The territory I concede to him for as long as this lasts.

He pushes hard between my legs, lost in it. He moves fast, panting with a rhythm only punctuated by a soft moan every few seconds. I know when that moan comes at shorter intervals, we're about to come. We, because I'm already touching myself so I come with him. Suddenly, he slams on the brakes and pulls away from me, holding his weight on his palms. He hesitates. A bead of sweat glistens on his temple.

"Should I stop and put one on?"

Ah, the condom.

"No," I beg him. "Keep going."

"Keep going all the way?" he seems surprised.

"No. No." I get scared. I don't know what day it is or if I'm on the Pill. Although...would a change like this have any consequences in the "future"? "Pull out first."

For a few minutes, the mattress creaks. We kiss so passionately it feels like an emergency instead of a slow-burning love. Sometimes I like it like that. I think he does too. Plus, it's healthy for a couple to fuck like a wildlife documentary every once in a while.

"Come…" I say when I can feel he's close. "Now, please…now." Tristan pulls back from me so he can thrust harder; he notices how I'm tightening around him, squeezing him harder, and he speeds up. Harder. Faster. Deeper. I don't understand how he can control himself and not fill me up…

My head falls back onto the pillow before I'm even aware I had lifted it. Sometimes I fly a little when I orgasm. I levitate above the mattress, above my body, above everything, and he knows it, so it's a signal for me to release him. Tristan rushes out of me, driving a knee between my thighs and soaking my stomach. And after the last moans, he stays like that, his erection in his hand, his head thrown back slightly and his eyes closed, breathing deeply…and he's so beautiful. Beautiful. Like this, naked and a little sweaty, shining like they must have done in the Roman circus when they were victorious. He's so hot. That mouth. That nose. The way his hair flops over his forehead. How thick his black hair is… The alarm clock on his phone punctures the moment, but he smiles as he opens his eyes and looks at me.

"Good morning," he says.

"Good morning."

"Good thing I set two alarms."

"Seems like you were pretty awake for the second one."

"Yeah, but right now, all I wanna do is curl up next to you and go back to sleep."

He jumps out of bed. I'm still thinking about his naked body when I hear the shower turn on. We take turns in the bathroom without much poetry. And we're rushing a little. Well, him more than me, because all I know is that today's a workday. I'm having fun not worrying, the Russian roulette of the days when I'm not forcing myself to find references that will bring me back to reality.

"Miri, I can't wait for you," he says as he looks at me in the mirror, leaning over his contact lens case.

"You're not even gonna drink coffee? It's still pretty early."

"Yeah, I know. But I have to get in early today."

"How come? Do you have court?"

"I have…stuff." He blinks. I wish I was even closer to him right now. Sometimes a few drops get stuck in his eyelashes, and I love how they shimmer, how it makes them droop.

He's already dressed when I come out of the shower wrapped in a soft towel. He's pulling his coat on over his suit jacket, and I know he hates how it gets bunched up, so I help him straighten everything out.

"Are we seeing each other today? Do we have plans?"

He has a wicked gleam in his eyes.

"Maybe. Let's leave things in the hands of serendipity."

He gives me a kiss on the arch of my top lip and winks at me. He doesn't need to say anything else. Now I know exactly what day it is.

The office is submerged in complete silence. The lights are still off, and nobody's come in yet. I appreciate these moments of calm, and I stroll toward my office unhurriedly. The wall is already sporting a few colorful layout pages. Spring is blaring, and we're joining the chorus from our magazine.

A couple of girls arrive at their desks, saying good morning and dropping their bags off before they head to the kitchen, where we have all the usual stuff: fridge, coffee and vending machines, two microwaves, sink, a few tables to sit down to eat…and there are always cookies, cereals, muesli…that kind of stuff. Almost all my coworkers have breakfast there every day, but I hate the coffee from that machine. I'd go for one at Dori's, but I don't feel like it. I'm a little nervous. Reliving today is a gift, but…I wish I could relive tomorrow too. This is making me a little greedy. I wonder, a little worried, whether I'll ever have enough. Maybe the answer is that we can never have enough of the good stuff.

Today is Friday, and we're still a couple of weeks away from closing, so we're not up against it yet. It's going to be a nice day, the kind that doesn't make you wonder if the job you love might kill you too. I know some people may think it's frivolous, but we still have the pressure of deadlines: delivery of material, layout, printing…but not today. Today, there will be no fire and no rush. Just a group of women writing about things they care about and like for other women who are interested in the same things.

At three o'clock in the afternoon, the magazine's receptionist will call me at the office; I'll be packing up to go home, but she'll ask me to wait a second for a last-minute visitor. The visitor will be Ivan, who will bring me a small suitcase with clothes to spend the weekend away…with Tristan. Tristan, who's arranged a surprise "just because."

"Because we're tired. Because we deserve it. Just because, for fuck's sake," he'll say, wrapping both arms around my waist at the hotel.

The rest of the day is going to be torture.

"Morning, Miri!"

Rita's clacking heels wake me from my reverie.

"Good morning, rat."

"Whoa! You look so pretty today!"

"I don't know if I should hit you with my bag for sounding so surprised!" I retort.

"No, no." She laughs. "Idiot. It's just that…I dunno. Your face looks like…"

"Someone who just got fucked?"

A silence falls over us before we both burst out laughing.

"You're so dirty…and so lucky."

"It's not like you can complain. Your new fling looks pretty good."

"Shut up, shut up. I don't want to get my hopes up yet, Miri."

She should. Within a year, he's going to ask her to marry her in one of the most romantic proposals in history. And her wedding will be beautiful.

"I'm going to get the Friday churros. It's my turn. How do you want your coffee?" she says on the way back to her desk, where she left her purse.

"I don't want any, thank you. I'll pass on churros today."

"Are you on a diet or what?" She raises one eyebrow.

"The term 'diet' gives me goose bumps even where the sun don't shine… I don't know if I'm making myself clear."

"Yeah, yeah…but you saying no to coffee and churros on Friday…"

"It's just that Tristan set up a surprise for me, and I'm nervous."

"A surprise? And you think you know what it is?"

"Yes." I turn back to the wall again with my arms crossed over my chest.

"If it's very romantic, don't say anything to me. I get all sprung about love, and then everything is a letdown."

"Well, I'm keeping my mouth shut. Even though it sounds like we're gonna go ho it up."

"That's my little slut."

I furrow my brow, not because of the filthy language but because an idea popped into my head while I was looking at the wall. I don't say goodbye when I stride toward my office; I need to check the folder with the topics we're preparing for the publication. When Rita comes back with the churros and coffee for everyone, I've already summoned Eva to my office, and between the two of us, we've dismantled the whole issue and rebuilt it.

"Girls." I poke my head in the door. "Could you eat your churros in the meeting room? We have a few changes."

"Fuck off."

I don't know who said it, because it felt like they all said it at the same time. And even if they didn't, I know they're thinking it.

Operation Bikini. Instructions: Put on a bikini.

All the reasons you shouldn't go on a
diet or exercise more or detox.
(Basically...you're already a goddess, girl.)

It's three years ago, and the body positive movement will be all over this special. I know. Soon, this will be much more common, but you never know whether companies are doing it because they genuinely want change or if they're just jumping on a bandwagon because they think it'll improve their bottom line.

The changes keep me busy all morning. I don't get to write that much anymore, besides product reviews or opinion columns and summer or end-of-year specials. But everyone agrees when I suggest they leave it to me. Deep down, I'm a journalist, and a journalist who loves to write. Writing and giving the world a little seed that maybe, if we're lucky, can sprout into something good.

So between calls to psychologists and nutritionists who specialize in eating disorders and reviewing brands that have expanded their size ranges and searching for examples of famous women with "bikini bodies" from size zero to thirty, the morning flies by. The two interns lending me a hand are pumped, and so am I. I guess reliving lets you highlight things you missed the first time. Three o'clock sneaks up on me and catches me completely off guard.

"Miranda...can you wait in your office for a minute? You have a visitor. It's personal. He's on his way there."

I smile as I stack papers on my desk and egg the interns on to go home. "Go on, girls, it's the end of the week, and trouble won't make itself."

I'm so excited I'd be happy to let them raid the beauty closet, but it would be like giving a kid sugar at bedtime. Like putting Mentos in a bottle of Coke. Like locking me in Chanel for the night. Like...

I forget all about the similes when I see Ivan. I wasn't prepared. I wasn't, and neither was anybody else, but everyone here seems to be used to it. That or they've gone temporarily blind and they can't see that he's wearing leggings. Zebra-print Lycra leggings. A studded belt. A shirt that (thank the gods worshipped in this world and others) covers the bulge of his anaconda. He has a scarf wrapped over his forehead like a turban. His hair looks like he stuck his finger in a socket but even more exaggerated. Like it's sticking up all over the place...but with bangs. He has bangs... He's the AliExpress version of one of the members of Europe in the mid-eighties.

"What?" he blurts out as soon as he comes into my office.

"The universe has a terrifying sense of humor."

"Are you back on that change of look as cosmic readjustment bullshit?"

I cover my mouth and crack up while I nod.

"Miranda, I don't know how to make this any more clear. I've always been like this."

"Like this" goes along with a sweep of his body from head to chest.

"Okay, okay. But today is just too much. They weren't even this eighties in the actual eighties."

He takes my criticism like a champ and shoves my bag at me.

"Take it. I'm not yelling 'surprise' or anything because...of course, you already know everything, right?"

"Sometimes I get the feeling that, even though I proved it with the Thalia thing, you still don't believe me."

"I believe you, Miranda, it's just easier to think you've got a screw loose in there." He points at my head. "But...I'm taking a total leap of faith. Because I'm your faithful squire, my queen. If you tell me you're time traveling..."

"Don't you think it's weird that you only remember this whole thing when you see me?"

"I don't know if I remember or I don't remember. I have a life, you know? I don't go around all day thinking about your shit."

"Okay." I let it be. I'm too happy to let this bug me. "Tristan booked a bubble hotel this weekend in a village near Toledo."

Ivan narrows his eyes at me.

"And you really don't know the numbers for the Christmas lottery?"

"We already talked about that."

"Well, we talked about the lotto."

"I'm going to do you another favor, now that I think about it: get your passport renewed. This winter, you're going to Colombia for work, and you're gonna end up stranded at the airport on the way back until they sort you out at the embassy. I already told you the thing about buying toilet paper in 2020."

"If any of this shit actually happens to me, it's your fault. You're jinxing me."

"You're the one jinxing yourself, you big dumb box of rocks. Actually, rocks are smarter." I jump back to dodge the punch he tries to land on my arm. "He's picking me up soon, right?"

"Yes, but we have time to grab a beer. He just messaged me saying that he's leaving work and he still has to run home to pick up his suitcase and get the rental car."

"You guys are friends now?"

"You introduced us one afternoon." He raises an eyebrow. "You don't remember that? I mean...you should know that, right?"

"Yes. Yes...but sometimes things change."

"Are you changing things?"

"It's impossible to live everything exactly the same way I did the first time, but on top of that...let's just say I insisted on doing it my way a few times."

"Ah, so that's why you're asking me, in case you created some awful butterfly effect and now we hate each other."

"If everything goes well and nothing changes, I'm giving you a heads-up that you're not exactly going to be besties."

"Don't we start getting along better over time?" he asks worriedly.

"I mean…not really. You get along, but you're not friends. You always tell me that he seems musty, very dry. You use the elegant excuse that 'he's very northern and I'm very Mediterranean,' but the truth is you never quite get the hang of his sense of humor, as much as I keep telling you he's the love of my life."

His face twitches… The kind of subtle shift only your best friend, who knows you better than you know yourself, would notice.

"What was that face?"

"Nothing."

"No, not nothing. What was that face?"

"An involuntary tic, probably."

I bite my lip and hold his gaze. We're locked in a staring contest.

"Tell me…" I groan.

He sucks his teeth and rests his fists on those hips wrapped in such tight leggings.

"He's not the love of your life, not even close."

I open my mouth to answer, but he puts his palm between us to force me to let him keep talking.

"I'm not denying how important Tristan is in your life, but, Miranda… he's not the love of your life."

"Why? Do you know something I don't?"

"Yes," he says and nods confidently, going back to his Power Ranger stance. "There's no single man destined to be in anyone's lives, and if there were, which there isn't, yours isn't Tristan. Period. Let's go get a beer at Dori's. I saw her on my way in, and she said they're putting out torrezno tapas."

"So I usually let myself be seen with you looking like that?"

"Yes. I just don't understand how I let myself be seen with an idiot like you."

Touché.

I don't think much about what Ivan said. Much or at all, actually. Because we barely have time to chug a beer and bolt down some bacon before Tristan shows up with the car. And of course, like all people dickmatized to an embarrassing level, nothing can rain on that adolescent parade.

I pretend to be surprised, but I guess I wasn't as believable as in the original version, because Tristan asks me over and over whether Ivan told me or whether he unknowingly gave it away over the last few days. I say no to everything and amp up my happiness a little, which doesn't really work either, because I'm the kind of person who instinctively responds with suspicion when someone surprises me. I don't know why. I don't know if it's because I don't like surprises that much or because I don't know how to react. I feel awkward. I feel ungrateful. I don't know.

But I must have done it right this time, because Tristan is smiling in that way that makes me so crazy, showing off those beautiful teeth. I would sacrifice myself as an offering to be eaten.

The bubble hotel was just a few kilometers from a tiny village in Toledo that took us more than an hour to get to from central Madrid and was made up of a main building, a tiny spa, a lounge and the reception, and a few areas delineated by fences made of reeds and bushes that preserved the privacy between one and the other. In each plot, there's a "building" in the form of a bubble, translucent (except in some areas, like the shower and the toilet) so we'll be able to gaze up at an amazingly clear sky full of stars tonight.

See how love and all that romantic stuff make us a little embarrassing sometimes? Why do we like looking at the stars so much when we're in love? Especially when it's so hard in big cities, with all the light pollution stuff. Couldn't we have been obsessed with something simpler? For example, watching the oven cook a tray of cannelloni.

Don't listen to me. That's the cynical Miranda talking, the one who's forgotten the vibration bodies in love emit. It's the kind that doesn't give in to external shame, that this "me" is trying to project onto her, but I'm a goner: I don't care anymore...again.

After we check in and one of the staff members explains how the hotel works, we settle into our bubble, and this, that little sentence, seems like a beautiful metaphor for that time in our relationship.

That year, Tristan and I were (are) in the middle of climbing Everest, and I think the lack of oxygen made us happier than either of us had ever been. I don't remember ever having been happier, not even in my most innocent childhood, when I believed my dad's stories about ancient flying carpets or songs that gave you powers if you could memorize them. So this bubble, this little "moon," as the hotel calls each of its circular and panoramic "rooms," is like a memory you treasure greedily and go back to when you have doubts or when the floor is too hard to go barefoot. When it becomes obvious that sometimes life is a bedazzled turd.

Tristan catches me off guard, circling his arms around my waist from behind, and I'm caught off guard because he was never that into cuddling. This is the same man who will spoon you in bed, especially before he gets up in the morning, or wrap his arm around your waist walking down the street or grab your hand for a little while, but he still thinks kissing in public is pretty much as bad as graffiti.

I'm exaggerating, but I think you get the idea.

"What are you thinking about? Oof...that's such a girly thing for me to say," he murmurs almost to himself.

"I didn't know questions had a gender."

He laughs.

"Touché. What are you thinking about?"

I'm thinking about how we'll make love here tonight, and I can't imagine a better place. How we're going to fill the bath, and when we both climb in, we'll make the water slosh out, but we'll think it's hilarious. How you're going to spend a while going back and forth to the door to make sure it's closed because they told us that if not, the bubble can deflate, and I'm going to love you a little more every time you do it for that sometimes obsessive-compulsive mania you imbue certain tasks with.

"Nothing. Just wondering what the plan is."

"Hmm, let's see..." His nose nuzzles my hair for a few seconds, almost covertly. Tristan is still Tristan...and he still has the same tics. "Tonight, they're going to bring us some dinner and a bottle of wine and...we can try to see something with the spyglass..."

"Telescope..."

"Telescope. And take a bath."

"And fuck."

"Dude...sometimes I can't help but wonder if you escaped from treatment for sex addiction."

I crack up. It's already pretty obvious that I'm a...um...very sexual woman. Or at least I was. It seems normal to me. I mean...I think anything is normal: having a lot of, a little, or no sexual appetite. But somehow, it surprises him. One night, when the only thing that brought us together was meeting up to fuck and drink wine, back at the dawn of our relationship, he told me that he had only met one woman with as voracious an appetite as me. It didn't seem right or wrong to me, just weird. Now I know that that hunger can fade a little over time, but I still can't figure out if that's good or bad. Whether it's calmness or apathy.

"What about tomorrow?" I ask.

And it's a masochistic question, because tomorrow will be an incredible day, but I won't be here, because ever since this started, I always wake up a few jumps away from the night before. And I want to relive these plans.

"Well, the sun will definitely wake us up." I can't see him, but I know he's making a face. He likes to sleep. "They'll bring us breakfast...at ten. Once we're done and we freshen up a bit, we can go take a walk. Just a short one...maybe into the village. Have lunch there. Get a few beers on some sunny patio."

"I like that plan."

"In the afternoon, we can go to the...what did they call it?"

"Call what?"

"The...the pool you float in."

How could I not fall in love with him? I've always liked men who are a little clumsy romantically.

"The floatarium."

"So we'll go float. And you can't fuck in the floatarium, so don't get any ideas."

I stroke his strong hands and his long fingers and laugh.

"I think I can control myself," I retort.

"But at night, we can do it again, if you let me get enough sustenance."

I turn around. I don't have to stand on tiptoes to kiss him; he's taller than me, but the height difference isn't that big, and I like that. Even though before him, I loved really tall guys. Even though my dream dude would be like six five. Even though I used to get hung up on dudes who were nothing like him. It's like nothing I liked before matters anymore. At least not now.

"You know what?" I say to him. "If someone had told me when I met you that you were such a sweet guy...I wouldn't have believed it."

"I'm sweet when the time is right, yeah?"

"A guy from the north."

"Don't stereotype." He grabs my ass, drawing me into him. "Our home-land can leave a mark, but…is it really that deep?"

"You keep surprising me with this stuff."

"What stuff?"

"I don't know, you're hugging me. Kissing me. Holding my hand. It still seems weird to me."

He furrows his brow.

"But is that good or bad?"

"I don't know. But it makes me throb."

17

~~

IT'S AMAZING, INCREDIBLE, AND THE FUCKING BEST

TRISTAN

This is what happens when you think too much, I'm warning you.

I hate light in the mornings. If I have to wake up early, fine, it is what it is. Sometimes it even helps. But if I have time to sleep in and a beam of light penetrates the room…sleep is over for me. A beam. One. So it's easy to imagine that with the nuclear bomb of sudden alertness that exploded in the room as soon as the sun started hinting at dawn, it's physically impossible to fall asleep again. I guess I could have put on the eye mask the hotel kindly left on the pillow, but…I just can't picture it on me. I've always had a hyperawareness of looking ridiculous even for stuff like this. Plus I don't think it'd be comfortable.

It crosses my mind a couple of times to wake up Miranda, who's breathing open-mouthed next to me with an expression that makes me laugh. I guess this is what relationships are all about, isn't it? The same girl can impress you, excite you, fill you with admiration, laughter, or fear of abandonment. The latter shouldn't be there, but I'm working on it. This is my first long-term relationship, and I still have to struggle, often, with the Tristan who didn't owe anyone anything and who hoped that one day, his time would come…the way it looks in the movies, not real life.

Love isn't anticlimactic, but it's like a wave that tumbles you around like a washing machine and makes you swallow water. It's good, it's not painful, it's not suffocating, it doesn't create anxiety or bad thoughts, but it is demanding. It demands from you. It demands from your partner. It demands.

And that's what being in love is about, right? I'm asking. This is my first love story, presumably the only one, the ultimate one, the one that will last. I fell in love a long time ago, a really long time, with a girl with straight, golden hair who drove me nuts and smelled like vanilla. I wore two earrings in my left ear, and she wore supertight pants. She had a tight little butt that my friends joked I could fit in one hand. I never understood why that was a good thing. But I fell in love, even though later I didn't want her anymore. I mean…that crush didn't translate into anything lasting. We would make out in parks, and we'd hide from her parents and mine, and we'd pilfer any free moment to sneak off to bed. Ah, those teenage hormones…

Miranda has never been comparable to anything, much less to that first love. She came in like a cyclone, turned everything upside down, and burrowed in deep down, where I couldn't kick her out. That's how it happens, isn't it? First, it settles in your head and in your stomach like a parasite. It's in every conversation, whether you talk about it or not. You think about her all the time. You want to spend any minute you can scrape together with her. And then, when you take it in, when you chew on it, when you let it set foot inside the circle of intimacy you defend from others, this comes along. Love. Trust. Laughter. The importance of imperfection. The admiration. The plans.

And I can't deny it even to myself: whether it scares me or not, I'm making plans. At least I am mentally, even if I don't share them with anyone. It's time. It's the right person. It's her.

Recently, on a quick trip back to Vigo, on one of those typical ragers where you end up with a kebab in one hand watching the sunrise, a friend told me that love is when you don't feel suffocated by the idea that every-thing you're going to do, you're going to do with her. I don't agree. I think that seems... I don't know. It's too reductionist. I'm not going to do every single thing in my life with her, but that doesn't mean I don't love her. Love doesn't chain you down; it doesn't mean your skin morphs and bonds you to each other like conjoined twins. And that's what I like most about Miranda: there's a piece of life she doesn't want us to share, that is our own, each of us. But like all the things we love most about each other, I know this is one of the reasons we might break up someday.

It's like extreme sports, right? If something can kill you but doesn't, it becomes special. We are special. It could go well, or at the last moment, the parachute could decide not to open.

I should stop. Get up, go out on the little patio, do some stretches. Get out of this warm bed that smells like her and where, since I can't sleep, I can't stop thinking. Thinking is overrated. Thinking complicates things and rushes them. I miss smoking; then I'd have an excuse to go out and stop the wheel from spinning.

The man who thought "relationships work best when they're short term" is thinking about the future. That must be what they mean when they say that you "mature" after thirty. When I was thirty, I bought an apartment in Vigo, and I felt like I was adulting. If you don't feel grown up with a mortgage, the only other option is being diagnosed with high blood pressure.

So I bought an apartment...and what good has it done me? My three-bedroom apartment in Vigo is now inhabited by a group of architects who pay the rent like clockwork every month, and I use it to cover the mortgage. And in the meantime, I live in Madrid, where drivers have never heard of a turn signal and everything is more expensive.

The goal was to beef up my experience with the firm and come back to the office in Vigo as a partner in a few years. Until I met Miranda, of course. Until I fell in love. I want to go back, but I know it's impossible to tear Miranda away from Madrid.

I miss the sea, the pace of life I had, my friends, the Tristan I am there, but Miranda makes up for everything. I look at her next to me, clutching her pillow. Her mouth is closed now, and her nose is crinkled with sleep. If I have to choose, I choose her. Her over me...at the risk of that destroying us too.

I wonder if you have to be old to be able to feel things as intensely as they sound in love songs. Maybe you just have to be in love to understand them.

So...well, I've always been an easygoing guy. If you have to change plans, change them. There are things that worry me, of course, like those days when she's even weirder than normal. It's not just that she's quirky, but sometimes she gives the impression that there's such a full and complete universe inside her head that it's hard for her to get out into the real world. But I'm not too worried about it either...maybe just for when I introduce her to the family. Well, first we'll move in together, and then I'll introduce her to my parents. Will she ever want to get married? I don't really care. And we'll talk about the rest...whether we want to keep living in the center, how long to wait before we consider becoming parents... Did I just think the word "parents"?

I push the quilt aside and jump out of bed to go wash my face. On the way back, I make as much noise as I can, trying to wake her up, but she's still curled up peacefully.

"Miranda..." I sit down by her side and stroke her temple.

"Mmm..."

Last night, she was resisting sleep like I've never seen anyone resist it. My eyelids were getting so heavy, but she wouldn't quit pacing around the room, like she was trying to scare off sleep.

She was telling me things about the stars, downloading apps on her phone to tell them apart, humming, trying to hold my hand. When she finally lay down, she seemed really sad. And I thought of the sadness that fills you when you realize you're living a moment that is so happy it's ephemeral.

See? You have to take off your armor to understand song lyrics.

"Miranda," I insist, "the sun's rising."

"Great," she mumbles, more asleep than awake.

"Seriously, it's beautiful."

"So take a picture."

I laugh. This girl is nuts. Why didn't I run in the opposite direction when I had the chance? Oh, right, I did. But I came back.

"Miranda…you're really gonna miss out on seeing the sunrise from a giant bubble?"

Something in those words seems to jiggle her conscience (which is not conscious), and she opens one eye, like the dragon sleeping on the dwarves' gold in *The Hobbit*.

"What did you say?"

"Look…" I point in front of us.

The bubbles are oriented so that the sun rises behind us and impedes our sleep as little as possible, but the dawn is tinging the sky with some fabulous colors. From the deep blue of the night, it turned into indigo a while ago, the color I woke up to. Then to mauve. And later lavender. Now that color is fading into a delicate orange that is sure to bring a soft yellow with it. I admit, I woke her up so I could stop thinking, but it would be a bummer for her to miss this show. It's one of the reasons I brought her.

Miranda sits up, propping herself on one elbow. One of her boobs has escaped from her nightgown. It would be more complicated for it to stay in with so little fabric. This girl's underwear and pajamas are like costumes for Toulouse-Lautrec's *Moulin Rouge*.

She looks at me again. She has a little spit dried on the corner of her lips, and she has crazy bedhead. I can't imagine a less romantic vision, but it reminds me again that love is made up of many more layers than what we see in movies. I adore her. Does she know?

Yesterday, she told me it surprised her when I was affectionate with her. And I wouldn't want to have things left unsaid. I know how I am, how I can be a bit harsh, especially for someone as completely over-the-top as Miranda, who was born with a fucking speaker on her chest that plays songs that make you want to dance. She is the queen of excess. And I'm the king of quiet enjoyment. Maybe I should make a little effort…a little more, to verbalize what I take for granted. I don't want to look like I don't care, even though…that's who she fell in love with, right?

"Miri…" I smile at her. "Your nipple…"

She adjusts her nightgown without looking at me, pushes her hair out of her face, and swipes the back of her hand over her mouth while she studies everything around her in amazement, as if it were the first time she's seen it.

"It's beautiful, eh?" I repeat.

"It's not beautiful…it's amazing!"

When she looks at me, her eyes are shining. Jesus…so intense.

"It's pretty, but…" I try to calm her down.

"No, it's not beautiful, Tristan. It's…amazing! It's incredible! It's the fucking best!"

I can't dodge her leaping onto me and plastering me to the mattress and kissing me passionately on the mouth.

I would have preferred us to brush our teeth first…but…what the hell?

She's right. Enough thinking. It's amazing, incredible, and the fucking best.

18

~~

"EVEN IF YOU'RE LIVING IT TWICE"

MIRANDA

"That was the most incredible sunrise I've ever seen in my life, you know? Tops everything. Lying in this bed with the sky above me, nothing but the sky..."

"And a layer of PVC."

In the chair opposite my table, Ivan is rolling his eyes. I'm so nervous, so excited, so content that I throw a box of paper clips at him. I don't know why.

"Ouch!" he complains.

"Shut it. I'm telling you we had nothing but the sky above us. Can you picture it? All those colors...the sky turned into a spectacular gradient. The birds fluttering around over our room chirping. And I was there, Ivan. I was there, not in another time jump. It's like...like I wanted it so much that I could control where I woke up. Can you imagine if I controlled where I woke up?"

"You control it?"

"No. I don't think so. Today, I woke up on a random workday...but imagine it! And then the thing is the whole day was...was even more incredible than I remembered. You have to go. It's a super special place."

"Well, I don't have anyone who wants to go with me..."

"Don't worry, this isn't your year, but…"

"Shut up! You're gonna jinx me!"

"The floatarium is super romantic." I get back on track. "Seriously. It's a tiny, covered pool, and you bob around like a cork. And the ceiling is… it's painted black, and it has LED lights in it and… I don't know. You're both just sitting there in silence. Holding hands. Cuddling. I swear I never remember Tristan being so touchy-feely."

"Something must have made you get with him," he says with the face of someone who's finding this all a little too mushy.

"Don't you think how hot he is would be enough?"

"You want the truth? No. And I'm pretty surprised you think so."

"No, not really. But you wouldn't kick him out of bed for eating crackers, right? He's so cute."

"If that's your type…" He's fidgeting with the box of paper clips.

"What type? The hottest ones with a mouth like a bao bun?"

"Seriously, Miranda, I really miss my best friend, the one who said romantic love is a social construct. Have you seen her anywhere? If you see her, tell her to hold on, I'll rescue her."

"You're a dumbass. I was saying that because…because…because I wasn't in love."

"Love is a pandemic," he quips.

"Not the pandemic you should be worried about, sweetie."

"Stop saying that, it scares me!"

"Ivan…it was incredible. And that night, we wrapped ourselves in a blanket and took a bottle of wine out on the little patio, stargazing, and…" I shrug, take a deep breath, and clasp my chest. I almost feel like my lungs aren't big enough for everything I need to breathe in. "And we laughed so much…"

"You laughed while you were stargazing? Look, girl, you two are weird as fuck."

"Yes. Because we were there, with our wine, in the dark, wrapped in a blanket, trying to find the Big Dipper…"

"You're both dopey as hell," he mutters.

"Suddenly…a shooting star flew by!"

"If I ever fall in love, slit my throat with a broken bottle."

"Listen to me!"

"A shooting star went by. And you made a wish. Okay. So what?"

"Well, so…suddenly he threw out that he thought it was a UFO, that he saw one the summer he turned eighteen. But he was so convinced, Ivan! And I couldn't stop laughing. He's such a cutie!"

"Miranda, seriously…kill me. You're so sweet, I'm gonna be diabetic by the time I leave this office."

I cross my arms, feeling abandoned. Why is it the only person I confided in about everything I'm going through is incapable of empathizing with what I'm feeling? If I had known, I wouldn't have hidden my laughter when I saw him come in with blond streaks, electric-blue contact lenses, and waxed eyebrows. Waxed to oblivion. Not to mention what he must be spending on tanning beds in this reality.

"Listen, Ivan, if I'm boring you…"

He sucks his teeth, rolls his eyes, slaps both armrests, and stands up.

"Miranda, for God's sake…you're my best friend. If I find you boring, I'm fucked."

"I don't know what's going on with you."

"What's going on is that my best friend once told me that she didn't recognize my look, that she's time traveling, and that she's falling back in love with a dude who, apparently, in a few years is going to destroy her heart. So maybe you can understand my reservations."

"Didn't we agree you were going to give me the benefit of the doubt?"

"And I am! But…" He shakes his hands, trying to find the words. "It's just that…I don't think…"

"You don't think what?"

"Well, if you're time traveling, you fucking crazy bitch, I don't think the goal should be falling back in love."

"So then what?"

"Well, I don't know. You're probably supposed to learn something, right? Or are you just gonna let history repeat itself?"

"I'm not repeating it. I'm living it with…with more emotion this time. More…attention. That's it. Attention. And that way, when the problems come, I can solve them."

He raises one eyebrow.

"Seriously?" he asks sarcastically.

"Yes. Of course. You said it yourself, right? If this is happening to me, there must be a reason for it."

"To learn something," he points out, thrusting his finger at me.

"To fix it. So that it doesn't end on that day in that café on Calle de Fuencarral."

"Listen, have you ever stopped to think about why you broke up?"

"Of course." No, no, I haven't. Of course I haven't. Why the fuck would I want to do that?

"Those two people…they're you. There's not some big thing that's going to change either of you, Miranda. It's just…it's time. Time made you into those two people!"

"All couples have problems, but I can avoid them."

"If you jump to the key days, right?"

"Well, yeah. But I trust that…"

"Miri…when you two broke up, did you like the relationship you had?"

"Yes," I blurt out without thinking.

"No buts?"

"It's a relationship, Ivan. There are buts, but it's not like we can aspire to perfection, you know?"

"No. I don't know." He sighs sadly.

The silence hovers over us. I don't like arguing with Ivan, but I don't understand why he's being such a hard-ass. He's my best friend. He's my confidant. Besides my dad, he's the person I trust most in the world. Finally, Ivan's face softens, and he comes closer.

"Miri, I don't want to be a party pooper."

"So don't be!" I smile at him.

"But let me say one thing…one last thing… Miri, listen to me," he insists, rolling his eyes again.

"Spit it out!"

"You know that thing about how we can't make everyone like us."

"Yes. I work at a women's magazine where we're constantly railing against the idea that we should even try."

"And that's very admirable, but…Miranda, when someone dumps you…maybe it's because it's for the best. And you have to pay attention to how they actually dump you, because sometimes we get hurt trying to make it work. You only live once, Miranda. You only live once, even if you're living it twice."

19

~~~

AND FOR US
TO PULL IT OFF

Tristan has never been very good at communicating when it comes to feelings, but he's really good about sending photos. All kinds of photos. I still have a folder hidden in my iPhone of some pretty…explicit ones. I swear he has the most beautiful penis I've ever seen, and nothing will ever change my mind.

When Ivan leaves, I go into the kitchen to wash our coffee mugs. When I get back, I collapse into my chair, and just as I'm starting to flip through my planner, searching for what's special about today or how I can make the most of waking up today, my phone screen lights up with a message from Tristan.

It's a selfie. He's sitting in the office he shares with three other colleagues. His tie is loose, his hair is a little disheveled, and the dark bags under his eyes are impossible to miss.

TRISTAN:

I don't think I'm ever gonna get out of here. The clock isn't moving.
How are you doing?

It's 3:30 in the afternoon, that difficult time…

I flip my camera into selfie mode and study myself before I take a photo. I look fine. My eyeliner is still in place. My hair, in messy waves, too. The red lipstick is a little dry, but nothing I can't fix by licking my lips. My eyelashes are on fleek. I smile and take the picture.

MIRANDA:
Not to be a dick, but my day is flying by.
Ivan came to see me after lunch and I have a ton of work.

He's online when I send it, but he still takes a few seconds, more than a few actually, to answer:

TRISTAN:
So pretty.
I'm going to have to send a résumé to your magazine to see if the days are magic there.
Should I pick you up when we're done?
I need a hug.

I glance at my planner again. I have a video call with the head of a brand who wants to contract an advertorial and needs us to finalize some details before we go over the final budget. I think I remember that whole thing being a huge pain in the ass.

MIRANDA:
I have a video conference at 6:45 and I think it might take a while.

TRISTAN:
How long?
It'll take me 15 minutes to get to your office from mine.

MIRANDA:

I'm scared to say yes in case it ends up taking forever.

TRISTAN:

If it takes a long time, I'll wait for you at Dori's having a beer

Actually it's looking like I'll need more than a quick one

after today...

MIRANDA:

Okay. Are we sleeping at my house after?

TRISTAN:

We'll see.

My need to be meticulous with time and have everything organized. His need to go with the flow. It crosses my mind that we've always been very different, and that idea makes a breeze whip around my office.

The cover shoot was kind of a disaster. We don't know how it could've happened. It was a photographer we trusted, but when we saw the photos, the lighting is hideous... We call an urgent meeting to decide if we should reshoot the whole thing, even though it would be so complicated to find a time when all three actresses on the cover can come in again or if it can be fixed in postproduction.

Plus the digital team are up in arms because I've vetoed some content that's always a big hit with certain recurring advertisers. And I feel like a witch for standing my ground about saying no. Marisol delegates certain responsibilities to me, and that's great because it shows professional growth and confidence in how I do things, but...it's hard. The truth is I'm not a writer anymore, so for a while now, ever since I was promoted to deputy editor, there's been some distance between my colleagues and me. It's normal. It's not like they're suddenly avoiding me or whispering behind my back; it's just that…well, you don't let off steam with the deputy editor in the kitchen, clutching your coffee, saying you're sick of how many hours you invest in your professional life.

These executive decisions don't make my relationships any easier, but at least I have the support of Eva, the editor in chief, and Cris and Rita, who, as the directors of beauty and fashion, always have my back.

We just got the sales numbers for last month, and…they're not good. And I know that curve is only going to get worse and that within two years, the pandemic will decimate us. I won't let my anxiety make me take a few girls aside and recommend they start sending their résumé around. It would cause panic…

I shut myself in the beauty closet, trying to find a moment of calm, but they find me and ask me to go to the "wardrobe" because Marisol has an event and she wants my opinion about what they've lent her. The look is a disaster, but we fix it, taking off layers and adding a few accessories. It's not like we have a huge selection, but we can make a few emergency fixes.

They're gonna give me a heart attack if they don't let me have a few seconds to myself.

The video call is delayed. The client asks me to start at 7:15 and…of course, the client's always right. As I wait, I scroll through the tweets that are scheduled for the week. Yesterday, apparently, was the night we were a trending topic…and not the good kind.

My phone saves me from the urge to scream the community manager's name from my office so she can explain to me what the hell was going through her head when she decided to tweet a joke about lactation to sneak in a collaboration with a yogurt brand. Sometimes I think the competition is paying her.

TRISTAN:

How's it going?

MIRANDA:

I'm half an hour behind...at least.

TRISTAN:

No worries, I'll wait for you. I'm here.

MIRANDA:

I'm going to get out super late. Why don't you go to my place and wait for me there?

TRISTAN:

What keys will I use to get in?

MIRANDA:

Mine. Come up for a second and I'll give them to you.

TRISTAN:

Nah, I have time.

I just ordered a drink.

Not a quick one. A double.

MIRANDA:

Tough day.

TRISTAN:

Is that a question or a statement?

MIRANDA:

A statement.

TRISTAN:

You can say that again. And I still need that hug.

It's bugging me that I can't remember this day. Why am I reliving this? Is it because it's important for him that we see each other today? Is it because I failed in his day and now I'm being offered the opportunity to fix it?

"Miranda..." Marisol appears in my doorway.

She looks gorgeous. I haven't seen her in a long time; it made me happy to spend a little time with her in the wardrobe, even if it was a crisis. Well...these time jumps are like life. Marisol is always running around a million miles a minute, and there are weeks when we don't see each other much or at all.

"Talk to me, boss." I smile.

"You're gorgeous, you know that, but go home soon. Stress takes a toll over the years, and one day, you'll wake up wrinkled like a raisin."

"I dunno about wrinkles, but gray hairs..."

She scrutinizes my head from where she is, but I waggle my finger at her.

"Not there."

"Ah!" She laughs. "Filthy."

"Have a good time."

"I'm not going to have a good time, but I'm going to kill it for the magazine."

"That's my Marisol."

When she leaves, her heels tap out the rhythm of the call coming into my computer. Finally...

"Good evening, Myriam. How are you?"

"Good evening, Miranda, sorry for the delay."

No problem... I'm used to it...

I leave the magazine at 9:15. Tristan already left over an hour ago and went home. And I don't blame him. I asked him if he wanted me to go by his house so we could go out, but he told me that he felt like he had been hit by a truck he was so exhausted. He wasn't angry. I know him. He's just tired.

He's not angry...right?

Today I wore a plaid shirtdress combined with flat boots made for walking, so I'm walking home. The late-spring breeze is tousling my hair in the side streets, and my mind is filled with frivolous stuff, like how I love that the days are getting longer and stretching into the night. That or how I don't understand how a city like Madrid, all exhaust, construction work, and crowds, can still smell like this in spring. Also how useful my habit of laying my clothes out ready for the next day has been in this "time travel" lark. My present self or past self, I don't know what to call it, makes my mornings so much easier.

When will it end?

Will "she" (me) be aware that I've gone through all this, or will she take it for granted that she lived the day the normal way I did in the original thread? Will she think she's going crazy? And what if...

I stop dead in the middle of the sidewalk. I don't know what unleashed this torrent of reflections all of a sudden, like a flood, pouring over me. It's a chaos of sounds, consonants, and exclamations, with no beginning or end, no rhyme or reason, gripping my chest. They are questions, even if they sound like exclamations, even though they don't have question marks with them. They're screaming fears, like a friend's WhatsApp written in all caps.

Stop. Miranda. Stop.

This doesn't make sense. It doesn't.

But if it doesn't and it's still happening, I have to do something. Beyond just putting out fires at the magazine. Beyond telling Ivan how I've fallen back in love. Beyond...today, for example.

Today.

I turn around and pick up the skirt of my dress, the sound of a few horns warning me the walking signal has turned red.

If he's surprised to see me at his door, he doesn't say anything. He just gives a restrained smile.

"Hi." He's wearing jeans and a speckled blue shirt. He looks great even though he's exhausted. "Come in."

"No, no." I shake my head. I ran up the four flights of stairs, and I'm out of breath.

"What do you mean, no?" He furrows his brow.

"I just came to give you that hug." I take a deep breath. "You're tired. And you had a bad day. And I owe you a hug, and…well…it's just a hop and a skip from the office."

He raises one eyebrow.

"You came here just to give me a hug?"

"Yes. And then I'm leaving."

I throw myself into his arms and bury my nose in his neck. The relief is immediate. The flood of doubts, fears, and worries is losing water.

Once, a prestigious perfume house invited us to a presentation. It was fun and interesting to learn more about all the notes that make up a perfume, like a symphony. They talked to us about how they sometimes try to give an olfactory interpretation of a moment, a memory, or a story. When I got home, out of curiosity, I looked up what Tristan's is composed of. Apparently it was trying to evoke the image of a night of an intense blue color. Intensity, mystery…all the stuff perfumers says about their "brews."

Ever since then, when I hug Tristan, I'm immediately plunged into a deep blue color, a pool of dense, fresh paint, that leaves me feeling hungry.

The hug is intense, and it feels like a goodbye, which gives me mixed feelings: the relief of being able to hold him and the sorrow of knowing he'll want me to stop. Actually, we had pretty much stopped when he dumped me. We didn't hug. We didn't kiss. We didn't cuddle in bed after we made love. We didn't even make love anymore.

"What's going on?" he whispers into my neck, landing a distracted kiss there.

"Tristan…let's never stop hugging, okay? Or kissing."

"Miri, I'm not mad that you left work late. Your work is important to you, and I understand that."

"But you are too."

"Miri…" He pulls back and forces me out of my hiding place in the curve of his neck and looks into my eyes. "I'm not mad, honestly. It's not a competition."

He raises his eyebrows, underlining his words. I nod, even though I don't know what exactly I'm saying yes to.

"Promise me," I repeat, like I didn't hear a word he said.

"Promise what?" he asks patiently.

"That we won't stop hugging each other. That when we start to forget, we'll make ourselves remember how good a hug can make you feel."

He laughs, and now it's his turn to nod. This guy isn't very into promises. He's firm. He's silent. He's honest. But words are not his thing. And I can see how uncomfortable he is right now not being able to say those two simple words: "I promise." So I decide to do what I always do and clear the air.

"Tristan, you have really straight eyebrows, you know that?"

A silent laugh escapes him, more of a puff from his nose, and he grabs my arm, like he's scared I'm going to run off down the stairs, while he takes his jacket off a hook. It's a light jacket, navy blue.

"Where are you going?" I ask.

"Don't you think it's weird that I'm in street clothes and not house clothes?"

I look at his jeans. Oh, right…duh.

"I was heading over to your house," he says, smiling. "I wanted to go by Lady Madonna first to pick up something for dinner and go see you. I needed this hug."

My expression must be full of laughter, because Tristan's smile spreads even wider.

"Thank—"

"Shut up," he says, coming a little closer and grabbing my other arm as well. "See? I wasn't angry, and we weren't going to miss our hug. I promise."

To hell with I love you. I just want him to promise. To promise me everything. And for us to pull it off.

20

I WISH I COULD SAY THE SAME

Tristan doesn't know how to be nervous. Some people bite their nails, chew their cuticles, play with their hair, or jiggle their leg. He shoves his hands in his pockets and hopes. Hopes that nobody will notice and, while you're at it, that it will pass. That's why I don't ask him if he's nervous or, actually, *why* he is, because I know him well enough to know he's trying to get away with it.

There's something kind of soothing about reliving things you did before you knew who you were. Today, I woke up thinking that if I could choose where to go on this temporal train, I would go much further back. Maybe to when I was fifteen. To all the doors I slammed in my dad's face because teenagers are the worst. Not to slam the door or cry because he bought the wrong conditioner but just to ask that pubescent girl what she wanted from life and not disappoint her. That's how I feel about this story. I don't want to disappoint the Miranda who fell asleep with her chest ripped open after Tristan told her he didn't want to be with her anymore. That Miranda who was broken enough to not shed a single tear or drop of blood.

Maybe that's why I don't care what I'm going to live through today. I provoked my own memory today, maybe actually the key to all this. What if I'm supposed to invent another ending? If you don't want to end up in the same place…you shouldn't walk the same path.

Let's speed things up. Let's force a memory. Let's live something we already lived outside its natural date.

It's a beautiful Sunday in June, and the forecast says it's not going to be too hot, and Tristan is here. I reserved a table for three in one of the restaurants on the edge of the Casa de Campo lake. So…Tristan is going to meet my father.

"He's really sweet," I say, looking at Tristan out of the corner of my eye while we wait to be taken to our table, because I think if he keeps shoving his hands into his pockets that hard, he's going to make a hole.

"I'm sure he is."

"He's not punctual, but he's very sweet."

"I think we're the ones who got here a little early."

"I'm surprised we didn't arrive yesterday considering how fast we were walking."

He laughs. Tristan walks too fast.

"Slow walkers should be illegal." He laughs.

"Put it on the agenda, Mr. Counselor. It would be good for us to comment on that later."

He gives me a discreet pat on the ass and then slings his arm around my shoulder. And that's the moment (pat included) that my father chooses to show up…behind us.

"Hey, hey, hey…you're gonna be reaching into the breadbasket with that hand."

Tristan's eyes are about to pop out of their sockets. The guy who has failed the subject of PDA since kindergarten, caught grabbing my ass. Caught by my father.

"Mr. García, it's a pleasure to meet you." He holds out his hand, pushing me away at the same time. "And please excuse the…display. It's not…

Well, it's just… Ha ha." He laughs with a more nervous guffaw than I've heard in a long time. "Just my luck. I swear I'm not even into PDA."

My father holds out his hand and laughs. He's nervous too.

"Well, that's terrible, Tristan. Life is very short."

"That's what your daughter says, Mr. García."

"Please, call me Isidro."

"Okay, Isidro."

They unclasp their hands, and both look at me. My brow is furrowed.

"What?" my father asks. "Why are you making that face?"

"Nothing. The sun was in my eyes."

They both look out the window, where a perfect and unseasonably warm sun is sparkling off the lake…but the glare is nowhere near my face. And I'm making that face because this is going exactly how it went the first time, even though back then, we lived it the next month.

"Are you okay?"

Tristan puts his hand on my back.

Essentially, I can change things like the how but not the fundamental of what. And that makes me think…

"Excuse me…" The waiter smiles at us. "If you'll follow me, I'll show you to your table."

When the food arrives, Tristan and my father are talking animatedly about my guy's work. I think it's the first time I've heard him verbalize something I always suspected. Maybe I should have paid more attention to these conversations in the past.

"I actually don't like being a lawyer, but I'm not sure I've ever had a clear vocation, so I wasn't going to sit at home waiting for the job of my dreams to come find me. All I knew was that I wanted to be successful. Most of my friends didn't even go to college. They got jobs straight out of high school, and everyone put a lot of faith in me... They were hoping I would be someone, and I...I don't know."

I don't like admitting it, but that comment makes me feel a kind of pity. A condescending pity. I don't want to feel superior for always having such a clear passion. It doesn't make sense. Is that what came between us?

"This seems to worry your daughter a lot."

Both of them start making fun of my expression again, so I immediately force myself to soften it.

"The only thing I'm worried about is the amount of meat they just brought out. Are you two nuts?"

As if I didn't know...it's not going to be too much. Not the meat, which is splayed pornographically in the middle of a tray, or the potatoes. Steak and fries. That's our style...Maybe that's why Tristan felt so at home. Give him good food, and you're already halfway there.

They talk about the shop, about the memories it holds. My father rambles a little as we eat, waving his glass of red wine and telling Tristan old family stories...all with my mother as the main character and the store as the backdrop. My father, trapped forever in a memory of my mother.

"Miranda never really liked her name, you know?" He points at me with the piece of meat speared on his fork.

"Tell him why you named me that. Let's see what he thinks..."

"My wife loved Mirinda... Do you remember Mirinda? It was an orange soda...like Fanta."

Tristan shoots me a side-eye, waiting for me to tell him it isn't true. I laugh.

"He's not joking," I pipe up.

"But her name is Miranda, not Mirinda."

"Of course, because we didn't want to fuck over the poor little thing's whole childhood."

I'm not giving him any points for that.

"It was that or Gwendolyne."

"Because of the Julio Iglesias song," I specify.

"If you had been named Gwendolyne...I don't know what nicknames I could've come up with."

"You would have called me Amparito because I would've changed my name. In Spain in the nineties, being called Gwendolyne would've been hard."

All three of us burst out laughing.

"Interesting..." my father says, focused on cutting up his meat. "Tristan and Miranda."

Two weird names.

"Two weird people." Tristan looks at me and smiles.

"I'm happy she found someone like her." My father nods to himself.

"Someone weird?" I ask him.

"No. Someone special."

Something makes my stomach clench harder than I'd like.

"Well...we'll have to start a list of weird names for our children to continue the tradition." Tristan drops the bomb and then shoves a potato the size of his fist in his mouth.

My father looks at him sidelong and jumps in to my aid.

"First, you have to make a list for the move, right? Or do you already live together and I just don't know?"

"True, true," Tristan agrees after he swallows. "To be discussed."

"Uh-oh. Better leave that discussion for when I'm not here," I say, trying to be funny.

It works. They both laugh.

After lunch, Tristan's phone chimes repetitively from his pocket, and after he glances at the screen, he makes a face and excuses himself to answer it.

"Work?"

"Worse. My mother."

I laugh at him with a slightly tense smile, but he doesn't sense the tension because he's already striding away, the phone pressed to his ear.

"You don't get along with his mother?"

"I don't know her." I shrug.

"Ah, you smiled like…"

My father tries to imitate me, baring his teeth like he's a horse at the dentist.

"Very funny," I respond sarcastically.

"What's going on there?"

"Do you want to be a grandfather?"

He smiles, this time without baring his teeth. He smiles like a father who actually already knows exactly what the deal is but is going to force the needed conversation to help you figure it out for yourself.

"Come on, if you're asking if I want to, of course I do."

"Sometimes I feel like the saddest part about not wanting kids…is that it means you're not going to be a grandfather. You were the best dad… Just imagine what you'd be like as a grandfather…"

"Ay, sweetie, that's a very personal decision. I would never tell you to have kids. Or not to have them."

"But I'm all you have," I mutter to myself, fidgeting with my napkin.

"You, the shop, my games on Saturday, and I decided I'm going to sign up for pottery classes."

"That's not what I thought you were gonna say."

"Anyway, Miranda, you should never make a decision based on 'missing out.' Do you want to have kids?"

I stare at him. I can't say that I've categorically decided not to be a mother, but I want so many things that aren't kids that I've had to give in to the evidence that maternity isn't on the list. I want to travel, dedicate myself to my work, read on Sunday morning while records are playing in a calm house and…and the thing is, I wouldn't be any good at it. I would worry so much, so incredibly much, about this creature that I would probably make them unhappy. They can call me egotistical all they want, a word that is somehow still bandied around when a woman decides not to be a mother. They can call me immature, egotistical, frivolous…whatever they want, but we all have baggage here. It's not trauma-based from not having a mother in my life. It's a firm decision, and if I change my mind one day, I'll embrace that too.

"You should tell him," my father says. "If you're pretty sure that being a mother isn't in your plans…you should tell him."

"I think he already knows."

"Well, the whole wanting to make a list of baby names doesn't sound like he's very clear on it."

"I guess he thinks it's a phase."

"Well, you have to disabuse him of that error."

I nod. Shit. Another minefield.

"One step at a time," I mumble.

"You'll do whatever's best, I have no doubt about that. But let me play the role of the annoying father and tell you that…if you're both clear on your positions, it wouldn't be smart to try to convince the other. Or convince yourself."

"Maybe he's right and it is a phase."

"Maybe, but timing is important too, and no one should have to experience feeling like they're waiting for the other." There's a pause, and he smiles at someone behind me. "Tristan, would you like a coffee?"

"Yes."

Tristan appears right behind me and pulls out his chair. I glance at my father, trying to glean whether he could tell if Tristan heard our conversation. He makes a pacifying gesture at me.

"Well, let's have a coffee, and then I'll leave you two to enjoy the setting. It's pretty, eh?"

The sunset surprises Tristan and me strolling around the banks of the lake. There are some pesky mosquitoes buzzing around too close, but everything else is perfect. The colors of the Madrid sky when the sun hides itself. The temperature. The affectionate way he's holding my waist. The smell of his neck.

"In Galicia, the sunsets are different," he says suddenly.

"Because of the sea?"

"I don't know. The colors are different."

"And which is more beautiful?" I ask.

"Don't make me choose between my homeland and my girl."

"I'm not Madrid."

"For me, you kind of are."

"Are you a little bit Vigo then? Because if so, you'll have to take me there."

"Soon," he says and nods. "First, we should stop wasting money on two apartments. I'm sick of having half my stuff one place and half in the other and spending my mornings like a nomad, packing up camp."

"When they gave you your law degree, they must have given you another degree in hyperbole that you should frame."

"I have it at my parents' house, right next to my graduation photo."

I laugh and nod.

"Okay. When your lease is up, does that sound good? How long do you have left?"

"Seven months..." he says, and I get the feeling that he's been thinking about this a lot already.

"Ah. That's a long time, right? Could you break it sooner?"

"Do you want me to?"

"I don't know. You're the one who understands the law. Check it over, and see if there's a clause that will let you break it early."

"There is." His fingers squeeze my waist.

I wish he were capable of leaning down, kissing my temple, giving me a cuddle. Maybe "capable" isn't the right word. This is his code. This is the way that he communicates. I can't ask him to do something for me that's not him.

"Tristan…"

My tone makes him stop.

"What?" he asks, sounding worried.

"I think I don't want to have kids. Actually, I don't think I've ever wanted to. I can't even picture it."

"Uh-huh." He nods slowly.

"It's possible that it's not a phase. What if I don't ever want to have them?"

"*Never* is a word that… Do you think we could figure it out? I mean…I believe you. I believe you when you tell me you might never want them. But your never is really a now. There's no way to know you'll never end up wanting them a few years down the line."

Ay…

The minefields.

Fucking Ivan. What if he was right when he said that the Tristan and Miranda who broke up are exactly the same people walking around the lake today? What if there's never anything that can make us prevent it? What if the only thing I destroy is the weight of time on the decisions we end up postponing?

"You know what?" he says, grabbing my hand again, a smile spreading across his face. "We don't even live together yet. You haven't even met my family. Maybe it's a little early to be worrying about this, right?"

"Of course…"

"Plus, we might move in together and then never want to see each other again after six months. Imagine all the energy we would've wasted talking about all this."

Ay…

"Wanna get ice cream?" he proposes.

"Yes."

Yes, I want ice cream. And you. So much, so much…that I'm wondering if I shouldn't just say yes right now, despite what my father thinks, to make you really happy.

"Lemon?" he guesses, heading to the kiosk with me tucked under his arm.

"Of course."

"Okay, so lemon…ah, and, Miranda…" He stops again and looks at me. He looks at me like a knight in shining armor in a movie. I look at him like I must be falling in love. Like I wasn't already crazy about him. "I'll work out the stuff with my apartment, we'll move in together, and we can think about where to escape on vacation."

"I thought you were going to say: 'And we'll think about when I introduce you to my parents.'"

"There's no rush."

"Are your parents the kraken? It's kinda weird that you're going to live with someone you've never even brought home."

He laughs.

"They trust my taste. But yes…you'll meet them. They're…terribly friendly."

"Friendlier than their son?"

"Even more."

"Will you kiss me?"

Hesitation shines in his eyes, but he leans in and gives me the quickest, most chaste kiss of our lives.

"I love you," I tell him.

"I love you too, Miri. I really do. And I'm not worried about a thing."

I wish I could say the same.

21

~~~

"EVEN WHEN YOU'RE SLIPPERY, I'LL TRY TO CATCH YOU IN YOUR DREAMS."

Moving is the worst. I don't know why this cosmic and temporal wheel is punishing me by making me live through our move again. I don't have very fond memories of it, to be honest. And the truth is Tristan didn't have much stuff to move, but he did have a lot of his own habits. But I'm not going to get ahead of myself. Maybe today will set the huge butterfly effect in motion that I've been waiting for for so long, and the little changes I've been making will collapse into a substantial change in our history... like, for example, transforming this adjustment period into a honeymoon period instead of a shitmoon.

But Ivan will probably be the only one who'll suffer collateral damage. He might wake up tomorrow and decide to wear a Teenage Mutant Ninja Turtles costume. Or get the urge to give himself a perm.

Fine. It wasn't that bad. Let's not exaggerate. I'll find the good part of all this in no time. It's just about not being as nitpicky as I was that day.

When I wake up, Tristan isn't in bed. For a few seconds, I'm not sure whether it's winter or summer. So you can imagine when it comes to the year...I can't even go there. The problem is he must have turned on the

AC before he left, and now there's a penguin walking into the bathroom. Any doubt about the details of the day disappear when I grab my phone and check it. It's Friday, and I have a message from him:

TRISTAN:

I was going to bring you coffee in bed, but since you took the day off for the move, I thought it would be better to let you sleep. Yes, sleep, that elusive thing that doesn't seem to be one of your physiological needs.
I'll be back soon. There's just a few boxes and some suitcases. I'll be all moved in before you even know it.

Great.

Moving is the worst, but the universe, karma, Vishnu, or who knows what other cosmic force wants me to relive it.

I open my laptop almost immediately. I took the day off, but I remember that we're in the middle of closing, and the girls are going to have questions. I like to be on top of things, so I try to get ahead of the worst by firing off a few "just in case, girls" emails.

When Tristan opens the door (I gave him a set of keys with great ceremony on a very lovely night that, of course, I'm not going to relive), completely loaded down with stuff, I've gone down a bit of a rabbit hole, and I'm checking a few pieces.

"Don't work. They're going to count it as a vacation day anyway."

I get up to help him right away... I will neither confirm nor deny whether "right away" means that I take a little longer than strictly necessary to stand up and tear my eyes away from the screen.

"Come on. The sooner we start defiling this temple, the sooner we'll be done," I joke.

"So sweet. To me, the guy who brought you a gift."

He holds out the white vase from Abe the Ape with the bouquet of flowers I forgot at his first apartment in Madrid, which he lovingly dried. "Welcome home."

Tristan isn't messy; that's the truth. I've said it before, he's a neat guy, which doesn't mean he has any fondness for housework. In the first move (this same one, but the first time around), I gave him a "house tour" of the few rooms in the house, explaining certain rules, as if I was welcoming a tenant whom I was going to share a bed with. It didn't sit very well with him. It wasn't that bad though. I think he just got a little sullen because he thought: "What the hell have I gotten myself into, for Christ's sake!"

And I don't blame him. I'm not going to make that mistake today.

I shove the hangers in my closet to one side. My past self was always meticulous about decluttering my clothes, and there are far, far fewer (I remember it took me all weekend and ten huge garbage bags), but there are still plenty. My apartment is cute but very small. A kitchen, the living room, just one bedroom, and an en suite bathroom. What makes it special is that it had been recently renovated when I rented it, it's not crazy expensive, and it has a lot of light thanks to the floor-to-ceiling windows in the living room and the bedroom. In the kitchen, there's a window that lets in good light, even though it overlooks the inner courtyard. So tons of light, but closets...that's a different story.

I carefully fold the T-shirts and sweaters in the drawers I emptied for him while I lovingly explain to him that winter clothes will have to be stored in special vacuum bags under the bed. He's hanging shirts up randomly (color-coordinate them for the love of the universe, can't you see the chromatic harmony of my closet?) and furrows his brow.

"But they'll be all wrinkled when they come out."

"They don't come out. You have to take them out." I bite my lip, trying not to be so blunt, but I just caught a glimpse of the box of research books he uses when he works from home, and they're going to hog a good portion of the shelves in the living room, and it's making me grumpy.

"I guess home automation hasn't gotten that far."

"They do get pretty wrinkled," I admit. "But it's the best solution for the space. Anyway, we don't have to iron it all ourselves. Don't worry."

"If we don't iron it, then who does?"

I'd forgotten this. I hid that someone cleaned my house and did the ironing. Why did I do that? Who knows? I think I wanted to project the image of being a superwoman capable of having it all. A mythological being. Who knows why it would be a problem for someone to work in your house doing things that you can't manage yourself? Why are we disappointed in ourselves if we can't do everything single-handedly?

"Well, I don't know why this has never come up before, but I have a cleaner. She comes once a week, for four hours on Thursday mornings."

"For such a small house?" He raises an eyebrow.

"I spend a lot of time out, at work." I shrug. "It's the best. She's really sweet. Sometimes, if there's not much to iron and I've kept the house more or less tidy and she has time left over, she makes me cookies. Because I don't know if you've ever noticed it...but I have an oven."

I'm very proud of my oven. When you see a lot of places to rent in central Madrid, you realize it's a real luxury.

"So basically, you're paying her to make you cookies," he points out.

"That's a straw man argument."

"Miri, there are two of us now. You spend a lot of time at work, but we can handle it ourselves. We have four hands. The weekend..."

I stand across from him, my hands on my hips.

"No, Tristan, I want to spend the weekend resting and having fun, not cleaning and ironing. It's a preplanned expense, and it's included in my budget. If you don't want to contribute to the payment, that's fine, but I'm not going to fire Yolanda."

"Yolanda."

"Yes. Yolanda."

He nods slowly.

"If that's the house rule…I'll comply. How much does she charge?"

"We'll talk about expenses later."

I'm not going to argue about it. I did that last time, and all that happened was I flipped out, and the end result was the same: Yolanda stays.

"You have a lot of clothes," he mumbles.

"Not really." Yes, I do have a lot of clothes.

"You do. Look."

I look at the wardrobe-dresser in my bedroom, where I have it all categorized by garment type and color; skirts, pants, dresses, blouses, and shoes.

"I work in fashion."

He mimes zipping his mouth shut, and I sigh. Memory is an incredible thing: it hoovers over the friction and the gray parts like an industrial vacuum cleaner and then strokes the good moments like someone holding a puppy.

Since I've been stuck in this time-traveling thing, I haven't had a chance to go shopping; when I do, sometimes I'll have to hide the bags and cut the tags off quickly so Tristan doesn't give me a lecture about hoarding clothes. I'll lose count of the number of times I'll lie and say no when he asks, "Is that new?"

"It's true I have a lot of clothes, but think about—"

"Yeah, yeah. I was just surprised because I remember how excited you were when you published that article about capsule wardrobes and the need to buy versatile garments."

He's a lawyer. Of course. He'll defend his argument to the death.

"Yes, you're right, but as I was saying"—I try to speak very calmly as I show him the empty drawer I left for his boxers—"I have a lot of events where I can't repeat the same outfit…"

"That's where the versatility part comes in." He smiles.

"Okay. You're just trying to rile me up, so I'm going to ignore you. What do you think about putting your books on the bottom shelf?"

"All the way on the bottom? They're research books. I'm going to break my back."

"I mean, look, if you do squats when you take them out, you can save on a gym membership."

I couldn't quite make out what he muttered as I headed out toward the living room, but whatever it was seems to make it clear I'm not making this move much more fun than the first time around.

"Universe, what have I done to deserve this?" I say from the living room, trying to get a rise out of him.

"You should've fallen in love with a Saudi prince, darling. When you put two people and all their stuff in a fifty-square-meter apartment, this is the result."

"Don't complain. There are people in Madrid living in thirty-square-meter apartments."

Oy, oy, oy. Let's not go there, because it's a very touchy subject for me. My apartment is the best. Was he this tedious the last time?

"I'm not complaining, but we have to be meticulous and prioritize the things we use the most to make the space more workable. My research books…"

I stick my head into the bedroom.

"Tristan…"

"Talk to me."

"Tristan, my love…"

"Talk to me, Miranda, my sweetie…" He smiles.

Ay. Fuck. That smile.

"I love this apartment. It's comfortable. It's updated. It's practical, and on top of that, I've made it beautiful. And you are wonderful, and even my liver is in love with you, which, just so you know, is the organ that holds your rage. You're smart, fun, good-looking. You're hot, and we both like our meat very rare, the beach, and drinking martinis on Sunday, which is just gilding the lily..."

"Don't forget the part about my cock."

"The most beautiful cock in the northern hemisphere."

"And the Yucatán Peninsula."

I raise an eyebrow.

"The Yucatán Peninsula? But what...? Look, it doesn't matter."

"I don't know where you're going with this." He leans against the wardrobe and crosses his arms over his chest.

Holy mother of God, what a man... I could even get over his research books. But I can't give in.

"This is where I'm going: the research books belonging to the lawyer I'm in love with are going on the bottom shelf of the bookshelf in the living room until 2020."

"Why until 2020?"

"Something tells me you're going to need to use them more often."

"Ay, Miranda..."

By nighttime, everything is unpacked in its place, and I've held up pretty well, even when he wanted to know the use of every little bottle I keep in the bathroom. On the actual "day," I felt like he was trying to point out that I didn't need them so I would get rid of them to open up more space, but I've learned that Tristan has a curious soul, especially with what he appreciates, with the people he loves. And today, he loves me a lot. You can see it in how he looks at me.

I really enjoy the way he's looking at me today. Maybe, in the rush to understand what was happening to me, with my thirst for revenge, with the successive days of blind love and Cupid's arrow, I haven't been paying attention to that look. Because those two eyes somewhere between brown, green, and gray follow me through what is now their living room with a kind of admiration, teasing, surprised. These two people who are opening take-out containers at the coffee table in the living room, sitting on the floor, can still surprise each other. They haven't resigned themselves, they want to make an effort, and they haven't yet settled into their comfort zone as a couple. Hopefully they never will. Maybe they can make it.

"Cooking is going to happen way more in this house starting now," he announces, bounding nimbly toward the kitchen.

"You assume I don't cook."

"I just peeled the protective plastic off one of the buttons on the stove."

He hands me a plate and sits down across from me again. I like that he likes the TV just the right amount. He doesn't ask me to turn it on while we're eating dinner; he wants us to tell each other things. I think it was the pandemic that brought that into our lives.

"Well…it's just that if I examine my consciousness, I don't have the patience to cook."

"Patience is important in cooking," he says seriously. "And cohabitating."

Our eyes meet, and we smile.

"We're gonna have a great time," I assure him.

"Another exercise in prediction? You haven't done that in a while."

"Because it comes in phases. My powers are fickle… They come and go."

"Phew, thank God. I was about to ask you for the winning lottery numbers."

In this world, we're obsessed with material things… I'm tempted to tell him that we could lose much more than we could win in the lottery if we don't get it right this time, but I'd have to explain too much to him. Explanations he wouldn't understand.

"Are there rules?" he asks, handing me a little bowl for soy sauce.

"For sushi?" I find it strange.

"For your house."

"Yes. The first one is to stop saying 'your house' because it's 'our house' now."

I arm myself with chopsticks and pinch them at him before I grab a little wasabi and dilute it in my soy sauce. It's time to break out the big guns.

"Second rule: being empathetic about each other's preferences and pet peeves."

"Seems easy enough."

"It's not gonna be that easy. I like lighting scented candles, buying novels when I still have some I haven't read yet, and blasting music on Saturday mornings while I tidy up the house. I never get rid of books, so I calculate that in approximately three years, they'll be in every corner of the house, including the floor and the windowsills."

He makes a face.

"I lay my clothes out the night before and put them on a hanger on the back of the bathroom door, and you're always going to be tempted to hang your towel there. Either there or on top of mine…making it damp. I put so much moisturizer on every night I end up as slippery as a bar of soap in the bathroom of a prison movie. And sometimes that's going to piss you off."

"Okay."

"But you'll have to remember that you eat like the world is ending and that on top of that, when you cook, because you have to eat a homemade meal no matter what, the kitchen will look like Chernobyl. Every time you put towels in the washing machine, you 'forget'"—I make air quotes—"to put in softener. You have enough hair to fill IKEA cushions, and it grows fast, so there will always be a reminder of your hair in the bathroom. Let's not even talk about the bathroom, okay? I want the evening to stay pleasant."

He lets out a chuckle that makes him choke on the maki he was eating. When he recovers, he nods.

"Understood. We'll both be annoyed by stuff about each other, and we have to be empathetic for cohabitating to work."

"Exactly. Third rule…"

"There's more?" He sounds surprised.

"Of course there are more. Way more. Make a mental note."

"Go on then…" He chooses a nigiri with seared salmon and looks at it suspiciously. He's more into classic flavors. I don't know how I convinced him to order sushi.

"We'll never go to bed angry without kissing each other. Sundays will be our special day. We're not going to spend all day rotting on the couch in pajamas or sweatpants. We'll make nice plans. Sunday is date day, no matter what."

"A date!" He laughs.

"We have to keep surprising each other. It doesn't matter how. A song, a note on the fridge, a coffee, a visit, sneaking into the shower when the other one is soaping up…"

"Phew, for a second, I thought you weren't going to mention sex." He laughs.

"It's important that we don't stop touching each other."

"That would never happen. And we'll hug each other every day," he adds.

"Yes." I put a maki into my mouth and then say with my mouth full: "Do you want to keep going?"

"No, no, you're the one who can predict the future here, so…"

"Ay, so funny." I grimace. "Well, I'll tell you these rules are important."

"Yeah? Do we have to pay a fine if we don't follow them?" He raises an eyebrow.

"I know you want me to say something about your mouth being busy between my thighs, but I'm serious. What happens if we don't follow the rules is that we're gonna take it up the ass."

"Fuck..." He opens his eyes wide.

I sigh.

"Miri..." He strokes my arm tenderly. "It's going to be fine. Don't worry."

"My father always says love is a full-time job, three hundred and sixty-five days a year, twenty-four hours a day, but I think it's more like a newborn that needs attention and care. It's not just about feeding it, protecting it from the cold or the heat, and keeping it safe... You have to rock it, pamper it, play with it, teach it to laugh, and console it when it cries."

Tristan has stopped chewing and dropped his chopsticks, which he can usually handle pretty well...and he's staring at me, like he's looking right through me.

"What?" I ask.

He doesn't answer. He stands up again and heads into the kitchen, where I hear him rummaging through one of the drawers. He comes back looking serious, with something hidden in his closed fist, and heads over to the record player.

"You're not going to tell me...?"

He shoots me a look over his shoulder as he picks out a record; there's something complicit in his expression, but his silence is so confusing. It could be anything. He moves the needle on the record player, looking for a specific song. He misses a few times, but finally he finds the one he wants: "You and Me" by The Cranberries. Then he comes back to the table, sits down, and clears the center, pushing the sushi containers to either side. In the middle, he puts a tiny candle and lights it.

"Ooh, so romantic," and I say it with surprise, not sarcasm, because I really wasn't expecting it.

"For a while now, I've been wondering if you're the type who wants to get married. To tell the truth, my mother even asked me that: 'But, Tristan, doesn't she want to get married?' I still have no clue. It's part of the magic between us, that there are mysteries that can only be discovered over time. And listen, I'm not the type who thinks marriage is the natural progression of love, but to these vows, I say I do."

I raise one eyebrow at the same time as a huge grin spreads across my face.

"Slather yourself in all the cream you want, Miranda. Even when you're slippery, I'll try to catch you in your dreams."

22

~~~

THE PIECE OF THE ATLANTIC OCEAN THAT KISSES CAPE FINISTERRE

I feel something pulling me out of sleep. Like someone shaking me carefully, almost like someone rocking me. I resist being pulled out of my current state. It's one of those tranquil dreams where you're gently swaying on something floating way up high. And there's no way to fall. I cling harder to my drowsiness. But there it is again. The rattling. What the fuck? Is Tristan moving the bed? How? Why? My eyes want to open, but I forbid them. Fuck no. I'm too comfortable.

Wait, wait…

I crack open my eyelids and find, right in front of me, glass and a car. A car coming straight at us, head-on. '

"Aaah!" I scream at the top of my lungs.

Something is shaking the space I'm in. It takes me a little longer than it should to figure out the space is a car and the shake Tristan jerking the wheel in fear.

"What are you doing? Why are you screaming?"

"Ay…"

This is new. Waking up in motion. Where the fuck am I? Where are we going? How is it possible that I woke up here?

"Tris…"

"Argh…"

He hates when I call him Tris. I don't do it very often.

"I don't know where I am, for fuck's sake. Be nice," I croak, my voice raspy from sleep. "That was terrifying."

I point at the tow truck in front of us, which has a few cars strapped to it backward.

"What did you think? That it was coming straight at us?" He cracks up.

"Yes." I rub my eyes, and when I let my hand fall, I see my knuckle is completely black. "Shit. Do I have eyeliner everywhere?"

Tristan takes his eyes off the road for a second to check.

"You're Voldemort."

"What does Voldemort have to do with this?"

"What do I know?" He pisses himself laughing.

This is life. This is being human. We're such creatures of habit that even though I don't know where the hell I'm going or how it's possible to wake up here at four in the afternoon, the thing I'm most worried about is my makeup running.

"Where are we going?"

"Ay, Miranda, for God's sake." He huffs.

I grab my bag from the footwell and rummage until I find my phone: March 15. I investigate a little further: two years ago. I look out the window, and everything is so green…

Of course, we're on the way to Vigo. We left Madrid at ten a.m. in a rental car. I had to work until five in the morning to make the day off possible. Tristan complained passive-aggressively about having to drive so many hours "with nothing but your snores as company."

Let's see…a twinge of pain in my neck is bothering me, but I know it's very important to make an effort. This trip wasn't easy. It was beautiful because I had only passed through Vigo before, and it's one of the most beautiful cities I've ever seen. So regal. So clean. So riddled with seagulls…

but I can get over the seagulls. In fact, all of Galicia is beautiful. Seeing it through Tristan's eyes was incredible. But…

Oh, the buts. There are big ones.

This is the trip where I met his parents. His mom thought it was borderline offensive that he had been with a girl for almost three years (if you count the first on-and-off year), he had moved into her apartment, and they still hadn't even met her. I agreed. And his parents were lovely, as they have always been with me. The problem wasn't his parents. It was his sister. Uxia became my archnemesis on that trip. And Tristan always took it on the chin…never her, of course not, because she's the "sister of all sisters." He was annoyed that I, as his girlfriend, as a girlfriend who lived a six-hour drive away, hadn't somehow found a way to build a thriving relationship in the few moments we'd had together. I explained to him so many times that relationships are a two-way street and there was nothing I could do if she didn't want me to, but he always said the same thing:

"Miri, it takes two to tango, especially when it comes to arguing. End of story."

Well, then tell her that, because she's got a grudge against me wasn't a good response. It was a possible response, yes, but it would cause a fight that would last hours. A fight with Tristan had nothing to do with spitting reproaches or yelling at each other. Not at all. Having a fight with Tristan meant listening to him sigh and snort and getting used to the static of his silence.

"How much longer?"

"We're near Melón."

I keep looking at him with a smile. He smiles too.

"The village is called Melón. What do you want me to do?"

A giggle slips out before I respond.

"But how long until we get there?"

"About forty-five minutes."

"When we get to Vigo, can you pass by El Molino?"

He shoots me a surprised look out of the corner of his eye.

"What did you say?" he asks.

"Can we stop by El Molino."

"The bakery El Molino?"

"Yes."

"Well…I wasn't planning on going through the center, to be honest. My parents live kind of on the outskirts."

"Yeah, I know. But…can't we make a detour?"

"Well…I guess so. I don't know if we'll be able to stop on that street."

"If you can't, just drop me there, and go around the block a few times."

"But…how the hell do you know about a bakery in Vigo?"

"I'm a journalist." I smile at him. "I have my sources."

"Well, your sources are excellent. It's my mother's favorite bakery." He chuckles to himself.

My source is him, of course. His mother and his sister like the chocolate-covered tuiles and the chocolates from that bakery. His father likes the tea cake, which in my opinion is delicious but very dense.

An hour and fifteen minutes later, we get to the neighborhood where he grew up, Teis, a ten-minute drive from the center of Vigo. It's a blue-collar town, like Carabanchel, where I grew up. The buildings have always reminded me of the ones on my parents' street: seventies-style buildings made of brick and concrete, no frills. Practical balconies, the kind where you can hang your clothes to dry and look down onto the street. A neighborhood without luxuries that, according to what his parents told me, has changed a lot in the last decades. Years ago, it didn't have a very good reputation, which is often the case where we working-class people live. I say we, because it's not like I haven't heard things about Carabanchel, and

I've seen people turn their noses up. I always say the same thing: I've only been mugged once, and it was in fancy-ass Salamanca. But from what my future in-laws have told me, it's possible that their neighborhood hides certain "treasures" that are better not to dig up.

Teis has a beautiful park I love, the A Riouxa Park, which is so intensely green it's impossible to recreate it. There's no Pantone for that color; it only exists here. It's something Tristan always liked to hear me say, that his Vigo has colors you can't find anywhere else. He's proud of his homeland. He says Galicians are travelers but they always end up coming home, and that's always bothered me. Vigo is beautiful, but it's not mine. Not mine at all. I only fit in here as a tourist.

Tristan has been quiet for a while. On top of not wanting to tell me that he's nervous about introducing me to his family, he's not very happy I kept him waiting in the car for twenty minutes while I got out to buy the desserts. He always moves slowly, but he doesn't like to be kept waiting. After I bought the pastries for everyone, I snuck into the Casa del Libro, which is on the next street over, to buy Uxia a book. She loves poetry, and I want to start off on the right foot. I've asked myself many times if I did something wrong, if I wasn't sweet or thoughtful enough or... I don't know. I need to know it's not about me.

"Stop making that face, come on. I'm just trying to impress them," I say in the doorway.

"I just don't understand all this superhuman effort. It's like you think my family has two heads and one of them eats Madrileños or something."

"You're upset I'm trying to get off on the right foot..."

"Well, don't make such a big deal, and I won't make this face." He raises his eyebrows. "They're nicer than me, don't worry."

"Well, that makes me feel better because, look, you can be awful when you want to be."

"And that's why I fell in love with you."

His mother opens the door and bounds out to kiss...me. To kiss me. At the time, I expected her to make a beeline for her son, not to me, but this time, I come prepared, and I respond with the same effusiveness. His father pokes his head out of the hallway and studies me up and down. Tristan never confirmed it, but I suspect I'm the first girl he ever brought home.

"How was the trip? You must be exhausted. Who drove?" his mother asks.

"Well, we were going to take turns, but Miranda fell into an irreversible coma, and I suffered through six hundred kilometers."

"It can't have been that bad," his mother chides him, giving him a hug and two kisses.

"She didn't wake up even when I stopped to get gas."

"I worked really late last night so I could take the day off," I say, making excuses. "I'm sorry...now he's all grumpy."

"I'm not grumpy," he grumbles as he shoves the bags from the bakery at his mother. "Here."

"Wow! From El Molino! That's so thoughtful, darling."

"It's all Miranda's doing. She did some research."

"Ay! Thank you, *miña xoia!*"

I flash Tristan a victorious smile as his parents pat me gratefully. In the bag. I've got it in the bag.

"What about Uxia? Is she here? I'm dying to meet her," I say.

"She's in the living room. Come in, come in..."

The rude cow...doesn't even come out to say hi.

Uxia is, far and away, one of the most beautiful women I've ever seen in my life. She's the female equivalent of her brother, but all Tristan's sharp, masculine features are softened on her face. She's brunette, has much greener eyes and a killer body. But Uxia's beauty is inversely proportional to how nice she is. I find her sprawled out on the couch, and she struggles to get up when we appear in the living room, not because of anything physical, just because she doesn't feel like it.

"Hi, Uxia!" I go over to her with a big grin. "How's it going? I'm Miranda. So nice to meet you. Your brother has told me so much about you."

"Miranda? I could've sworn your name was Amanda."

I side-eye Tristan. In this version, she's almost ruder than the first time.

"Close." I laugh. "Tristan told me you like poetry, so…I brought you a book."

"It's not my birthday." She takes the bag I hold out to her reluctantly, which is actually a euphemism meaning with "a face like she's smelling shit."

Actually, it's fair to say that's her usual face; she always gives me the feeling that someone is holding a piece of shit under her nose and she's permanently smelling it.

"Well, it's just a little welcome present?" I say.

"Yes. To the family."

And it's dripping with irony. She drops the book onto the coffee table in front of the couch and throws herself into Tristan's arms in an overly effusive way. It almost seems like she's hamming it up just to show how much I gross her out.

"Mr. Lawyer!"

"Mr. Legal Eagle." He smiles.

They both laugh. Their adoration for each other is tangible. The same thing happened the first time I lived this: I'm dying of jealousy. I want to have someone who's flesh of my flesh, blood of my blood, to adore. And someone to talk shit about this girl with me.

"I left the sweater you forgot at my house on your bed," she says to him.

"I'm not sleeping here this time."

"Why not?"

"My childhood bed, a twin, might be a little bit of a stretch for two of us."

Tristan looks at me sidelong with that beautiful smile.

"You're not sleeping here?" his sister repeats.

Come on, dudette, what's so hard to get? That I'm not a chihuahua and I'm not going to sleep curled up at his feet?

"No," her brother replies. "We booked a room in that hotel…the one in the port. I can't remember the name."

"The fancy one?"

"The fancy one." He laughs.

"Well, I saw some of your friends at the bar on my way here, and they're convinced you're going to grab a drink with them tonight."

"That's the plan." He laughs and tugs on her hair, which she has in a low pony.

"And you're going to try to get in there wasted?"

"He's not going to the hotel wasted or anywhere, because I don't think your brother gets blind-drunk at his age like he did when he was eighteen," their mother says.

Tristan shoots me an embarrassed look.

"Chill out, Mama."

"I'm not going to chill out. I know what animals your friends are."

I do too. I do too…

"I'll drive. He can drink all the beers he wants," I say to ease the tension.

"Umm…how kind," Uxia mutters.

"Are you coming with us?" I ask her. "To meet them for a drink?"

I smile like a saint, but she glares at me…she stares at me…she stares at me…and she doesn't answer. I search for Tristan with my gaze…and I don't find him. He reappears carrying a tray loaded down with cups of coffee.

"I was just asking your sister if she was going to come have a drink with us tonight."

"She probably has plans," he says. "What about that boyfriend of yours with the long hair?"

"He doesn't have long hair. It's just that you, my boy, with that haircut you've had since communion… I'm sure if you tried the part on the other side, it would chap your ass."

"I don't have a part on either side, you nerd."

But he laughs. They laugh together. And I'm just standing there, looking at them with a shit-eating grin on my face.

"Miranda, sweetheart, you really hit the bull's-eye with everything you brought," his mother thanks me. "How do you like your coffee, lovely?"

"Black like the night and with sweetener," Tristan says, coming back over to me and looping his arm around my waist. "Like her soul: dark but slightly cloying."

"You can say that again…"

I look at Uxia, waiting for her to laugh, but she doesn't. The book I bought is sitting there, tossed aside, on the coffee table.

"Your sister hates me."

Tristan is slumped against the car window. It's not like he's a lightweight, but he's had a lot of beer. I had two stubbies at the beginning of the night and then a lot of sparkling water. Apparently, drinking sparkling water is frowned upon in this circle, and I got a little heckled. His sister, who finally decided to grace us with her presence, didn't miss the opportunity to make a joke that didn't exactly sound like a joke.

"She doesn't hate you," he slurs.

His eyes are drooping. He's tired.

"She despises me. She looks at me with disgust. I don't know what I did. I tried to be nice, to bring up topics she'd like, to take an interest in her stuff…but nothing." I'm honestly frustrated.

"Maybe…"

"Maybe what?"

"It doesn't matter. Let it go. You're gonna let your imagination run wild."

"No, no." I shoot him a look. "Tell me. I want her to like me."

"Maybe that's the problem." He sighs. "You're trying too hard."

"Too hard? Define too hard."

"Just…too much. I don't know. You know what I mean."

"Too much like when someone is sprung on you and they won't take the hint and it's super annoying?"

"Something like that." He presses his left hand to his forehead.

"Does your head hurt?"

"A little."

"Do you want an aspirin? I have some in my bag. It's the kind you can take without water."

"You're doing it again."

"Doing what again?"

"Trying too hard. I'm your boyfriend. You don't need to be like that. I already love you."

I shoot him a questioning look. The GPS is telling me to turn left on the next road, where I'll find the hotel parking lot.

"Are you gonna start being mean now too?"

Tristan gives a muffled laugh.

"No, of course not." He reaches out to stroke my neck. "I'm just saying you're so nervous. Like…next level."

"Overhyped?"

"You said it, not me. But maybe that is the right word."

I suck my teeth.

"You think this is all so fucking funny…" I lose my cool.

"A little. You always seem so…I don't know, so over-the-top."

"I seem over-the-top?" I'm scandalized.

"Well, you know. Like you're prepared for everything. I think what happens is you have to be such a hard-ass at work and ready to adapt to any situation."

"Well, yes, I do," I grumble.

"Don't get mad."

"Your sister was really rude, Tristan."

"She wasn't rude. She's just...herself. And I'm her only brother."

"And that's why she had to treat your partner like a piece of shit you dragged into the house on your shoe?"

Tristan sighs. He sighs and...

"You're going too far, Miranda."

"Tell me what I have to do to get your sister to like me."

He laughs, but it sounds kind of bitter like someone thinking "again?"

"You really wanna know?"

"Yes, please, because I'm hoping for some nice...years."

"Here comes the fortune teller again."

"Come on. How can I make her like me? Or at least tolerate me with a good sense of humor?"

"Nothing."

I look at him, surprised, and he turns back to me with a tired smile.

"I'm her little brother, and she'll never think anything is good enough for me. None of the girls I've dated before, from college, from home, Vigo, Madrid, my car back when I had a car, my vacations... She always treats me like I'm not striving hard enough and I'm missing out on opportunities. I could fall in love with her best friend, and she'd be just as bummed as she is about anyone, including you. Plus now she has someone to blame for not getting to see me as much."

I stop the car on the access ramp to the parking lot and look at him as I roll the window down to take the ticket.

"Great." I raise my eyebrows to underline my sarcasm.

"Yeah, yeah, I know, Miri, but this is the deal and…I hate to break it to you that you're just gonna have to put up with it. You live far away from each other, and you're going to see each other from Easter to Palm Sunday… It's not that hard to put on a good face and suck it up."

"That's pretty egotistical of you. You'll be fine, just grin and bear it and never bother you with it again, right? Don't burden you with it."

"Miranda, that's not what I'm saying. I'm saying there's no solution except resigning yourself to it."

"Well, I'm not really one for resigning myself," I mutter.

"So what can we do?"

"You could say something to her. Ask her to be nice to me, for example…or at least to answer when I speak to her."

"I could do that, yes, but then she'll just be even madder at you because she'll think you asked me to yell at her. I'm saying it for your own good, Miri, babe."

"There has to be something that…"

"Miranda, for God's sake…" He recoils. "I'm not my sister's keeper. She's thirty-six, and she's a grown-up. This isn't a classroom, and I'm not the teacher."

"Fine then, we'll settle it in the ring. Or in a duel. Whoever survives gets to keep you."

"God…considering how little I like drama, I don't know how I ended up with the queen of tragedy."

I have the urge to slam his head against the dashboard, but I resist it and park.

"Now you're mad?" he asks, gobsmacked.

This thing with some men…what's their damage? Do they come from the past, from another planet, or from the earth's core? No. I'm not stereotyping. The male species is stupid sometimes. End of story.

We drag our suitcases over to reception, which is deserted at this hour. A smiley girl is waiting for us behind the desk. We check in in silence, and while she types away on her computer and activates our electronic key cards, I start thinking how this is like that Bill Murray movie where he's always living the same day, *Groundhog Day*, but instead of always waking up in the same temporal point, I'm jumping from situation to situation, and I can change the way things happen but not the outcome. It's frustrating. That giant whore Uxia stole the night from us again. And here I was wanting to celebrate my triumph by nuzzling into his sweaty chest after an intense fuck session…

Our room is on the third floor, and it's beautiful. A little dark and impersonal, like almost all hotels at night, but pretty. It has views of the port, which will definitely make everything look better when I wake up. I don't know what tomorrow holds, but I'd be sad if I drag this feeling of defeat around the whole weekend, even subconsciously. It's still Friday night. We can come back from this. I can fix all this. I can strip his sister of the power to fuck over what's left of our trip, because I'm playing with an advantage; if this were a war, I have a certain strategic superiority. What can I do?

Wait…

I grab my phone and look up a few things.

Yes.

That's it.

"Tristan…"

He comes out of the bathroom, his pants unzipped, looking scruffy.

"Are you over it yet?" He looks at me for a second but then heads straight over to our luggage. "Do you have any idea where I put my contact lens case?"

"Can you listen to me for a second, look me in the eyes, and shut up?"

"There's no way you're demanding sex? Because I would really flip out, after the way you…"

"Shut up and get dressed again," I demand.

"Why?"

"Because we're leaving."

"Where?"

"Somewhere."

"I'm exhausted, Miri…" he groans, sliding off the bed and slumping against the side of it.

"Please, Tristan… I'll drive."

"Drive? Miranda, it's almost two in the morning."

"Do we have plans to get up early tomorrow?"

"No, but I got up early today, and…you slept in the car, but I had the hassle of six hours behind the wheel."

"I said I'll drive," I repeat. "You can sleep. And it's not going to kill us. Don't make that face."

"But where do you want to go?"

"Can you just listen to me for once in your life?" I try to make puppy-dog eyes at him to see if he'll soften. "It's important… I don't normally do stuff like this."

"No. You're usually a little more normal."

"Well, time for me to stop being boring… Button your pants, and grab your jacket."

Before we leave, I make myself a coffee from the capsule machine on the table opposite the bed, because I want to fix this, but I don't want to kill myself on the way…

Tristan falls asleep twenty minutes in, and he doesn't even wake up when I open my window so the crisp night air perks me up. I'm not tired. I wouldn't have risked it if I were, but it feels good. He sleeps like a log and gifts me some very funny snores as a soundtrack. In profile, asleep like this, he's halfway between ugly and very funny. I mean, he can't be ugly, because I'm sure even his spleen is beautiful, but in that pretty comical position, his head tipping back, his mouth ajar, and totally out of it…he's not exactly handsome.

A bump in the road jolts him awake, but we're only a few minutes away…at least to the closest point to our destination where we are allowed to leave the car. The first thing he does is look at the time and then at me. It's four in the morning.

"Wait, where are we?"

I don't say anything until the car is parked. Then I turn on the lights and roll down the windows. Then the sound of the waves crashing against the rocks down below us floats in. He must have already recognized the place, because he scans the darkness in silence, no questions asked.

"Couples always say super romantic stuff like in the movies. Things like they'll love each other even after they die or they'd cross the whole world just to be together," I say, looking out into the night as well. I'm generating power from this burst of romance. "I don't know how to say these things. I could try to write them, but I'd probably get terrible secondhand embarrassment saying them to you."

"Not secondhand, firsthand," he points out.

"Yeah. Exactly."

I fall silent, and the sounds of the night waft inside, mingling with us and the unbroken darkness. Soon our eyes will adjust, and the stars will glow even brighter.

"Go ahead…" he nudges.

"I'm saying I don't know how to say these things, but…if I have a car and an opportunity, I'm capable of taking you to the end of the world. Maybe our love is that kind of love…a slightly apocalyptic love."

We turn back to each other again. His eyes are drowsy, but they look as beautiful as ever. We smile at the same time and reach for each other's hands at the same time.

"I'm not going to tell you I'll love you even after we die."

"Thanks," he says with a teasing smile.

"But I'm going to tell you that I love you at the end of the world. And I think that's worth something."

The kiss that comes after is clumsy, because kisses in the front seat of cars always are, navigating the steering wheel, gear shift, and emergency brake. But it's a happy kiss. A kiss of two people in love who get angry, who snore, who are going to fight dozens of times, and who one day, maybe, will throw in the towel, but they are two people who love each other like they've never loved anyone else before. And discovering how deep love can go, even though they're over thirty, is amazing. It's unstoppable. Because I guess we're all capable of loving more.

Sunrise is still at least three hours away, so we decide to snuggle up in the back of the car. It doesn't take long for clothes to ride up a bit, and I end up on top of him, unable to take my eyes off his face, his expression of pleasure as he penetrates me. The same girl who once frantically asked him to slap me during a sex marathon, I find myself stroking his hair as I ride up and down on his lap. His hands clinging to my hips are like an anchor to real life in the midst of the strange thing my existence has become. And when the moment to stop comes, I don't want to, and I ask him not to. Not to pull out, to keep going, to fill me up. I tell him I want to feel him empty out inside me. I want to have him so deep inside me that I can never erase his footprint. And when he does, when he comes inside me for the first time, I feel like I would do anything to change how our story ends.

At 7:48, the sun breaks over the end of the earth, the piece of the Atlantic Ocean that kisses Cape Finisterre.

23

~~~

WHERE VERY FEW THINGS HAVE THAT EFFECT ON ME

TRISTAN

When we wake up, I have six missed calls from my mother, but I'm more worried that we missed breakfast. It's 1:20. This is what happens when you get back to the hotel at 9:30 in the morning after sneaking off to Cape Finisterre in the middle of the night and you're so exhausted…that the whole eating breakfast before you fall asleep thing doesn't even occur to you.

I'm not very romantic. That's the truth. To me, romance means sharing your Wi-Fi password. But what do I know? I can't picture myself going to pick Miranda up brandishing a bouquet of flowers, and it's not because I think that would be bad. It's just that…those kinds of gestures are hard for me. It's not my style. I try to express that stuff in a different way; I hope the message gets through, even if it comes with fewer frills.

I want to take Miranda to get some martinis and then to the A Riouxa Park, which I know she'll love. It's not like driving two hours in the middle of the night just to say "I love you" at Cape Finisterre, but it's something. Tonight, we have plans to meet up with my parents at four and then go to dinner. Uxia isn't coming because she's busy, but maybe it's better that way. There hasn't been much harmony between my sister and my girlfriend. I'm not going to say I wasn't expecting it. Uxia has always been…special. She can be a hard pill to swallow when she puts her mind to it. Sometimes, we seem a lot alike, like the siblings we are, but other times, we're like the sun and the moon. Yesterday, she wasn't very friendly with Miranda, and I guess I should have done something about it, but it seemed aggressive to me. I've never been a big fan of confrontations. I've only gotten in a fight once in my life, and to be honest, all I really did was push away some asshole who was coming at me. Although…this isn't about punching anyone; it's about telling my sister to please stop being a jerk.

I have a lot to do today.

Miri comes out of the shower wrapped in a towel. I took a shower first, and now I'm dressed, taking the opportunity to message someone on WhatsApp.

"Will I be okay in a dress, Tristan? Because I'm guessing we're not coming back to the hotel before dinner with your parents, right?"

"We can come take a siesta midafternoon if you want."

"Okay, but will I be okay at dinner in a short dress, tights, boo—?"

"No," I cut her off.

She turns and gives me a confused look, and I laugh.

"I mean, of course, silly. You always look good. You don't have to ask me what to wear."

"It's for your parents." She wrinkles her nose shyly. "Sometimes, in Madrid, I get carried away with the trendy stuff, and I don't want them to think I'm wearing a costume."

"You always look good," I insist. "Don't worry about what they think. They already liked you yesterday."

She keeps talking about how important clothes are for first and second impressions, but all I can focus on is the lingerie she's putting on. Jeez, it should come with a pair of free sunglasses, because the color could burn your retinas.

"You know? Because the second impression can either confirm the first or prove it wrong."

"Does that underwear glow in the dark?" I joke.

"Yes. I wear it when I'm going to be in a dark room so everyone can spot me."

I sit on the edge of the bed and focus on putting my shoes on.

"You're ready?" she asks. "I'm going to need a little more time. I have to blow-dry my hair, put my makeup on…"

"Yeah, I'm ready, but… I'm going to head out for a minute. Is that okay?"

I sit down next to her, opposite the mirror, and she studies me in silence.

"What?" I ask.

"Where are you going?"

"I just wanna go say hi to my ex-boss. He messaged me that he's in a bar with the other partners and…"

She raises her eyebrows doubtfully, but she nods and shrugs.

"Of course. I'll wait for you here?"

"Yeah. Or…if I take a long time and you feel like going out to grab something to eat, feel free…"

"But are you going to take a long time?"

"I mean, I don't know, Miranda. I don't think so."

"I don't know why I'm even asking. You're always late," she grumbles.

"Like you at the bakery yesterday when you were buying the sweets, right?"

"Wait, what's up with you?" she exclaims.

"Nothing's up with me, Miranda, for God's sake," I complain. "You always get so defensive."

"I'm not getting defensive, Tristan. It's just that…"

"It's just what, exactly?" I lean against the table and cross my arms over my chest.

"You're handling me with exfoliating gloves. If you could be a little sweeter when you talk to me, I wouldn't be so defensive."

"I thought you said you weren't defensive."

"Oh, fuck off."

I sigh. Ay, Lord, what a woman.

"I don't like it when you sigh instead of saying what you're thinking or how you're feeling," she insists.

"Miri, my angel, you can't change a donkey," I say to try to make her understand, with all my affection and love.

But she doesn't answer. I pat my pockets to make sure I have everything and throw on my jacket.

"I'm leaving."

She doesn't respond. This time, I don't sigh. I snort.

"Miranda, please…make things a little easier on me. What's the biggest complaint?"

"I don't have a complaint, Tristan. It just makes me a little sad that we can't find a middle ground between your way of showing love and mine. That's all."

"Well, don't be sad."

I go over, kiss her on the temple, and wrap my arms around her briefly.

"I'll be right back. I won't take too long."

I know sometimes she's right, but right now, I feel like Miranda adopted a fish hoping it would bark.

When I get there, she's sitting at the bar. I can tell it's her from her hair, which she's wearing loose, wavy, and very long. She turns around when I swoop in next to her and smiles, leaning against my chest affectionately in a kind of brief hug.

"I could smell your aftershave from a mile away."

"It's cologne," I quibble.

"Did you really just wake up?"

"I was glued to the sheets. I went to bed really late last night."

"How come? You were out partying?"

I suck my teeth and order a stubby.

"I don't have much time," I warn her.

"You lied to her, didn't you? You made up an excuse to get out."

"Well, yeah." I nod, leaning backward against the bar and looking at her. "Because I wanted to talk to you alone and…"

The bartender serves my beer, and after I thank him, I stare at her with a calm smile.

"You can't keep picking fights with her," I declare with a lot of self-restraint.

"You've always been so freaked out by conflict."

"I avoid mess that isn't worth it. There's a difference."

My sister rolls her eyes. I'm afraid this seems to be a gesture we make a lot in my family.

"Did she send you to yell at me?"

"Do you think I'm twelve years old, Uxia?" I say this a little more seriously, trying to make her get it. "You don't have to watch over my life choices."

"So what if I don't like that girl? Then what?"

"Then you grin and bear it."

"Yeah?" she says, livid.

"Well, yeah, Uxia, but for a whole bunch of reasons. For one, because I live in Madrid and you're not exactly gonna have to see her every Sunday. And…"

"The girl from the big city…" she says snidely.

"And," I insist more bluntly, "because she's the woman your brother fell in love with, and you can keep your mouth shut because it's none of your business."

"You're my brother, so it kind of is my business."

"Yes, your little brother, but that doesn't mean you have to inspect everything I do with a magnifying glass and judge me." I soften my tone a little. "Uxi...I'm asking you please."

"What a crybaby, that babe..." she mutters.

"She didn't say anything to me," I lie. "But I have eyes and ears, and what you did yesterday was"—I throw my hands up—"uncalled for...and I'm asking you to do this for me, if you can't find a reason for yourself. Smile at her, talk about the weather, I don't care, but don't bust my balls."

She sips her martini and scowls.

"You really like her that much?"

"Well, yeah." I nod, and in spite of myself, I get the giggles. Sometimes my sister...she still acts like a teenager.

"What the hell are you laughing at, you clown?"

"The fact that I have to explain to you that I like her a lot." I laugh. "It's not that I like her. I love her."

"Wait, you're not going to propose, are you?" Her eyes bulge.

"I mean, I don't think so, but only because I can't picture her in a white dress walking down the aisle. She's"—I waggle my head, being funny—"she's not that kind of girl. But we live together. Doesn't that give you a hint? We're making plans."

"Like adopting a dog and going vegan?"

"You're such a dumbass," I say impatiently. "I don't know why you have so much beef with someone you don't even know. You're being a little provincial, and I never thought you were such a bumpkin."

She flips me off, and I take some cash out of my pocket and give it to her.

"This is on me. I've gotta go. She's waiting for me."

"Who, Amanda?"

I flick her on the forehead, just like when we were little, and she laughs.

"What if she makes you choose?" she says, and I can't tell whether she's joking or serious.

"Then I'll choose the one who's not making me choose."

I kiss her on the forehead, right where I hit her (gently, *hit* isn't really the word), and wink as I down the rest of my beer.

"Go take a nap. Don't show up at Mama and Papa's house with that depraved face like you've been up all night screwing."

I let out a chuckle.

"Nothing could be further from the truth."

"You didn't get laid?"

"She took me to Finisterre to watch the sun rise," I confess with a mix of shame and pride.

"That's so beautiful," she says sarcastically.

"It was. Try feeling something human. You'd be surprised. Take your boyfriend to Finisterre, and tell him that you can't promise him eternal love, but you can take him to the end of the world to tell him you love him right here and now. And then try to fuck in the back of the car to see if it wipes that bad mood off your face."

"Yuck."

That's the last thing she says to me. Then I just kiss her on the cheek and leave. But I still have one more stop to make before I meet Miranda...

I find her sitting on a patio, in the weak sun shining over Vigo today. I glanced at the weather forecast, and it's supposed to rain this afternoon. We'll make the most of it until the first drops, and then we'll go to the hotel to sleep, fully clothed, listening to the drops pattering against the window, until dinnertime.

"Hi." I lean down and give her a kiss. Her lips have a trace of vermouth on them.

"I didn't order you anything in case you took a long time."

"No worries." I sit down next to her and squeeze her leg affectionately.

"How's your boss?"

"Good. Like always. Walking the thin line between being a jerk and a psychopath."

That gets a smile out of her, and I show her the little bag resting in my lap.

"What's that?"

"I stopped by the pharmacy. It's for you."

I give it to her. She peeks inside and recognizes the medicine. It's the morning-after pill. I came inside her yesterday. We've been doing it without condoms for a year, but I always pull out. And we never actually settled on a contraceptive method. Then we did tests to make sure we were healthy...it's too tempting. We both get carried away in the moment, even though we've never taken it as far as we did last night. And yes, I know all about how "it sprinkles before it rains," but that's part of the risk we take on.

"Ah..." When she fishes out the box, she seems a little disoriented, like she doesn't remember last night, but she quickly nods to herself. "Of course. Thank you."

"I didn't buy it because I think you... I mean...you know I..." God, I'm so bad at this stuff. "If you don't want to take it, please, don't think I'm pressuring you. I know you... If it were up to me..."

Miranda smiles, opens the box, and asks me to call the waiter over.

"Order your beer and a tap water for me."

"How do you know I want a beer?" I return the smile.

"Because I know everything about you."

And that declaration scares me. And makes me feel warm. Warm, too, right in the part of my chest where very few things have that effect on me.

24

~~~

"COME OVER HERE FOR A SECOND, AND I'LL EXPLAIN EVERYTHING."

MIRANDA

You know when you wake up and you get the feeling the whole day is going to be shitty, and then everything is shitty? Well, try adding the bonus of knowing exactly what's going to happen and when. Some things I can solve; for example, the pigeon poop that dribbled down my hair, forehead, and raincoat, which I avoided by waiting for my cab under a bus shelter. The mischievous bird, which was waiting for me majestically perched on the lamppost in front of my door, was shit out of luck. But… will I be able to prevent anything else?

Today is Tristan's birthday. His thirty-fifth birthday. It should be a happy day, but it's not going to be. Why? Because today is the deadline day for closing the next issue, and there are a lot of problems that I could've fixed if I had woken up yesterday, but today they are going to make the newsroom go straight to DEFCON 2.

The first time around, not only was I a shitty girlfriend who didn't plan anything special for him, like a surprise party or something like that, but I was also very late for the "celebration," which was nothing more than a beer party with the four dudes from the office he gets along with. Well, kind of. Let's just say he can stand them.

He didn't like my gift at all, by the way: it was a beautiful black Saint

Laurent shirt with white guns printed on it. He took it out of the box, unfolded it, studied it, and looked at me very slowly before he declared, "But, Miri…you don't know me at all."

To be fair to Tristan: the shirt was amazing, but it wasn't his style at all. I don't know why I bought it for him. Sometimes we project ourselves onto our partners. Or maybe it was the kind of gift you give because you would love it yourself and you don't stop to think about the other person's taste. Maybe I didn't even have time to think it through.

Let's see what we can do today.

First of all, the office seems to be in flames. We're closing today, and Marisol (poor Marisol, who didn't even want to but succumbed to the peer pressure) trashed a four-page article. And she must have had her reasons.

"Girls, we have to come up with something else. That article isn't relevant at all anymore."

"That's what they said when they said paper was going to become obsolete," Marta, the digital director, pointed out.

And that's where the panic started. And the shit-talking. Because even though we all do a little bit of everything, there's still a kind of rivalry (which I've always thought was healthy, for what it's worth) between the people who work on the physical issue and those who work on the digital issue. This rivalry has created some friction today because…

We have to pull four pages of content out of our asses.

A huge ad campaign came in, and we have to redo the whole thing.

We're waiting for the photos for an article that still haven't come in, and we're waiting…and waiting…and waiting…

We all know this means staying really late. And these girls have lives beyond these four walls.

And I have a boyfriend, and it's his birthday.

I set up camp in the meeting room with the heads of each section to try to find solutions. No one's listening to each other, Marta's not helping with her digs, Marisol has a lunch with Guerlain, and I keep thinking about how to fix Tristan's birthday and worrying about being late. It's a madhouse right now.

I propose the topics that got us out of the predicament back then, because suddenly, a beam of light flashes in the hemisphere of my brain where this information is stored, but it turns out they don't quite work for Eva.

"We did something similar four or five months ago."

"Oh, go suck a dick," I answer tersely.

Marisol shoots me a look and then glances at her Cartier Tank watch.

"Sorry, Marisol," I apologize, putting my hand on her forearm. "But we have to find a solution."

"It's not a problem. I trust your judgment, my love, but let's watch how we talk to each other. I know the whole 'we're little ladies' thing is pretty outdated, but...let's speak to each other with the respect we deserve."

"You're right, you're right. Sorry, everyone," I address the table.

They nod. They're nervous too.

"What's the problem with the topic, Eva?" I try to mediate conciliatorily.

Outside, from their desks, the girls are all watching like this conclave is going to decide something life or death.

"We can't be constantly talking about skin care routines and hydration."

"I couldn't agree more," Cris pipes up. "We have a lot more to say from the beauty section."

"Under other circumstances, I would see it the same way you are, but we're up against the clock, and it's not a good day. We have to make executive decisions."

"But we're beating a dead horse."

"So find a hot take," I suggest. "'Skin care routines according to your age or your budget or whether there was a crescent moon when you were born.'"

"Come on, what's going on with you, Miranda?" Rita laughs.

"Isn't this enough?" I raise my eyebrows and sweep my arm across the expectant office.

"It is. But this happens every month."

"Yeah, but it doesn't fall on my boyfriend's birthday every month. And I bought him a shirt I know he's not gonna like, and I'm gonna show up late to his party, and I'm gonna be in the doghouse for at least five days, and he'll refuse to touch me with a barge pole for two weeks. Look, this affects me and all of you."

"How does you not getting laid affect the rest of us?"

"Because I'm going to make your lives a living hell."

I widen my eyes to emphasize my words.

I guess they don't believe my threats for a second, because they know me too well. Although I can get pretty annoying complaining about stuff, which isn't exactly fun for anyone.

"Girls, go ahead with the facial routine. Try to put an original spin on it, do something with a wink to our brand partners, and fashion can do their bit too," Marisol declares.

"What about an editorial debunking fashion myths?" I suddenly suggest.

"Such as…?"

"Well…the whole 'dress for the job you want,' 'only appropriate for a certain age,' every season some headline comes out declaring the 'new black' and it never is…"

"Said the eternal widow."

Everyone laughs. I do too. I can't help it. Today I'm wearing a black tube skirt, an oversized sweater that is also black, cinched at the waist with a black-and-gold belt, ankle booties with the same finish, and…can you guess what color my trench coat and bag are? Bingo.

"Sounds good to me. Let's adjust the pages and sections. I'll leave it in your hands. See?" Marisol stands up and adjusts her blouse. "See how we don't need to get trashy with each other?"

I laugh and nod. She points at me with her perfectly manicured hand. "I'm leaving you in charge, as always. I'll be back as soon as I can. Don't skip out on me. We're either going to close this together or not at all."

A sigh lodges in my chest when I realize how much I like this, how attached I am to my job. Tristan, the end version is right. It's one of the loves of my life, and sometimes I spoil it…

"Ah…" My boss turns in the door of the meeting room and looks at me again. "About your boyfriend's birthday… Do you know what really gets men excited?"

"What?"

"Same as us: feeling special. Gift him your time."

"Great. This is the perfect day to find a ton of time for him." I sigh.

"You'll figure out how to do it. You're a clever girl."

I love her, but right now, I feel like strangling her.

I dole out the content to write as fairly as possible, and I leave a few tasks for myself. I ask the poor interns to find images that we haven't used before to illustrate each new article.

After two calls trying to get them to send us the missing photos for the article (that still haven't come in yet), I shuffle off to the kitchen to pour myself another coffee and, while I'm at it, sit with my head in my hands to see if I can come up with something that won't fatally disappoint my partner. I've been hunched over racking my brain like this for ten minutes when the first batch of editors and interns come in for their caffeine fix.

"Hi, Miri," they all chorus.

"Hey, girls." I barely lift my head.

"You okay?" one of them asks.

I straighten up with hair like Eduard Punset and shake my head.

"We're going to get home super late tonight. You all know that, right?"

"Yes," they respond in chorus again before they all burst out laughing.

"Well, we'll take the hit in salary order, so the lowest paid will have the honor of going home as soon as they finish their work."

"Very considerate."

I take a bow.

"It works great for me because today is my boyfriend's birthday."

I look at the girl who said this like a caged dog looking at a bunny.

"Did you plan a surprise for him?"

"Well…" She shrugs, embarrassed. "Something."

"Will you tell me?"

They all look at each other timidly. Let's not forget that when Marisol isn't here, I'm the boss.

"If you want…"

"The thing is…it's my boyfriend's birthday too, and I haven't organized anything. I feel terrible and I know…"

"Did you say happy birthday this morning?"

I nod.

"And I brought him coffee in bed. But he had a meeting really early, and he barely had time to drink it."

Of course, I can't tell them that I was the one in a hurry because I realized what day I had woken up in, and I knew all the shit we were going to suffer today.

"I booked a table at a restaurant, and we're going to meet up at the bar where we met." She smiles politely. "I don't know if that'll give you many ideas. It's not very original."

"Right…it's just that I'm going to get out of here so late."

"Can't one of us fill in for you so you can leave earlier?"

"No, no. If closing is delayed, it's on me."

They nod gratefully, but I keep staring at them, stupefied. I just had an idea.

"Ooh, ooh…" one of them murmurs.

"Wait... You can't fill in for me on the closing, but..."

"Miri, I'm not going to flirt with your boyfriend," one of them pipes up.

"Have you seen him?" Another one elbows her. "I'll go, I'll go."

"You're all filthy!" I laugh. "Let me think. I might ask you for a couple of favors."

Twenty minutes later, I run into the newsroom like a nutjob, still looking like a mess, a hot mess.

"Raise your hand if you're not wearing heels today!"

After confused looks all around, six hands emerge timidly.

"Not you," I say to Rita. "I need you to close this fucking issue. You." I point at an intern. "I need you to do me a favor."

"And what are you going to give her in exchange?" Cris calls out from her desk, trying to bug me.

"Listen..." I lower my voice, and they all listen closely. "Today is closing day, and as you know, it looks like we're all going to get out of here veeeeeery late. But...to take our minds off it, the ones who have the least work are going to help me with my boyfriend's birthday. In exchange... you can all fill a bag full of products from the beauty closet."

There's a round of applause and whoops.

"Almudena, come over here for a second, and I'll explain everything."

25

~~

STROKING MY FACE

TRISTAN

I miss smoking. At least when I smoked, I had an excuse to get out of the office for ten minutes every hour and a half. Well…it's not really an office. It's one of those huge, old apartments that has been converted into a law firm. It looks like a fancy notary, which makes sense because I guess we're a fancy firm.

The bedrooms have been turned meeting rooms and offices. The kitchen is big, and we have an office kitchen with a coffee machine and some tables where we eat lunch when we bring food from home. The ceilings are high. We have three bathrooms. The walls are white and smooth, and the decor is classic and elegant. There's only the occasional landscape painting in the halls, and the furniture is made of good wood. You could say it's a good place to work, even if I find it stifling. I guess, at least as far as comfort is concerned, I'm lucky. There's a balcony off my shared office, and when we open the door, voices from the street, the smell of the season, and a thin thread of connection to real life (as in the life that takes place outside the walls of this office) waft in on the breeze. I've never really gotten the concept of living to work.

It's not a terrible environment. I just don't like what I do. It's taken me a few years longer than it should have to realize that I'm good at it, but I don't enjoy it. The only saving grace is the fact that I have no idea what else I could do.

The balcony door is open today. It's my birthday. And it's turning out to be a pretty gloomy one.

Last year, I could go home to Vigo because it fell on a weekend. The year before, I don't remember. But this year…well, Miranda is closing today, so I don't even have much faith she'll be able to come grab a beer with my colleagues later; she'll get home really late and exhausted. And I don't have many other friends in Madrid. Plus, I have barely any work today, but I can't leave the office. I'm a little down. I feel homesick.

"Tristan."

I look up from the computer and see the firm's receptionist. He doesn't usually talk to me much, only if the partners leave some note to share with me or if a document comes in addressed to me. But this seems different… He's wearing kind of a sneaky smile.

"Can you come out here for a second?"

"Why?"

"Is it your birthday?"

Oh God…

"Um…" I can feel my cheeks reddening under my beard. "Yes. Why?"

"There's a girl here…"

Before I can run out there to make sure Miranda hasn't shown up at my office with some crazy idea, a little blond girl, who's pretty cute, by the way, sticks her head out behind him, smiling. She has a box with two helium balloons in the shape of "35" attached to it.

"I'm gonna kill her," I say very seriously before breaking into a mortified laugh.

The girl comes over without asking permission, and I sit in my chair again, although I guess saying I collapsed into my chair would be more faithful to reality.

"Hi, Tristan. Happy birthday."

She resolutely pushes aside some papers and carefully puts the box down. The balloons bob over my desk to the delight of all my colleagues, who burst into applause, laughter, and cheers. I don't like most of them very much (too much ego, too much nonsense, too much competitive-ness), but their laughter is contagious.

"Thanks," I say to her. "She sent you?"

"It's closing day, Tristan. It's like if you were all in the middle of an important trial." She smiles like a saint. "We can't lose our best Amazon at the height of the battle. Plus...she sent me because I'm wearing flats."

That Miranda. I cover my face, rub it, and then laugh again mid-sigh.

"Okay. Thanks so much..."

"Almudena."

"Thank you, Almudena."

"For you, Tristan." She holds an envelope out to me. "Have a happy day."

"Sounds like a threat."

She answers with a giggle as she heads to the door. I catch a glimpse of her flirting with the receptionist on her way out. I love the spark of people in their twenties, when you think the world is yours and...it probably is. I open the box and find a beautiful, tempting spread, including coffee, a juice, a cinnamon roll, and a slice of tortilla de patata. I get the giggles.

"What'd you get, Galicia boy?" one of my colleagues asks.

"Breakfast."

"What about the card?"

"It's probably just a happy birthday card."

I open the envelope and take out a white card that just has a few words written on it and Miranda's signature.

A happy birthday breakfast.
I love you.
You probably won't feel the same about me tonight.

Miranda

I raise my eyebrows. Jeez. That does sound like a threat. I'm scared of her. I'm really scared of her, but in a smiling way.

"You sharing?" A colleague sticks her head over to see if she can snag something. It's 11:30, and everyone's getting peckish.

"No fucking way."

Miranda knows me, everything about me, and she knows I can be easily seduced by food.

At 12:15, a shaft of light cuts across the room, leaving a trail of golden dust mites dancing in its path. We're all slightly entranced by it because it looks so peaceful, like the plastic bag floating in the wind in *American Beauty*. We're joking about what would happen if a client saw us looking like this when the receptionist comes back in.

"Tristan…"

"Oh God. In person or a delivery?"

"In person."

I jump to my feet.

"Okay, I'm coming."

"You don't need to come out."

"I'm coming, I'm coming. I'll grab it by reception." I'm trying to prevent the ceremonial entry of the messenger or chosen intern coming to my desk, whatever Miranda might have thought of sending me now, but I see him shake his head, enjoying himself.

"It's easier if the messenger wheels the cart in."

"What cart?"

A messenger dressed in midnight blue comes in whistling and pushing a cart holding three boxes. Three boxes and an envelope.

"Tristan Castro?"

"That's me."

"I need your signature here."

I'm in disbelief.

When the messenger leaves, I gesture for scissors from my desk mate, who takes the chance to jump up and crane her neck over to see what the boxes are hiding.

"Your girl sent those too?" my colleague from the back of the office pipes up.

"Who else?"

"Your girlfriend is...enthusiastic."

"Enthusiastic? She's a hurricane."

When I lift the flaps of the first box, I take a step back and put my hands on my hips, chewing my bottom lip. I can't believe it. She's nuts.

"What is it?"

I don't answer. I push the box aside and open the other one. Identical. The content of the bottom one must be the same. I grab the envelope and tear it open.

Dear Tristan,

I'd tell you to store them in a dry place out of direct sunlight, but first you have to find the clue.
You've always had a big sweet tooth, right?
Happy egg birthday.

I love you,
Miranda

"What are they?"

When I look up, my colleagues have gathered around me.

"Kinder eggs."

The laughter must have been loud enough to reach the other side of the office, because another handful of colleagues suddenly appear. And that's a good thing, because I'm going to need help.

We count 210 Kinder eggs in total. There are seventy in each box. We split up into groups to inspect each one carefully to find "the clue." Whoever finds it is supposed to raise the alarm so the rest can stop searching. We thank our lucky stars that the bosses are insanely busy today and there are no fires to put out.

"Your girlfriend is the shit," one of my colleagues murmurs as she pushes aside the chocolates that have already been checked.

"Don't get your dirty mitts all over them. I plan on eating all of them," I say, holding up the one I've already bitten into.

"You could have chocolate every day until you turn thirty-six."

More like forty.

"Here it is!"

The shout comes from the next room, so dozens of footsteps ring out on the parquet as everyone stampedes in there at the same time. I have to jostle through the crowd to get to the colleague who found the clue and has probably already read it.

I don't know if I'm dying of embarrassment or laughter.

"Ooooh," howl a couple of the morons who already managed to catch a glimpse of it.

"Argh, you're all so gross. Give it to me."

I hear several mouths chewing as I read it.

Don't eat too many…
    You don't wanna ruin your appetite.

                    Happy and hot thirty-five, my love.
                    Miranda

Come the fuck on.

"But that isn't a clue!"

"That's a declaration of intentions."

My colleagues don't hold back. An elbow digs into my side, and I roll my eyes as I fold the slip of paper and tuck it into my pocket. When I get back to my desk, I'll put it in my wallet, next to the other notes.

"Okay, okay, thanks everyone. You can take a few eggs each. Who says this firm doesn't have perks?"

"Or ovaries, right?"

"True, true." I bow subtly to a few colleagues, who take the chance to give me a deserved slap on the back of the neck.

I spend the next half an hour organizing boxes of Kinder eggs. This has been the most bizarre birthday of my life. But there's no rest for the wicked, so just when I finish and go back to my seat, the receptionist sticks his head in again.

"Tristan..."

"No way!" I exclaim.

They all burst into laughter and applause.

"Messenger or intern?"

"Interns..."

Three girls in outfits so trendy they look like they've come from the future appear, each holding a little box and giggling uncontrollably. They're the modern version of the Three Kings, except it's not Christmas.

"Hi, Tristan," they greet me in unison.

"Hi, girls." I sigh.

"He's so cute," they murmur through their giggles.

"Happy birthday."

All three hand me their boxes, but I hesitate.

"Do I need to open them in a specific order?"

"Miranda says it doesn't matter, that…what was it again?"

They look at each other until finally one widens her eyes with a clear "Eureka!" look.

"You never seemed that into protocol when it comes to this."

"Oh, Lord…" I murmur to myself.

By the time the girls are heading for the door, my desk is surrounded by expectant colleagues. I can see where this is going, but I don't know how to get out of it. Curiosity killed the cat.

"It'd probably be better if I open this one by myself."

The jeering doesn't intimidate me, but they're not going anywhere.

"Come on, don't any of you have work to do or something?"

"Open it!"

"Go eat a Kinder."

There's no way out of it. I pray that Miranda wasn't being herself too much when she chose this gift.

I open a tiny corner. It's definitely small, so I don't think it can get me in too much trouble or make me blush. I'm not quick enough on the uptake to see how wrong I am.

It's two dice. Two red dice, each about the size of a nut, but instead of numbers, there's something written on each face. Actions on one of them, body parts on the other.

"No fucking way…" I mutter through clenched teeth, trying to shove them out of view at the same time.

But it's too late. My colleagues caught a glimpse of the words "lick" and "nipples" too.

There's another round of applause, and I want to dig a hole down to the first floor and run out to the street below to catch a bus. But it's all in good fun, because it's impossible not to laugh. The crowd keeps growing unstoppably, and they're cheering and clapping out a beat. *Miranda, I'm gonna kill you.*

"Open them! Open them!"

"The partners are going to come out, for God's sake. Quiet down!" I beg, but the partners are either blasting Vivaldi or they're not here. I figure it's probably the latter.

I put the boxes under my desk and try to use reason to dissuade the mob, but finally I have to jab at them with the umbrella printed with the firm's logo that we all keep under our desks for rainy days to get them to leave. When I think there are no prying eyes around, I duck under my desk to open the other two boxes. First the medium one: handcuffs…but not the regular kind. I have to study them for a while before I figure out they must be for the headboard. Or who knows, they'd probably work on any piece of furniture. There must be steam coming out of my ears. I don't know if I have the balls to open the big one. Please don't let it be what my friends call a "strap-on," because I'm not saying I wouldn't like it if I tried it, but I don't feel like parading it around here… It'd provide fodder for the office banter for years to come. Not that I really care what other people think about my sex life, but…I'd rather they didn't think anything at all.

Inside the box, there's another very pretty black box, adorned with a ribbon that curls all the way down to the floor. I have to push aside some scented tissue paper to see what's inside, and I discover…

I slam the box shut, push everything back down next to my feet, and rest my forehead on the desk. Fuck. The golden whore.

There are so many straps and buckles on this lingerie I have no idea how she'll even get it on. But I get the impression that it's…a lot more out there than what she normally wears. It's not the kind of getup she would wear under her clothes to work. She'd put it on to go out to dinner and whisper, in a very sultry voice in the middle of dinner, that she's wearing something underneath that I'm going to like. Like that one time. I slid my hand under the table stealthily while she was leaning forward to talk to me, feigning interest in her coffee, until I reached her left breast and fondled it. We almost fucked in the doorway after. And today, just like that time, I can't stand up, because I'm hard. She knows this stuff really turns me on.

I look up from my computer and realize that my colleagues I share a room with are all smirking at me.

"Lingerie?" one of them ventures a guess.

"Yup."

The chuckle is contagious. Damn Miranda. She drives me crazy.

At two, when I normally go out to eat lunch, my colleagues suggest going to a burger place nearby to "celebrate." I feel like telling them we're already going to "celebrate" with a few beers at the end of the day, but I don't know how to pull that off without seeming like an asshole, so I agree. I don't feel like sitting and eating a greasy burger. Look, any other day, it wouldn't gross me out, but today, I'm just not really craving it, with this huge crowd of acquaintances. I like some of them, but I have to be honest and admit that I haven't deepened my relationship with any of them. I have colleagues here, but I don't think I would call any of them a friend. That's just how it is sometimes. It's not like I'm an idiot; I tried, but…we just don't click. They think anyone who isn't obsessed with learning to play golf to impress clients and climb the ladder fast is a total loser. There are a couple of guys and girls I like well enough, but they have very different lives, family lives.

I walk down the stairs with a few of them; normally they'd be talking about work, soccer, theater, or some TV show, but today, my birthday is monopolizing the conversation, much to my utter discomfort. I smile and shove my hands as deep as I can into my pockets, trying desperately to come up with a topic that will distract them. But…

When I step onto the street, Madrid's yellow spring light blasts me in the face, and I squint. I guess that's why I don't spot her right away. At first, I can only make out a silhouette dressed in black leaning against the car parked in front of the awning. But that red-painted smile can only belong to one person. My stomach leaps, and I smile. She makes me tingle. She makes my palms, my stomach, my cock, my lips tingle. My whole being yearns to be close to her, to smell her, to kiss her, to caress her.

A brief, amused murmur slips out from behind her huge sunglasses. I like them...sophisticated without trying too hard. And like so many other things I love about us, it also kind of scares me. I'm scared I'll get tired of it. I'm scared she'll want me to be like that too and... I won't be able to keep up for long. Or at all.

"You're crazy."

I mouth the words silently, but she can read my lips.

"You guys go ahead without me, okay? We'll celebrate tonight."

They slap me on the back like I'm a bullfighter heading off to face the big one, like they suspect, as I do, that under her trench coat...Miranda's wearing nothing at all.

"Tell me you're not naked under there," I whisper, pressing my nose into hers.

"Are you crazy? Of course not. I came to eat lunch with you, not to eat you."

"No idea what part of your last three gifts could've confused me."

"Kiss me."

I put a hand on the hood of the car and look around to make sure my colleagues have turned the corner. Then I press myself into her, trapping her between the vehicle and my body, moving my hips so she notices how I always react when I smell her. I kiss her. I kiss her passionately, really passionately, but I keep it brief. I want to leave her as hungry as I was after getting all her little gifts.

"Bastard," she moans when I pull away from her and dodge her trying to kiss me again.

"They say relationships need a little mystery to make them healthy and sustainable." I give her a roguish smile. "What are you doing here? You must be really stressed with closing the issue."

"I am, but I still have to eat, right? Everything's going wrong today. If Godzilla shows up in the newsroom demanding right of pardon, I wouldn't be surprised."

"He couldn't do much there. I don't think there are any virgins to sacrifice."

"Depends what orifice we're talking."

A snort escapes through my nose.

"I'll never get used to it." I linger near her mouth again, enjoying teasing her.

"To what?"

"To you."

"That's good. Then you'll never get bored."

Sometimes I think Miranda can read my mind. There are days when it seems like nothing about me could be foreign or strange or indecipherable. Like I'm an open book. Or a white page she's writing on herself.

"I'm really sorry," she says remorsefully. "I only have forty-five minutes. An hour tops. I would have loved to set up a picnic for you in Oeste Park…near that little stream you like, but it's impossible. And it's not because I don't love you or I love the magazine more. It's just that I have a responsibility."

"It's fine," I say sincerely.

"So…I booked us a table at Nagoya. It's near both of us, and I know, even though sushi's not your fave, you do like their food."

I want to tell her it's perfect, exactly what I was craving even if I didn't know it yet, but I just take her hand and tug her a little in the direction of the restaurant.

Lunch flies by. Or that's how it feels at least. I'm aware of the effort Miranda is making to not check her phone every five minutes. It makes me sick that she's doing this, because this is childish, but it makes me feel invisible, unimportant, in the way. Like she's going to say: "Just gimme a second. This is grown-up stuff." And I want to be her grown-up stuff, although I want to have my own stuff too, but I don't. We say goodbye at the door of the restaurant, where she hails the first cab that goes by. She has to go harass I don't know who owes her I don't know what photos.

"I'm worried they forgot to edit them and now they're rushing to get it done. I can't publish a bunch of bullshit."

I don't really know what she's talking about, but like so many other times, there's no time to explain. She's like a fashion superhero. She has her obligations to the world.

Once the taxi she's in disappears around the corner, I start heading back to the office, but I've only gotten a few meters when a message from Miranda sounds:

MIRANDA:

Check your right pocket.

I bury both my hands in my jacket pockets, even though her instructions were very specific, and I discover a little slip of paper that I read immediately. It's just an address:

Calle de Modesto Lafuente, 31.

I open Google Maps, which tells me it will take seventeen minutes to walk there. If I pick up the pace, it won't be more than fifteen. I'm a little sweaty when I get there, but there's a nice breeze that makes it more bearable. The address is for a small bookstore that is a play on the street name: Modesta Librería. And it fits because the space is so tiny and modest. I don't know what I'm doing here. Does she want me to buy a book? Is this a hint to get me to read more? Does she want me to buy something for her? I hesitate, but curiosity wins out, and I go in. A boy is reading behind the counter, sitting on a stool.

"Hello," I say to him.

"Hi…"

He doesn't just look at me. He scrutinizes me. His brow furrows under his floppy bangs.

"Are you looking for anything in particular?" he asks me.

"No." I can't help but smile, a little embarrassed. "The truth is…"

He takes a book out from under the counter and hands it to me. It's a small book; on the cover, on a green background, there's a black-and-white photo of a girl who looks like she could be the protagonist of a silent film, holding a heart with flowers growing out of it. *Primero de Poeta* by Patricia Benito.

"I think this belongs to you."

"Um…" I hesitate.

"Because you're Tristan, right?"

I smile. Yes, yes, I am, especially when she's the one saying my name.

I should already be back at my desk, getting back to work after my lunch break, but I decide not to rush. It's just one day. I sit on a bench in a little plaza near the office with my book in my hand. I notice it has an inscription, simple and perfect, which she scribbled as fast as she could with the blue pen she always has in her bag and left a tiny smudge when she started writing:

I just wanted to give you something that would last a long time.

I don't think there's anything more lasting than printed words, especially when they're about love.

The one who
loves you,
Miranda

I flip through the pages in search of a note, a clue, something, but the only thing I find (which is a lot actually) is a dog-eared page. I figure she wanted me to read this poem.

For so long I've only known
one-night stands
under Monday moons full of darkness
I can't imagine any other way.
For so long I've only known
treating my pain with lime,
healing myself with salt,
erasing with tequila.
For so long I've only known
weekend permissions,
loveless orgasms,
spaces without warmth.
For so long I've only known
treading slowly,
entering noiselessly,
fleeing without an embrace.
By myself for so long,

so many nights without you,
I can't imagine any other way.
Then you come along,
and I understand why spring
comes after the cold
and it seems impossible
for winter to return.
Now any old groundhog day
sounds just perfect with you.

Miranda...how much effort did it take to create you?
I don't want to bore you with the rest. Just...
At five in the afternoon, a huge bouquet of flowers arrives for me with a note that says:

Flowers don't have a gender.
They're just beautiful.
I love you.

At six, a messenger with a box of colorful, elaborate filled donuts.
At five past six, an email with a link to a song by Zahara..."Tú me llevas."
At six thirty, when almost everyone from the office is heading to the bar on the corner to toast with a few beers, the bartender pulls me aside to tell me that half an hour earlier, a girl came in, paid him a hundred euros, and told him this was for my celebration. He asks me if I want to order any food.
"We have bacon from Soria..."
At ten, when I get home, a trail of LED candles guides me to the bathroom, where there's music playing (for God knows how long) and there

are little fairy lights hanging from everything and a note stuck to the mirror:

You're right that every house should have a bathtub. I wanted to run you a bath so you can relax, but all I can offer you is a shower.

If you're still hungry, there's dinner waiting in the oven. The iPad is on the bed, all set up so you can watch that really boring show you love.

I can't tell you I'll be home soon, but I can promise you I'll be home. Always and wherever you are. It doesn't matter how late. I'll be there.

I love you,
Miranda

P.S. When I come in, if I find the lingerie I sent you hanging from the bedroom doorknob, I'll know it's okay to wake you up so you can tie me to the bed.

Maybe better to save it for Saturday, when you'll be well rested and have more time to enjoy (me) (us).

My pajamas are laid out on the bed, next to the iPad, and they smell like fabric softener.

I fall asleep watching the show, and I forget to hang the lingerie on the door, but I wake up when she's pulling the tablet out of my lap and slipping stealthily into bed. Right now, I don't have enough energy to fuck her in a way that would be worth remembering, so I put it on my to-do list for tomorrow.

Miranda snuggles into my back, putting her arm around my waist; I notice how she smells me through the cotton of my shirt. She sighs, like my scent soothes her, but softly, because she thinks I'm asleep.

"I'm sorry," she says quietly.

"Thank you for the best birthday of my life."

I roll over to face her, and we kiss. She seems like a mixture between sad and relieved, but it's very dark, and this is just a fleeting impression.

I fall back to sleep with her fingertips stroking my face.

26

~~

AND THE GAZPACHO SUDDENLY DOESN'T TASTE AS DELICIOUS ANYMORE

MIRANDA

I wish I could've woken up exactly how I fell asleep, with his arms wrapped around me, enveloped by his scent and my hands on him, but I'm alone in bed, and the alarm clock is drilling into my temples like a machine gun. My head hurts like hell, and I don't know what day it is.

There's a lot of light streaming in through the window for seven o'clock in the morning, so I deduce that it's the middle of summer. My phone confirms it: July 5.

I sit on the edge of the bed and feel a heaviness in my head, eyelids, and shoulders. I finally muster enough strength to get up and head to the bathroom, and I barely recognize myself in the mirror. I look terrible. My face looks gaunt, my eyes are puffy, I have deep, dark circles under my eyes, and my hair is pretty dirty. Pretty dirty is a euphemism…it's filthy. You could fry croquettes in it.

I can't tell if I've lost weight, gained weight, or neither, but my body has changed, and my face looks like death. Is this a consequence of so many time jumps? But wait…what year is it?

An internal alarm makes my heart race, and I put my hand on my chest, like I could squeeze it into not beating so fast, and study my surroundings.

My house. A house exactly like last night, except for a few subtle, very subtle, changes.

Tristan's soap isn't in the shower. I can't see his electric razor either or his shaving cream, his toothpaste, or his comb in the medicine cabinet. The wardrobe is much emptier than usual: his clothes are missing. And his shoes. I rush into the living room: his books aren't there or his records or the record player, and neither are our photos. But...have I gone further back? Have I gone back to before I met him?

"No, no, no, no," I say over and over with a tinge of rage in my voice.

All this effort is killing me; I'm exhausted. Everything was going so well...

I open the calendar app on my phone and collapse.

July 5, present time.

Tristan dumped me three months ago.

"Fuck!"

I have a delayed reaction. All I want to do is climb back into bed, close the curtains, and sleep until all this is over. I don't know where I want to wake up tomorrow, but I want to be anywhere but here. The possibility that I could wake up tied to a bed in a mental institution, with a doctor telling me this was all a dream, occurs to me more than once. Or maybe the Matrix exists, and the simulation they've put me in is glitching.

The only thing I know for sure is that today is Monday and, as far as I know, I still work for a living. I can call the magazine, tell them I'm sick, and then send a message to Ivan, asking him to come over. Maybe he...I don't know. Maybe he can somehow explain what's happening. He's really smart, he always has been... He probably understands it.

I could also go to work, and... I have this nagging feeling that's what I should do. But first...I'm going to change the sheets and air out this room. Everything seems to indicate that I've spent the whole weekend rotting in bed. It smells like... Let's just say it smells stuffy.

The fridge is empty. There's a teetering pile of take-out bags next to the trash. All very healthy, of course... The pimples I noticed on my chin and temples were born to a mother of "burger and onion rings" and a father of "fried chicken combo." The sink is full of glasses, cups, spoons, and the occasional plate. The washing machine is empty, and the laundry basket is overflowing. The sink is full of hair. A giant dust bunny is staring at me gravely from the corner, judging me. It seems like it's saying: "You've hit rock bottom, bitch."

When I leave the house, I've finally made everything halfway decent... enough so the neighbors don't feel the need to call the Health Department to shut down my house as a threat to public safety. Yolanda isn't coming until Thursday, so something had to be done, or I'd be living in filth for the next four days.

I put on the only clean clothes in my closet that weren't party clothes: a midi, short-sleeved cotton dress. I add a necklace to show I made some effort to "look cute." I wash my hair, but I put it in a low bun so I don't have to do much with it. I'm not wearing a scrap of makeup. I can't be bothered, so my eyes are still puffy; apparently I spent most of Sunday crying. I look like Mad-Eye Moody from Harry Potter.

I could have finished off the look with heels as a final touch, but I decided to go for some low black Converse instead, opting for comfort. I'm carrying a big bucket bag. As I got dressed, I realized I have slimmed down in certain places... My boobs have shrunk, and maybe my thighs too, although they're also flabbier. I feel numb and soft in equal parts. But my belly is swollen, and so is my face, like my body is changing its shape piece by piece instead of all together. I know my body, and even though I'm not worried about the aesthetic effect, I know all this is a consequence of months of not taking care of myself at all. Months of neglect. And that's enough now...

I forget to take off my sunglasses when I get to the newsroom and keep them on until I'm safely ensconced in my office. Well...actually I forgot I was wearing them for a few seconds, and then I thought it was best not to take them off so I wouldn't scare anyone. A few eyes follow me to "my quarters," but I don't meet them. I just throw a generic "good morning" out into the air. No motivational phrases or endearments. I feel the instinct to hide, like a nocturnal rodent in the sun. I watched so many vampire movies I ended up becoming one.

I turn on my computer, open my planner with the intention of getting to work right away, and... God...it's a disaster. Everything is full of chaotic, scribbled, unreadable Post-its. I can't understand any of it, but it seems like we have a lot of work to do. I don't know where to start. I'm plagued by a kind of compulsive thought, one that I recognize and that haunts me whenever I'm not doing well, when I set my sights on goals that are too lofty and then I fall apart when I don't achieve them. It goes something like "This is a mess, and I feel helpless about doing anything to improve it. I don't want to do it. I would have to expend a titanic effort, which I'm not prepared to do." Instead of all that drama, I could just sigh and...just start, little by little, to try. It's better than nothing. But I can't see it clearly.

Someone knocks on my office's glass door, and I beckon them in without looking up to see who it is. It's Rita.

"Love...how are you doing?" she asks gently.

"Fine...well... I gave up trying to understand my handwriting from last week, so you caught me seriously considering contacting a specialist in cuneiform writing to see if anyone can decipher all these unhinged Post-its."

I look at her and smile in a way that's probably disturbing because it's not genuine. She gives me back a sad smile.

"You smell good," she declares.

"Um..."

"Showering is a good step, but…you don't look great, Miri."

"Yeah, I noticed."

Wait…have I not been showering at all lately?

"I know that's a shitty thing to say." She grabs the chair in front of my desk, sits down, leans in, and says in a conciliatory tone, "It's not like I'm saying it maliciously. 'Ooh, your face looks terrible' or 'Are we packing on a few pounds?' That's not it. You know me, and you know I'm not like that."

"I know, I know."

"But let me just say: I'm a little worried about you."

I stare at her, not knowing how to respond.

"Did you just get in?" she asks.

"Yes." And I say it like it's the best evidence in the whole history of humanity.

"It's past eleven. You never get in that late."

"Well, I wanted to use the flexible hours for once…" And yes, I'm being defensive even though I know that she has good intentions and we trust each other enough for her to be able to say stuff like that.

"Yes. It's fine, Miri. I'm not saying this as a colleague, I'm saying it as a friend. It's just not like you, and I'm scared it's a symptom that things aren't improving. It's been three months…"

I want to explain to her that for me, it's been much less, that yesterday, I buried my nose in his back in bed, that pain doesn't have official, logical deadlines that we all have to meet, and that I'm time traveling, jumping from one moment of my relationship to another, so I have the right to show up however the coin flips. There's no one checking our schedules or hoping for better grades. And I'm scared and crestfallen, because I thought I was fixing things. But I don't say anything.

"Why don't you take a few days off? Maybe you can go somewhere with Ivan. Maybe even spend a few days in Tarifa like you did before."

Ivan…what's he going to look like now? Has all this change made him sprout wings from his back? Maybe he's decided to dress like a Tibetan monk?

"Tarifa will be packed. Nobody'd be able to book a room right now. Can you imagine El Tumbao? It'll be like Primark on a Saturday afternoon." I shrug, pretending it doesn't matter, that everything's fine and we're just chatting about vacations.

More knuckles rap on the door, but the person they belong to doesn't wait to come in. They just barge in. That gives me a clue who it is before I even see her. It's Marisol.

"Hi, my girls. Happy Monday."

"Happy Monday, Marisol."

"Ooh! It smells good in here, right?"

Okay. I've definitely been slacking on my personal hygiene for a while now. I try as discreetly as possible to sniff inside my clothes. Everything is in order…at least today.

"Rita, can you give me a second with Miranda?"

"Of course…"

A lecture is looming.

"Oh, and, love…I hate asking you to do this, but…could you ask someone to bring us some of those really nice teas from the kitchen?"

"Of course, lady. No problem."

When the door closes and we're left alone, Marisol looks at me tenderly, so tenderly that I want to do her a favor and break the ice.

"I look terrible, I know."

"Hmm…" She crosses her legs elegantly. "You showered, brushed your hair, and got dressed to come in to work. That's all a really good start."

"Do I not normally do that?" I ask, alarmed.

An image flashes into my head of me sitting in this same chair in pilled leggings, a sweatshirt with a stain that looks suspiciously like mayonnaise, and a bun like a Yorkshire terrier trying to "hide" the grease; a few flies and a green cloud float over me. That last part is a figment of my imagination, I admit.

"We both know the last three months have been hard for you. A loss is a loss, even when it's not a death, and it needs a mourning period," she says patiently.

"I know."

"But you have to take care of yourself."

"I'm trying." I have no idea if I actually am.

"You have to try harder. For yourself. Because when you're better, you're not going to like looking back at this."

I don't agree. Loving someone, respecting them and admiring them, doesn't always mean that you're going to have the same opinion. I've always advocated that if you need to be bad without punishing yourself for it, that's part of the healing process. Just like we'd never think of telling someone who's broken his leg that he should start running with a cast on, we shouldn't do that when the pain isn't something physical. I don't know if the soul takes more or less time to heal itself, but I think it deserves to set its own timeline.

But still…she's my boss.

"I've been letting work slide," I'm assuming. But it's pretty clear, even though I haven't exactly been here.

"Well, yes, but this magazine is a community, a united family, and so we're here to back you up and make a human chain with the things that are left unfinished, because you've led the charge to do the same for us in the past."

"I don't like leaving things unfinished in my wake, but I don't feel very capable right now, Marisol. And I'm sorry about that. I shouldn't have let my personal life invade my professional one."

"And you haven't. It's just that it's very hard to lead a normal life with a broken heart."

I feel a lump in my throat. But I was doing everything right... How did it not fix what was broken? How is it possible that all the effort of reliving and fixing still left me feeling like this?

One of the interns slips into the office quietly with two tall glasses of ice and tea with lemon. She worked hard on the presentation, dropping a slice of lemon into each and adding a colorful cardboard straw. In the editorial kitchen, we always have nice things to cheer us up. Maybe I should take refuge in the frivolous for the rest of the day.

"You smell so good!" she exclaims when she comes over to put the glasses on the table.

Ay, Saint Christian Dior...

"Thanks so much," I say. "I swear your whole internship isn't going to be making tea and coffee."

"Yes, poor thing, we're also going to ask you to research prices," Marisol says, being funny but sheepish at the same time.

The girl smiles.

"Well...the truth is I love researching prices. I find it really soothing."

"That's my girl, always finding something positive in everything." Marisol gives her a pat before she leaves the office.

We're both aware that this short exchange of words has brightened the girl's day. But reality barges back to the forefront again.

"Miranda, I need you to do me a favor." She takes a sip of her tea and invites me to do the same, but I don't really feel like it.

"Of course."

"I need you to take the week off. I can't give you extra days, but I've been looking at the quarter, and you haven't taken any vacation since Christmas. You have plenty."

"If I don't need to come in to work, I'll go crazy at home."

"I know, my love, but doing things halfway ends up costing double, because that way, you're not healing your pain, and you're not conquering it like you should either. I'm sorry to be so harsh."

"I've always liked it when you are. You do it affectionately, and that gets the best out of us."

"Miri…take the vacation days. Come back next week ready to create a new life. If all that means is taking care of yourself more, that's fine by me. Because we can only take baby steps down that path."

I don't like those kinds of phrases from a self-help book, but I chew it over and nod.

"One day," I haggle.

"Three."

"Two."

She raises a hand. She knows I'm stubborn, and…it's not like under other circumstances, days off wouldn't seem like ambrosia to me, but right now, I feel, more than ever, like I need my work.

"Rules for my return to the grindstone: shower every day."

We both laugh.

"Darling…" She reaches out her hand and takes mine. "It's shitty losing a love, especially when it is something as special as you and Tristan had, but life is long, and we have a lot to give. Right now, you might think it's impossible, but one day, you'll love again. And when that day comes, you'll love yourself, which is wonderful."

When people say the word "time" to someone with a broken heart, that word becomes a rosary burning your throat. Because when its fresh, time is relative. Rest is fleeting, nights are too long, memories too deep. Time is what you feel you don't have, what you've lost. You're in a hurry, yes, because the pain squeezes so tightly, but you have no idea what this "time" really means. And as painful as it might be, it couldn't be more real.

I turn off my computer, close my planner, and smile at her.

"Well, I'm going home then. Who's in charge? Tell them to call me if there are any questions or fires to put out..."

"I'm in charge, sweetie. I think I can handle it."

I find my father sitting in the wingback chair in his little shop, reading a book that looks older than him. Next to him, on a small round table, like a Parisian coffee table with wrought-iron legs, sits a Victorian-style teacup full of herbal tea.

"Dad...I know I always ask you this, but...is it normal that you're always using the stuff you should be selling?"

"I sold that Castilian chest you've always hated today."

"You didn't answer my question, but I'm glad to hear it. It's looked like a vampire sarcophagus from the thirteenth century."

"Four thousand euros." He raises his eyebrows and leaves them really high while he smiles at me. "And...I sell old things. What does it matter if I use them in the meantime? It's just so they don't get sad."

We both smile. He still tells me stories even though I'm grown up.

"They sent me home from school. Two days off," I announce.

"Vacation or unpaid?"

"Vacation. I'm scatterbrained, but I'm a good person. I'm not on the path to being a delinquent yet."

"A drunk but not a punk."

We both laugh.

"Well..." He puts his book down next to the cup of tea and stands up to give me a kiss. "I think you're looking a little better. Mmm! And you showered! You smell great."

"Clear something up for me... From one to ten, how have I been these last few months?"

"The first two months, you were fine. This last one, we were thinking about staging an intervention. The thing is, it was like this really sour smell."

I'm horrified.

"Dad!"

"Ay, sweetheart, don't ask if you don't want the truth."

My father offers to order some food, Korean or maybe Thai, and eat it in the shop while we talk, but I'm worried about my nutrition.

"I think everything I've eaten in the last few months has come from a package or been delivered in a paper bag."

So he resolutely pulls the curtain closed on the store and takes me to his favorite bar, the bar where he's had coffee every workday since he opened his business and where he's built up a friendship with the owner over the years. Even though it's a bar that feeds many people, the food is still homemade and good. Today, they're serving gazpacho and roast chicken. It tastes so good I could cry.

Dad struggles to broach what he's worried about; I see him watching me out of the corner of his eye, gauging how and when would be best to tackle it. I could give him a hand and bring it up myself, but I find it amusing watching him work out his plan. A plan that could be summed up as "trying to rob the Bank of Spain without being noticed and end up smashing the car into the window of a Mercería Lola and taking twenty euros worth of stockings."

"Look, I think it's great that you're back to showering."

I'm glad I swallowed my spoonful of gazpacho before he started talking.

"Go on…" I laugh.

"You had us worried."

"You and who else? You know the memory of Mama doesn't count as a physical presence, right?"

"You're really silly when you want to be," he replies seriously. "For me, she's much more than a memory, but it's complicated, which you understand." He sighs. "I'm talking about Ivan."

"I'll call him later."

"Call him, and go do something fun. Go to a spa or get a massage. Something."

I nod and keep eating.

"You were really little and you won't remember, of course, but when your mother lost your grandmother... Ay, your grandmother was the best. Super fun and very sweet...but as I was saying...when your grandmother died, Mama was destroyed. At first, she resisted the pain. She told me we had to take care of you and the store and she couldn't collapse, she didn't have time. I remember her face when I asked her if it would work for us to send her grief on vacation so it wouldn't disturb her. She had a temper... I guess you do know that because you inherited all of it. The thing is, she resisted, but pain is like an avalanche. You might think it'll be quick, but it can bury you under layers and layers of snow. It's not predictable at all."

"Why are you telling me this?" I don't look at him when I ask.

"Because I'm proud of you, and I'm sure Mama would be too. You let a few important things fall by the wayside, yes, but you've embraced your grief, and that..."

"Wait, wait...you're congratulating me because I've embraced the shit and I don't know how to get out of it?"

"No." He laughs. "You're so full of quips, sweetheart. I'm telling you I'm very proud that you're self-aware enough to put yourself first."

Ay...

"Dad, I haven't been neglecting work and my hygiene to prioritize myself. It's just that...I didn't know how to do any better. I've been under the avalanche, thinking I was warm."

"But look at you. You smell good now."

Mother of God.

"This is like when your mama was going through it," he goes on. "The first month, she was absent, but because she needed to accept everything first before she could..."

I stop him. I don't need more sad stories.

"Papi...let me ask you something. It's something nice, eh. It's not a dig."

"Of course, sweetie."

He strokes my hair. Sometimes I think we express love in my house like we're dogs.

"Don't you get tired of remembering Mama?"

I don't think he was expecting that question, because he stays silent for what seems like a long time, looking at me. Little by little, he gets his smile back and shakes his head.

"No. I don't. But it has its stages and...its choices."

"What do you mean by 'choices'?"

"You're not asking me about the stages..."

"No. I'm guessing you're talking about the stages of grief."

"Yes. And that has to do with the choices I'm talking about. And the thing is...when you're overcome by grief, it's normal to revisit the past all the time. I found it pretty overwhelming, but I wasn't always aware of it, because I had my grief and I had you, and you were demanding a lot of attention at the time. You were only four, and being left without a mother, it makes sense you needed your father."

"Yeah." I nod.

"I was really angry at first because I thought that maybe, if we had been more attentive, we could've done more for her. When I understood we couldn't...I started revisiting all the happy moments, bargaining a little with memory, building frozen rooms, like...like in that movie I liked so much, you know the one I mean? Where people get stuck in other people's dreams."

"*Inception.*"

"Yes, exactly. I built a mountain of memories that I made a huge effort to furnish to the very last detail, and I went back to…well, I go back to. It's a way of having a part of her with me. And you know what? One time, in the shop, a woman came in to see if I was interested in her father's book collection, and she told me she had read somewhere that our memory finds a way to reinterpret and rewrite our memories over time so that what happened and what we wish happened coexist in peace. And that's when the choices come in."

"How so? Say more."

"I decided to lead two parallel lives: one with you, in the present, and another with her, in the past."

"But, Dad…" I clutch his forearm and fiddle with his old watch. "That's sad because…you didn't give yourself the chance to experience anything else in the future. You could have remade your life and…who would've blamed you? There's not just one love of your life. You can't just love…"

He stops me, putting his time-mottled hand over mine. His smile is tinged with sadness, and it breaks my heart.

"I decided to stay in those rooms built out of memories, Miranda. I chose to split my life between what you're describing and what you and I are living and what I'm telling you about Mama and what I lived with her. But that was the choice I made, and…I don't want the same for you."

"But…"

"I'm proud you took a good shower…"

"Dad…" I complain, tired.

"You smell amazing, you're well dressed, and you're embracing your grief so you can see how big it is and learn how to manage it. I just want to tell you…don't stay and live in the past. You have time to get your life back. But…you have to choose yourself. And now…let's eat. Here and now."

"Dad, wait, how do you know that?"

"Time's up."

"No, Dad. I need… Listen, this thing that's happening to me… Did it happen to you too? Is that what you're trying to tell me?"

"Miranda, sweetheart, let me return to the present now, please. I need to."

I don't think it's crazy to think that my father knows exactly what he's saying to me, but when I try to keep insisting, he refuses to budge. The only thing I can get out of him is…

"Everyone rewrites their memories however they want. That doesn't mean it solves what happened in the past."

And the gazpacho suddenly doesn't taste as delicious anymore.

27

~~~

IN STRIDE

When I hear or read the word "ocean," I always picture the Mediterranean. Not the Cantabrian or the Atlantic or the Caribbean. My head flies direct and nonstop straight to its shores, and I see it. I smell it too. I don't know a single Madrileño who doesn't have love, games, and sorrows buried in its sand, like in the Joan Manuel Serrat song. I could pick its color out of dozens of different seas because it's the only one that can be dark, blue, green, black, or turquoise all at once. That's why, as soon as I see it through the windows of the hotel, I know what day, what year, and what moment of my life I've woken up in. There's no doubt.

Tristan is still asleep, so I allow myself a moment of reflection in the living room of our suite. But first I drink in my view for a few seconds: him, hugging his pillow with his back to me, swimming in the middle of a wave of white sheets that make his skin look so tan. His back. The top of that tight ass hidden down below…looks good enough to be an oil painting. Or a snack.

Have you ever felt anxiety and relief well up in your stomach? If your answer is no, you're probably wondering how it's possible to feel anxiety and relief at the same time and…well, human beings are amazing…especially when it comes to contradictions.

On one hand, I'm relieved to be traveling backward again. Yesterday, in the right year, I fell asleep wondering what would happen if I couldn't do it again. And I was really overwhelmed by it. Grief, disorientation, and anxiety are just a few of the feelings even the possibility provokes, but...

On the other hand, I'm stressed not knowing what I'll do if all this doesn't stop. I makes me anxious to think my life is over, that I'll only have an occasional glimpse, like yesterday, of the present. Or the future. I don't even know what timeline I belong in anymore, but it scares me that I can only evoke the past and exist clearly in my memories.

Plus, 2020 is looming. And everyone knows what happened then.

Today is May 17, two years ago, and we're in Barcelona. We took an AVE yesterday and arrived in the Condal City around 10 at night. We went straight to eat some tacos at the Gastro-Taquería Mexicana on Calle de París, and after dinner, we dragged our wheeled suitcases to a taxi, which took us to the Hotel Arts Barcelona, overlooking the ocean. I'm here for work, but the magazine always knows how to give me perks that make it feel like the opposite.

The issue that will hit the stands next month has a nostalgia theme, and the only article left to go to print is my review of the concert I'm going to tonight: the Backstreet Boys are performing at the Palau Sant Jordi, and I was a big fan back in the early 2000s. While I'm at it, I'm going to take advantage of the hotel's invitations to see its facilities, and I'll write a short article about them for the "Escapes" section. So we have the Mediterranean suite on the thirty-second floor, with stunning ocean and city views, all to ourselves.

Tristan and I are both telecommuting from here for the day...which essentially means we'll be more or less tethered to our email in case there's a fire to put out until cocktail hour.

Today is one of those memories that my father was telling me about: dormant rooms, every detail furnished by memory, the smells, the colors, the kind I wish I could stay and live in, good days, happy days. This doesn't mean they're not real, but they wouldn't exist without balance. I'm thinking about my dad's words when Tristan appears in the living room, his thick head of black hair mussed and his lips even fuller than usual, swollen by sleep.

"Hey…" He clears his throat, but his raspy voice still makes him sound like a bad boy. "Why didn't you wake me up?"

"It's early. It's only eight thirty."

"I have to be on the computer in half an hour." He rubs his eyes. "Do we have time to get breakfast if I jump in the shower?"

"Probably not." I shake my head very seriously. "You're going to have to choose, although there are several combinations: shower and sex, shower and breakfast, sex and breakfast. You can't have it all."

He cracks up and spins on his heel to head to the bathroom. His tight little butt winks at me, encased in white boxers that make it…it's crazy.

"Shower and breakfast, babe. This machine doesn't work if you don't give it fuel."

We'll see about that…

His back is pearled with drops of hot water when I sneak into the shower. A roar escapes from his throat when I kiss his spine and drape my arm around his waist; he lifts his face into the water falling over him, arching with pleasure… That pleasure you feel when you stretch or someone hugs you, not the kind I'm planning on him feeling in a few minutes. I press my breasts against his back, and my skin, cool from the hotel's AC, warms against his. I can feel the heat of the water just how he likes it… scalding.

"Miri…what are you doing?" he plays along.

I could play the "fortune teller" with him and tell him that it'll be fine, that the sex is going to be good, even if it's a quickie, but I'd rather be more direct.

"Ah…" He gives a short moan when I grab his cock firmly.

"This. Looks like you were thinking about it too."

"I'm always thinking about it. I'm just like you… I just hide it better."

"That's not true."

"Oh yeah? Try me."

From the tone of his voice, I'd say he's even hornier than I remember.

"What do you want me to try?"

He turns around before I even put the final question mark on the sentence and devours my lips; our tongues chase and find each other, but before the kiss goes on for too long, he slips his hand into my hair and drags me back, pulling away.

"No. Let me," I beg when I realize he's stopping me from leaning in to kiss him again.

"Put it in your mouth."

His hand travels down a little, and…you don't have to be a genius to figure out what he wants.

"You want a blow job?" I call him out.

"I want a blow job. The kind you like."

"Oh yeah? You're going to shove your cock in until I choke on it?"

His hand tugs the hair at the nape of my neck down again, this time a little more forcefully. I moan with pleasure.

Everyone has their vices. This is my vice: when he gets a little rough during sex. And when he obeys when I'm the one who wants to dominate.

I get on my knees and open my mouth. He keeps a firm grip on my wet hair. With his other hand, he pushes his erection toward the tongue that's waiting for him hungrily and slides it back until it makes me gag. He wants to apologize. Deep down, he wants to, but he knows it would ruin the mood I love so much, so he withdraws slowly, enjoying every inch of my wet mouth…and starts thrusting again. I moan. Sometimes it seems wrong how much I love sucking his cock.

We rock back and forth like this for a few minutes, me alternating between my lips and my tongue, which I trail down his cock to tease him. I try to use my hands, but he pulls them away; when I grip the back of his thighs, I feel him get even harder in my mouth.

"You like that?" I ask when he pulls out after an intense thrust, scared he's going to come already.

"I love fucking your mouth, Miranda, but now all I can think about is spreading your legs and licking you until they tremble."

I'm stubborn. I like rough sex, but deep down, I love being the one in charge: deciding when we do something, when we stop doing it, and when we start doing something new. Even if that something new is pleasuring me. So I move my mouth closer until the tip brushes my lips, and then I devour it even more eagerly. He almost comes three times before I give in and let him carry me to the bedroom.

I leave a wet mark on the cover of the armchair where he puts me down, but I don't care. When I put each leg over the armrests, the last thing I'm thinking about is whether it'll dry before someone comes to clean the room or if they'll suspect the reason the chair is damp. And even less when he kneels in front of me and buries his head between my thighs. I think he likes licking me almost as much as I like blowing him.

For a few minutes, the only sound is his tongue between my wet folds. That and my moans. He knows exactly what to do to get me close to coming and then leave me there, hanging in the air, in no-man's-land, on the brink. He does something with his mouth… No one else has ever done it. He sucks and licks, and it even feels like he's vibrating down there, attached to my clit.

"Fingers, Tristan…please…"

I'm not even fully aware of it, but I beg like a cat in heat because I need to feel him penetrate me with them.

He goes slowly at first, just one finger. A caress, a brief penetration that he does again and again and again before he picks up speed and stops pulling out, staying inside me and pumping rhythmically. I don't know how he knows exactly when to put another finger in, but he does and...so much pleasure bursts inside me that my legs usually squeeze shut.

He pulls his mouth away and wipes it on the inside of my thigh; I've always liked that way of cleaning himself, intimately, on the way up to my mouth. We kiss like two crazy people, like we're depraved, as his strokes slow down. His fingers move up and down until we hear a splash, and suddenly I can't hear anymore because I'm lost, soaring toward the ceiling.

I'm close, so, so close, when he takes his fingers out and wraps both hands around my ankles, yanking me up. When he has me on the floor, he parts my legs and penetrates me hard. We both let out a roar. For a few minutes, we fuck like wild animals.

"Don't stop..." I beg him, even though I know he won't.

"Pounding you drives me crazy."

We smile at each other wolfishly and speed up. Our skin doesn't crash. It explodes against each other. And I writhe as my fingers grip his ass.

He pulls out suddenly, probably because he's starting to feel that tingling in his back, that heat that makes him throb even harder. And he doesn't want to. Not yet. So I take the chance to sit up, but before I can pounce on him, he throws me onto the mattress, on my stomach, and pulls my hips to the edge of the bed. In that position, I feel him everywhere, deep, strong, hard as a rock. In that position, sometimes the pleasure can make me lose control.

His hips thrust until he's deep, so deep. He thrusts over and over without pulling out, as if he wants to stay inside forever.

"Harder..." I beg him.

"Wait, wait…" he pants, his chest pressing into my back and his lips on my neck. "If I keep going, I'm gonna come."

"Come."

"Wait."

"Come inside me."

My right hand gets lost stroking myself, and his grab the flesh on my hips so hard it almost hurts. Almost. The thrusting becomes feverish; it's a pathway to pleasure that…well…never misses.

I know he's close because I can feel him throbbing. Much more than I've noticed in any of these relived times. He wants to let go, but he doesn't know if he should yet; he's waiting for me.

My moans get louder when the tingling starts, and it acts as a starting gun to his instincts; he's not stopping now. He's not stopping…until I feel the explosion inside me. His orgasm and mine intertwine.

He groans…or more like roars, a few expletives. I think "fuck" and "ah," but I'm gone, so it could've been half the list of the Gothic kings. How can I not be gone when he groans and thrusts that hard? Even though he's moving to a different rhythm now, until there's nothing left inside him and I'm completely filled.

I collapse onto the bed, my legs trembling and my clit on fire. He does the same on top of me and kisses my neck, my shoulder, and my back before he sits up again.

"Fuck…" he pants.

When he pulls out, I can see his semen leaving a trail from my thighs to the bed.

"They're gonna have to burn these sheets," I say when I see the stain we left.

"They can burn the whole room down if they want."

I lie down next to him with a satisfied smile. It's like a drunken torpor. The ecstasy of a saint that has come close to God. The happiness of a child surprised by candy.

"Even your eyelids are heavy." I run my fingertip gently across his forehead until I get to his eyes.

This would be the perfect moment for an "I love you" or an "I can't imagine life without you," but it's Tristan, and I've never even heard something like that come out of his mouth. But the smile he gives me feels the same.

"I'm going to take a shower...for real this time," he says after he kisses me.

"I need one too."

"And the people on the floor below, probably."

I whack him on the arm, and he bursts into laughter.

When I sit up, Tristan holds me before I can get up.

"Hey..."

"What?"

"I love you."

And I feel like my father was right; maybe revisiting your memories somehow lets you rewrite them.

We get to El Nacional at happy hour and perch on stools at the oyster and wine bar at the back. Despite our postcoital breakfast, we eat as if we've never experienced such delicious flavors in our lives. The oysters are soft, salty, and delicious. They're like every bit of sea that trickles down your throat and leaves a tasty note in its wake. The sparkling wine bubbles tickle us gently as we chatter away. And we laugh as if it's all hilarious, because we have our own language. Funny or not, we're in love, and that's what matters.

I know he wasn't that hyped about this trip at first because he thought he'd have to follow me around everywhere like a fanboy and then go to a concert he had no interest in at all.

"But do it for me. I loved them when I was little," I said to him at the time.

"Don't you have some girlfriend who likes them too and who'll jump at the offer?"

"My friends were more into NSYNC. They're traitors."

He reluctantly accepted, clearly, mostly because I laid on the emotional blackmail pretty thick. But back then, neither of us knew that this trip would become a sweet memory.

"Doesn't seem so terrible now, does it?"

"I never said it seemed terrible." He laughs, holding his glass with a little smile. "It's just that…I didn't think it was really my thing. It sounded more like a…girls' night."

"Just wait and see. You're gonna have a blast at the concert."

"If I'm gonna be watching four dudes in their fifties doing intense choreography, I probably will have a great time."

"There's five of them, and they're mostly in their forties. Don't be a snob. Age is just a number."

He rolls his eyes and takes a sip of his drink.

"If it makes your inner child happy, let's give her whatever she wants."

"My inner child wants you to dance to 'I'll Never Break Your Heart' or, even better, the Spanish version, 'Nunca te haré llorar.'"

"For the love of God…" He covers his face with both hands. "So cheesy."

"It was the end of the nineties…and I was really young… I still think it's a banger."

He dies laughing, leaning into me.

"I think this stuff makes me fall more in love with you."

"What stuff?"

"Well…this stuff. How you can be cold, burning hot, or tender enough to admit that you still like a song you listened to when you were eleven all at once."

"I was really in love with Brian, you have to understand."

"I don't even wanna know the age difference."

"I had planned our wedding down the very last detail."

"Nutjob."

He kisses my forehead and my nose.

"This nutjob makes you nutty," I say brazenly.

"Definitely. But I think I'm actually the nutjob. I've been crazy about you since the day I met you and...here we are. About to go to a Backstreet Boys concert. It will be a beautiful memory we'll treasure for the rest of our lives."

I know he's being sarcastic, but I can't help but think that this memory... we will actually treasure this memory. Until the day it starts to fade.

"Your face changed. What happened?" he asks. "Was I being a dick again without realizing?"

"No. It's just that...my father... He told me that over time, memories can be rewritten."

"That makes sense." He turns on his stool again. "Do you want another oyster?"

"Do you think time can make memories grow more valuable but also less valuable?"

He raises his eyebrows, and his fingers strum the bar rhythmically. He moves his head, not really sure.

"Maybe it's like...a coin when a country goes through inflation."

"What?" I ask petulantly.

"Yeah, you know...like when prices keep going up and...so in the end, the coin loses value in a reflection of the loss of acquisitive power."

"But what does that have to do with this?" It would piss me off that he was making these comparisons if I didn't know this was his way of being romantic.

"Well, maybe the value of memories depends on...the availability of resources, which in this context would be the person you love and time with them. Is that what you mean?"

"Tristan…" I pout. "Do you really have to answer the question I just asked you in economic jargon?"

"I know a little something about the economy, eh…"

"Tristan!" I groan.

"Ay, babe…what I'm trying to say is that memories are probably only worth their weight in gold when they're the only thing you have left of the person you lived through them with."

"Or when they love each other a lot, right? Because time passes quickly…and people are scared of running out of it."

"You're a romantic." He smiles. And he smiles nicely. "Yes. Probably. And that's why, when I'm ninety and I'm very, very, very wrinkly, today's concert will seem like a wonderful memory to me."

"Because the only thing lovers should be afraid of is being left without time to love each other."

Tristan looks at me slightly condescendingly. I know he doesn't feel the same way, that his romanticism only stretches to much more practical matters.

"What? Are you making fun of me?" I ask him, unbothered.

He furrows his brow but keeps his smile.

"No. Of course not. I was just thinking that…I wish you had designed the world, because you would've made it beautiful."

I don't know if the world would've been beautiful in my hands when it was just a ball of clay waiting to be transformed, but I do know that, hours later, this man gives the girl I was what I was so afraid I would never live again.

It's not during "I'll Never Break Your Heart," and it happens in the solitude of a half-lit hallway, while we're on the way back from the bathroom. I'm running ahead of him, hustling because I don't want to miss anything, when the first chords of "As Long as You Love Me" ring out. The Palau Sant Jordi is shaking with the audience's applause. And Tristan pulls me back.

"I'm missing it! And I love this song!" I complain, red from the beers we drank earlier and nostalgia and excitement and love and heat and…

Then I understand that he just wants to dance where nobody can see us. He wants to slow dance to a song that doesn't seem like it would work for a slow dance. Maybe I'm about to tell him we shouldn't be ridiculous, but here, in the dwindling light of a deserted hallway, my inner child shoves me aside, takes over, and hangs from his neck. She laughs like a bell, happy to have found a love like they talk about in songs.

She, the girl, dances excitedly with the hot boy from the story while I think about the lyrics from the song. No, I don't care who he is…or where he's from or what he did… I don't care, as long as he loves me.

And now that I know he's going to stop one day…I should abandon the refuge of these happy memories. Stop clinging to them. Especially because 2020 is waiting in ambush around the corner. And we all know what that means for us. Although, maybe this time, we can take it in stride.

28

~~~

THAT'S MY PROBLEM

What I'm about to say doesn't mean that I'm sick of all this. No. Not at all. But…I miss when days were consecutive, you lived a month all in a row, and you wished for vacations to come sooner because you were tired and totally alive. I'm tired and totally losing my mind, especially when I wake up and realize I'm in Vigo. In Vigo, in the home of Tristan's parents, who have deigned to change the single bed from his childhood into a bigger one. Full-size, not exactly a double, but at least we can sleep there together and not waste money on a hotel every time we go see them, and that's cool.

Cough, cough, cough…

Sorry about the cough. I didn't know how else to make it clear that this was Tristan's opinion: I would have preferred staying in the hotel.

Tristan's parents were (well, are) wonderful people, but they're not my parents, they're my future in-laws. That means they're fake family, a "rental" (or bought with a mortgage, depending on how you look at it), which means you have to learn all their traditions from zero. You come from your house, from your relationship with your father, your familial obsessions, and your mutual habits, and now you have to pretend like you belong to their zip code and share their last names. And I don't see Castro or Souto anywhere on my license.

So when I open my eyes and see the drawn blinds, the old bookshelf, and the wooden artist mannequin, a shiver runs down my spine. Because of where we are and because of my suspicion of when we are. Today is the day that his jerk of a sister is going to try on wedding dresses. And we're going to get in a fight. A bad one.

Or maybe not. Maybe since I'm rewriting our story, like I did when I met her for the second time, a few days ago, I improved the original conditions and now we're BFFs. But when Tristan wakes up, that hope dissolves like the cocoa his mother is making. I don't remember saying I liked cocoa…

"Babe…" Tristan has the exhausted voice of someone who's just woken up and is already tense, trying to figure out how to say something uncomfortable. "Can you come here for a second?"

"Oy…that's quite a way to say good morning. Whatever you have to say to the girl, you can say it here, because we're women, you know that, Tristan? We support each other. Collective spirit." Tristan's mother holds up her fist, and I smile at her because I want to kiss her and kill her at the same time.

"Seriously, Mama?"

"Well, of course, with that tone of yours I know so well."

"What if I have to say something in *private to my partner* that I don't want you to hear?" He emphasizes the words he thinks are key and hopes will make his mother react.

"I'll respect that bond when you put a ring on her finger."

I wave my hand proudly, especially the finger where the gift he gave me that year glints, but she quickly pushes it down.

"Very pretty, dear, but that doesn't mean anything. I'm talking about an engagement ring."

"Well, I want to talk to her about weddings, but not ours. Come here for a second, Miranda?"

And since I'm not that brave, I drag my feet back to his childhood bedroom in my Garfield pajamas. What? Don't judge me. It's not like I'm going to strut around his parents' house in a set of my raunchy ones.

"Talk to me."

Tristan closes the door behind me and smiles like butter wouldn't melt in his mouth.

"My love."

"You've never called me 'my love' in your life." I pretend to be shocked. "What do you want?"

"I just want to talk to you. Come here, make yourself comfortable, darling."

"Ah, no…" I say to him. "You're really freaking me out now."

"I just want to ask you for a favor. A small thing."

He sits me down on the bed, still procrastinating, and kneels in front of me. He refuses to spit it out. All he does is stroke my legs, trying and failing to conceal how nervous he is.

"I need you to try to be patient and…"

"Patience? Is this about your mother? Your mother is a sweetheart. You don't need to say this stuff to me."

"No, I'm not talking about her. It's about Uxia."

Okay. If I was still harboring a tiny wisp of faith deep down, it just vanished. I didn't get us to be besties in this timeline either.

"I'm always patient with Uxia, Tristan."

"She's more anxious than usual. She's wedding planning and…"

"Don't worry," I say. "But anyway…why are you asking me to be more patient and not her to be more friendly?"

"Well, because…that's what I'm saying, Miranda. She's stressed about all the wedding stuff, and you don't get along at the best of times…but if her little brother shows up in the middle of all this chaos and starts droning on about how she has to treat her future sister-in-law, it's going to be a mess. I'm trying to achieve the opposite effect."

"It'll be a mess, yes. But that's not why. It's actually because we don't even have the freedom to ask someone to behave like a normal person and not a rabid animal."

"Hey, don't take it too far." He's suddenly serious. "That's my sister. She has her issues, I know, but…"

"But I'm your girlfriend. And even if I weren't, she should treat me well. Like she would any other human being, jeez. I'm not Pol Pot."

"Or Mother Teresa."

I roll my eyes. I can't with her.

"What's the problem?"

He sucks in air through pursed lips. He doesn't know how to tell me, even though I already know. I should make it easier on him…but I don't feel like it. I was hoping I had changed this "future," even just a little, when I made such an effort when I met Uxia, but it seems like everything is exactly the same.

Right before I showed up in the kitchen, Tristan had read a message from his sister in which she let slip that maybe it would be better if I didn't go with them wedding-dress shopping. Could she be more of a coward and a cunt?

If it doesn't seem that deep, it's probably because, in order to fathom the depths of my disappointment, I'd have to reset the scene of the moment he proposed the trip to me. I was excited, but at the same time, I felt a little lost. He told me he didn't know if he was really going to fit in with the whole going to look at dresses, but he wanted to go.

"I don't know if I'll be any help really. Will she be expecting me to? It's just that I don't get any of this stuff. I don't know. It all makes me pretty nervous. The good thing is that you'll be with me, and…when you're there, I feel safe."

Even so, knowing how much Uxia hates me, I kept insisting that he should make the trip alone. I told him it was a special thing for siblings, for a family, it was private, that I had nothing to do with it... I repeated it so many times that he ended up getting pissed off and snapped that if doing these things with his family was a pain in the ass for me, all I had to do was admit it. A pain in the ass? I don't have a mother. I don't have siblings. I would have loved to do this with them, but I was aware that she, Uxia, didn't want me there. And she was the star of the day. But still, I went. And when she wrote him that message and he reluctantly asked me to go get a drink and wait, I swallowed my pride and tears of rage and just nodded, and I didn't even say I told you so.

But here's the funny part...because she wasn't happy, the girl, the bride, the star, the biggest sister, she decided to make a scene with me during lunch with her parents. Why? Because I didn't go with them to the store. Schizophrenia? No. Just a bad temper.

She started with the less offensive bullshit, wondering if the reason I didn't go was because I was jealous because Tristan was never going to walk down the aisle, not even drunk off his ass, which wasn't even true. If one of us was more into the traditional path of love, it was him. I didn't answer, and I tried to change the subject, but because she kept hammering away at it, her brother asked her to shut up. He said it affectionately but firmly, and even though she's almost two years older than he is, she threw a tantrum like a ten-year-old child who's not allowed to be the tyrant she normally is:

"The little lady, who works in a fashion magazine in the capital, thinks she's too good to slum it looking at wedding dresses with a girl from the suburbs. Is that it? Or is it because you know you're never going to get married in your whole fucking life so it makes your blood boil?"

The more her brother reacted, the more venom she spat and the quieter I was. I don't remember ever being more embarrassed in my whole life. Her mother burst into tears. Her father's voice trembled as he asked her to go outside and get some fresh air, and I, bearing the brunt of an attack like that, could do nothing but get up and hide in the bathroom, where I sobbed until Tristan came to get me, put me in the car, and, without even packing our suitcases, headed back to Madrid. He didn't say a word.

It took three hours before we spoke again, and the whole time, he was too embarrassed to explain that he had never been mad at me, that he didn't talk to me the whole journey because he was afraid of falling apart, because he didn't know what to say, and because he was ashamed. I understood, I forgave him, and I hugged him...but I swallowed my rage when I heard him saying goodbye sweetly on the phone to his sister. Sweetly. Tristan. Anyway. Family can bring out the worst in us.

So...that's the day I'm going to relive if I don't do anything to change it. And you tell me. Sitting here, in his teenager bedroom, wearing pajamas I bought just to trick his parents into thinking I'm a modest girl who doesn't usually sleep butt naked (and, whenever possible, spooning their son), I feel like someone who's handling enriched uranium. This memory is the equivalent of a nuclear bomb.

"Tristan..." I smile, stubbornly staying sweet. "What's the problem?"

Hesitation flickers across his face for a millisecond, but I catch it.

"I don't know if Uxia is going to feel comfortable with this...with so many people there. Do you understand?"

Understand you, yes. That piece of dry shit that is your sister, no.

"Did she mention something to you?"

He sighs.

"Tris..." I goad him.

"Ay," he complains, "please, don't call me Tris."

"Then answer me."

"It's not that she said anything, Miranda," he lies, "it's just that...well, think about it... You work in a fashion magazine in Madrid, and she... I guess she feels insecure."

"She feels insecure because I work in a fashion magazine in Madrid?"

"I don't know. I guess she's scared you're going to judge her for the dress she picks. Or maybe she'll get overwhelmed with so many people there."

"Stop saying 'I guess' if you know that's what's going to happen."

"But I don't know. She just might have mentioned..."

I suck my teeth and stand up from the bed.

"Where are you going?"

"To talk to your mother."

"Miri... Miri!"

He catches up to me in the kitchen, but I'm already tactfully bringing it up:

"Sabela, I have a question, between us... Tristan thinks Uxia might get uncomfortable if I go with you to look for dresses. I'm not asking you because I want you to say yes, but...don't you think she'll get offended if I don't go?"

His mother, who was slicing up bread for toast, turns around, surprised.

"Ay, no, dear, how could she be uncomfortable if you come with us? She wants you to come. She told me. Her exact words were 'Tell Tristan to bring Miranda.'"

"Don't bring her into this," Tristan warns me gravely.

He skirts around us and heads to the Moka pot and pours himself a cup of coffee.

"I know she did want me to go, and I understand she could have changed her mind. That's understandable."

"So then why are you going around in circles about it, for fuck's sake?" he snarls, annoyed, with his back still turned.

"The 'for fuck's sake' is too much, Tristan," I snap.

"I totally agree," his mother backs me up. "*Miña neniña*, you're completely right. If you don't come, she'll ask why you didn't come. I know Uxia because I'm her mother and...look, this is how Tristan came into the world, quiet, chewing his words, but mostly because I think his sister took them all. At least they were good kids."

"Mama…"

"I adore your sister, Tristan, sweetie, but when you're a father, you'll understand. You love your kids more than yourself, but you don't always understand them. Or approve of them. When you were sixteen, I would've happily slapped you silly."

"She doesn't want Miranda to come with us," he fesses up, tired of rehashing the topic.

He slams his coffee cup down on the table nervously and rudely, and some of the liquid sloshes over the edge; a sand-colored stain spreads on the tablecloth around the cup, but he ignores it and keeps going.

"She messaged me and said she's not sure she'll feel comfortable. What am I supposed to do?"

You grow some balls, because either way, I'm the one stuck between a rock and a hard place here.

"But, Tristan…do you understand why I'm asking your mother? You can be blind about this. And I just want to do the right thing."

"Well, if you want to do the right thing, don't come. I'm telling you. Because if you do, she's going to flip out on me."

"No, Tristan," his mother replies very seriously. "Miranda is completely right. Nothing your sister is saying makes any sense, because if Miranda doesn't go, she's not going to like that later. End of story!"

I go into the bathroom while Tristan's in the shower. He hasn't said more than a handful of words to me since the thing in the kitchen, so I imagine he's pissed off, but if all these years have given me anything, it's patience. I'm not the girl I was that day two years ago anymore.

"Tristan…" I close the door and sit down on the closed toilet.

I can see his body through the beveled glass. Nom nom.

Focus, Miranda.

"What?"

"I just want you to listen to me for a minute, okay? You're mad that I asked your mother, but I needed..."

"You put me in a pretty good position, eh?" His tone is dripping with more sarcasm than the showerhead is water.

"You think it's normal to get this mad about asking her when she agrees it could seem like a middle finger if I don't go? Because you weren't going to explain to her that it's because your sister doesn't want me to, right? I kept saying I shouldn't come when you asked."

He shuts off the water and opens the door. Oof. He grabs a towel, dries his face and his hair, and wraps it around his waist. Then he leans against the sink, finally stopping to listen to me intently. At least I have his attention.

"I warned you I shouldn't come, you took it badly, and I gave in, for you, because I love you. And now your sister turns on a dime and decides it'd be better if I don't, and you throw me to the wolves. And I don't have the right to ask your mother, who is part of all this too, what she thinks? And on top of all that, you get mad at me. Well, you'll have to forgive me, but I'm not going to end up on bad terms with your mother all because of your sister."

He bites his upper lip but doesn't say anything.

"And you wanna know the worst part?" I insist. "If it weren't for me, your parents wouldn't even know that it's your sister who doesn't want me to go. Because you're used to covering up for her all the time, even all the shit she puts me through."

He hangs his head, looking downtrodden, which is difficult to see in Tristan, and after a few more seconds in silence, he nods. When he turns back to look at me, he seems regretful.

"It's just that I don't know how to finesse this stuff so she doesn't have it in for you even more," he confesses.

"I know. But the way you're trying to solve it is cowardly."

"Okay."

"And when you do it like that, you're not respecting me. You're prioritizing her. If that's what you want, fine. I can accept it and stay or reject it and leave. But if that's not what you want…"

"It's not what I want."

"Then you're making a mistake."

He sighs, overwhelmed, and I stand up and go over to him.

"She's the one putting you in this situation. You know that, right?"

"But it wouldn't be that hard for you to make it easier. The thing with my mother…"

"I'm sorry you didn't like it. I didn't know what else to do."

"Okay."

I give him a kiss and pat his damp forearms.

"Look, why don't we try this: I'll get dressed and go with you. I'll give your sister a kiss, I'll gauge her face when she sees me, and if she's pouting, then I'll say dress shopping is very intimate and just for family and that…"

"But you're going to be part of this family."

"Yeah, well, she's not that into that idea."

We both chuckle softly.

"You'll see. We're going to fix this."

When Uxia sees me show up with her parents and her brother, she doesn't look like she's going to have a stroke. But she doesn't have a good poker face, and everyone can see it. Miranda: 1, Uxia: O.

I go over politely, kiss her on both cheeks, and give her a brief, affectionate hug, faker than a wooden euro. I want to cackle and have the lightning strike the sidewalk behind me to make the scene more theatrical, but it's fine how it is. She glares at me the whole time she greets her family until she gets to Tristan and pinches him on the arm.

"Ow!" he yelps, not understanding where the aggression is coming from.

"Uxia..." I go back over. "Listen...your brother and I were talking, and I said to him I feel like this going dress-hunting thing is very intimate... I don't know. You'd probably be overwhelmed having all of us crammed in there. So what do you think about me going to grab a drink and waiting for you all?" I wave at the busy street full of cafés next to us. "But if your brother gets stubborn about his opinions or you need a tiebreaker...I'll be happy to run right over and be on your side."

I wink at her, smiling.

"Miranda..." their mother begs.

"No, really, Sabela, I think she's going to be calmer this way. And that's what's most important. You have bridal store appointments, right? Well, I'll wait for you here, and then we can go celebrate when you've found your dress. And if not, we'll buy some magazines and you can flip through them. You still have plenty of time."

"The truth is I'm a little nervous; The fewer people, the less noise," Uxia says. "I really appreciate it."

"No problem. Totally understandable. Plus...I don't really know much about wedding dresses, and I'm sure you'll look great in all of them."

Impeccable performance. The Oscar goes to...me!

She spits out a thank-you that even makes her brother smile as he leans over to give me a kiss.

"I'll see you really soon."

"No rush."

I wave a smiley goodbye and head toward my destination, a martini and a plate of fries, but Tristan pulls me back to whisper:

"You're the best."

They come in looking happy after two long hours I spent engrossed in reading a book I grabbed from Tristan's room and I only understand half of because I've always had trouble staying focused when I read nonfiction. But I've been entertained and serene, especially with the expectation of a peaceful lunch and the certainty that they're going to find exactly the tacky thing his sister is looking for, tighter than Ned Flanders's ski suit and more sparkles than all the weddings in *My Big Fat Gypsy Wedding* put together.

She was right about one thing: I was going to judge her choice, but silently and smiling, with the pleasure you get from watching your enemy look like a sledgehammer on one of the most beautiful days of her life. Anyway, I won't be able to go to her wedding, because someone in Wuhan is going to start coughing and feeling under the weather, and the rest of the world is going to have to wait at home for a global pandemic to end. And I'm not trying to make light of it; it's going to be the most fucked-up thing I can ever remember living through.

When Tristan and I break up, Uxia and her boyfriend still aren't married.

We get the car again and go to a restaurant to celebrate the snake finding her dress with her future husband, the weirdest guy I've ever met in my whole life, who I've barely heard string two words together, but... listen, all that matters is that they understand each other. Tristan and I go get our rental car, and she goes with her parents in their gray sedan.

Tristan is surprised I'm so happy on the way there, but all I'm thinking about is stuffing myself to the gills with seafood and white wine and then taking a nap on the sofa at his parents' house, snug as a bug in a rug. He tells me everything, and he seems happy too, even emotional, which is a lot for someone as restrained as Tristan.

I can't believe I dodged this bullet.

When he was planning this trip, Tristan asked me if it was all right if he treated them all to lunch. I told him of course, he didn't need to check with me, and he proudly reserved a table for six at Silabario, a restaurant with a Michelin star on the sixth floor of a very central building in Vigo, which is crowned by a pretty spectacular avant-garde dome of glass and steel. The view of the city from there is incredible, and his parents insist that I sit by the window (more like a glass wall) so that I can enjoy it because I'm the guest. Opposite me, Uxia has been bestowed the same honor because it's her day.

We order a couple of bottles of white wine and toast to the future bride and groom with joy, a joy that is becoming increasingly tense because, honestly, it seems like the "happy bride" is pissed off by my smile. But I think, naively, that the amount of food Tristan ordered would relax anyone…although judging by his sister's sour face, you might think that instead of eating it, someone suggested shoving all this seafood up her ass. I take my chance when the groom goes to the bathroom to try to win her over by broaching the topic of the day:

"So…tell me about the dress! What's it like?"

"Um…it's white," she says, passing it off as a joke and not just her being rude as usual.

"Ah…but white white or off-white?"

"It's white, silk, and body-con." She shrugs. "I was going to choose a princess cut, but then I thought about how a lot of women would die to be able to wear a mermaid cut and not have to hide their big hips with a poofy skirt, so since I can…"

I let it go. I make like I don't know that these "big hips" she's talking about are probably mine.

"Well, sounds like you did great. Are you going to wear a veil?"

"I haven't decided yet."

"She has one from my beautiful mother," Sabela pipes up, very emotionally. "That way, her bare shoulders won't be exposed in the church."

"Is it sleeveless?" I ask.

"No. It has a neckline…what did the girl call it?" Their mother can't find the word.

"Hunter," Uxia says like a smartass.

I stifle my laughter, because what she means to say with that air of superiority toward her mother, who doesn't remember the term, is *halter*, not *hunter*. But I stay quiet as a mouse.

The groom comes back.

"Okay, quick, let's change the subject," her mother says. "We don't want to ruin the surprise."

Her mother winks at me from across the table, and I wink back. Judging by her glare, it seems to turn Uxia's stomach. They bring the first plates over, and the table is groaning under all the delicious food. There are few things that make me as happy as having Tristan, white wine, and good food all in the same place, and you can tell. That and knowing I'm safe from her making a scene this time. Finally, I'm going to be able to enjoy this restaurant.

Or not.

"So…do you want to get married?" Uxia asks me.

"Me?" I'm surprised.

"Yes. I already know my brother's opinion. Asking you is more fun."

I can sense that Tristan is signaling frantically at her but she's ignoring him.

"Well…we haven't discussed it, right?" I look at him with the most neutral face I can find in my repertoire, which transforms into a smile when one spreads across his face. "Ay, you devil, don't look at me like that."

"But do you want to?" Uxia insists.

"Well, it's just that…" *It's just that my opinion is very different from yours, you little shit stirrer, and I don't want you to use it to start a fight, can't you see that?* "The truth is I've never put much thought into it."

"Come on!" she teases. "This is a safe space. You can say it… We're not going to laugh."

It's not like you have a record.

"Well, look…" I grab my glass and pluck up my courage. "The thing is I've always thought romantic stuff is a very personal matter. I understand the traditional discourse around weddings as a symbolic act of the culmination of love, but…it's just not that important to me."

"You don't want to marry my brother?"

I scratch my head. She's making me nervous. Of course I want to marry him. Not in a wedding like the one she would plan, but still. Even though he never asked me. And I never asked him.

"I wouldn't hate it, but it's not something I'm losing sleep over," I reply, feeling a stab of pain.

"You heard her, Tristan."

"You didn't have to goad her into saying that. I already know. I've been dating her for three years, and we live together. I know her."

"But you gave her a ring…and it's not an engagement ring."

"No. It's an oval-shaped aquamarine." I'm trying to be funny.

"It's beautiful," Tristan's mother says, trying to settle the subject. Poor thing.

Uxia keeps going.

"And how did you figure out a way to give it to her without her thinking it was a proposal?"

"Uxia, why aren't you eating?" Tristan snaps.

"Take a breath, dude." She grins at him.

Trying to make me uncomfortable is actually just annoying her brother, and she just noticed. That's the only thing that could stop her, and I'm relieved, but the sharpness of Tristan's voice left even me speechless.

"We had already talked about it," I explain to her, because it leaves a bad taste in my mouth to leave her hanging. "Your brother has his own way of being romantic too…and he's even more practical than me. So… I told him that if he ever wanted to propose, he had to…"

"Don't…" He laughs.

"We're so dumb." I laugh back.

"Totally."

We fall into complicit giggles, but everyone else is waiting for the answer.

"I told him he had to do it with a ring made of a coin and a pair of wires. You know? Those coins that have a hole in the middle. And he accepted. So when I opened the box and saw this ring, I just thought how…how incredibly thoughtful your brother is and how much I love him and some other stuff about how he must have bought it at auction. He knew I would go crazy for it. It's from 1929, and it's been passed down for years. My father is an antiques dealer and…"

"Your brother is a romantic in his own way. I couldn't escape your peer pressure entirely." Tristan puts a piece of duck and sea urchin croquette in his mouth and waggles his eyebrows at his sister.

They both smile.

I sigh. Come on, come on…please let us get out of this unscathed.

"Your brother told me your wedding is going to be in a really beautiful manor house."

"Yes," she replies, refusing to make eye contact. "The ceremony's going to be in a tiny chapel and then the reception in the garden. We'll put some marquees up, but hopefully we'll get lucky with the rain, like today."

"Hopefully," I add, ready to shut my mouth for the rest of the lunch.

"You'd like a manor house, right?" Tristan asks me.

"For my wedding?"

"Our wedding."

The whole family is looking at us slyly, and I swallow.

"If there's a ring made of coins, wherever you want, playboy."

A general chuckle relaxes me. Oh my god. I'm clenching my ass so hard from nerves that I don't know where I'll wake up tomorrow, but I know I'll be sore. But no, Tristan, not in a manor house. I want to get married in an open field. And I want Ivan to marry us. Or my father. Nothing over our heads but verbena bulbs and the moon, and just a handful of good friends and close family. You, dressed in jeans and one of those T-shirts that look so good on you; and me, with some nice cleavage and red lips. No rings. And for the wedding dance, "Sesenta memorias perdidas" by Love of Lesbian. We'll eat delicious food, and we won't care whether it's on trend, and we'll drink Coke from glass bottles and sparkling wine in coupes. And we'll be the happiest couple anyone has ever seen get married. Why haven't I ever told you? Why haven't we ever talked about this?

"Hey…" Tristan wakes me from my reverie with a soft elbow.

"Yes…what?"

"You were in la-la land," he whispers.

"I went to my own planet for a minute."

"And what did they tell you there?"

I kiss his shoulder to disguise a sigh and focus on the conversation at the table again. My future mother-in-law is talking about the wedding planning…the real one, not the one I was imagining that will probably never happen.

It makes me sad to think about how disappointed she'll be when she has to postpone all this for more than two years because of COVID. Uxia will want to get married when restrictions on these kinds of events are lifted, so it will take a long time. But honestly, it makes me sadder to think that despite loving each other as much as I know we do now, Tristan and

I never daydreamed out loud about getting married, and somehow the moment passed us by. And even though he doesn't know it, after this year, we'll be mercilessly mowed down by the grayest part of this relationship, and we won't have any time to make plans first.

Miranda…eat. Focus on enjoying yourself in the most hedonistic way possible. Eat, drink, and then try to seduce Tristan into having a drink. Enjoy everything you couldn't that day. The Galician steak tartare is to die for. And the anchovies from Castro Urdiales. The oysters. And the cockles. I'm going to get some. Langoustines, beware. Somebody stop me with the crab. By the time the meat arrives, I'm about to go into a permanent coma.

And one piece of advice…never let the enemy see you weak…even if it is due to a massive seafood intake. Make sure to never let your guard down, because when you least expect it, right then is when the final blow will fall.

"Hey, squirt." Uxia turns to Tristan. "Fine, you're not going to have a wedding, but aren't you going to make me an auntie?"

Dumb bitch.

Tristan side-eyes me for a split second before he takes his napkin and elegantly dabs at his lips.

"Well…" he mumbles.

"Well, what? Ay! Don't tell me you're pregnant!" she says to me. "I knew it!"

The big dumb bitch.

"No, no…that's just the kilo of cockles I ate." I pat my stomach.

"Can't you see she's drinking wine?" pipes up her brother, who's starting to blush, I don't know why.

"Ah, sorry, sorry. It's just that…the way you said that 'well'…"

"No. I said 'well' because time will tell with these things, right?"

"Miranda, how old are you?"

I sigh. I'm done hiding how sick I am of her trolling me. I finally make it clear that this question is a huge pain in the ass for me. Especially because I have to calculate how old I was at that point…

"Thirty-one."

"Well, you have some time…but you're not exactly a teenager."

I resist the urge to ask her how old she is, because I'm not like that. What worries me isn't my biological age; what worries me is that I don't care at all. Tristan knows without a doubt that he wants to be a father. As much time as I've asked for to figure it out, all I've found is internal silence and panic. I think the last year and a half of our relationship was based solely on the hope that I would suddenly get some clarity on it.

"I always thought he would have kids before me, you know? You can't imagine how good with kids he is. They love him. Whenever we meet up with the crew, he ends up with some friend's kid in his arms. Or he's down on the floor playing with them all at once. He's like…the Pied Piper. He's gonna be a great father."

"Uxi…" Tristan mutters. When she looks at him, he wrinkles his nose affectionately. "Leave it."

"Ah, you don't like them anymore? You changed your mind? You don't want to be a dad anymore?"

Tristan looks at me out of the corner of his eye, trying to gauge how uncomfortable I am.

"Yes. Yes, I still want to, Uxia."

"So? Come on, kids. Repopulate the planet! There aren't enough children, everything is terrible, and kids always make everyone happy."

She's doing it on purpose, that's obvious. I don't know when he must have told her that I'm not sure I want to be a mother, but I'd bet my right hand that they've already had this conversation and she's reminding her brother the reasons why letting this drag on with me doesn't make sense.

I hate her. And I know that haters are the worst, but I'm going to allow myself this indulgence for today.

"Well, Uxia, the two of us will see about that, don't you think?" he retorts.

"Yeah, yeah. I'm not saying anything."

She mimes zipping her mouth shut, and I wish I could sew it like that with my own hands.

I should say something, something like "there's no rush," but nothing comes out. My face falls, probably like hers did this morning when she saw me show up at the store. And just like Julieta Venegas sang, or close enough: I don't know if I deserve it, but I don't want it.

After lunch, there's no siesta. His witch of a sister and her flying monkey of a fiancé go home, and Tristan says he wants to show me something. I guess he wants to shake off the lingering feeling after the clusterfuck of a conversation about kids. And I get it.

"It's a half-hour drive, but it's beautiful."

"Of course," I say and nod, even though I don't know if I actually care anymore.

"Ay, I know where he's taking you. You're going to love it, girlie. You're going to love it," his mother says, her eyes shining.

And she's right, even though I know it already because I've been there, even though he already showed me on another trip to Vigo. I remember how that day when his sister made me cry, he was planning to take me to spend the afternoon there. Today, he's finally going to pull it off, even though Uxia left her mark in a different way.

There's something special about the Enchanted Forest of Aldán, beyond the lush greenery and the crumbling castle. Beyond the families with children playing and shouting war cries, pretending to be pirates from another century attacking each other. There's something about it. A halo of magic that envelops people in love. That and a damp that gets in your bones. It's like nineteenth-century ghost stories...creepy and romantic at the same time.

Tristan wraps his arm around me and rubs mine like he can sense how the cold is already burrowing into my flesh and soaking in deep. He walks along quietly, though I know him; he's ruminating. He chews on his words like cows chewing cud because it's the only way he understands how to carve out sentences without leaving scorched earth in his wake. I don't know if I'm making sense.

It takes him a while to work up to it. It takes him a while, but when he does, he hits the bull's-eye.

"My sister's a dick."

"She is." I smile.

"Sometimes I feel like you provoke her, like you're in a duel, but I have to be fair and recognize that today, you didn't... Today had nothing to do with you."

"I appreciate that. But?"

"But?"

"There's a but."

He smiles sadly.

"There is, but you already know it."

"Yes."

We keep walking arm in arm, in silence, scared. Sometimes if you don't put a tagged collar on your fear, if you let it run free, it gets away from you. But you're still responsible if it bites someone, because it's up to you to muzzle it.

"Miranda...we never talked about it again since back then."

"Yeah, I know."

"But I haven't changed my mind. I understand that you haven't either."

I don't answer. I keep my eyes trained on the ground covered in soggy leaves and branches. I swallow.

"Sometimes I wonder if we're not sweeping it under the rug on purpose because we don't want to make a decision about it. I worry that if we let too much time pass, we'll end up getting hurt."

He stops.

"I want to be a father. It doesn't have to be now, but if it were up to me, I would. I would do it with you right now. But if you're never going to want to be a mother, maybe we should reconsider things."

"That day at the lake, I told you. You were the one who didn't want to look at it, who swept it under the rug."

"I know. But now that Uxia brought it up... I don't know. I have to be honest...I think about it sometimes."

"I do too."

God...I feel like I'm swallowing handfuls of pointy rocks.

"And?" he asks with a trace of hope.

"I can't help feeling like this is an ultimatum."

"It's not. It's just that...when you love someone, sometimes you have to let go even if it tears you up inside, because to love someone is also to let them go."

I furrow my brow. What? "Are you dumping me?"

"No. No, no, fuck. I don't want to. It's just that..." He shrugs and sighs. "I feel like if you're dead set on not being a mother, you should say so. And we'll have to talk about it, put it all on the table...and there are a lot of other things...like our pace of life and how long we're going to stay in Madrid. It wouldn't be fair for either of us to give up when it comes to this. It's too important."

And he's right. I nod. I swallow another fistful of rocks.

"So?"

"So..."

The first time we had this conversation, when he brought it up again, I asked him for time. I told him that I thought I might not change my mind, that I was sorry, but I asked him to give me time.

"Time for what?" he asked me.

I had no idea, but he gave it to me. And I'm sure that was the day we started to die. Maybe not us, but our "us," yes.

"Okay," I hear myself say.

"Okay?" He's surprised.

"Yes. Okay."

"But okay…to what plan? Okay, it's too important for either of us to give in? Or okay, let's be parents?"

"Okay, let's be parents."

"Okay, that's it?"

A giggle slips out. It's a terrified giggle, sad but tender, because I love him.

I would do anything so I won't lose him. Even fail myself, my word, my will, the way I understand myself and the world around me.

"Okay…just give me…give me a little time."

"A little time? Eh…" Tristan moves a little nervously. "Fuck, yes, of course. But…" He laughs. "This is amazing. I…I wasn't expecting this. Will you kiss me?"

And I kiss him, clinging to him like this is the last memory I'm going to have of him. In a way I wish everything could stay frozen here. But it can't.

Once again, I'm holding a fistful of time that I don't know what to do with.

Convince myself. Resign myself. I don't know.

Time…that's my problem.

29

~~~

"INCLUDING YOU"

The first time I saw a photo shoot, I was pretty starstruck. It felt like exactly how I had imagined it. It's funny. Sometimes the things that are closest to our expectations can be overwhelming. Everything feels like a movie… The "click" of the shot and the strobes popping over the music blaring to make the star of the shoot feel comfortable. Photography studios are usually cold, with high white ceilings. Some have cycloramas; others have neutral backgrounds and floors that are removed after each session. And they're almost always bustling with people: stylists, makeup artists, brand representatives, people from the publication where the shoot is going to appear, managers, production teams, lighting crew, technicians… They're not ideal for shy people.

Luckily for him, Ivan is not. Apparently, according to him, he used to be back at school, when being different was scary and the other kids made fun of him. Maybe he was more self-conscious there. But for a long time now, he is who he is, and not much can make him feel less than…especially when he's working. Because he's good. He's really good. That's why I've never felt like hiring him for editorials or magazine covers was nepotism. Marisol agrees: yes, he's my best friend, but I met him in a professional environment, he has an impeccable portfolio, his résumé speaks for itself, he's reliable and trustworthy, and he works fast and gets the job done. That's why, whenever we have an especially important cover, we call him. Today, we're doing a cover shoot of someone who will become one of the hottest actresses over the next few years, but I'm not supposed to know that. Not me or anyone else, but of course, I come from the future. We're going to get a lot of praise for this cover because she's talented, because we didn't wait for her to be on top to feature her, and because she's not what the heteronormative cover girl profile dictates. This issue, starring a relatively unknown actress who is only five seven and plus size with big boobs (at least as far as fashion dictates), is going to be a symbol of change. And we're going to be a vital part of the movement.

Today is Thursday, December 12, two years ago. I remember this shoot vividly. It was relaxed and fun, and the photos came out great. We were all thrilled. On the magazine's side, Rita, as fashion director, and I are in charge. Ivan is the stylist. Makeup artist Natalia Belda is responsible for the glam. The photographer is a great guy who we're constantly fighting with *Harper's Bazaar* over. I hope I get to enjoy this second go-round... if Ivan lets me.

"I mean, seriously, Miranda, I can't believe you."

He's been livid ever since I told him that yesterday, in my last time jump, I told Tristan that I did want to be a mother, that I just needed a little more time. He's not mad because he doesn't want me to have kids out of some kind of jealousy or who knows what. It's just that he knows me well, and he knows why I did it. And I do too.

But fine. We're all suffering here, you know? For example, I haven't said a word about how, in this parallel reality, he looks like a Bond villain from the seventies...if the film had been set in the futuristic era. He's wearing a black frock coat with a Mandarin collar, matching trousers cuffed at the ankle, and silver Doc Martens; his hair is cut with a very strange gradient; he's missing one eyebrow, which I don't know if he shaved off in a moment of insanity or if he's just that trendy now; and he's wearing white contact lenses and a silver cap on one tooth. What do I do? Kill myself?

"When you get all serious and grumpy in this getup, you look like a cult leader."

"Don't be funny, Miri." The photographer comes over, directing the actress, and Ivan crouches down to him. "Carlos…what do you think about trying a few head-on? The dress has amazing sleeves. Maybe you can play with them."

I go over too. Rita is at the village, the table where all the computers and everything else are set up so they can see the images as they come in. She gives me a glance that I understand immediately, and in a whisper that doesn't sound like a whisper, I say to the photographer:

"Carlos, I agree with Ivan. Let's try a few head-on, with sleeves or without sleeves. That way, you can all see it too. Her posing in profile like that is flattering, I know, but…it's not what we're going for. We want her to be her. Just as she is. We're looking for a powerful image, sexy, strong. The way her energy fills the room as soon as she comes in."

The photographer nods and smiles.

"Gotcha. Sounds cool to me."

Ivan and I take two steps back and cross our arms across our chests at the same time. "Djadja" by Aya Nakamura is playing…the remix with Maluma hasn't come out yet.

"Mara, babe, we're going to try a few from the front, okay? Stand with your legs apart a little like a powerful bullfighter…just like that! That's it!"

"Wait a sec while we adjust the dress… Vero, can you do it?" Ivan asks his assistant.

"Of course, Ivan."

"Don't be mad at me," I whisper to him.

"It's not my life. I can't be mad if you want to fuck it all up."

"Listen to me."

"You're making me nervous," he says with clenched teeth, biting his words.

"What if that's why I lost him?"

"So what if it is?" His glare is full of rage. "Tell me, if that's why you lost him…then what?"

"Well, I've probably been avoiding the question of motherhood out of Peter Pan syndrome or…I don't know, narcissism."

"Next are you going to ask who's going to take care of you when you're old if you don't have kids? Because I don't think I can flip out more than I'm flipping out right now."

"I can't ask myself questions about things that go a little deeper?" I ask, catching the suit jacket I'm wearing on my shoulders, never putting my arms in, before it slips off and falls to the floor.

"Of course," he says, dodging the question, "you look stunning in maroon. I don't know why you don't wear color more often."

"Because black is my color."

"Well, the whole 'fit in French maroon looks incredible."

"French maroon?"

"Yes. That shade of maroon is very French, right? Our Spanish one is more…more carmine. You know? More crimson."

He lightly brushes the sweater I'm wearing with the monochrome suit, in the same shade, and nods his approval when he confirms it's cashmere.

"Acceptable?" I ask sarcastically.

"You do love good wool."

"Does that win me some points?"

"No, because you like good wool, but you're still a jerk who's putting your boyfriend's needs before yours, even though they're going to make yours take it up the ass."

"Being a mother isn't the end of the world."

"Of course it's not, you giant whore!"

Suddenly, everyone is staring at us. The flashes popping, the directions, the buzz of conversations all grind to a halt. All that's left is the music and a ton of eyes on us. We mime our apologies, and the shoot starts again.

"Being a mother isn't the end of the world, of course not," Ivan goes on, "but it's not what you want. At least it's not what you want now. If it were, you'd be totally sure about it, don't you think?"

"Well, I dunno. These big decisions always freak me out... Give me a second."

I go over to the photographer and the village. Rita shows me a few of the photos on the iPad, and I nod.

"Her expression is so cool." I point at the actress's face on the screen. "She looks kind and sure of herself. That's exactly what we're going for."

"Let's try another look, yeah?" Rita suggests.

"Yes." I look quickly at Carlos, who's trying to get our attention. "Talk to me."

"She looks stunning. Are you into the pose?"

"Love it."

"Do you want to put the fan on for a bit?"

"Mara, are you into having the fan on?" The girl gives me a confused look, and I laugh. "Like in a Paulina Rubio video?"

"Oh, for sure!"

"Let's do it then."

"Should we do a few more poses with this dress and then try the other Dolce & Gabbana one?" Ivan asks.

"Perfect," Rita confirms.

Ivan and I retreat to one side again. Vero, Ivan's assistant, runs to readjust the star's clothes. We both give her a thumbs-up at the same time when they're right. Rita laughs, iPad in hand, making jokes about whether we really are twins separated at birth.

"I'm sure we were kidnapped by that nun who stole babies, and…you went to Boston, and I went to California."

"You're animals at this magazine." The photographers laughs.

We ignore the dig.

"What if I lose the love of my life out of fear and miss out on the most gratifying and fulfilling experience of—"

"OMG, Miranda." He sighs.

"What?"

He turns to me.

"One…" He squints, very focused. "This is a very evocative song."

"Yes, it is."

"Sorry. What was I saying?" And to my disappointment, he gets back to the topic, shoving a solemn finger in my face. "One. The whole love of your life thing… Don't you think that idea of romance is a little… outdated?"

"That's what romance is, Ivan."

"Oh, well, bring back the corsets then."

"You're such a dick," I groan.

"No, seriously, Miranda. 'The love of your life'… Okay, and when do you find that out? Because it feels like a title of that caliber should be given on your deathbed, right? But go off."

"You're very practical."

"No. Not at all," he says desperately. "I'm a whore for romance, Miranda, way more than you, even that embarrasses the shit out of me. I fall hard, and that's exactly why I don't even try to trick myself into thinking that whomever I'm with is the only one for me. He's just the one I want. Jesus…that's a lot more romantic! Don't be cynical."

He looks at the finger he's holding in my face and laughs like a kid who just discovered his hand.

"What are you laughing at?" It spreads to me.

"The other day, someone told me a joke, and I just remembered it."

I shoot him a murderous look.

"What's the best thing about fingering a psychic on her period?" He holds two fingers up.

"Ugh, I don't know. What?"

"You get your palm red for free."

He waggles his fingers lasciviously, and I can't help but burst out laughing. Well…I'm not the only one. His assistant, the light tech, one of the people in the village, and Mara, the actress, all start cackling. The photographer quickly snaps a few shots. One of them will end up being the cover shot.

"You're all filthy eavesdroppers," I complain. "Carlos, Rita, have we got it? Should we try a new look?"

"Perfect."

The producer takes the lead, showing Mara to the dressing room, and we follow a few steps behind. I think I've wriggled out of the ass reaming when my best friend grabs my arm and holds me back.

"I'm not going in," I splutter. "I know I have to give the girl a little privacy."

"Two," he says, putting up his middle finger too.

"God, no…"

"God, yes. Come get coffee with me."

He literally throws me toward a table where someone has set up a carafe of hot water.

"Miranda, a woman's worth can't be reduced to motherhood."

"For fuck's sake, I know that." I'm indignant.

"So why can't your position on having kids be valid?"

"Because I don't know if I want them or not."

"And isn't that valid too? Especially because, babe, I've known you forever, and you've always been closer to no than yes."

"I mean…"

"I mean…" He imitates me, making a cocksucker face.

"I don't have my whole life, Ivan. It's not that hard to understand. He's clear about it. He wants to be a father. And I lost him once and…" I see the face he's making, and I feel hopeless. "You don't get it."

"You're the one who doesn't get it, Miranda." He seems genuinely crushed, like he can't understand why I'm being so stubborn about something like this. "It should be fuck yes or nothing at all. That goes for everything. The whole 'if it scares you, do it scared' thing is fine for some stuff, but sometimes it's way more complicated than that. And so what if it's not a no and it's just a not yet? You're not going to respect your own timing? And what if it is actually a no?"

"I guess you never know for sure with these things."

"Yeah, you're right, but there shouldn't be another person pushing you into the decision."

"It's not another person. It's love."

"Ay…love."

"Yes, love. Who's being cynical now?"

"How many cowards have hidden behind that word, 'love'?"

I snort and concentrate on pouring myself coffee. He does too. Our silence doesn't even last a minute.

"I just don't want you to be pressured into making the decision… fuck." He interrupts himself and put his hands on his hips. "I know you'd never regret it if you had a kid. It would be your kid, you'd adore it, and I'm sure you'd be an incredible mother, but I want… I want you to make that decision one day because *you* make it. For *yourself.*"

"Well…I asked him for a little time. It's not like I'm downing folic acid with my coffee every morning. Take a breath."

"When was that?"

"When was what?" I look at him, confused.

"The jump 'you just came from.'" He does air quotes.

"October."

"I just can't believe you didn't say anything to me until now." He blinks, surprised, and shakes his head disapprovingly.

"The me of the real timeline either didn't know about the change or was more cowardly than me."

"Or she knew that it was all bark"—he points at his mouth—"and no bite."

"What does that mean?"

"So you asked him for time…and he said yes, not knowing how much you were asking for. Knowing you, you're going to use that to your advantage."

"When you put it like that, I sound like a con artist."

"Miranda, if that kid…who isn't such a kid anymore, by the way, wants to be a father and you're not sure, you have to make that clear to him. He's giving you time so you can think about it, and he deserves to have all the information before he does that."

"Ah! You're so smart! Thanks so much for the advice! I had never thought of that! I did that the first time!" I say, finally losing my shit.

"And?"

"Do I need to remind you why I'm time traveling?"

"Yes, please." And he crosses his arms over his chest.

I stare at him, bewildered, because I don't actually know how to answer him. I grab a mini croissant and stuff it into his mouth. Nobody freak out…it's tiny and Ivan has eaten much bigger things with no complaints. And I'm talking about a fried chicken sandwich with fries…

"I have no idea!" I yell and then lower my voice. "But if I do things the way you're saying, spoiler alert: he dumps me at the end."

Once he manages to swallow the croissant, I get a ten-megaton slap that undoes my bun in one blow. Bobby pins go flying.

"Ah!" I yelp.

"You're crazy, deadass. Let me tell you something." He comes over, pursing his lips like a baboon's ass. His lips are covered in crumbs. "You can't... You can't let your whole life be swallowed up by love."

"And I'm not!"

"Fuck my life, your life, and Mercury retrograde, Miranda...so now what?"

"I don't want to spoil what's coming next, but it's not good."

"Yeah, yeah, I know. Every closet in my house is full of toilet paper and cans of stew, meatballs, and peaches in syrup."

"You should've bought canned vegetables too."

"You're scaring me."

I bite my lip.

"You know how people are starting to talk about a flu...in China?"

"Yeah, the one in Wuhan."

"Well, it's not going to stay in Wuhan...or in Asia. It's going to travel around the world like Willy Fog. Remember this word, because you're going to be using it a lot: 'pandemic.'"

He makes a face.

"Are we all going to die?"

"Yes. But before it was all over, Prime Minister Pedro Sanchez decided to put me in a time machine and send me back to talk to you, because you're the only one who can save us, Ivan."

He gets very quiet. I think for a few seconds he might even believe it, until I start laughing.

"You're a jerk, you know that?" he spits angrily.

"You fell for it."

"Look, girl, you've been telling me since 2016 that sometimes you're from the future, and when you don't tell me, magically, I forget all about it. Either this is the longest and best played prank in history, or I believe everything you tell me at this point."

He sighs and, clutching his coffee, heads toward the changing room, which he pokes his head into after a few light taps on the door.

"Ah, fuck...spectacular. It looks even better than I thought."

I stick my head in too. The girl looks incredible, but Ivan fits the garment to her body with a few safety pins until it looks like it was sewn onto her.

"Rita...what do you think?" I ask.

"I think she looks great." She's intrigued when she sees me. "You let your hair down?"

"Ivan let it down for me."

"I knocked that shit down, so be warned."

They all burst out laughing.

"What do you think?" I gesture with my chin toward Mara, who really is spectacular.

Ivan makes a gesture that I understand to mean he's got it under control. Rita, Natalia Belda, and he move aside and discuss something about the mood board they sent to the photographer. They want a really "Italian" look. Mara goes to hair and makeup again, and I take a second to relax and eat a bun with my coffee. But of course...I dropped a bomb on Ivan, and he's not going to just let it go.

"Are we all going to die?" he pesters me.

"No. We're not. But..." I make a bad face. Truly bad. "Let's not make light of it."

He nods. I don't know how he can believe me blindly. Sometimes I think that, deep down, he doesn't. He's just acting.

"Let me ask you a question, Miranda." He leans against the wall next to craft services and crosses his arms. "If all this is true...and I don't doubt it is, but if a global crisis is looming and we're even fearing for our lives and the lives of the people we love...how is it possible that knowing everything you know, you're still worried about all this frivolous shit?"

I stare at him, not knowing whether this is a real question or a value judgment; I don't know how to answer.

"I'm not judging you," he clarifies. "It's just that..." He looks around. "We're here, doing such pointless stuff..."

"The world needs these things to keep turning. And love."

"Yes, but crisis has to serve for something, right? Whether it's a pandemic or a breakup. To put things in order. To put things in the place they deserve."

"Well, that's what this is all about. That's what I'm trying to do."

"No, Miri. You're not putting things in their place. You're fleeing," he says sadly.

"Fleeing isn't the right word, Ivan. It's complicated."

"Miranda," he insists very seriously. "He dumped you, and you fled to a warmer place, to your memories. You're ditching everything else, trying to reconstruct it. Everything. Including you."

30

~~

SHE'S SCREWING
EVERYTHING UP

TRISTAN

It's ten thirty, and it has already been pitch-black for hours. Nights in Madrid, in the winter, are long and orange. The cold is so dry it's easy to get lulled into a false sense of security.

I got home around eight thirty. I walked unhurriedly, bundled up warm, listening to music, absorbed in work things that won't leave my head until I throw them out. When I go in, the apartment is warm and dark like a uterus but empty. I don't feel like it, but I change, grab my backpack, and head to the gym. I have to fill the time with something while Miranda's at work.

Now, back at the house, after a shower, in comfortable clothes (jeans and a sweater, in case Miranda wants to go out to eat), I wait for her, sipping a beer. But it's really late already. I should call her.

She picks up on the second ring, but she's distracted.

"Six, seven, eight… Eight, Cris, there are eight!" she says to someone who must be in her glass office. "Hey, handsome."

"Are you still at the magazine?"

"Yes. But I don't think I'll be here much longer."

"Are you closing?"

"Yes."

There's a lot of chaos around her. I catch the word "poke."

"I'm tired, but I can come pick you up and we can grab a burger some-where around there."

"The thing is, we still have to send it off, and everyone's acting like they're green." She clears her throat. "I'm sorry, babe. It's just that…it'll probably take a while, it's cold…it's a pain in the ass for you."

"Should I make something at home and wait for you?"

"No, my love. That's the last thing you need. I get home super late, and you have to take care of everything on top of that? Don't worry about it. Plus I'm gonna be catatonic when I get home. Can we leave it for tomor-row? Today, all I can think about is thigh-high boots and polyamory being in this season."

"Polyamory?"

"An article in the issue we're closing today. Don't worry about it."

"I'm not worried. It's physically impossible for your job to leave you time to have another relationship, so…"

She laughs. That laugh makes me smile.

"Don't make anything for dinner," she says. "I'll send dinner for both of us. Put mine in the microwave, and I'll eat it when I get home."

"Should I wait up so we can watch a movie?"

"Don't wait to go to bed if you're tired."

"But didn't you say it wouldn't be much longer?"

"I don't know, Tristan. I can't guarantee it."

I rub my forehead.

"Okay. Well, see you in bed."

"Great. See you in bed. I'll be the one in underwear that shows my whole ass, okay?"

I crack up.

"It's winter, for God's sake. Don't wear those ones."

"What do you think, my butt cheeks are going to catch a cold?"

"Now I'm trying not to picture them sneezing."

I hear a kind of cough, and I realize she's choking.

"Okay...I'll let you go. I don't want to bug you," I insist.

"I'll see you soon. I love you."

"Yeah..." I sigh. "I think I can almost remember the last time I saw you too."

"I'm sorry. You're right. I'll make it up to you soon."

"Blow job?"

"I was thinking more like whisking you away to a hotel with a fireplace, but if a blow job is all it takes..."

"Miranda!" I scold her. "Don't say that out loud! I can tell someone's in your office."

"Do you think I talk any less dirty to my other boyfriend?"

I blow her a kiss, one of those liquid I love yous that leak from couple's mouths, and I hang up.

I look at the living room, calm, organized, lit by a pretty, trendy lamp in the corner, and... I don't know what to do. But it's fine. A good day is one where there are no surprises, right? A good day is a day when nothing happens.

I dig out the book I've been making slow but steady progress through for weeks: *How the Mind Works*. I hope when I finish it, I have a slightly clearer idea...because sometimes I don't even understand myself.

"Hey..."

My sister has a knack (for better or worse) for always calling when I'm alone at home, bored, with nothing to do. In a way, it's good, because it keeps me entertained and makes me feel connected to the world...but it gives her too many tools to doubt how I'm doing things.

"You picked up on the first ring. Is your life that interesting?" she asks.

"You caught me with my phone in my hand. I was scrolling on Instagram. I'm reading, but… I don't know what's going on with me lately. I can't concentrate for more than fifteen minutes in a row."

"Yeah…and apart from that, what can you tell me?"

"Well, not much. Same as every day."

"Have you solved your work problem yet?"

"Yeah, the hard way. I don't know what's going on with the bosses. I think when you get to a certain point, after a couple of years, like a computer programmed to become obsolete, you start to malfunction."

"Isn't your girl the boss?"

"You're the worst," I say very seriously.

If I laugh even half-heartedly about this, we're in trouble.

"Have you seen the news? Seems like this flu is going to get complicated. Are you going to come see us?"

"You say that like we're all going to turn into zombies in a few months and I have to say goodbye. Like in *Apocalypse Z*. I loved those books…"

"Yeah, right. I'm just saying…judging by how you're always so happy and surrounded by people there…"

"It's Tuesday. It's normal for Miranda to be working."

"As far as I know, you work too…and you're at home. It's almost eleven."

"Ah, and you didn't think it was too late to call at this hour?"

"Tristan…"

The doorbell rings. Saved by the bell. I buzz them up without checking who it is.

"Is it the princess?"

"It's dinner. Miranda sent it, and by the way, she's not a princess, she's the queen."

"Argh, so gross. Saying stuff like that is really not a good look."

"I must be hangry. I don't know what she sent, but right now, I'm so hungry I'd even eat that disgusting soup Papa makes with spinach."

"Not even the dogs eat that, Tristan."

I laugh and open the door when I hear the sound of the elevator arriving on our floor. I take the bag the messenger hands me and thank him with a smile. Burgers. I doubt it sometimes, but Miranda does listen to me.

"I'm gonna go eat," I say to Uxia. "I'll call you tomorrow."

"Wait, Tristan...one second."

I put the bag down on the kitchen counter and wait for my sister to keep talking.

"You spend a lot of time alone."

I lick my lips. Here comes the lecture.

"I never had the social prowess to make friends."

"What about your girl?"

"My girl does, but Miri's friends are her friends. And the truth is I've always felt like they look at me kinda weird. I'm a dry guy, Uxi. Of course I'm not their favorite dude."

"Have you talked about the kid thing again?"

"No."

"I never thought I'd say this about a woman, but...do you think she's a commitment-phobe? I think she's traumatized by the whole dead mother thing."

"First of all, that's grossly misogynistic. I can't believe I have to point that out to you."

"True. The first part was badly constructed," she admits. "But I stand by the trauma thing."

"She doesn't have any trauma."

"Well, she's going to end up traumatizing you. Or not. You'll just end up a bitter old man in your fifties, always wondering whether."

"Uxia..." I stop her firmly, annoyed, "I had a shitty day. Don't make it worse."

"It's just that...if you don't tell me anything..."

"What do you want me to tell you? I hate my job. I don't know why the fuck I listened to everyone and became a lawyer, and even worse, I don't know how I can be so good at it when I hate it so much."

"What does that have to do with…?"

"Let me finish! I'm a guy from the sea living completely landlocked, surrounded by people from the drylands. The only good thing I have, apart from you three, is Miranda. Are there things that aren't so great about our relationship? Of course there are. She avoids certain topics, she's in love with her work, and sometimes it seems like she totally spaces out and returns to her planet, but I'm crazy about her. Do you get it? And if we broke up one day because…because…I don't know. Because I can't stand my shitty job, this city that isn't mine, the little time I have by her side, and I discover my life's purpose is to raise children…if all that happens all at once and I leave her…even then, with all those reasons, it'll still be the hardest fucking thing I've ever gone through in my life. And I'm probably not a very romantic guy, you know? And I can't tell her this, but sometimes I think we can fall in love many times, but each time is going to be completely different, and I want to spend the rest of my life in love the way I am now. Exactly like this. With this person. So stop being a pain in my ass about it, for fuck's sake."

Uxia doesn't say anything, but she hasn't hung up, because I can hear her breathing on the other end of the line. I close my eyes and lean my forehead against the cold counter, next to the paper bag full of our dinner. I don't think there's anything else to say. She can't stand Miranda because she's everything my sister will never be and we always hate what we envy. And that's a fact. But it doesn't mean we always envy what we hate. I decide to cut the conversation off there, but affectionately.

"Good night, Uxi."

"Good night, Tristan. I'm just worried about you."

"I know. But please stop. You're making me feel worse."

When I hang up and unwrap the burgers, I'm not even in the mood anymore. But I eat it.

I miss Vigo. And not just Vigo. I miss Galicia. It's like a pull deep inside me. Because you can take the boy out of Galicia, but you can't take Galicia out of the boy. Sometimes this landlocked phase is painful, this hiatus to "grow up." If it weren't for Miranda, I would've been back by now. I wouldn't have stuck it out, but we all know that she's not omnipotent, even if for a while now, I've started thinking of her more and more as a deity I worship and thank every night, every morning.

I'm starting to see the cracks in this approach. And I need something, some kind of proof. Like Saint Thomas, I want to put my finger in the wound on the relationship's side to give me faith that everything will pay off. I need her to give me something in return for everything I feel, maybe unfairly, that I'm giving up for her. Because I'm here with her, even though she never asked me to be. I need more. I don't know how to tell her anymore. I don't know how to bring it up again. I'm afraid to insist, because deep down, deep, deep down, I know what she needs and wants and what I need and want. And they're not compatible. Even though they should be. They say love conquers all...

Not long ago, a woman I work with whom I was venting to for some reason told me that Miranda was a spoiled brat and that she must not love me that much if she wasn't capable of growing up and starting a family. I answered her calmly but sharply:

"No. Not at all. Miranda's just a woman who thinks differently than you do, but that doesn't make her worse. And I'm not just saying that because she's my partner. I think it's pretty logical. In any case, it's a question of empathy. You just have to understand, as much as it kills me that we're not on the same page about this, that my partner needs other things to feel like her life is full. I want her, but I want a family too, and a peaceful life, a house in the suburbs, and probably, if I can dream, to go back to

Galicia with her and get out of here and never come back. She wants me, she loves her job, she wants to travel, keep growing and learning, finding time for herself, time to spend with me, time to decide, she adores her apartment right in the center, the noise of Madrid, and some day, she wants to feel like she accomplished something big. Does that make one of us better than the other?"

She didn't answer me. I didn't add anything else. I wasn't really responding to her and her rudeness. I was talking to myself, making it clear that it is what it is and that as much as everyone likes to say it, love doesn't conquer all, because that would mean steamrolling a ton of other things that are important too. If love conquers all, where does that leave us? Where does that leave what we choose, who we are?

When Miranda gets home, I'm half-asleep watching a show in bed, but I try to perk up a bit and get up.

"Ay, no," she says, her face looking pained. "Don't get up, please. I feel awful."

"Don't worry about it. I was awake. I want to sit with you while you eat."

"I'm not even hungry." She rubs her face.

She looks…oof… I almost feel tired just looking at her. There's hardly anything left of the flawless makeup she put on this morning. She has deep, dark circles under her bloodshot eyes. I hug her.

"Don't hug me, please," she begs. "When I'm this tired, I get really sensitive."

"I know. And it's fine."

"I'm the worst girlfriend in the world."

I notice the shoulder of my pajamas getting damp where she's curled up against me, so I squeeze her tighter. I don't mention the tears, because I know she just needs to get it out a little. A minute of weakness and then she's back on track…that's how she is. When she calms down, she straightens up and smiles at me.

"All better. I'm a dumbass."

"Never say you're the worst girlfriend in the world again. You're exhausted, and you have no reason to feel bad for not having the gift of omnipresence. Babe." I smile at her. "You're doing the best you can, and that's always much more than you need to. Because you're amazing, okay?"

She nods, pouting.

"You are too," she moans.

"Me?" I laugh. "The sad lawyer."

"No." Tears well up in her eyes again. "You just haven't found the thing that will show everyone how amazing you are yet. But you already are to me."

And this is why I say love doesn't conquer all, because it can also be a liar and convince this woman that she doesn't deserve me and that she's screwing everything up.

31

~~

"I'M GOING TO MAKE LUNCH"

MIRANDA

Tristan gently shakes me awake. The first thing I see is that he's wearing a pilly brown sweater and old jeans. I'm confused. The light coming in makes me think it's early but not early enough that we shouldn't both be at work. Is it the weekend?

"Miranda...wake up..."

"What time is it?"

"Eight thirty."

"What day?"

"Friday."

"Shit, I'm gonna be late," I say, sitting up.

"Don't worry, don't worry...we're working from home, remember?"

I look at him from the bed. My head is still super foggy. I grab my phone automatically, and all my suspicions are confirmed: Friday, March 13, 2020. The government is about to declare a state of emergency because of the coronavirus.

"But still, it's not early."

"You stayed up working really late last night, getting ahead of things. You don't need to rush," he reminds me. "Miri...the office just called me."

"And?"

"Get up, please. I think you need coffee before we talk about this."

A cup of steaming coffee is waiting for me on the kitchen counter. All I'm wearing is a nightie and a silk robe. I sit on one of the high stools and take a sip, which warms me up immediately. Tristan is hopping from the bedroom to the living room, pulling his shoes on at the same time.

"Come on. What's going on?" I call out, even though I already know.

"Umm…well, you know how one of the partners at the firm has a lot of connections, right?"

"Yes." I nod.

"Well…someone tipped him off that they're serious… They're really going to lock us in our houses."

"Define 'lock us in our houses.'"

"The government is going to decree a state of emergency, and they're going to limit leaving the house to essentials only: buying absolute necessities, going to the doctor only when it's an emergency, and work that can't be done virtually. Something like that. They asked us to come into the office to get any documents we need to work from home."

"But you already brought your stuff home, right?"

"Yes. But I have to get a few other things. It's probably going to last a while."

I debate between playing dumb and continuing to ask questions or shutting up.

"Miri…it could last weeks. Go see your dad today. Ask him if he wants to come stay here or if he needs anything or…I don't know."

"I have to call Marisol to see how we're going to handle it at the magazine. Luckily we installed VPN this week so we can access the computers in the office remotely. Otherwise, I have no idea how we would've done layout."

He nods and put his hands on his thighs. He's very solemn.

"Did you talk to your parents?" I ask.

"No. I was going to call them now. My mother's going to lose it."

"She's a good planner. I'm sure her pantry is stocked already."

"Yes. There'll be no shortage in their house." He smiles tensely. "It's just that he's a restless ass, and they're both retired…"

"Don't worry. As long as they have a deck of cards…"

He smiles and kisses me.

"I'm heading out."

"Yeah. I'm going to drink this coffee and then go see my dad. Do you want me to buy anything?"

He looks at me, not sure how to answer. I know he feels like he's getting carried away by the collective hysteria right now and he's embarrassed, but in the end, he succumbs to it.

"I'm going to stop by the pharmacy again to see if they have any paracetamol. Just in case. We only have a half-empty box left," he says.

"See if they have any approved face masks."

He makes a face. At this point, it still all sounds so weird and extremist. "Okay."

"Should I go to the supermarket?" I insist.

"I'm scared, Miri. People are going crazy. You already saw what the shelves were like at the supermarket yesterday."

"That's why. We don't have much at home. I could at least try to see what I can find."

My father lives in Carabanchel, in the same apartment I grew up in. An apartment with the seventies charm of the public buildings in working-class neighborhoods. No frills but comfortable, with floral tiles in the kitchen and bathroom, which are ugly but coming back into fashion… because everything in fashion is cyclical. But I know that if I want to find him, I should forget about going there and head to the store instead. He refuses to close, even though no one has been there for days. The scene I stumble into is a man calmly reading the newspaper, sitting in a winged armchair and sipping coffee.

"Dad, this is ridiculous. Are you living under a rock, or are you so cool you think this global pandemic has nothing to do with you? As far as I know, you're not part of the Avengers."

"I think they're kinda blowing this whole COVID thing out of proportion."

"Well, I think I don't want to end up without a father, so get up and get your stuff, we're going."

"Jeez Louise."

I grab his sweater and shake him.

"Dad, I'm not fucking around. They're sending everyone home. The government is going to declare a state of emergency tomorrow. Don't act like a child."

He raises his eyebrows, making like he's scared.

"A state of emergency?"

"Yes. They let it slip to Tristan at work. It's serious. It's not a rumor. This thing is going to get ugly. The emergency rooms in hospitals are getting overwhelmed. A lot of people are dying, Dad. Don't make jokes about it. Don't make light of it."

"Miri…"

"What?"

"I have lunch at home, and the sheets on your bed are clean. Do you want to come?"

I can't help laughing.

"No, Dad. I have a house. Do you want to come to mine? Tristan suggested it. He's worried that you're alone."

"Well, tell him I'm not senile, I'm seventy-five years old, and I can whip his butt in pelota."

"Nobody plays pelota anymore, Dad."

"Well, then paddle tennis."

"They call it pickleball now."

"Whatever it is."

"Do you want to come to our house or not?" I blurt out desperately.

"What am I going to do shut up with my daughter and her boyfriend in a house that's not mine? No, no. If you want, you can both come to mine. Plus, there's only one bedroom in your house."

"But if it'll stop you being lonely, we can all make it work. Or if that will just make you more anxious, we can both come to yours."

He shakes his head.

"It'll just be for a few days. I don't want Tristan to be uncomfortable."

"He won't be," I lie.

"Miri, it's only going to be a few days. You have to relax, sweetheart. You're making me nervous."

"Okay." I sigh. Yeah...just a few days. "Do you remember how to FaceTime from your iPad?"

"Dear child"—he's starting to get pissed off—"just because you're so clever, that doesn't mean your father is an idiot, okay?"

I give up.

"Close up shop, and take everything you need. We won't be back for a long time. And we're catching a cab."

The pharmacy is mayhem, just as I remembered it. There's almost nothing left. People are mostly trying to find prescription drugs for chronic diseases. My father takes tablets for his gout, and I force him to ask his pharmacist for enough for three months. And we manage to find some anti-inflammatories in case his knees act up and paracetamol. The mask thing is still in the realm of science fiction.

We carry the groceries (what little we were able to buy) up the stairs, just like I remember us doing the first time, because I wanted to avoid the canned air in the elevator. I also remember the paranoia and fear that I felt, and I appreciate knowing what I know now: that my father will be okay. I had a really hard time leaving him all alone. With everything unpacked in the kitchen and the bathroom, I make sure he charges his phone and his iPad, but I'm not satisfied.

"You should really come to our house."

"To toss and turn on a couch, right?"

"It's a pullout. We'll sleep on the couch bed, and you can sleep in our bed."

"No way. A couple needs privacy, and I'm going to get anxious. I'd rather stay here, Miri. If you were alone, you'd come here, and that'd be that. But having Tristan, you should be with him. He's alone in Madrid, and his parents are far away. He must be worried. Go on, go be with him. We'll see each other in a few days."

"Don't go out. Okay? Don't go out for anything in the world. I'll have groceries delivered for you, they'll drop them at your door, and you can pick them up when they're gone. And then you wash them all well, like I told you. Understood? And none of those games with your neighbors and all that stuff."

"Don't worry. I'll be fine here with your mother."

I think that worries me even more.

I call Marisol on the way out of my father's house. We had some foresight, and we've been preparing ourselves for this situation for the last few weeks. Hard times are coming, but at least we won't need to go into the office. It's all under control.

When I get home, carrying what I was able to make off with at the grocery store, I find Tristan sitting on the couch, in front of the computer, with his phone pressed to his ear.

"No, Mama. I can't see you. You're doing something wrong. Look. It doesn't matter. I'll show you another time because it looks like we're going to have a lot of free time." He looks up at me and rolls his eyes. "No, Mama, you're getting hysterical. Okaaay. Okaaaaaaaay. Okay!"

He hangs up and throws the phone onto the coffee table and then rubs his face roughly.

"Please tell me it went better with your father."

"Yes. Everything is under control." I sit down next to him. "Don't worry."

"How can I not worry?" He looks at me sidelong. "Have you heard the death count today? And my sister is saying: 'I don't know. Look, don't you think it's all a setup?'"

I laugh and lean on his shoulder.

"You have to be patient."

"That's something I don't have much of lately."

"Well, you're gonna need it, Tristan." I kiss his shoulder and look at him. "Because we're going to spend a lot of hours locked up inside here and long days without much information. And it's going to be desperate and claustrophobic. And sad sometimes."

He throws me a look that I translate as a very sarcastic "thanks, you're a big help."

"Yeah, I know. But I want us to be realistic."

He sucks his teeth, staring unseeingly at the back of the room, and doesn't answer.

"What?" I prod him to speak.

"Nothing."

"No, come on, don't go all silent. What's going on?"

"You don't think this is a big deal?"

"No, I do. But you got all… I don't know. Tell me."

"Nothing." But he drags out the vowels reluctantly.

"Babe…we have to be realistic."

"And we'll die from realism, my love." He stands up and heads to the kitchen. "I'm going to make lunch."

32

~~~

"MY DREAM LIFE TOO"

I could've woken up remembering our trip to Lisbon. Or the day of Rita's wedding. Or maybe when we went to that festival in Valencia, the day Vetusta Morla and Zahara played the same night, and he got a little drunk and said into my ear that I had made him understand love songs. I could have woken up again and again on lazy Sundays lounging in bed and on the couch, the ones where we binged whole series, ate terribly, and fucked like it was a sport. Or on those Saturdays when we tried to cook recipes that came out disgusting, but we ate them anyway. Or the Wednesday nights, getting undressed in our bedroom, talking about the day enveloped in that intimacy and normality calm love provides. Maybe in the honeymoon period, when you smile too much, when you make such an effort to be the best version of yourself without realizing that the best version will always be the whole one, even though you have your shadows.

But no.

I'm determined to invent my own song, which will be called "Go to Fucking Hell," and the lyrics would be: "In the neurotic's bingo game, I haven't had much luck, because out of all the days, I landed on one in the middle of COVID." And it'll be a global hit. I'll be a star in Korea.

Just my luck. Of all the days in the world, I have to relive the fucking pandemic. At least living through it the second time, I can be grateful the fear of the unknown is gone…for me but not for him. Tristan is scared, as we all were, but unwilling to admit it. I guess he was always too proud to show his weaknesses. And I was too optimistic to see ours.

To be honest, lockdown was not our greatest era as a couple. The apartment is small, and we both had a lot of work to do. I didn't handle the lockdown well, and he really struggled with the distance from his loved ones. Having something imposed on you can make it unbearable.

The first ten days were easy, even peaceful in some twisted way. We took advantage of the chance to be together more than work had ever allowed us before. But the first month as a whole…was not easy. Tension loomed over our heads like a thick, gray, rain-laden cloud. I remember thinking that we wouldn't make it all the time, that our relationship would be collateral damage of the situation, like so many others. We were fighting about cleaning and mess. About cooking. About doing the dishes. About if one of us was breathing too loudly or the other one was clearing his throat too much. And parroting the news to each other at the same time. About whose turn it was to take the recycling downstairs. Sex took a hit, of course, although it had already taken a hit since Tristan saw me take the Pill one morning around Christmas. It's not like I was sneaking it. We just had never had that conversation, and things left unsaid are like that frenemy who's always talking shit about you behind your back.

But a little over a month after lockdown started…the sun came out. They say human beings are capable of adapting to anything.

Wait…hold on. Let me rewind.

When I say the sun came out…I don't mean a rainbow, little birds singing, bunnies hopping behind dew-covered bushes, and deer drinking water from a spring. It's more like…like those gray days when you can see light through a thin layer of clouds and it stops raining.

And there we are. That's where I woke up today. Shitty luck.

Today, we celebrate thirty-five days of lockdown, and we've sunk into a more comfortable but eerie calm. Even I'm aware that the Miranda and Tristan who were crazy in love are in the distant past, and I don't really know what happened. Maybe nothing. Maybe that's exactly what happened to us: nothing.

I come out of the bathroom and pass behind him, typing away with his headphones on. I can hear that he's listening to "Eternal Summer" by The Strokes. If I'm not mistaken, it just came out, and Tristan loves it.

I lean over and kiss his neck. He takes out one of his headphones, a little surprised by the affection.

"What's up?"

"Nothing. I just wanted to give you a kiss." I smile at him. "I love that you still wear cologne even though we're stuck in the house."

"I have a female to seduce," he jokes.

I vaguely remember a comment like that causing a fight; if it wasn't today, it was a day like today. I guess I considered it cruel, given the circumstances, or I took it as an opportunity to throw how he never touches me in his face. Or who knows?

I take a deep breath and gesture at his computer screen.

"What are you doing?"

"Drafting an email for a client who doesn't understand the proceedings. And it's complicated because"—he turns around to look at me properly—"I barely understand it myself."

We both smile.

"How are you doing?" I ask him.

He sucks in air. He's wearing the old jeans that I like so much and a white cotton T-shirt. Have we talked about how hot white looks on brunettes? No, probably better not to.

"I'm just like I was yesterday…and the day before yesterday…and the day before that." He pulls his hands apart, drawing a straight line.

I drag the chair back and sit sideways in his lap. He's about to pull his left headphone out, but I pick up the cable and put the other one in my right ear. I smile at him.

"You like routine," I point out.

"Yeah. I guess so. If the situation out there weren't what it is…and if I weren't so worried about my parents and how things will be when everything goes back to normal…well, it's ideal, right? Both of us at home. Chillin." He says the last word in English.

"Wow, you're so cosmopolitan."

We both fall silent, not really knowing what to say, while I stroke his earlobe, the same one where, years ago, I laughed when I discovered the two piercings from his teenage years.

"Change the song," I ask him. "The electric guitar is making my head pound."

"I thought you liked getting pounded?"

"Only by you."

He lets a soft laugh escape as he turns back to the computer.

"Wait…I'm going to show you something super romantic that I'm sure you don't know."

He selects a song with a double click of the mouse and then settles down to watch me as the simple, rhythmic sound of the guitar strumming starts and then a male voice quickly joins.

"It's by a singer from Mexico."

For the next three minutes and forty-five seconds, we don't say a word. We just listen to the song. I can't decide if it seems sad, hopeful, romantic, or painful, and from now on, it will always taste like him. I already knew that. It's the first time I've listened to it since, and it hurts like hell. I'm surprised to find there's so much of the truth about us in the lyrics…so much truth we don't know yet.

"I like it," I say when it ends.

And my voice sounds weak, because it made me sad, like someone crying in front of a painting or listening to a poem written by someone who has nothing to do with them.

"I knew it."

Another song plays.

"Listen, Miri…" He absentmindedly strokes the part of my neck exposed by my nightie. "I kinda meant what I said, you know?"

"Which part?"

"The thing about how if a global pandemic weren't the reason we were trapped in the house…this wouldn't be so bad."

"You're not dying to go out? You don't feel like the walls are closing in on you?"

"I kinda miss going out for dinner or…I don't know…playing sports in the fresh air. Strolling around. And seeing my family, of course…but this has been good for making me realize that"—he moves his head—"I'm a pretty calm boy."

"Everyone knows you're a calm boy."

"So what are we gonna do about that?" he asks, tenderly pushing my hair off my forehead. "What can we do about a calm boy in the capital?"

"You'd have to ask the calm boy, right? What does he want?"

"He wants the high-strung girl."

"Yeah…the high-strung girl glued to the city."

"But the boy doesn't want the city. Can we unglue her? Or are they conjoined twins who share vital organs that make living a separate life impossible?"

I use a smile to disguise how much what he's saying scares me. After everything I've worked so hard on, we're back here again.

"And what would you do with a girl from the city without the city, calm boy?"

"You've never thought about leaving all this?"

"Leaving what, exactly?" I ask, still stroking his hair, his neck, and his earlobes.

"Leaving Madrid. It's fine, eh. I'm not saying it's not. And I'm not asking you to consider it right now, but…you've never thought about it?"

"In what context? Because, I don't know, we all fantasize about winning the EuroMillions and spending our lives traipsing around on a never-ending vacation."

"No, not like that. I mean a change of scene. Taking a different turn in the road. Working for some small publication in the 'provinces' or…or going back to writing, leaving the managing part aside. Being freelance. Or a correspondent from outside Madrid. Living in a little house…a little house with some land. And a dog. You love greyhounds. You always say you'd like to adopt one and walk it around in a scarf in the winter." I start to say something, but he cuts me off. "A few more years here achieving our goals and then…living life. Real life."

I had never realized, but for Tristan, living in Madrid was always like being plugged into a Matrix. A kind of simulation of what he considers real life, a surrogate for fast fashion, something "just for now." Like the fast, flashy car you buy when you're young without even thinking about whether it's practical.

I stroke his temple and sigh.

"That sigh sounds like a no." He smiles sadly.

"For me, this is real life too."

"Working twelve-hour days, coming home with just enough energy to wolf something down and then go straight to sleep? Or rushing to get changed for some event. A brand presentation. Some awards show. A premier. And not for pleasure. Thirty vacation days enjoyed where you have your ass clenched the whole time, worrying the shit will hit the fan and they'll need you when you're not there… Is that really your dream life, Miranda?"

Is that how he sees it?

What about the pleasure of my fingers on the keyboard, the sensation of holding the printed magazine, seeing a girl reading it on the subway, being lauded as a driving force of something good for the youth, participating in causes we believe in... What about the fun we have at those parties we're sometimes obliged to go to? And the conversations held with hundreds of interesting and brilliant people who you can meet in different functions or activities? I've eaten dinner behind closed doors at the Louvre. I've visited the atelier where they design the couture looks that are heading down the runway in the Dior show. I've given a master class in journalism. I met with all the directors and subdirectors at the international headquarters in New York. I've watched Adele sing a cappella at an event...

Fuck. And that's just one part of my life. That's my work. My job has immaculate vibes. But...

I have Ivan, the guy who can drink a bottle of Larios with Coke Zero in two hours and dance "Paquito el Chocolatero" with strangers, with whom I can make lemon cookies and watch funny movies on a Sunday at his house. Someone to travel with, to confide in, to love. And he's not the only one of my good friends I would call to help me bury a body.

I have my father, who endlessly tells me tales from a life I didn't live and keeps me anchored to a part of my history.

I have Madrid, which on one hand is a huge city that dresses up in fancy clothes, and high heels, invites you to parties, plies you with cocktails, is cool, cutting-edge, reads, participates in life, in culture, in the future, and sparkles...and on the other hand is home, a Sunday with hot chocolate and churros, a calamari sandwich in La Latina, coffee shops where you feel at home, old bookstores, cobbled streets, history, tradition.

Should I go on?

And he's asking if this is my dream life?

"Yes," I answer. "Yes, it is."

To make up for how sad this conversation is, I kiss him. I melt into an intense kiss, nipping his full lips, letting my tongue caress his while I muss his hair. He responds shyly at first. But soon he's matching my intensity with the same desire, the same need.

I've always been fascinated by how easily a kiss can make you breathless. Not any kiss. But a good one. And right now, our breathing is like heavy machinery chugging up into full operation.

My fingers are intertwined in his black hair, and his fingers are on my neck and my ass. The pressure of his thumb, right in the valley drawn on the bottom of my throat, turns me on so fast it makes me moan. And that moan makes him moan. I grab the hand he has on my ass and put it on my breast, but he lets go…so he can slip under my clothes and grab it again with nothing between his skin and mine. My whole body is awake, and so is his under my thighs, so I sit up, still kissing him, and straddle him.

As we move, the headphones tumble to the floor, and our mouths pull apart for a fraction of a second. As our lips reconnect, I sense the shift…

"Miri… Miri…" He pulls away a little and moves back.

"What?" I ask, panting. "Should we move to the bedroom?"

"Miri…it's noon. I have to work. I was in the middle of sending an email."

Years ago, the old Miranda, with the fire I was born with that burned even brighter as I grew up, would've probably insisted. But the one straddling a boyfriend who just used an excuse to reject her is tired. Very tired. Tired, sad, and frustrated.

I know he wants it too. I'm not the problem. He's not either. The problem is one of the ghosts that will haunt us in the future…and they're starting to let their electronic voice phenomenon be heard.

"Okay." I pat his chest, breathing hard. "Okay."

I stand up, not bothering to hide my frustration, and Tristan doesn't make much effort to hide how he's adjusting his erection under his pants.

"I'm sorry, babe…it's just that…"

"It's fine." I fix my nightie and my hair and go to the corner where my desk is. "I have to send some emails too."

A terrible silence fills the cramped but open-plan living room and dining room, which is actually the same room. As soon as I get to my desk, I say his name.

"Tristan…"

"Yeah?" He doesn't turn around.

"What we have, you and me…that, this, is my dream life too."

33

~~

"YOUR PILLOW SMELLS MORE LIKE YOU THAN YOU DO YOURSELF"

I hear Tristan taking a shower, and I check the time. I should have logged in already, but who cares? I don't feel like getting out of bed. I checked the date on my phone, and the world is still stopped out there, so it doesn't matter if I keep lying here. I hug my pillow, which smells like him, and it makes me think about how it smells more like him than he does. Sometimes memories are the same. I don't know if that makes sense. It's like he's fading away, like he's ceasing to be a tangible person. I hear the shower turn off, and then the bathroom door opens, and Tristan comes out in his boxers.

"You're still in bed?" He sounds surprised.

"No, I'm a hologram."

He pouts affectionately, pulling on sweatpants in an award-winning balancing act, and then comes over and sits down next to me.

"It's hard for everyone, Miri. But we're getting closer to the end of all this. It'll be over soon."

I nod.

"Can you get in bed with me for a little bit?" I ask him. "Five minutes."

I know he considers it, at least for a second, but then he says no.

"I have a call. I can't. I'll make coffee?"

I take forever to say yes. By the time I say it, Tristan's already halfway to the kitchen.

I feel like a weirdo, but I can't stop staring at him during his Zoom call. I'm frozen there watching him, like a sentry, with my headphones on, hugging my knees to my chest in the wicker chair I usually sit in to work.

"Falling" by Harry Styles is playing in my ears, and it's playing really loudly. I can't hear anything but his voice. The world is silent, and even the wind sounds like piano.

Tristan is wearing a white polo for the "meeting," trying to look a little more professional, even though he's sitting in his living room, in front of the only bare wall in the house. I can't hear what they're saying or what he's saying. I just see him nod seriously and watch the way his lips move with the rhythm of some words that look firm. He smiles, and it makes his eyes squint. His left hand fidgets with the skin on his neck, meandering back and forth in a kind of nervous gesture. His hands will smell like cologne later, but I won't dare smell them, shove all the papers off the desk, sit on it, and tell him I want to breathe him in until I drown. Only couples who still have a lot of hope left, who aren't tired, can say stuff like that.

I'm tired. I can't deny it.

I've revisited our story patiently, affectionately; I put my life on pause to do it. And it's not fixed. It doesn't work. What will become of me now? Am I going to be trapped here? Am I going to be the ghost, the hologram of the girlfriend I used to be in a couple that doesn't exist anymore?

Who am I without him? I know I'm someone. I was before him, I was during, and I will be if he leaves in the end, but I can't be bothered to discover her again. I just want to climb back into bed.

And for this time-traveling thing, all this coming and going to end. I don't care how, but it needs to end. It's exhausting analyzing, assigning blame, reliving every episode looking for the seams to try to resew them with needle and thread, trying to make them stronger this time, and finally seeing that there's no point. And here I was thinking the problem was that I had fucked up. I thought I could patch it up.

Tristan is saying goodbye. He smiles, waves, and closes the laptop screen so he can take a deep breath. His shoulders fall, his smile disappears, and the shadows under his eyes become more visible.

You'd have to be blind not to see that he's burned out and worried about something. And I know it's like I disconnect at night, like I'm not there, but I travel back in my memory and remember how we spent those nights warming the mattress, tossing and turning, sighing. Awake.

Do you remember what happens with things left unsaid? Well, they have an even crazier friend: things left undone.

Tristan waves his arms to get my attention, and I take off my headphones. The world goes back to having real edges, and Harry Styles is left trapped back in the playlist I listened to on repeat during the pandemic when reality wasn't enough.

"What's up?"

"Should we make lunch?"

"It's so early," I grumble.

He raises one eyebrow.

"It's almost three."

"How long did your call last?"

"Two hours. I had two. One was one hour, and the other was two hours. I'm dead."

Me too, but in another sense. I stand up agreeably, trying to make up for all the heartache.

"I'll make lunch. You…relax."

"You're going to cook?" he teases.

"Yes." I go to the kitchen pretending to be in the mood, skipping a little, and I open the fridge. "I'm full of creativity and ready to cook something for you...um...let's see..."

I glance at the potential ingredients, but when creativity was doled out, I didn't get in the line dedicated to cooking skills. I make a face.

"Spaghetti?" I suggest.

"I think you need a sous-chef."

"Maybe. Every master needs young blood by their side with new ideas. You know."

Within a few minutes, a frying pan is steaming on the induction burner, browning an onion and some minced garlic, and Tristan is straining crushed tomatoes. I want to stop the world. And yeah, he's just making spaghetti, but he's going to do it right, with his homemade Bolognese.

"It'll be done in no time."

"In no time, you can open a jar of tomato sauce, babe. Bolognese is in a different category."

"We'll be eating in twenty minutes, you'll see."

"In twenty minutes, I will have nibbled away all the cheese in the fridge. Silently. Like a termite."

"But I'm the one who had to remind you it was lunchtime! Jeez..."

A phone buzzes on the coffee table, buried under scribbled pages.

"That's mine. Can you grab it for me?" he asks.

I run to catch it in time, even though it's not far from the kitchen to the living room.

"Who is it?"

"Your sister." I pretend to gag, taking advantage of him not being able to see me.

"Pick up and say hi!"

I swallow. Every call with his sister during lockdown has been a huge kick in the ass. Supremely stupid. Unbearably strained. Now I know what day it is today. Of course. I wasn't going to wake up just to watch desire fade.

"Hi, Uxia," I greet her. "How's it going?"

"Is my brother not there?"

"We're in lockdown, like the rest of the world. Of course he's here."

"Can you put him on?"

I stop in front of Tristan, who's putting the ground beef in the pan.

"Put him on," Uxia rudely insists.

"I was just trying to…" I justify myself.

"I have to tell him something."

Go fuck yourself.

"'Hi, Miranda, how's it going? I'm fine. How are you? How are you feeling?' That's the bare minimum, right? Even if you're just being polite and you don't actually care."

Tristan only lifts his eyes, his head frozen in place, and holds his arm out toward me.

"Give me the phone."

I hand it to him.

"She hung up."

He stiffens up, unlocks the phone, and redials her without looking at me.

"Don't even think about being pissed off at me," I warn him.

He slowly licks his lips and turns off the stove with a gesture that seems to say he's not pissed off…he's beyond that.

"What was that?" he says when his sister answers. "I'm sick of this. No, no, Uxia, I'm sick of it. Of both of you. Both of you!" His voice rises.

He glares at me.

"If you're sick of it, imagine how sick I am of your brat of a sister," I toss out, my mouth full of rage.

"Shut up. Please shut up." He puts a hand up between us.

"Don't tell me to shut up."

"One thing at a time, I'm begging both of you."

With the phone pressed to his ear, he strides over to the bedroom and slams the door. Great. I was totally in the mood to reunite with my teenage boyfriend.

The conversation gets loud...really loud. I guess it gets louder than ours will, because you can't argue the same way with a girlfriend as you can with a sister. At least I hope so, because I would never tolerate a boyfriend speaking to me that way. Not even him. Not even from his lips.

I catch a few words that help me build a map of the situation while I wait in the kitchen, my arms crossed: fed up, babies, tired, ruin, future, bitter, not enough, competition, protection, adult, embarrassed, unbearable, trapped.

When he comes out, he's shaken.

"Come on," he says. "Your turn."

"I'm not going to tell you where you can shove that condescending tone, because we've never argued like that, and we're not going to start now."

"It's not condescending. You seemed like you had a lot to say, right? So talk."

"No."

"Oh, no? Now we're going to play silent treatment? Very mature."

"I have nothing to add right now, because this topic doesn't merit discussion. That's it."

Tristan rubs his forehead.

"I pick up the phone, try to be friendly, she gives some snotty answer, and I'm the one getting yelled at?" I say, livid. "No, sir. That's your sister, your problem, not mine."

He slumps onto a kitchen stool, his head in his hands.

"Well, you did have something to add, right?"

"Should I tell you to go to hell, Tristan?"

"I'm already in hell, sweetheart. There's no need."

"Very nice," I spit.

"You have to put up with her…how many times a year?"

"That's not what this is about, because I don't have to put up with anyone as rude as your sister for even thirty seconds. And on top of that, she makes it clear how disgusting she finds me every chance she gets with total impunity."

"She's thirty-eight." He looks at me with his eyes wide. "What am I supposed to do? Make her copy it a hundred times?"

"Ay, look, Tristan, it's just that…" I get desperate. "The problem is that we're arguing about this in the first place. Because we shouldn't be. If I heard Ivan talking to you that way…" I bite my lip.

"Ivan is a friend. Uxia is my sister. I didn't choose her; we came as a package deal. And I know what she's like. She has a weird way of showing affection, I know. She thinks it's her way of protecting me as a sister because I'm her little brother and…"

"No, Tristan. You sister has an inferiority complex, and she needs to get that poison out before she withers away. She hates everything that represents what she's not. Obviously, nobody's ever going to be good enough for you, but you have to admit that the bulk of the problem is that Uxia isn't who she wants to be, and she hates the rest of us for striving to be who we want to be…because she doesn't dare. And you refuse to tell her that."

Tristan doesn't answer. I had never, ever laid it out that clearly for him. I had thought it a thousand times. The idea had been forming in my head and gaining power like a summer storm, but it might be the first time it's ever materialized in my mouth. And he still has his right hand pressed into his forehead and his eyes clamped on the counter.

"I'm just asking to stop arguing, Miranda," I hear him mutter.

"The thing is, sometimes you have to."

"But I don't want to argue about her."

"Well, then take her out of it. This is between us."

He snorts.

"I'm never going to ask you to choose between your family and me, but I can't tolerate being treated like this. And you shouldn't either. And that's it," I say.

The silence hovers over our heads for a few minutes until it lands on the kitchen floor with a deafening clatter. And it stays there, with us, until I can't stand it anymore. I try to leave, but when I pass by him, one of his arms shoots out and wraps around my waist. I could keep going, because he's not holding on very tightly, but I'm weak, and I hear a ghostly "tick tock" in my head, so I stop and let him pull me over to him. When I bury my face in his neck and smell him, I feel a sad relief that ends in an embrace.

He doesn't say "I'm sorry." I don't either. Deep down, neither of us is sorry, because I'm clinging to the truth for dear life, and he's clinging to his resignation, but neither of us wants this to be the reason we end. I guess we have too many of our own issues to fall down at this hurdle.

"Hey…" He makes me look at him. He smiles timidly, and his bao bun lips look even more beautiful than ever. "I'm going to finish making this sauce, and we'll eat lunch listening to music, okay? None of that TV stuff. Just a little music to relax us."

Light music… I remember the Italian song Ana Mena will make a Spanish version of next year, which talks honestly about this, about the need to put on music that distracts us and lightens the painful silences.

"Sound good?" he insists.

I nod.

He makes a face.

"Say something," he begs. "Please."

"Your pillow smells more like you than you do yourself."

34

~~

IN MADRID

There are so many ways to be woken up. To the sound of birds or rain pattering against a window. With a gentle song you like. With the knowledge that today is your first day of vacation, your birthday, Christmas morning…or with two lips on your neck, right below your earlobe, and two arms wrapped around you. Not just any two arms. No, the two arms of the person you love.

That's how I wake up. With a gentle nudge that pulls you out of sleep like the hand guiding you through a crowd at a concert. My feet are moving lazily in sheets that are so soft I can immediately tell it's a hotel bed. The sun is peeking in timidly through the thin gap between the opaque curtains covering the huge window opposite me. The room's temperature is perfect, but I'm grateful for the warmth of Tristan's nearly naked body pressed against my back.

Besides my recent rude awakening three months after all this started, I've always traveled forward chronologically from one point in our history to another. So I can only be in one place. I don't even look at my phone to check. We're in Tenerife, at the end of July, and we're on vacation.

"Good morning," I say.

"Shh…"

I turn around to look at him, and he gives me a kiss. There's a lot of bedhead going on…

"What are you…?"

He quiets me again with his mouth and tugs on me until I turn over and instinctively sling my left leg over his hip. We look at each other, because sometimes looking at each other is a complete action that doesn't have to imply anything more than how nice it is…or it does. His right hand slips under my panties slowly, giving me time to decide whether I want to stop him, like a declaration of intentions. I bite my lip and arch to make it easier for him. He smiles, his eyes on my tits.

"It's going to be fast," he says throatily.

I nod. That's how I like it in the mornings. No foreplay. Sometimes we like to tease, holding each other's gazes, testing little by little how and how far he's entering me. Very slowly at first, making me desperate, rubbing, teasing me, and pulling out when my body has barely opened for him, until I'm completely soaked and then he speeds up. Today it takes a little while. Or we're moving faster. I don't know, but our bodies don't quite line up with each other. Sex isn't always perfect; it's worth remembering, or you'll get frustrated.

"Ah…" I moan, putting my open palm on his chest.

He rubs my clit with the head of his cock, and I nod with a purr.

"Shh…"

He tries again. He pushes in a little farther. He pulls out. When he pushes in again, he thrusts so deep it leaves me breathless, and we hold each other in a kind of sideways embrace.

"I'm not gonna stop until I fill you up," he growls into my ear.

I throw my head back and moan, loving the way he's grabbing me, how he braces me with his palms and fingers on my body before he fucks me hard.

"Don't stop," I beg.

"I'm not going to," he groans. "Catch up with me."

I hope the adjoining rooms are empty and their inhabitants are down by the hotel pool, on the beach, or at the buffet having breakfast, anywhere but listening to this spectacle. It's a short show, that's true, but intense. And traumatizing for minors under eighteen. Possibly for those of age too.

The headboard is slamming against the wall, Tristan is gasping, and even though I'm trying to prevent it, I stifle some screams in his neck and bite it because I don't know how else I can absorb this much pleasure.

In less than ten minutes, at least seven rooms on this floor hear Tristan curse before he keeps his word and fills me up. I lost track a couple of minutes ago, because my orgasm left me half-unconscious after I felt his hand hovering around my neck, on top of how hard he was pounding me.

But he keeps thrusting for a few seconds, eyes closed, until he seems to calm down, nuzzles into me, and collapses, burying me.

"I think I love you," he says, completely spent.

All I can do is laugh.

"Sitting down kinda hurts," I whimper as I climb into the rental car.

Tristan lets out a laugh.

"You're silly."

"I'm serious. What did we do last night?"

"You're asking me?" He puts on his seat belt and yawns. "I started worrying you thought I was your sex slave instead of your boyfriend."

"Seriously, Tristan…everything hurts when I sit." I put on my seat belt and start the car. "I don't know how to be any clearer."

He settles in and rubs an eye.

"Should I sketch it for you? Do you have amnesia all of a sudden?"

I look at him, trying to understand why I'm in so much pain. He raises his eyebrows.

"Listen, girl, I'm just a dude in love. My girlfriend asks me to do things, and I step up to the plate and do them to her."

"What do you mean, 'do them to her'?"

"I mean, I do them to her." He laughs. "You can't say I wasn't careful, I was a bundle of nerves, and I kept telling myself 'slllooooooooowwww.' Still...there's no lube left."

I turn back to the wheel 100 percent sure I don't want to delve any deeper into the subject. This is how Tristan is; he's not the most communicative guy in the world, but you know that topic that you're embarrassed to talk about? Well, that very thing will be the topic he treats without a hint of euphemism. Not one. Not even out of mercy.

After a twenty-minute journey with the windows rolled down, we get to the diving port. I'm happy. After all the days I've relived, I needed this; he did too. He looks so relaxed it's easy to forget that not long ago in lockdown, we wanted to battle to the death.

We hired a small boat with a captain to take us to see pilot whales in the open sea and swim near a cove, surrounded by nothing but fish. We could have booked it with a group of people and it would've been much cheaper, but when we were organizing the trip, Tristan looked at me, shook his head, and said:

"Better alone. It's not because I plan on making this a special memory to bring up when life becomes sad and gray. It's just that after this whole lockdown thing, I've developed social anxiety."

And I understood that it was the most romantic way he knew how to say it. It was a "You're all I need."

The captain, accustomed to groups of friends who want a lot of beer, a lot of wine, and reggaeton and are constantly whooping, greets us like we're godsent. He asks us what kind of music we like, what time we'd like to eat, and if we're celebrating anything.

"Well...I think just life. This year showed us everything is worth celebrating," Tristan confesses, putting his arm around my shoulder. "Don't you think?"

That's so Tristan. It can take him decades to feel comfortable in a group of friends, but he can immediately open up to strangers he'll never see again in his life.

We start slathering ourselves head to toe in sunscreen...even though he's reluctant. He says he doesn't burn. No. Of course not. The thing is, when he does get burned, there's no turning back, and he doesn't complain. But he should've found another girl to spend the day on a boat with if he wanted to soak up the August sun.

Putting lotion on his back, spreading lotion and kisses in equal parts, his scent mixing with the floral sunscreen, is one of my favorite memories. When I experienced it, I wasn't aware it was on clearance. I don't even think I realized exactly where we were heading as a couple, yet I felt as happy as a little kid.

The wind tousles our hair, and we settle on the bow, sipping cold beers and listening to Tristan's Spotify playlist called "Get to work, for the love of God" that I love. He Bluetoothed his phone to the speakers before we departed, and now Khalid's "Better" is playing. And...fuck, it really hits the spot, because I don't think there's anything in the world that could be better than this. The sea is darkening to cobalt, and shards of sunlight sparkle on it. Everything is perfect.

As we get closer to where the whale sightings usually happen, the skipper turns the music down until it's barely more than a faint murmur and slows down to a crawl. He explains that we might not see them, which we know, and as we wait and move almost by inertia, he tells us about the whales that are native to the area.

"They usually travel in pods," he tells us. "And they're pretty big. They can measure...I don't know, easily four or five meters, the biggest ones. They're actually from the dolphin family."

"Do they eat humans?"

Tristan covers his face when he hears my question, and the captain bursts out laughing and shakes his head vigorously.

"No, not at all, but unless you have very bad luck and you fall overboard, you're not going to find out, because this area is very protected and controlled. Very few boats are allowed in the perimeter, and swimming isn't permitted. For their protection."

"That's really good to hear," I admit.

I remember how I was dying to ask him the first time. Now I'm sure people aren't in their diet. And it's a relief, because they're beautiful but enormous, and it's scary to think about falling out of the boat with them so close.

Right then, he gives us a signal.

"There. Right there. I think there are two of them."

When they come closer, it doesn't take us long to see there are six of them. Enormous, amazing, and incredible. Their skin shines like the sun when they come to the surface, and we can make out the shape of their heads. Just like the first time, it almost brings me to tears. They say nature, as in the entire concept of it, doesn't interact with us, but I think it does, in the same way the concept of beauty does.

"They're so beautiful!" I yelp. "Tristan…aren't they beautiful?"

He beams at me.

"What?"

He laughs.

"They look so soft. I mean…they're huge, but…"

"You're the one who's beautiful."

He puts his arm around me, and I rest my head on his shoulder. His skin is warm from the sun, and the boat is swaying on the waves, the engine turned off, rocking us like we were in someone's arms trying to get us to sleep.

"Do you know how much I love you?" I ask him when I see the skipper moving away toward the stern.

"Of course."

"No. It's impossible for you to know."

He leans back to look at me.

"Of course, just like it's impossible for you to know how much I love you."

"You never say it."

"Don't start," he begs me with a tired look. "I wish we all spoke the same language about this, but that's just not how it is. It's not my style, but that doesn't mean that I don't love you as much as or more than you."

"How much do you love me?"

He smiles.

"So much…so much…so much…that I'll volunteer to tell your cousin we're not going to her wedding."

"Nooo…" I let out a moan mixed with laughter. "Tristan, for once, just this one time, I'm asking you to say something to me. I'm even asking you explicitly. And you're on a boat surrounded by whales. There's no escape. Tell me, how much do you love me?"

He looks at me, and his lips twist into a smile. He strokes the skin between my eyebrows and then runs his finger down my nose and my lips. When he gets to my chin, the smile has turned into a slightly more ambiguous look.

"I love you so much, Miranda, so much, enough to let you go if we get to a point in our lives where I suspect I'm not making you as happy as I can and you deserve."

"It's not your responsibility to make me happy," I reply.

"I know. But I shouldn't do the opposite either, right?"

"Of course."

"So we do understand love the same way."

The kiss is short. We're interrupted by the skipper, who didn't notice our intimate moment.

"Hiya, should we head off again? We might be able to spot some dolphins farther that way." But when he sees how closely we're sitting… "Sorry."

"No worries." We laugh.

"We'll eat lunch next to a cove, and you can swim. Okay? It's starting to get hot."

We didn't end up seeing dolphins, but I already knew that, just like I knew Tristan was going to have some ups and downs when we leaped into open water. He has slight vertigo, and sometimes he can't prevent the feeling in really deep water.

"Just concentrate on floating," I say.

"Jesus," he splutters. "That sounds easy, but we have a fucking void under us, Miri."

Still, by the time we get back in the boat again, we're cracking up. When we get to the port, we feel like we're coming back from summer camp. One of those special summer camps where you made friends, they showed you how to recognize stars, and someone even kissed you.

On the way back to the hotel, windows down again, the wind ruffles our salty hair, and we're blasting Foxes. Tristan's driving, and my fingers are in his hair while I sing along in my terrible English. "Let Go for Tonight" is playing when he says that, if I feel like it, we could go for a walk after dinner tonight.

"A walk?"

"A walk." He glances over at me. "Don't you miss smoking sometimes?"

I never used to smoke in the car, but right now, I'd love a smoke…

"Yes." I nod. "Sometimes. Some moments are made for cigarettes."

"A walk," he broaches it again as he downshifts, brakes, looks in the rearview mirror, accelerates, changes lanes, and shifts gears again.

"Go back. I dropped my underwear a hundred meters back."

"All you dropped is your shame. I can't with you anymore. My dick is gonna fall off. I swear it's starting to hurt when I take a piss."

I get the giggles.

"Focus. You were saying something about a walk."

"Yes. Fuck." He gives me a vulgar look. "You don't want to marry me. You don't want to have kids with me. We're still just boyfriend-girlfriend at our age…well, we're going to do boyfriend-girlfriend things. We're going to walk on the beach. Actually…"

The tires screech as he suddenly swerves to take the next turn, where there's a sign advertising a supermarket.

"What are you doing?" I say, hanging on wherever I can.

It's not that he drives badly…he just drives hard.

"We're going to buy calimocho." He cracks himself up. "And we're going to get wasted on a beach."

I burst out laughing. I had forgotten all about the calimocho on the beach. We did go on a walk from the hotel, but I don't know why I thought we had bought the drink somewhere around there…

Another sharp turn.

"Actually, we should probably buy it there. I'm too old to drink it warm, and I don't wanna lug around a cooler full of ice."

Just as I was saying.

"Tristan…" I mumble.

"Mm?"

"I never said I didn't want to marry you."

The moon is full and beautiful when we walk down the slope at the back of the hotel holding hands. I look at our clasped hands and smile. The hard guy who "isn't like that" and who dreams of a house with a little land in

Vigo, with kids playing in a yard full of bicycles, balls, dolls, a family car, a peaceful life…clinging to my hand.

"What are you looking at?"

"Our hands. Do you remember the whole 'we're not that kind of couple' thing?"

"I'm not, You are. You could see it on your face like you were wearing a sign." He laughs. "I think the first time I did it was just so you wouldn't be disappointed, and then I thought…that's ridiculous? Why shouldn't I hold her hand if it makes her happy?"

"The other day…" I hesitate.

"The other day what?"

"I was remembering that kiss you gave me in Paris."

"I've given you a lot of kisses in Paris." He looks at me out of the corner of his eye. "Come on. I'm actually pretty mushy."

"I was talking about the first time we went together, when we were there for fashion week. We weren't even official yet."

"Oh yeah. You were a real handful on that trip." He laughs. "I kissed you, and you smudged lipstick all over my mouth."

I side-eye him.

"I think it was the best kiss of my life."

"That doesn't say much about our relationship." But he throws it out like it's nothing, like it actually doesn't matter to him at all.

"No. But…those kisses in the beginning are the most romantic, right? The most exciting."

"Kisses are always beautiful when there are more to give." He looks at me and smiles. "Isn't that what it's about?"

I don't know why. That affirmation should have made me deliriously happy and given me hope, but it makes me sad. There's something…something, something small, malignant, that has wrapped its tentacles around our words and is staining every letter with a poison that I can't get rid of.

"Do you want to kiss other women?"

Tristan stops in the middle of the street. He doesn't seem angry or annoyed by the question. He seems completely disoriented and confused.

"Wow."

"What?" I ask.

"I don't know. I wasn't expecting that. Not from you."

"What does that mean?"

"I don't know." He starts walking again. "Let me think up an answer."

"To which question?"

"I find it pretty disturbing that you're asking me that, I guess. I thought the first question would've been answered more than four years ago."

We don't talk much; we're a little tense but not annoyed, maybe the word is uncomfortable, at least until we get to the beach. We find a hut that sells us a few drinks we can take with us in plastic cups, and we venture out onto the sand. I take my shoes off first. He drags sand under the soles of his white shoes until we sit down a good distance away from a group of friends who have gathered with a very similar idea to ours, but slightly more…social.

He takes off his shoes ceremoniously while I hold his drink and take a few small sips of mine. I hear a few girls with a pretty accent saying it's almost one. We took it easy today during dinner and cocktails at the hotel before we came for this stroll. I'm worried that Tristan is bothered by my question, and that feels weird. I don't know how to explain it.

"Tristan…are you mad?"

"Nope," he answers right away. "All done. Hand it over, thanks."

He takes his cup and gives me a kiss on the lips. I relax until I hear the next thing he says:

"But…"

"Fuck."

"Listen, Miranda, for God's sake..." He gets surprised. "I just wanted to say that asking me if I want to kiss other women is the last thing I thought would come out of your mouth. It's not like you at all."

"How is it not like me at all?"

"At all." He stares ahead, out to sea, leaning his forearms on his knees. "Ever since I met you, and not just then but through our whole relationship, you've always been a woman with no jealousy. You have your insecurities, like everyone else, but you're aware that if I'm by your side, it's because I want to be. We both know the door is open for us to leave, and that's why what we have is so valuable, right?"

"Yes."

"Asking me if I want to kiss other women is questioning if I'm where I want to be."

I blink, surprised, and look out to sea.

"Well, that's not what I was thinking about when I asked you that."

"I understand that, but that's what I heard behind that question."

"Okay." I nod.

"Do you have doubts?"

"About what?"

"About me."

Yes. Because in seven months, you're going to dump me in a soulless café on Calle de Fuencarral.

"No."

"You say no, and I hear yes."

"Maybe that's because we're so close to the ocean?" I raise my eyebrows, hoping it sounds gentler filtered through a joke. "I don't know. Maybe we just have to admit that the last few months have been hard."

"Yes. They have. But just because our relationship goes through rough patches, that doesn't mean I want to sleep with other women. Plural, to make it worse. Multiple women. Maybe even all at once."

"I'm sure you want to sleep with a bunch all at once when you're jerking off in the shower." I attempt another joke.

"I'm sure you want to do it with Harry Styles."

"Duh. Who doesn't?"

He laughs.

"Miranda..." He sighs. "Things get hard because we both want this to work, not because we want to break up."

"I don't know if what you just said makes much sense."

"Of course it does." His smile is tinged with bitterness. "I realized a little while ago. And I'm sure you'll come to the same conclusion. We're so different that the whole 'opposites attract' thing doesn't work with us. And when fire and ice dance...oof, Miranda, it's really complicated. Because you melt me. And I extinguish you. Where's the balance? Is there one?"

A sigh lodges in the middle of my chest. I don't want to cry, but I don't know if I can hold it in.

"Hey," he says softly. "We'll keep trying, right? But only because, despite the laws of physics, this ice doesn't have any intention of kissing other people. So...Miranda...I don't know. What if we just dance?"

I let him tuck me under his arm. I don't cry, even though I want to, because right now, more than anything, I want to dance. Dance until the end. And it feels like the music is going to stop playing any minute.

"Can we stay here until dawn?"

"All night?" It's a question, but he doesn't seem surprised.

"Please. I want to see what happens."

"Can I give you a spoiler? In the end, the sun comes up."

"What I want to know is if I'll still be here."

"You're nuts." He laughs.

"No way! Listen...do you remember that time you made me steak tartare at your house? In your first apartment in Madrid."

"Fuck. Of course. You were so weird. I couldn't decide for a long time whether you were crazy or the most interesting girl I had ever met in my life. Do you know what else I thought? Come here. Let's get comfy."

We spend the night talking, remembering together and revisiting details and corners I hadn't traveled to. Now that something is telling me the music is going to stop playing, I'm scared I'll end up without a chair when the game ends. And hearing these things come out of his mouth decapitates the shadows that were lying in wait around the corner. And they're not so scary anymore, but they are sad. Very sad.

About the sunrise, if you want a spoiler, as Tristan says, when tints of pink are streaking the sky, I close my eyes. When I open them again, I'm in my bed. In my apartment. In Madrid.

35

~~~

I'LL SLEEP ON THE
COUCH TONIGHT

One of the things I like most about my job is going to the new season pre-
sentations from some of the biggest fashion brands. In the past, Marisol
and I used to go together, but with COVID and the reduced number of
seats, we had to start switching off. Now she goes to a lot of them, and
I go to the others because my boss has always considered me to be the
other visible face of the magazine. We divide the events according to the
brands we like the most and the friends we have who work for them. That's
another great thing about this job: you meet lovely people with whom you
share hobbies, chitchats, hours of work, favors, and exhaustion, and over
the years, you get pretty tight with them.

If I'm remembering correctly, the year after the pandemic, Marisol
went to Louis Vuitton, Chanel, Loewe, Valentino, Roger Vivier, Bottega
Veneta, and Etro. And I went to Balenciaga, Saint Laurent, Miu Miu, and
Prada. Sometimes I meet up with Ivan at the stores or the spaces the brands
have rented out for the occasion in a kind of "personal-professional" get-
together. I care about his opinion, I trust him, they usually serve sparkling
wine, and as a stylist, he has to see the new looks. It's a win-win.

Today is no exception, because it's the Prada presentation for the new
season, and I have a meeting with Xabier, the department manager of the

women's store (sweet, handsome, fun, and has a great ass, by the way) at seven thirty. With him and with Ivan.

The rest of the day, everything that's happened up until now isn't worth wasting my breath on. That's just how time traveling is. Sometimes, you're lucky enough to fall into the memory of something that shakes your foundations or shines a light into a pitch-black void. Other times, it's like regurgitating something that was bad for you. I don't know if I need a drink or an Alka-Seltzer.

The top floor of Prada's boutique on Calle de Serrano is all set up to show off the new season's iconic garments to its best customers, stylists, and publications. It's not hard to spot Ivan, because it's not very crowded and the whole floor is open-plan. Plus you can't miss him: he's in front of a rack bursting with the brightest fabrics.

"Look, there he is," Xabier points out with a smile. "I'll go grab us some wine and leave you to it for a bit."

"See you in a minute."

Normally, I would kiss him on the cheek before he left, but the whole mask thing has reduced human contact. I miss traveling to 2016, where people sneezed without covering their mouths and you weren't afraid of catching dengue fever.

"You're like a magpie," I say to my friend.

He doesn't even look at me. He just yanks a dress off a hanger and shoves it in my face.

"Look, it's for your next cover."

"Will it read well in a photo?"

"Will it read well in a pho—? Jesus. Don't insult me. You don't hire me because of my hair or even because I'm your best friend."

That's true.

I don't comment on his look, because for the first time in a long time, Ivan is Ivan. The original Ivan. His black hair, speckled with gray here and there, is styled in his usual haircut. His brown eyes, framed by thick dark lashes, are the same as always. He's wearing a black FPP2 mask, like the ones he always wears, matching his outfit. We're the "cockroaches," eternally dressed in mourning from head to toe. He's wearing Doc Martens, jeans, and a black sweater. I don't need to touch the sweater to know it's high quality. But it's Ivan; you'll never see him wearing a brand logo.

"What's up, cutie? Why are you looking at me like that?"

"You're back to being you," I blurt out giddily.

"What are you talking about?"

"Your look. You look how you always look today."

"You look how you always look too." He winks, puts his arm around my shoulder, and kisses my temple, even though he's wearing a mask. "What do you think?"

"Well, I haven't even had time to take a look yet. Got any spoilers for me?"

"I don't want to influence you. Let's start from that rack, and then we'll do a lap of the whole store."

Xabier comes over with a beautiful wooden tray laden with two mini bottles of sparkling wine that he uncorks for us. He walks alongside us and tells us about the collection just how we like it, honestly, with style and deep knowledge of what he's talking about. He throws in references to the history of the house, to previous collections, to what inspires the designer to make the garments one way and not another and we give him back the same honesty in return.

"You know I can't with performance fabrics," I confess. "That 'froufrou' sound it makes when it brushes against things…it makes my hair stand on end."

"You couldn't be more old-fashioned," Ivan accuses me. "High-quality technical fabric is modern, cosmopolitan. The garments are versatile and really comfy."

I wrinkle my nose, but he brushes right past me and holds up another hanger.

"But this dress is beautiful," I remark.

"You're more basic than a pumpkin spice latte," Ivan splutters.

"Coming from the guy who wears the same old black day in and day out."

"I can't with you two," Xabier teases, just as a client beckons him over from behind us. "Excuse me. Today is crazy. Keep browsing. I'll be right back, but you better hit me up for a drink one day soon, please."

We start laughing and encourage him to go, but it's always the same when we come in: we hog him. We keep moving along the rack. I stroke the garments, and Ivan studies them down to the very last detail.

"What's going on?" he says after a silence.

"I spent the day in Tenerife yesterday."

He side-eyes me sadly.

"This has to stop, Miri. You can't leave your life behind and just keep hiding out in happy memories."

"I know. That's what I'm saying. Yesterday, I was in Tenerife with him, and we were super happy…but no. This morning, I woke up all lovey-dovey, and he was cold as an iceberg. He told me his head hurt. And I don't know what comes over me when I can tell he's tense. It's like it raises my hackles. It's almost like I get embarrassed, you know? Embarrassed that I was trying to cozy up or be conciliatory, and my stupid streak comes out. More than usual. So in the tiny window between the alarm clock ringing and us leaving for work, we got into three fights. About the towels in the bathroom, because it fills me with rage when he puts his wet towel on top of my dry one. Then because there was no milk, and apparently I'm a fucking disaster who forgets everything that's not about my friends or my professional life. And finally because…I don't even know what the last one was about. Bottom line, I slammed the door on my way out."

Ivan puts the garment back on the hanger, pulls his mask down for a second, and takes a sip of wine as he nods, encouraging me to go on.

"You know me. By midmorning, I had calmed down because I'm a pushover and I get over things in two minutes, and I called him to say sorry. As soon as he picked up, he said he didn't have time to argue on the phone and to please not make a scene while he's at work."

"I can't imagine how you took that."

"Well, I was going to take it like a hydra…but I restrained myself."

"Yeah?"

"Until he freaked out because I told him I had to come to Prada to see the new season's showcase at seven thirty. He asked me why I didn't schedule the visit earlier, and I told him it was because I wanted to be here at the same time as you…and, well…it all got messy again."

"Why?"

"Because he says I prioritize seeing you over him. I didn't like that. But I told him he should come. And he said, 'I don't give a fuck about your clothes.' My clothes. And then…I did go"—I shake my head and sigh—"a little crazy, Ivan. Totally crazy actually."

"Have you talked since?"

"It's not going over my head that you're asking bland questions and not giving any opinions. You know that, right?"

"You're my best friend. You're intelligent."

I start laughing bitterly.

"I wouldn't be your best friend if I were a bimbo?"

"Obvs not, but seeing the shoes you're wearing today, I'm starting to think you might be."

I look down at my feet. I'm wearing the Prada boots that went viral years ago; they're not exactly chic. But I love pairing them with more "ladylike" looks. That's why I'm wearing them with a floral dress. He hates them.

"Argh…are you even listening to me?"

"Of course I'm listening. I just wanted to lighten the mood a little. So? Have you talked to him since?"

"I messaged him to ask if he wanted me to stop by somewhere on the way home and pick up dinner, and he wrote back that he's sick of eating junk. I think he's sick of a lot more than eating junk."

"We already talked about that. You shouldn't be so surprised."

"I don't eat that much junk. I'm just always in a rush. I ate tuna tartare today, for example."

"That's not what I'm talking about. Your nutritional regime is not my main concern here. I mean Tristan is done with Madrid, and we've already talked that to death."

"We were so good in Tenerife…"

"Ay, Miranda…" He rolls his eyes.

"What?"

"I mean…you were on vacation."

"Couples that are in a bad place have arguments on vacation too, you know?"

"Couples that don't love each other argue on vacation."

"Can we just agree that all couples argue?" I point out.

"Yeah, of course they do, but I've been here these last few months, Miranda, and…ever since you got back, everything's a problem. Going to Vigo to see his family, meeting up with friends, making plans for the weekend, sex, the right way to show affection, how much time you spend at work, even what's in the fridge."

"We're going through a rough patch." I'm clinging tooth and nail to that idea, even though it's starting to sound ridiculous even to me.

Ivan steps back from the rack and focuses all his attention on me. He looks at me with his big, beautiful eyes, and even through his mask, I can hear him suck his teeth.

"Miranda…I just want you to be happy."

"I know."

"Well, you're not. And he's not either."

"But I love him."

"Yeah, but since when does that guarantee success?"

I look over all the garments again and snap photos of a few that I want to show Marisol because they could fit in with a special we're doing in the next issue. Now Ivan and I are sitting on a patio in Plaza de la Independencia, under the red glow of one of those outdoor heaters, drinking wine and gossiping. We haven't talked much about Tristan, my life, or my relationship. We're catching up about work and a few projects we have on the table, like some still lifes we hired him for. He's great at still lifes, and in the next issue, we're going to produce two on shoes in the magazine's studio. I know it sounds like a baroque painting of pheasants and oranges, but it's still an artistic, aesthetic, and beautiful composition highlighting the accessories. We also talked about a night out we were planning with my group of friends from the old neighborhood. And about the guy he's kind of excited about, even though he won't admit it. But all signs point to it going great.

I get home at ten, and yes, I'm a couple of wines in. And when I say a couple…a couple of couples. I drank enough wine to notice that my tongue's a little thicker than usual, and I'm afraid Tristan will be pissed off because on top of getting home late, I've been out "partying." But these moments with my people do me good, not because I don't need him but because they're part of finding balance. I love him, but my life needs other things to be complete, not just him. I find him on the couch, reading in his pajamas. He stares at my hands as I put down my keys. There's no hello.

"You didn't bring dinner?" he asks tensely.

"Didn't you tell me not to bring you anything?"

"Me?"

"Yes. You. You said you were sick of eating junk?"

"There's nothing in the fridge. I said that too."

"Ay, Tristan"—I feel desperate—"it's just that sometimes I feel like I need a psychic to understand you or a Ouija board or something."

He stands up, visibly annoyed, walks over to the freezer, and wrenches it open angrily.

"I'll order sushi if you want."

"No, I don't care."

"Tristan, don't get like this. I'll order sushi, and it'll be here in twenty minutes."

"But I've been hungry for an hour already," he spits.

"You should've told me."

"You have to be told everything. You have to be told that the fridge is empty, that cooking is normal"—he's gaining speed as he talks and paces around the kitchen—"to remember to call and confirm the dinner for Saturday, to turn the washing machine on, that I have a job too, a life, that I'm tired, that relationships require time, that I feel alone stuck here at home while you go get drunk with your friends, and that this is the most exhausting relationship of my entire fucking life!"

He throws a dish towel down onto the counter, turns around, and, before I can even say anything, storms to the bedroom and slams the door. No. I'm not following him. It's the first time in a long time that I agree with someone yelling at me: this is exhausting. And I'm tired. Very, very tired.

I'll sleep on the couch tonight.

36

~~

LOVE

TRISTAN

It feels like there are two forces brutally pulling my organs in opposite directions. Not all my organs. Just my heart, my lungs, and my stomach. Sometimes my liver too. I live in a constant arrhythmia, in a dance between the "I'm done" and "I love her too much." Between the not-at-all-liberating mouthful of air that fills me when I suck in oxygen, pressed into her neck, in bed, or when I wake up, and the suffocating oppression of feeling like I'm alone. And there are echoes everywhere. I've lost weight. I don't know how much. I don't weigh myself, I don't really care, but I can see it in how my clothes fit and in the mirror; my face is gaunt. I've been told at work and even in court. I think I'm internalizing all this shit and starting to look sick. Madrid makes me sick. It's not her, it's not our relationship, which is sick too, it's Madrid. I don't know. I can definitely feel my liver in the bile that rises up in my throat all the time, especially when I'm filled with rage, when I spit certain words that I don't feel. Or I feel them, but I don't mean to say them.

I love her, but this isn't sustainable.

I love her, but not like this.

In this context, "like this" has a lot of faces. It's a ten-sided decahedron. "Like this" means "here," in the most concrete sense of space. I've built up a visceral hatred for this apartment I used to like so much. I don't understand why, considering my salary, I have to live in fifty square meters without even the option of stepping out onto a little balcony. With our salaries. But that's Madrid. And that's where the other face of "here" comes in. I can't handle this city full of lights, music, and life. For me, it's nothing more than a cacophony of honking horns and exhaust pipes, rushing around, and constant pressure on my temples. I can't be objective. It's not Madrid's fault. It's just that Madrid isn't my home, and I've never been able to turn this city into my home. I'm the problem.

"Like this" also means time, and time is unfurling like a fan with many different nuances. Five years have passed since we met: I need to move forward, to feel like what we have is growing and it's not just frozen like an eternal love waiting for something, who knows what. I don't even know if that something exists. Still, I've realized at this point that getting married isn't going to fix anything, and neither will having kids, because…that's where the other nuance of time comes in: there's already too much for the hours we have in a day. Her work is a ravenous baby constantly suckling at her tit. And mine. Her world, the whole thing (family, friends, work, interests, downtime) is an industrial machine, a monster that gobbles up time with its mouth full. And compared to her, I'm the workshop of a medieval carpenter. And she's not the problem. The problem is that she has a life, and the only thing I've managed to carve out here is her. And that… There's no way out of that.

"Like this" is also the state of our emotional health. We're in the red. We haven't had any time to dedicate to loving each other. We lack tenderness, probably out of shame. We live in a time of extremes: either you belong to the half that practices emotional pornography or the half that feels shame expressing his own emotions tenderly. I'm a blockhead incapable of telling my girlfriend that I love her so much that sometimes it doesn't fit in my chest. I can never find the words to express it.

"Like this," finally, is also the hidden face of the moon that I've turned into. She's the earth; I'm her satellite. And suddenly, I find myself loving her so much that I hate her, because I don't understand why, even though she loves me, she doesn't want the same things I do.

But I still have enough awareness to know, not "like this." It shouldn't be like this. It doesn't deserve to be like this. I don't deserve it like this. Love is not like this.

37

~~~

SENSE

MIRANDA

Waking up feels strange but gentle. I'm awoken by the light streaming in through the half-open blinds. The light is coming in from the left, but there's something different about it. I'm even more confused when I sit up in a springy, supercomfortable bed, but I don't recognize the bedroom, not even in my memories. It's a large, pretty room that's still a little shabby chic, with beautiful, original hardwood floors. Across from the bed, on the left, there's an old but restored double door painted white, with beautiful golden knobs, open to the rest of the house; between this door and the window, there's a banana tree in a very nice wicker pot.

"What…?"

I get out of bed, where the blankets are only mussed on one side. The floor is cold, and on the right side of the room, there's a large built-in closet. There are boxes with a moving company logo stacked up in front of it; some are open and half-empty, and the others are still sealed. I see another door in a corner that I open stealthily and timidly and discover an updated bathroom. It's huge and has a really cute, vintage vibe. There's a clawfoot bathtub and a shower. Sorry…a clawfoot tub? That's going overboard.

A practically nonexistent hallway connects the room to another door, which leads into a much smaller room filled with boxes where someone has scrawled the word *BOOKS* in screaming capital letters. The only thing in there is a light-wood, slender-legged desk with two shallow drawers pushed up against a wall and already housing…my computer? The walls sport wallpaper with a print of eucalyptus branches in a subtle green.

The living room is another chaos of boxes and mismatched furniture, including a very loud pink armchair and at least seven framed pictures waiting patiently for someone to hang them. A bar connects it to a kitchen that also looks like it was recently renovated while trying to maintain an echo of past decades. I smile when I see the fridge; it's one of those retro ones, impractical for a family but perfect for someone like me who doesn't cook much and lives alone.

Light is pouring in from two balconies overlooking a plaza, which I find out when I throw their doors open.

"What the hell is going on?" I smile.

Two more doors, near the entrance, enclose a small, nice, and practical half bath and a nice closet for storing coats and out-of-season clothes without them getting wrinkled.

I really like my apartment, but I'm not exaggerating when I say that this is pretty much my dream home.

A picture framed in very pretty turquoise wood catches my eye, and I go over; it's the gang. Well…me and the gang: a mix of all my best friends, the ones from the neighborhood, the ones from work, the ones from life. And I'm in the middle, smiling, in a black blazer and a lacy bodysuit, basically lingerie, underneath. I'm wearing red lipstick and eyeliner that must've been the work of a professional, because there's no fucking way I could've pulled it off. It's flattering, I look good…probably because I look happy. My mouth is open, like I'm laughing, surrounded by all my friends, who all look very glam too. Ivan, next to me, is looking at me complicitly, laughing.

It's a happy scene. I know you should never trust photographs, which are just a two-dimensional depiction. Sometimes we get hooked on images, aspirations, dreams, and we cling to them like they are stills from a movie...and we idealize everything that happened around them.

I contemplate this as I flop down on the couch covered in a sheet with the picture in my hands. I don't want to idealize it, but the best part of it, the most special, is that it's a glimpse of something that hasn't happened yet. And in it, in the future, I'm happy.

Marta is holding up a bottle of champagne; it must be a celebration of something for the magazine, but my friends from the neighborhood and Ivan are there too. Some are laughing, others are looking at each other, and some seem to be calling to someone off camera. In the background, Rita is blowing one of those bubble wands for kids to create a beautiful backdrop. It's nighttime. Everyone looks beautiful, happy. I feel something inside, a tingle from seeing us. Together. Happy.

No. Tristan's not there, but now is the time to accept that he started leaving a long time ago, that the goodbye stretched on for too long. The best part of us isn't always the most beautiful.

In the fridge, there are two different bottles of wine, good ones with a red cap, and in the freezer, there's a tray of Eiffel-tower-shaped ice cubes and a bottle of Larios. I start laughing. Definitely Ivan's work...

I wander through the house looking around, not knowing what to look at, what to think, what to do, but there's a calm feeling in my chest. I go back to the bedroom. I flop back onto the bed again and open the drawer on the bedside table, where I find a torn envelope holding a handwritten card. It's Ivan's handwriting:

I told you everything would turn out okay, and you didn't believe me, so now I can be the proud messenger of that shitty phrase that for once gives me pleasure to say: "I told you so."

Congratulations. Everything you have is yours. All this happiness. All this light. It's all yours and only yours. Take these two bottles, and share wine and fire with all the people you love. Now that I think about it, you'll need more wine.

Fire, you'll have plenty of.

I love you,
Ivan

P.S. To new beginnings.

In the end, it must be true what they say about time: you can't expect it to heal wounds without lifting a finger, the bastard. Even if we try to rush it, even if it hurts like hell, even if the word "time" sounds like a placebo to a broken heart, there's no other answer. Let it happen, let it heal, let it soothe you.

That reminds me of "Lodo," the song by Xoel Lopez; it must be true that the tallest flowers grow out of mud.

I wish I could look much further than these four walls to find out the details of how my life is going or what day it is today, but maybe it's better like this. Just a glimpse, a ray of hope, just an exhale, a small, short moment of lucidity, where the words "everything will turn out fine" make sense.

38

~~~

EVERYTHING WILL
TURN OUT OKAY

When Tristan asks me to meet up outside work, in a café between his firm and the magazine's office, I suggest meeting up at home instead. He insists, refusing to go into details, sadly but affectionately, avoiding the four funereal words that foreshadow any breakup: "We need to talk."

"I think it's better if we meet up somewhere else. Can you do it? I feel like…we need some air."

"Tristan…it'd be better at home. Really. Don't worry. We'll do it right."

I notice his voice is trembling much more than mine, but that doesn't mean it's not hard for me.

When my alarm clock rang this morning and I saw the date on my phone, I understood that this was coming to an end. This journey, this evolution through memories, has reached its final destination. And it's natural, because the trip lasted exactly as long as it should have. Now I understand the point of all this perfectly: everyone needs their own deadlines, their own time, their own processes, to come to understand and get over things. Grief is complicated.

Please, let's not try to impose a calendar on pain. It has its own. The heart doesn't understand rushing. I wish it could, but it's a grumpy, stubborn old man who shares a house with a child who laughs as much as he cries.

Everything is ending today. And we'll do it right. Today I'll say good-bye to Tristan, and there will be no more Tristan and Miranda. Actually, there will be no more Tristan, because taking refuge in my memories was fine for a while, but in the end, it healed me. When wounds start turning into scars, you have to pull the lever to stop the conveyor belt. And if I have to choose between the future or living as my father does, I choose what is to come, especially since there's no one I need to pass down the legacy of my history of Tristan to.

I was going to say we die today, but I'm afraid we're already dead and even buried. Today we're spreading the ashes between his Atlantic Ocean and my fire.

When I get home, he's already packed up some of his stuff. It doesn't bother me, because we both know what's coming, and it doesn't feel like a betrayal. It's just about making it easier, shorter. But when I drop my keys down on the hall table and look at him, he stops pulling books out of the bookshelf like he was caught red-handed. I want to tell him not to worry, but my voice won't come out. He stands up and looks at me with tears welling in his eyes. I nod, as if that could transmit to him that I'm sorry too, that I'm really sorry.

He takes a step toward me and hesitates, like he's asking permission to hug me. Before we sink into a tight embrace, I can see that he's holding back a sob. We rub each other's backs in a dance that doesn't make sense anymore, because we've already proved that when ice and fire dance, they destroy each other.

"I'm sorry," he says.

"Me too. I'm so sorry."

"We tried."

"I know."

"I can't do it anymore," and his voice is ragged around the edges like the pages of a very old book, "but the truth is it's not about you. I would stay for you my whole life, but you don't deserve the part of me that would stay, Miranda."

"I know."

"I hate myself for not being able to, but I can't."

"I understand."

"I hate you too for not wanting the same things I do, and you don't deserve that. But I admire you." He pulls back a little and looks into my eyes. "I admire you for staying true to what makes you happy and being who you are. And I know I should learn from you."

I sob. For a few minutes, there are no words, just wishes that will never come true ricocheting off the walls and the floor in the form of tears and sobs.

"I thought you weren't going to understand," he says, wiping away his tears. "And you were going to hate me."

"I already went through that phase."

He looks at me like he doesn't understand, and that makes sense. I pat his arm, go over to the couch, and collapse onto it. He hesitates before he comes over and sits next to me, like he's doubting whether he should.

"I don't know what to say," he adds.

"Say what you feel. Or don't say anything." I shrug. "Actually, if you think about it, it's all been said already."

He nibbles his bottom lip.

"I ended up being nothing more than a man who loves you," he mumbles. "And you deserve more than that. Your world turns too fast for me. I tried to speed up, but I don't know if it's because I don't know how or if deep down, I don't want to. And I started to get bitter."

"I know."

"I loved you so much." He takes a deep breath. "I still love you. But I don't have the strength to try anymore, especially because the truth is I don't believe in this anymore. I don't know when I stopped, but I don't think you and I can really work. And I don't want to wake up one morning in ten years and think that I'm just the inertia of what I didn't do. I want things, but I can't have them if I'm with you."

I burst into tears.

"The last thing I want to do is hurt you," he croaks.

"I know. It's just that…it's painful."

"Miranda…" He clears his throat, banishing his tears. "If you came with me…if you came with me, I wanted to grow old with you, but I can't ask that of you. Not that, and not you being a mother. Not in a house in the suburbs or…"

We grab each other's hands and hold on tightly.

"Stay," I beg him in a flash of weakness. "Stay, and we'll get married, and I'll get pregnant, and we can move…even if it takes me an hour to get to the magazine."

We hug.

"Is that what you want?" he asks.

"No." I confess. "But I want you."

"And I want you. And I love you so much, so, so much, that I could never accept being a little happier if the trade-off is you being a little unhappier."

"Is this about the kid thing?"

"No. Yes, but no. I would wait for you, Miranda, in case you want to be a mother at some point, but life has gotten sick of sending us signs that this is impossible. Unsustainable in the long run. Because for us to exist, one of us would have to let go of too much. And neither of us deserves that."

I nod. He's right.

"These have been the best years of my life," he whispers. His voice doesn't seem to work anymore. "I came to Madrid a pretty gray dude, and I'm going back with a garden inside. But, Miranda, I'm going home. I never ended up feeling like this was home."

"Thank you for…"

"Don't thank me for love, Miranda. You shouldn't thank someone for love."

"It's a gift."

We both stifle another sob and nod.

"I need to ask you something," he says. "I know I'm not in the position to ask you for anything. But I think I'm actually asking for both of us. Or at least for what I want to hold on to from all this."

"Go ahead." I wipe my tears, my makeup-streaked tears on my dress sleeve.

"Let some time pass. Don't call me. Don't write to me." He presses his lips together so hard his whole jaw clenches too. He swallows. "I need to get some real distance or…or I'll be weak. Because I don't want to leave… I want to leave here but not you. It's been really hard for me to make this decision, so I'll fall if you call me. And I'll show up at your door and beg you to love me the rest of your life and never let me go again."

The last words get muffled by tears and a tight hug. Caresses. By the echo of the words that won't be said anymore in this apartment. Almost unconsciously, we kiss each other, and I wish we hadn't, because now our last kiss will always taste salty. I don't believe in goodbye kisses, because those two words shouldn't fit in the same phrase. It's a sad kiss, and kisses should never be like that. A kiss that reminds our mouths of the reason we'll never have each other again.

Tristan jumps up from the couch with a deep sigh.

"Tomorrow, the place will be empty, okay? I won't bother you at all."

"I'll help you."

"No. No way. We did the first move together, but this is different; you're not going to help me leave. I don't want this memory to be part of our story. It's not a fair ending."

"Where are you going to go?"

He puts his hands on his hips and looks at the floor.

"I'm going to Vigo."

I swallow.

"Right now?"

"In a few weeks. Everything is all arranged."

Well, I have to admit he's made a lot of effort to do things right. I should have done the same.

I stand up.

"I'm going to…to leave you alone."

"Where are you going?" he asks, alarmed.

"To my dad's house, okay? You…no rush. Take your time."

"I found an Airbnb…"

"That's not necessary." I smile sadly. "Let me grab a few things, and I'll go stay at my dad's, seriously. You can stay here until you need to leave. You can pack up in peace. I guess you have to send these boxes to Vigo."

"Yes."

"Well, that's that then." I head to the bedroom.

"I'm not going to kick you out of here. I feel awful."

"Why? I'll spend a few days at my dad's house, and he'll take care of me. We did it right, but I have a broken heart, and I need him. So you can pack up at home, and nobody needs to…" I roll my eyes and swirl my hand, trying to make it clear I'm not going to drag it out.

"It's your house."

"But it was yours too."

While I pack up some clothes and toiletries in the bedroom, I realize the significance of that "was." And sometimes, the verbal tense can be the most tangible proof that yes, everything will turn out okay.

The last time I see Tristan, he's standing in the living room, his hands in the pockets of his old jeans, with big bags under those eyes whose color I still can't identify after five years. I get a sudden flash of the memory of the jovial gleam in his eyes that made me swipe right on Tinder when I met him for the first time…and then I shove aside the Tristan who showed up at the office that first day five years ago. How little we knew back then… about ourselves.

We could have gotten caught up in prosaic details that would lighten the mood a little, like how he can leave his set of keys, with the key chain I gave him when we decided to move in together, in the mailbox, but I think neither of us want to rob the moment of its importance. It's not a solemn occasion, but it still deserves tenderness and respect. It was love.

"Goodbye," I say.

"Goodbye," he says back.

"Take care of yourself."

He sucks his teeth and looks at the ground, biting his lips.

"You too."

I turn my back to him, holding in a sob, clenching it between my teeth until I drag my suitcase to the door. As I'm opening it, he calls out to me.

"Miranda…"

"Yeah?"

"In the end, it was without me."

"Yes."

We both smile, maybe because for a moment, we travel back to the Enchanted Forest of Aldán, to making plans that were a lie. Leaves crunch under our feet, the walls disappear, and we see glimpses of the crumbling walls of an abandoned castle through the greenery. And even though the ghosts somehow haven't caught up to us there, we're promising to love each other so much that if we need to, we'll learn how to let go.

"Be happy, please."

"Promise. You too."

"Promise."

I close the door very slowly, like I don't want him to hear it clicking into the frame.

The sob tears out of me before the elevator has even reached the third floor.

Accepting it doesn't mean it's not sad. Just because it's necessary doesn't mean it's not hard.

But if I've learned anything after this journey, it's that everything will turn out okay.

Epilogue

~~~

I LOVE YOU

TRISTAN

My office smells like old man. I've been saying it ever since I moved in. My colleagues have turned it into a running joke. Every so often, someone shows up at my door with the latest remedy, because the truth is everyone agrees it smells funny. It doesn't smell like you'd expect a law firm office to smell. At least not a good one. I've tried every kind of air freshener, an energy cleansing ritual with salt, candles, and leaving the windows open all night long… The only thing we achieved with the latter, by the way, was waterlogging the parquet floor.

It smells like a gentleman. Like a grumpy man who chews licorice loudly. But I like this office. In the morning, beautiful light filters in through the wooden Venetian blinds and leaves a diamond-shaped patch of sun on the desk. It's a tiny office, crammed with mahogany furniture older than me, nothing unique; a single frame hangs on the wall. When I moved in, it contained a stale print, the kind you'd expect to find in a doctor's office, but I didn't think I could live with it, so I replaced it with a print of Banksy's *Flower Thrower*. Yeah, I know. Unoriginal, but around here, it's an absolute showstopper, especially since I kept the fancy, gilded frame. It's my way of making the place my own; it reminds me that the kid from the suburbs, the little punk with two earrings and a rough voice from Teis, not only graduated against all odds but has also figured out how to succeed.

Not long ago, I finally understood that maybe that's where all the problems started: the need to prove to myself or the world that I can do it, regardless of the brick-and-concrete block I grew up in. I will not fall into the trap of defending meritocracy and say things like: "See, I'm a neighborhood kid with my own office in a fancy law firm in Vigo. If you want to, you can." But it makes me happy to show the twenty-year-old Tristan who felt like a nerd for being the only one in the gang who spent his weekends in January studying that it was worth it.

Anyway, despite the suit and how I've softened the tone of my naturally gravelly voice, I'll always be the boy from Teis here. I don't mind, for the record. But I do mind not being able to get the smell of rancid old man out of my office.

Some knuckles rap against the door, and the firm's receptionist immediately pokes her head in. She's a lovely girl who spoils us all. I wish I loved my job as much as she does. I wish she wasn't already married to her wife, because otherwise I'd propose.

"Good morning, Tristan. Here's your cortado with one sugar."

"Thank you, Paz." I smile at her. "Good morning."

"And your schedule."

She puts a highlighted sheet on my desk, and I can't help but laugh. I've been here more than a year, and there's no way of dissuading her.

"Yeah, yeah, I know. I know you do it all on your digital calendar, but I'm used to printing it out for the partners, so…and it's no trouble. It probably helps point things out to you. What do I know? Sorry. It's habit."

"No worries. I do always end up noticing things, but it's mostly out of ecological responsibility."

"I think you're the only person in the office who knows what those two words mean."

"Together or separately?"

"Don't get me started. Listen…the Madrid office called for you a few minutes ago."

"Okay…" I give her a quizzical look. "Why didn't you put me through?"

"Coffee first, Tristan. What are we, animals?"

I burst out laughing and thank her.

"Did they tell you what it was about?"

I'm guessing they want to check in with me about some client I brought in when I was there; sometimes they do that, and I like being able to flip through my notes before I return the call, because I don't have everything memorized.

"Well, it's weird because they wanted to transfer a call for you."

"From Madrid?" I furrow my brow.

She nods and shrugs.

"I'll put you through to them in ten minutes. You drink your coffee and check your emails in peace. You have a busy day ahead."

Ten minutes later, the phone in my office rings, and I pick it up without looking. I cradle the phone between my shoulder and my ear, still typing the response to an urgent email.

"Hello?"

"I'm transferring the call from Madrid."

"Perfect. Who is it?"

"It's the receptionist from Ortega. She's new. The one you knew retired."

"Can we send him flowers? He helped us with that disaster with Lopez," I suggest.

"Great. I'll take care of it. This one is called Monica."

I hear a click and then nothing.

"Hi, Monica, this is Tristan Castro. How can I help you?"

"Hi, Tristan, sorry to bother you so early. We got a call from an old client of yours who urgently needed to check with you about something.

To tell the truth, the client is still represented by the Madrid firm but insisted that you helped with a very similar task in your time and that it seems wrong to bypass you, even though you are no longer in Madrid, out of professional respect and personal affection. I would have insisted on handling it from here, but…"

I look up from my computer screen and my hands on my keyboard.

"No worries, that's fine. Yes. Um…is she on hold?"

"How do you know it's a she?" she asks.

I smile.

"Put her through. Thanks so much."

The silent seconds feel eternal, like they could hold two entire lifetimes. Two completely different possibilities are born in the static reaching my left ear and shoot off in opposite directions, leaving rainbow-hued trails.

"Good morning, Tristan," I hear a cordial, affectionate, and slightly shy voice. "How are you?"

"Very good. Well, just good, without the very." I laugh idiotically. "You?"

"Meh…you know. Sorry for calling so early and especially about something like this. I could have done it with the new 'Tristan' in the Madrid office, but between you and me…"

"You're not that into him?"

"I'm not that into him." She laughs. "He calls us 'sweetheart.' They've already chewed him out for it once, and we don't want to be responsible for him getting fired."

"That would be his own fault."

"Yeah, true."

"Don't go on a date with him, even if he insists," I joke. "Not even if you bump into him a hundred times in one weekend."

Her laugh travels into my ear.

"He doesn't have your rizz. Hey…" The filler word hides a long sigh. "Can I tell you something to see what you think, or does that seem totally inappropriate to you?"

"Of course not. Tell me…"

I turn to a clean page in my planner and grab a pen. For the next three or four minutes, I jot down some information, and when she finishes, I analyze my notes in silence before I say anything. I scratch my chin.

"It's the same as that other time," I inform her. "If you want, we can prepare one of our classic texts that covers your ass and throws them off. Ask your assistant to send us."

"Tristan…" She laughs. "I don't have an assistant."

"The one from the magazine, silly."

I hear her cackle.

"Don't be a clown," I say and smile, noticing how I'm blushing.

"I'm stupid, but it made me laugh. Yes, we'll make copies of all the emails and the signed contracts, and I'll send them to you. Do you still have the same email?"

"Um…yes. And the same phone number," I throw out there spontaneously. "You could have found that out today, by the way."

"Yeah…but it was a work thing, and I didn't want to abuse the trust imbued in me by the ex-girlfriend title. And that way, you had the option to redirect my call to Madrid if that's what you wanted."

"Very considerate."

"You asked me not to call you, not to text you, and you said that we couldn't see each other, and I accepted that. I was scared to break my word, but it just seemed ugly not to call you about this."

"You were incredibly elegant." I nod to myself. "And I don't think you're breaking your word looking me up for this. It's been more than a year."

"A year and five months, you gem."

"Are you keeping track?" I raise my eyebrows.

"Like you're not."

One year, five months, and eleven days.

"How's everything going with you?" I change the subject.

"Not much new around here, Tristan." She sighs. "Well…Marisol is threatening to retire, and I'll have a stroke if she does. I still need her to run everything. I'm too young to take on the whole magazine by myself."

"You're not by yourself. All those girls you love so much are there."

"And they blow me away. They do. But the brands and the ads, the investors… I can't handle all that. You know I'm better at galvanizing the masses and writing articles about period underwear."

"Don't make light of your work. I think you inspire a lot of people to make the world a better place."

"Thank you, Mr. Castro. You see me with rose-tinted glasses."

"At your service."

"How are you?"

"Me… I have my own office. Can you believe it?"

"Barely," she teases. "Are you a partner?"

"No, not yet. In a few years. If I can put up with a few years…"

"You still haven't discovered what makes you tick?"

I bite my lip and close my eyes, running my fingers through my hair.

"There are a lot of religions in the world ready to give you an answer to that question, apparently," I decide to answer her.

"Yeah. But I don't really see you as very devout. Are you having fun?"

"Yes. I sold my apartment, I paid off the mortgage, and now I'm renting a decent studio and saving for a house with a garden for when I pull my finger out and figure out what I want to do with my life. I think that pretty much sums it up."

"What are you wearing?"

"Is this that kind of call?"

We both crack up.

"I just wanted to know if you're on the brink of a midlife crisis and your next move is gonna be buying a stupid motorcycle or a convertible."

"I'm wearing a navy suit with a light-blue shirt. My tie's in the drawer. It's navy blue too."

"You've always been very put together."

"I don't know if you're aware, but I dated the deputy editor of a fashion magazine for five years. Either you learn or you *learn*."

She lets out a kind laugh. I wonder who's listening to these laughs now.

"Are you still living at your apartment?" I put my hand on my forehead and swallow.

"No. You're not gonna believe it. I'm a homeowner. Well...the bank is a homeowner, and I swore that if I pay them every month for thirty years, I'll be the owner of a two-bedroom apartment in Plaza de las Comendadoras."

"Living it up, yes, sir."

"It has original hardwood floors. Are you fucking kidding me? I had to buy it."

"It was an offer you couldn't refuse."

"Exactly."

We fall silent.

"And you live alone?"

Another silence.

"Yes," she answers. "And I'm going to be really honest, Tristan. It was really hard for me to move on, but now that I've done it, living alone is great. Really great."

"I'm really happy to hear that." I sit up straight and take a deep breath. "I know you didn't ask, but I've also found a kind of peace in being alone too."

"I hope you're not always."

"No. I have the gang and my family, but...you know? Throwing myself into getting to know someone would have been like trying to get a red wine stain out with white wine. That old Spanish saying is very wise, but I think it would be a mistake here."

"You already got the stain out?"

"Well…yes and no."

I hope that answer is enough, but of course, it doesn't hold water.

"You're going to have to say more, darling."

"Come on…" I groan.

"I didn't catch that."

"Oooff," I snort. "Well, fine, here goes: I still think about you, but every time, I feel less pain about what could have been and more happiness about what was."

"That's very beautiful. Thanks for sharing it. I'm going through something similar."

"Yeah?" That makes me feel better. I felt vulnerable and ridiculous saying it.

"Yes. I'm sorry about it, and I'm grateful too, because we could have kept trying so hard to make it work, and that would have been incredibly painful. I was ready to risk it, and I'm grateful that you loved me enough to leave that part intact."

"That's very beautiful too."

We fall silent again, but it's not an uncomfortable silence. It's almost happy. Almost.

"We did it right," I confirm.

"Yes. It hurt like hell, but we did it right. I'm sorry if…if it took me a little while to accept it. I'm sorry if I isolated myself for the next few months in that process that was so dark and so…I don't know, so opaque. But I needed to revisit it to understand it."

"Grief is fickle. Everyone goes through it in their own way."

"You're right."

A bitter laugh gurgles up out of my lips, and she's surprised.

"Are you laughing at me?"

"No, no, not at all. I'm laughing at how absurd it sounds now that I think about trying to drag you out of the city on my back."

"And me trying to take the north and the sea out of you. But what could we do? We were in love."

I want to tell her that sometimes I still am, but I think my therapist would tear her hair out if she heard me, because it's probably just an outburst of nostalgia and a tantrum from the wound that's still there. We love each other, but we're not in love anymore. Or we're almost not in love anymore. I listen to her and still feel an army of springs growing in my stomach. But I have to remember that with her in them, those springs would never blossom in a green garden in Galicia, filled with children.

"You still don't want to live a peaceful life in a manor house with a man raising your children, right?"

"Right." She laughs.

"Sorry. I had to ask."

"And I'm glad you did, honestly. You still don't want the hustle and bustle of life in Madrid?"

"I'm sorry." I smile sadly, because I've asked myself that question many times, as many as nights that I've missed her, but I can't go back.

"Look...let's make a deal. If I ever feel the irrepressible desire to retire from the madding crowd to live surrounded by the incredible Galician greenery with a wonderful man who can fuck my brains out, not just for hedonistic reasons but for reproductive ones, you'll be the first to know."

"Go to hell." I laugh.

"I'm happy to hear your voice, Tristan."

"Me too..."

"You can say my name. I don't think I've heard you say it once the whole call."

"Yeah, right."

"I'm serious," she insists between fits of laughter.

"If I get over my aversion to the capital and the city rat race, can I call you too?"

"Yes, but I won't be holding my breath, just like I trust and know you won't either. So…"

"You're so wise."

Some voices bubble up in the background and snap our telephonic thread in half, and she answers evasively in monosyllables.

"I have to go. But…it was good to hear your voice, you know? I needed this, and I didn't know it. And this'll probably seem totally out of line to you, but I feel like I should tell you that I'm not sad, that I'm a happy woman, and I never stopped believing in love, because if you and I were capable of loving each other like this, how can it not be real? So…thank you, okay? For these minutes. I'm not going to thank you for the professional part, because your firm is charging by the minute. I know you people. But you? I want to thank you for everything, Tristan. I was lucky to fall in love with someone so good, and that kind of luck stays with you forever, whether it lasts or not. And now…do me a favor. Don't say anything, okay? I have to go. Big kiss. Take care of yourself."

I take a deep breath. She's gone.

"You too. Be happy, Miranda. I love you."

Epilogue

~~~

Calle de Santa Engracia is pretty quiet at this hour. This part of it always is actually. You have to go a hundred meters farther down, where it feeds into Alonso Martínez, to find any kind of hubbub. The sun sparkles on the stone of the stately buildings and the concrete of the sidewalks. There's hardly any traffic; it's almost exclusively taxis seductively flashing their green lights.

Suddenly, a woman barrels out of a doorway at top speed. She looks like she's in her thirties and seems to be in a hurry. She's not wearing heels, but her shoes tap against the ground, and she's going so fast they take on an almost Latin rhythm. She's toting a big, black bag on her arm. Her hair is scraped back in a ponytail, with a middle part, although she's been thinking for a while that this style makes her face look rounder. She can't deny that her last breakup left her with the gift of a few extra pounds in the wrong places, but she doesn't think it matters very much. Especially not today, when she's so happy.

A gust of wind travels up Cuatro Caminos, rustling the leaves on the trees on its way past and licking her face, even caressing her eyelashes despite the huge sunglasses she shoved on as she left the office. And the air makes her pump the brakes, because the smell brings back memories. Ever since a few months ago, she's had an almost reverential respect for memories, because she's discovered that they can hold a kind of healing power.

Memory transports her to the door of her high school in her first year of the baccalaureate. She can almost feel the laminated plastic book covers in her sweaty hand while she waits for him to get out of class and take her home, just like he promised. It's the memory of her first love. She smiles, fishes her phone out of her bag, and taps out a message:

MIRANDA:

I talked to Tristan, and it was like pulling out a splinter I didn't know was there. Take a breath, Ivan, there's no drama. Abort the "best friend to the rescue" mission. And anyway, I'm running to fix a shit show, and I'm slightly hungover because of the event last night, but...life is beautiful, you know? And mine is exactly how I choose. And that's magic. I'm so lucky. And I believe in love.

She drops her phone back into her bag and picks up her pace again, matching the one she hurtled out onto the street with, but the light of a taxi seduces her, and she lifts her hand to hail it. She puts on her mask carefully so it doesn't get smeared with the lipstick she just touched up, which still feels a little damp, and as she climbs in and gives the address to the driver, her phone chirps to tell her she just got a message.

It's from Ivan, her best friend.

IVAN:

Miranda...are you high?

The taxi turns the corner, rolling down Calle de Génova toward Colon, as she cracks up.

In the end, she thinks, *life is a never-ending dialogue between the people we were, the people we are, and the people we will be. And even though sometimes we might think otherwise, the only thing we should really worry about are the things left unsaid. I hope we can look in the mirror and answer the me of today's questions with a simple:* "Wait, here's everything I'll say to you tomorrow."

ABOUT THE AUTHOR

Elísabet Benavent is a graduate in audiovisual communication from the Universidad Cardenal Herrera CEU in Valencia, and she has a master's degree in communication and art from the Universidad Complutense de Madrid. She worked in the communication department of a multinational company until she became a full-time writer. She is an international bestselling author of twenty novels, and she lives in Valencia, Spain.

Website: betacoqueta.com
Instagram: @betacoqueta

A PERFECT STORY

Two heartbroken people from different worlds go on a fake-dating vacation of a lifetime. What could possibly go wrong?

Margot Ortega always struggled to be the princess in her own fairytale: A successful career, a huge salary, a gorgeous apartment, and a perfect fiancé. But on her wedding day, she suffers a major panic attack and has to call it off. Devastated and ashamed, Margot decides to drown her sufferings in a wild night of alcohol and dancing.

The next day she goes back to the sleazy club to retrieve her sister's cell phone and finds David Sánchez, the handsome, fun-loving bartender who persuades her to pretend to be his new girlfriend to make his ex jealous. David recognizes the sadness in her eyes, and together they conspire to help each other get their exes back.

A trip to Greece together is a much-needed getaway. But what starts as a simple rouse becomes complicated when their deep feelings for each other pulls the two lovers in different directions and forces them to make a life-altering decision.

For more info about Sourcebooks's books and authors, visit:

sourcebooks.com